WHO
FEARS
DEATH

WHO FEARS DEATH

NNEDI OKORAFOR

HARPER
Voyager

Harper*Voyager*
An imprint of HarperCollins*Publishers* Ltd
1 London Bridge Street
London SE1 9GF

www.harpercollins.co.uk

First published by HarperCollins*Publishers* 2018
1

A catalogue record for this book is available from the British Library

ISBN HB: 9780008288709
ISBN PB: 9780008288716

Printed and bound in the UK by CPI Group (UK) Ltd, Croydon CR0 4YY

MIX
Paper from
responsible sources
FSC™ C007454

To my amazing father, Dr. Godwin Sunday Daniel Okoroafor, M.D.,
F.A.C.S. (1940-2004).

"Dear friends, are you afraid of death?"
—Patrice Lumumba, first and only elected
Prime Minister of the Republic of the Congo

Part I

Becoming

Chapter 1

My Father's Face

MY LIFE FELL APART WHEN I WAS SIXTEEN. Papa died. He had such a strong heart, yet he died. Was it the heat and smoke from his black-smithing shop? It's true that nothing could take him from his work, his art. He loved to make the metal bend, to obey him. But his work only seemed to strengthen him; he was so happy in his shop. So what was it that killed him? To this day I can't be sure. I hope it had nothing to do with me or what I did back then.

Immediately after he died, my mother came running out of their bedroom sobbing and throwing herself against the wall. I knew then that I would be different. I knew in that moment that I would never again be able to fully control the fire inside me. I became a different creature that day, not so human. Everything that happened later, I now understand, started then.

The ceremony was held on the outskirts of town, near the sand dunes. It was the middle of the day and terribly hot. His body lay on a thick white cloth surrounded by a garland of braided palm fronds. I knelt there in the sand next to his body, saying my last good-bye. I'll never forget his face. It didn't look like Papa's anymore. Papa's skin was dark brown, his lips were full. This face had sunken cheeks, deflated lips, and skin like gray-brown paper. Papa's spirit had gone elsewhere.

The back of my neck prickled. My white veil was a poor protection from people's ignorant and fearful eyes. By this time, everyone was *always* watching me. I clenched my jaw. Around me, women were on their knees weeping and wailing. Papa was dearly loved, despite the fact that he'd married my mother, a woman with a daughter like me—an *Ewu* daughter. That had long been excused as one of those mistakes even the greatest man can make. Over the wailing, I heard my mother's soft whimper. *She* had suffered the greatest loss.

It was her turn to have her last moment. Afterward, they'd take him for cremation. I looked down at his face one last time. *I'll never see you again*, I thought. I wasn't ready. I blinked and touched my chest. That's when it happened . . . when I touched my chest. At first, it felt like an itchy tingle. It quickly swelled into something greater.

The more I tried to get up, the more intense it got and the more my grief expanded. *They can't take him,* I thought frantically. *There is still so much metal left in his shop. He hasn't finished his work!* The sensation spread through my chest and radiated out to the rest of my body. I rounded my shoulders to hold it in. Then I started pulling it from the people around me. I shuddered and gnashed my teeth. I was filling with rage. *Oh, not here!* I thought. *Not at Papa's ceremony!* Life wouldn't leave me alone long enough to even mourn my dead father.

Behind me, the wailing stopped. All I heard was the gentle breeze. It was utterly eerie. Something was beneath me, in the ground, or maybe somewhere else. Suddenly, I was slammed with the pained emotions everyone around me had for Papa.

Instinctively, I laid my hand on his arm. People started screaming. I didn't turn around. I was too focused on what I had to do. Nobody tried to pull me away. No one touched me. My friend Luyu's uncle was once struck by lightning during a rare dry season Ungwa storm. He survived but he couldn't stop talking about how it felt like being violently shaken from the inside out. That's how I felt now.

I gasped with horror. I couldn't take my hand from Papa's arm. It was *fused* to him. My sand-colored skin flowed into to his gray-brown skin from my palm. A mound of mingled flesh.

I started screaming.

It caught in my throat and I coughed. Then I stared. Papa's chest was slowly moving up and down, up and down . . . he was breathing! I was both repulsed and desperately hopeful. I took a deep breath and cried, "Live, Papa! *Live!*"

A pair of hands settled on my wrists. I knew exactly whose they were. One of his fingers was broken and bandaged. If he didn't get his hands off me, I'd hurt him far worse than I had five days prior.

"Onyesonwu," Aro said into my ear, quickly taking his hands from my wrists. Oh, how I hated him. But I listened. "He's gone," he said. "*Let go*, so we can all be free of it."

Somehow . . . I did. I let go of Papa.

Everything went dead silent again.

As if the world, for a moment, were submerged in water.

Then the power that had built up inside of me burst. My veil was blown off my head and my freed braids whipped back. Everyone and everything was thrown back—Aro, my mother, family, friends, acquaintances, strangers, the table of food, the fifty yams, the thirteen large monkeybread fruits, the five cows, the ten goats, the thirty hens, and much sand. Back in town the power went off for thirty seconds; houses would need to be swept of sand and computers would be taken in for dust damage.

That underwater-like silence, again.

I looked down at my hand. When I tried to remove it from my Papa's cold, still, dead arm, there was the sound of peeling, like weak glue flaking off. My hand left a silhouette of dried mucus on Papa's arm. I rubbed my fingers together. More of the stuff crackled and peeled from between them. I took one more look at Papa. Then I fell over on my side and passed out.

That was four years ago. Now see me. People here know that I caused it all. They want to see my blood, they want to make me suffer, and then they want to kill me. Whatever happens after this . . . let me stop.

Tonight, you want to know how I came to be what I am. You want to know how I got here . . . It's a long story. But I'll tell you . . . I'll tell you. You're a fool if you believe what others say about me. I tell you my story to avert all those lies. Thankfully, even my long story will fit on that laptop of yours.

I have two days. I hope it's enough time. It will all catch up to me soon.

My mother named me Onyesonwu. It means "Who fears death?" She named me well. I was born twenty years ago, during troubled times. Ironically I grew up far from all the killing . . .

Chapter 2

Papa

JUST BY LOOKING AT ME, everyone can see that I am a child of rape. But when Papa first saw me, he looked right past this. He's the only person other than my mother who I can say loved me at first sight. That was part of why I found it so hard to let go of him when he died.

I was the one who chose my Papa for my mother. I was six years old.

My mother and I had recently arrived in Jwahir. Before that, we were desert nomads. One day, as we'd roamed the desert, she stopped, as if hearing another voice. She was often strange like that, seeming to converse with someone other than me. Then she said, "It's time for you to go to school." I was far too young to understand her real reasons. I was quite happy in the desert, but after we arrived in the town of Jwahir, the market quickly became my playground.

Those first few days, to make some fast money, my mother sold most of the cactus candy she had. Cactus candy was more valuable than currency in Jwahir. It was a delicious delicacy. My mother had taught herself how to cultivate it. She must always have had the intention of returning to civilization.

Over the weeks, she planted the cactus cutlets she'd kept and set up a booth. I helped out the best I could. I carried and arranged things and called over customers. In turn, she allowed me an hour of free time each day to roam. In the desert, I used to venture over a mile away from my mother on clear days. I never got lost. So the market was small to me. Nonetheless, there was much to see and the potential for trouble was around every corner.

I was a happy child. People sucked their teeth, grumbled, and shifted their eyes when I passed. But I didn't care. There were chickens and pet foxes to chase, other children to glare back at, arguments to watch. The sand on the ground was sometimes damp with spilled camel milk; at other times it was oily and fragrant from overflowing perfumed-oil bottles mixed with incense ashes and often stuck to camel, cow, or fox dung. The sand here was so affected, whereas back in the desert the sand was untouched.

We'd been in Jwahir only a few months when I found Papa. That fateful day was hot and sunny. When I left my mother, I took a cup of water with me. My first impulse was to go to the strangest structure in Jwahir: The House of Osugbo. Something always drew me to this large square-shaped building. Decorated with odd shapes and symbols, it was Jwahir's tallest building and the only one made entirely of stone.

"One day I'll go in there," I said, as I stood staring at it. "But not today."

I ventured farther from the market into an area that I hadn't explored. An electronics shop was selling ugly refurbished computers. They were small black and gray things with exposed motherboards and cracked cases. I wondered if they felt as ugly as they looked. I'd never touched a computer. I reached out to touch one.

"*Ta!*" the owner said from behind his counter. "Don't touch!"

I sipped my water and moved on.

My legs eventually brought me to a cave full of fire and noise. The white adobe building was open at the front. The room inside was dark with the occasional blast of fiery light. Heat hotter than the breeze wafted out like the breath out of a monster's open mouth. On the front of the building a large sign read:

OGUNDIMU BLACKSMITHING—WHITE ANTS
NEVER DEVOUR BRONZE, WORMS DO NOT EAT IRON.

I squinted, making out a tall muscle-bound man inside. His dark glistening skin was darkened with soot. *Like one of the heroes in the Great Book,*

I thought. He wore gloves woven from fine threads of metal and black goggles strapped tightly to his face. His nostrils were wide as he pounded on fire with a great hammer. His huge arms flexed with each blow. He could have been the son of Ogun, the goddess of metal. There was such joy in his motions. *But he seems so thirsty*, I thought. I imagined his throat burning and full of ash. I still had my cup of water. It was half full. I entered his shop.

It was even hotter inside. However, I'd grown up in the desert. I was used to extreme hot and cold. I cautiously watched the sparks burst from the metal he pounded. Then as respectfully as I could, I said, "*Oga*, I have water for you."

My voice startled him. The sight of a lanky little girl who was what people called *Ewu* standing in his shop startled him more. He pushed his goggles up. The area around his eyes where the soot had not fallen was about my mother's dark brown complexion. *The white part of his eyes are so white for someone who stares at fire all day*, I thought.

"Child, you shouldn't be in here," he said. I stepped back. His voice was sonorous. Full. This man could speak in the desert and animals from miles away would hear him.

"It's not so hot," I said. I held up the water. "Here." I stepped closer, very conscious of what I was. I was wearing the green dress my mother had sewn for me. The material was light but it covered every inch of me, all the way to my ankles and wrists. She'd have made me wear a veil over my face but she didn't have the heart.

It was odd. Mostly, people shunned me because I was *Ewu*. But sometimes women crowded around me. "But her skin," they would say to each other, never directly to me. "It's so smooth and delicate. It looks almost like camel's milk."

"And her hair is oddly bushy, like a cloud of dried grass."

"Her eyes are like a desert cat's."

"Ani makes strange beauty from ugliness."

"She might be beautiful by the time she goes through her Eleventh Rite."

"What's the point of her going through it? No one will marry her." Then laughter.

In the market, men had tried to grab me but I was always quicker and I knew how to scratch. I'd learned from the desert cats. All this confused my six-year-old mind. Now, as I stood before the blacksmith, I feared that he might find my ugly features strangely delightful, too.

I held the cup up to him. He took it and drank long and deep, pulling in every drop. I was tall for my age but he was tall for his. I had to tilt my head back to see the smile on his face. He let out a great sigh of relief and handed the cup back to me.

"Good water," he said. He went back to his anvil. "You're too tall and far too bold to be a water sprite."

I smiled and said, "My name is Onyesonwu Ubaid. What's yours, *Oga?*"

"Fadil Ogundimu," he said. He looked at his gloved hands. "I would shake your hand, Onyesonwu, but my gloves are hot."

"That's okay, *Oga*," I said. "You're a blacksmith!"

He nodded. "As was my father and his father and his father and so on."

"My mother and I just got here some months ago," I blurted. I remembered that it was growing late. "Oh. I have to go, *Oga* Ogundimu!"

"Thanks for the water," he said. "You were right. I was thirsty."

After that, I visited him often. He became my best and only friend. If my mother had known I was hanging around a strange man, she'd have beaten me and taken away my free time for weeks. The blacksmith's apprentice, a man named Ji, hated me and he let me know this by sneering with disgust whenever he saw me, as if I were a diseased wild animal.

"Ignore Ji," the blacksmith said. "He's good with metal but he lacks imagination. Forgive him. He is primitive."

"Do *you* think I look evil?" I asked.

"You're lovely," he said smiling. "The way a child is conceived is not a child's fault or burden."

I didn't know what *conceived* meant and I didn't ask. He'd called me lovely and I didn't want him to take his words back. Thankfully, Ji usually came late, during the cooler part of the day.

Soon I was telling the blacksmith about my life in the desert. I was too young to know to keep such sensitive things to myself. I didn't understand that my past, my very existence, was sensitive. In turn, he taught me a few things about metal, like which types yielded to heat most easily and which didn't.

"What was your wife like?" I asked one day. I was really just running my mouth. I was more interested in the small stack of bread he'd bought me.

"Njeri. She was black-skinned," he said. He put both his big hands around one of his thighs. "And had very strong legs. She was a camel racer."

I swallowed the bread I was chewing. "Really?" I exclaimed.

"People said that her legs were what kept her on the camels but I know better. She had some sort of gift, too."

"Gift of what?" I asked, leaning forward. "Could she walk through walls? Fly? Eat glass? Change into a beetle?"

The blacksmith laughed. "You read a lot," he said.

"I've read the Great Book twice!" I bragged.

"Impressive," he said. "Well, my Njeri could speak to camels. Camel-talking is a man's job, so she chose camel racing instead. And Njeri didn't just race. She *won* races. We met when we were teenagers. We married when we were twenty."

"What did her voice sound like?" I asked.

"Oh, her voice was aggravating and beautiful," he said.

I frowned at this, confused.

"She was very loud," he explained, taking a piece of my bread. "She laughed a lot when she was happy and shouted a lot when she was irritated. You see?"

I nodded.

"For a while, we were happy," he said. He paused.

I waited for him to continue. I knew this was the bad part. When he just stared at his piece of bread, I said, "Well? What happened next? Did she do you wrong?"

He chuckled and I was glad, though I had asked the question in seriousness. "No, no," he said. "The day she raced the fastest race of her life, something terrible happened. You should have seen it, Onyesonwu. It was the finals of the Rain Fest Races. She'd won this race before, but this day she was about to break the record for fastest half mile ever."

He paused. "I was at the finish line. We all were. The ground was still slick from the heavy rain the night before. They should have given the race another day. Her camel approached, running its knock-kneed gait. It was running faster than any camel ever has." He closed his eyes. "It took a wrong step and . . . tumbled." His voice broke. "In the end, Njeri's strong legs were her downfall. They held on and when the camel fell, she was crushed under its weight."

I gasped, clapping my hands over my mouth.

"Had she tumbled off, she'd have lived. We'd only been married for three months." He sighed. "The camel she was riding refused to leave her side. It went wherever her body went. Days after she was cremated, the camel died of grief. Camels all over were spitting and groaning for weeks." He put his gloves back on and went back to his anvil. The conversation was over.

Months passed. I continued visiting him every few days. I knew I was pushing my luck with my mother. But I believed it was a risk worth taking. One day, he asked me how my day was going. "Okay," I replied. "A lady was talking about you yesterday. She said that you were the greatest blacksmith ever and that someone named Osugbo pays you well. Does he own the House of Osugbo? I've always wanted to go in there."

"Osugbo isn't a man," he replied as he examined a piece of wrought iron. "It's the group of Jwahir elders who keep order, our government heads."

"Oh," I said, not knowing or caring what the word *government* meant.

"How's your mother?" he asked.

"Fine."

"I want to meet her."

I held my breath, frowning. If she found out about him, I'd get the worst beating of my life and then I'd lose my only friend. *What's he want to meet her for?* I wondered, suddenly feeling extremely possessive of my mother. But how could I stop him from meeting her? I bit my lip and very reluctantly said, "Fine."

To my dismay, he came to our tent that very night. Still, he did look striking in his long white flowing pants and a white caftan. He wore a white veil over his head. To wear all white was to present oneself with great humbleness. Usually women did this. For a man to do it was very special. He knew to approach my mother with care.

At first, my mother was afraid and angry with him. When he told her about the friendship he had with me, she slapped my bottom so hard that I ran off and cried for hours. Still, within a month, Papa and my mother were married. The day after the wedding, my mother and I moved into his house. It should have all been perfect after that. It was good for five years. Then the weirdness started.

Chapter 3

Interrupted Conversation

PAPA ANCHORED MY MOTHER AND ME TO JWAHIR. But even if he'd lived, I'd still have ended up here. I was never meant to *stay* in Jwahir. I was too volatile and there were other things driving me. I was trouble from the moment I was conceived. I was a black stain. A poison. I realized this when I was eleven years old. When something strange happened to me. The incident forced my mother to finally tell me my own ugly story.

It was evening and a thunderstorm was fast approaching. I was standing in the back doorway watching it come when, right before my eyes, a large eagle landed on a sparrow in my mother's garden. The eagle slammed the sparrow to the ground and flew off with it. Three brown bloody feathers fell from the sparrow's body. They landed between my mother's tomatoes. Thunder rumbled as I went and picked up one of the feathers. I rubbed the blood between my fingers. I don't know why I did this.

It was sticky. And its coppery smell was pungent in my nostrils, as if I were awash in it. I tilted my head, for some reason, listening, sensing. *Something's happening here*, I thought. The sky darkened. The wind picked up. It brought . . . another smell. A strange smell that I have since come to recognize but will never be able to describe.

The more I inhaled that smell, the more something began to happen in my head. I considered running inside but I didn't want to bring whatever it was into the house. Then I couldn't move even if I wanted to. There was a humming, then pain. I shut my eyes.

There were doors in my head, doors made of steel and wood and stone. The pain was from those doors cracking open. Hot air wafted through them. My body felt odd, like every move I made would break something. I fell to my knees and retched. Every muscle in my body seized up. Then I stopped existing. I recall nothing. Not even darkness.

It was awful.

Next thing I knew, I was stuck high in the giant iroko tree that grew in the center of town. I was naked. It was raining. Humiliation and confusion were the staples of my childhood. Is it a wonder that anger was never far behind?

I held my breath to keep from sobbing with shock and fear. The large branch I grasped was slippery. And I couldn't shake the feeling that I had just spontaneously died and returned to life. But that didn't matter at the moment. How was I going to get down?

"You have to jump!" someone yelled.

My father and some boy holding a basket over his head were below. I gnashed my teeth and grasped the branch more tightly, angry and embarrassed.

Papa held his arms out. "Jump!" he shouted.

I hesitated, thinking, *I don't want to die again.* I whimpered. In order to avoid my subsequent thoughts, I jumped. Papa and I tumbled to the wet iroko-fruit-covered ground. I scrambled up and pressed myself to him trying to hide as he took off his shirt. I quickly slipped it on. The smell of the mashed fruits was strong and bitter in the rain. We'd need a good bath to get the smell and purple stains off our skin. Papa's clothes were ruined. I looked around. The boy was gone.

Papa took my hand and we walked home in shocked silence. As we trudged through the rain, I struggled to keep my eyes open. I was so exhausted. It seemed to take forever to get home. *Did I come that far?* I wondered. *What . . . how?* Once home, I stopped Papa at the door. "What happened?" I finally asked. "How'd you know where to find me?"

"Let's just get you dried off, for now," he soothingly said.

When we opened the door, my mother came running. I insisted I was fine but I wasn't. I was falling into oblivion again. I headed to my room.

"Let her go," Papa told my mother.

I crawled into bed and this time tumbled into a normal deep sleep.

"Get up," my mother said in her whispery voice. Hours had passed. My eyes were gummy and my body ached. Slowly, I sat up, rubbing my face. My mother scooted her chair closer to my bed. "I don't know what happened to you," she said. But she looked away from me. Even then I wondered if she was telling the truth.

"I don't either, mama," I said. I sighed, massaging my sore arms and legs. I could still smell the iroko tree's fruit on my skin.

She took my hands. "This is the only time I will tell you this." She hesitated and shook her head, saying to herself, "Oh, Ani, she's only eleven years old." Then she cocked her head and had that look I knew so well. That listening look. She sucked her teeth and nodded.

"Mama, what . . ."

"The sun was high in the sky," she said in her soft voice. "It lit everything. That's when they came. When most of the women, those of us older than fifteen, were Holding Conversation in the desert. I was about twenty years old. . . ."

The Nuru militants waited for the retreat, when the Okeke women walked into the desert and stayed for seven days to give respect to the goddess Ani. "Okeke" means "the created ones." The Okeke people have skin the color of the night because they were created before the day. They were the first. Later, after much had happened, the Nuru arrived. They came from the stars and that's why their skin is the color of the sun.

These names must have been agreed upon during peaceful times, for it was well known that the Okeke were born to be slaves of the Nuru. Long ago, during the Old Africa Era, they had done something terrible causing Ani to put this duty on their backs. It is written in the Great Book.

Though Najeeba lived with her husband in a small Okeke village where no one was a slave, she knew her place. Like everyone else in her village, if she lived in the Seven Rivers Kingdom, only fifteen miles east, where there was more to be had, she would spend her life serving the Nuru.

Most abided by the old saying, "A snake is foolish if it dreams of being a lizard." But one day, thirty years earlier, a group of Okeke men and women in the city of Zin rejected it. They'd had enough. They rose up rioting and demanding and refusing. Their passion spread to neighboring Seven Rivers towns and villages. These Okeke paid dearly for having ambition. *Everyone* did, as is always the case with genocide. On and off this had been happening since. Those rebelling Okekes that weren't exterminated were driven East.

Najeeba had her head to the sand, her eyes closed, her attention turned inward. She smiled as she held conversation with Ani. When she was ten, she joined the journeys along the salt roads with her father and brothers to trade salt. Since then, she'd loved the open desert. And she'd always adored travel. She smiled wider and rubbed her head further into the sand, ignoring the sound of the women around her praying.

Najeeba was telling Ani how she and her husband had sat outside the night before and seen five stars fall from the sky. It's said that the number of stars a wife and husband see fall will be the number of children they will have. She laughed to herself. She hadn't a clue that this would be the last time she'd laugh for a very long time.

"We don't have much, but my father would be proud," Najeeba said in her rich voice. "We have a house that sand is always getting into. Our computer was old when we bought it. Our capture station collects only half as much water from the clouds as it should. The killing has begun again and is not far. We have no children yet. But we're happy. And I thank you . . ."

The purr of scooters. She looked up. There was a parade of them, each with an orange flag on the back of the seat. There must have been at least forty. Najeeba and her group were miles from the village. They'd left four days ago, drinking water and eating only bread. So not only were they alone, they were weak. She knew exactly who these people were. *How did they know where to find us?* she wondered. The desert had erased their trail days ago.

The hate had finally made it to her home. Her village was a quiet place where the houses were tiny but well built, the market small but well stocked, where marriages were the biggest events that happened. It was a sweet harmless place, hidden by lazy palm trees. Until now.

As the scooters drove circles around the women, Najeeba looked back toward her village. She grunted as if punched in the stomach. Black smoke plumed into the sky. The Goddess Ani hadn't bothered to tell the women that they were dying. That as they had their heads in the sand, their children, husbands, relatives at home were being murdered, their homes being burned.

On each scooter rode a man and on several a woman accompanied the man. They wore orange veils over their sunny faces. Their expensive military attire—sand-colored pants and tops and leather boots—were probably treated with weather gel to keep them cool in the sun. As Najeeba stood staring at the smoke, her mouth agape, she remembered how her husband had always wanted weather gel for his clothes when he worked up in the palm trees. He could never afford it. *He will never afford it*, she thought.

The Okeke women screamed and ran in all directions. Najeeba screamed so loudly that all the air left her lungs and she felt something give from deep in her throat. She'd later realize that this was her voice leaving her forever. She ran in the opposite direction from her village. But the Nurus made a wide circle around them, herding them back together like wild camels. As the Okeke women cowered, their long periwinkle garments fluttered in the breeze. The Nuru men got off their scooters, the Nuru women behind them. They closed in. And that was when the raping began.

All of the Okeke women, young, prime, and old, were raped. Repeatedly. Those men didn't tire; it was as if they were bewitched. When they spent themselves inside one woman, they had more to give to the next and the next. They sang as they raped. The Nuru women who'd come along laughed, pointed, and sang, too. They sang in the common language of Sipo, so that the Okeke women could understand.

The blood of the Okeke runs like water
We take their goods and shame their forefathers.
We beat them with a heavy hand

Then take what they call their land.
The power of Ani belongs to us
And so we will slay you to dust
Ugly filthy slaves, Ani has finally killed you!

Najeeba had it the worst. The other Okeke women were beaten and raped and then their abusers moved on, giving them a moment to breathe. The man who took Najeeba, however, stayed with her and there was no Nuru woman to laugh and observe. He was tall and strong like a bull. An animal. His veil covered his face but not his rage.

He grabbed Najeeba by her thick black braids and dragged her several feet from the others. She tried to get up and run but he was on her too fast. She stopped fighting when she saw his knife . . . shiny and sharp. He laughed, using it to cut her clothing open. She stared into his eyes, the only part of his face she could see. They were gold and brown and angry, the corners twitching.

As he held her down, he brought a coin-shaped device from his pocket and set it beside her. It was the sort of device people used to keep the time, the weather, to carry a file of the Great Book. This one had a recording mechanism. Its tiny black camera eye rose up, making a clicking and whirring sound as it began to record. He started singing, stabbing his knife into the sand next to Najeeba's head. Two large black beetles landed on the handle.

He pulled her legs apart and kept singing as he bore into her. And between songs, he spoke Nuru words that she couldn't understand. Heated, biting, snarling words. After a while, anger boiled up in Najeeba and she spat and snarled right back at him. He grabbed her neck and his knife and pointed its tip at her left eye until she grew still again. Then he sang louder and bore more deeply into her.

At some point, Najeeba went cold, then numb, then quiet. She became two eyes watching it happen. She'd always been like this to an extent. As a child, she'd fallen from a tree and broken her arm. Though in pain, she'd calmly gotten up, left her panicking friends, walked home and found her mother, who took her to a friend who knew how to set broken bones. Najeeba's peculiar behavior used to anger her father whenever she misbehaved and was beaten. No matter how hard the slap, she wouldn't make a sound.

"This child's Alusi has no respect!" her father always told her mother. But when he was in his usual good mood, her father praised this part of Najeeba, often saying, "Let your Alusi travel, daughter. See what you can see!"

Now her Alusi, that ethereal part of her with the ability to silence pain and observe, came forward. Her mind recorded events like the man's device. Every detail. Her mind observed that when the man sang, despite the song's words, his voice was beautiful.

It lasted about two hours, though to Najeeba it felt like a day and a half. In her memory, she saw the sun move across the sky, set, and come up again. It was a long time, that's what matters. The Nurus sang, laughed, raped, and, a few times, killed. Then they left. Najeeba lay there on her back, her garments open, her pummeled and bruised midsection exposed to the sun. She listened for breathing, moaning, crying and for a while, she heard nothing. She was glad.

Then she heard Amaka shout, "Stand up!" Amaka was twenty years Najeeba's senior. She was strong and often a voice for the women of her village. "Stand up, all of you!" Amaka said, stumbling. "Get up!" She went to each woman and kicked her. "We're dead but we won't die out here, those of us still breathing."

Najeeba listened without moving as Amaka kicked at thighs and pulled at women's arms. She hoped she could play dead well enough to trick Amaka. She knew her husband was dead and, even if he weren't, he'd never touch her again.

The Nuru men, and their women, had done what they did for more than torture and shame. They wanted to create *Ewu* children. Such children are not children of the forbidden love between a Nuru and an Okeke, nor are they Noahs, Okekes born without color. The *Ewu* are children of violence.

An Okeke woman will *never* kill a child kindled inside of her. She would go against even her husband to keep a child in her womb alive. However, custom dictates that a child is the child of her father. These Nuru had planted poison. An Okeke woman who gave birth to an *Ewu* child was bound to the Nuru through her child. The Nuru sought to destroy Okeke families at the very root. Najeeba didn't care about this cruel plan of theirs. There was no child kindled in her. All she wanted was to die. When Amaka got to her, it took only one kick to get Najeeba coughing.

"You don't fool me, Najeeba. Get up," Amaka said. The left side of Amaka's face was blue-purple. Her left eye was swollen shut.

"Why?" Najeeba said in her new voiceless voice.

"Because that's what we *do*." Amaka held out a hand.

Najeeba turned away. "Let me finish dying. I have no children. It's best." Najeeba felt the weight in her womb. If she stood up, all the semen that had been pumped into her would splash out. She gagged at the thought and then turned her head to the side and dry heaved. When her stomach settled, Amaka was still there. She spat on the ground next to Najeeba. It was red with blood. She tried to pull Najeeba up. The pain in Najeeba's abdomen flared but she kept her body limp and heavy. Eventually, frustrated, Amaka dropped Najeeba's arm, spat again, and moved on.

The women who chose to live dragged themselves up and walked back to the village. Najeeba closed her eyes, feeling blood seep from a cut on her forehead. Soon there was silence again. *Leaving this body will be easy*, she thought. She'd always loved traveling.

She lay there until her face burned in the sun. Death was coming slower than she wanted. She opened her eyes and sat up. It took a minute for her eyes to adjust to the bright sun. When they did, she saw bodies and pools of blood, the sand drinking it up as if the women had been sacrificed to the desert. She slowly stood, went over to her satchel, and picked it up.

"Leave me," Teka said minutes later as Najeeba shook her. Teka was the only one alive among the five bodies. Najeeba sat down hard beside her. She rubbed her aching scalp where her assailant had pulled her hair so brutally. She looked at Teka. Her cornrows were encrusted with sand and her face grimaced with each breath. Slowly Najeeba stood and tried to pull Teka up.

"Leave me," Teka repeated, looking at her angrily. And so Najeeba did.

She trudged back to the village, only going in that direction out of habit. She begged Ani to send something along to kill her, like a lion or more Nurus. But it was not Ani's will.

Her village was burning. Homes smoldered, gardens were destroyed, scooters were aflame. There were bodies in the street. Many were burned, unrecognizable. During these kinds of raids, the Nuru soldiers took the strongest Okeke men, tied them up, doused them with kerosene, and set them afire.

Najeeba saw no Nuru men or women dead or alive. The village had been an easy conquest, off guard, vulnerable, unaware, in denial. *Stupid*, she thought. Women moaned in the street. Men wept before their homes. Children walked about confused. The heat was stifling, radiating from the sun and the burning houses and scooters and people. By sundown, there would be a fresh exodus east.

Najeeba softly said her husband's name when she got to their house. Then she wet herself. The urine burned and ran down her bruised legs. Half of the house was on fire. Their garden was destroyed. Their scooter was on fire. But there was Idris, her husband, sitting on the ground with his head in his hands.

"Idris," Najeeba softly said again. *I'm seeing a ghost,* she thought. *The wind will blow and he will blow away with it.* There was no blood running down his face. And though the knees of his blue pants were crusted with sand and the armpits of his blue caftan were dark with sweat, he was intact. This was him, not his ghost. Najeeba wanted to say "Ani is merciful," but the goddess wasn't. Not at all. For, though her husband was spared, Ani had killed Najeeba and left her still alive.

When he saw her, Idris shouted with joy. They ran into each other's arms and held each other for several minutes. Idris smelled of sweat, anxiety, fear, and doom. She dared not wonder what she smelled like.

"I'm a man, but all I could do was hide like a child," he said into her ear. He kissed her neck. She closed her eyes, wishing Ani would strike her dead right there.

"It was what was best," Najeeba whispered.

Then he held her back and Najeeba knew. "Wife," he said, looking down at her open garments. Her pubic hair was exposed, her bruised thighs, her belly. "Cover yourself!" he said pulling the bottom part of her dress closed. His eyes grew moist. "C-c-cover yourself, *O!*" The look on his face grew more pained and he held his side. He stepped back. He looked at Najeeba again, squinting, and then he shook his head as if trying to ward something off. "No."

Najeeba just stood there as her husband stepped away, his hands held before him. "No," he repeated. His eyes spilled tears but his face hardened.

His face was blank as he watched Najeeba go into the burning house. Inside, Najeeba ignored the heat and the sounds of the house cracking, popping, and dying. She methodically gathered a few things, some money she'd hidden away, a pot, their capture station, a hand game her sister had given her years ago, a photo of her husband smiling, and a cloth sack of salt. Salt was good to have when going into the desert. The only picture she had of her deceased parents was burning.

Najeeba wasn't going to live for much longer. To herself, she became the Alusi that her father said had always lived in her; the desert spirit who loved to wander off to distant places. Once in her village, she had hoped her husband was alive. When she found him, she hoped he would be different. But she was an Okeke. What business did she have being hopeful?

She could survive in the desert. Her yearly retreats with the women and her Salt Road journeys with her father and brothers had taught her how. She knew how to use her capture station to pull condensation from the sky for drinking water. She knew how to trap foxes and hares. She knew where to find tortoise, lizard, and snake eggs. She knew which cacti were edible. And because she was already dead, she wasn't afraid.

Najeeba walked and walked, searching for a place to let her body die. *A week from now*, she thought, as she set up camp. *Tomorrow*, she thought as she trudged along. When she first realized she was pregnant, death was no longer an option. But in her mind, she remained an Alusi, controlling and maintaining her body as one controls a computer. She traveled east, away from the Nuru cities, toward the wastelands where the Okeke lived in exile. At night when she lay down in her tent, she'd hear Nuru women's voices laughing and singing outside. She'd voicelessly scream back at them to come in and finish her off if they could. "I'll tear off your breasts!" she said. "I'll drink your blood and it'll nourish the one who grows inside me!"

When she slept, she often saw her husband Idris standing there, disturbed and sad. Idris had loved her dearly for two years. She would wake up and have to look at his picture to remember him as he was before. After a while, this didn't help.

For months, Najeeba dwelled in limbo as her belly grew and the day of birth approached. When she had nothing else to do, she sat and stared into space. Sometimes she played her Dark Shadows hand game, winning it over and over, a higher score each time. Sometimes she talked to the child inside her. "The human world is harsh," Najeeba said. "But the desert is lovely. Alusi, *mmuo*, all spirits can live here in peace. When you come, you will love it here, too."

She was a nomad, traveling during the cool parts of the day, avoiding towns and villages. When she was about four months along, a scorpion stung the heel of her foot while she was walking. Her foot painfully swelled up and she had to lie down for two days. But she eventually got up and moved on.

When she finally went into labor, she was forced to admit that what she'd been telling herself all these months was wrong. She wasn't an Alusi about to give birth to an Alusi child. She was a woman in the desert all alone. Terrified, she lay in her tent on her thin mat in her desert beaten nightshirt, the only item she had that fit her swelling body.

The body that she had finally admitted to being hers was conspiring against her. Violently pushing and pulling, it was like battling an invisible monster. She cursed and screamed and strained. *If I die out here, the child will die alone,* she desperately thought. *No child deserves to die alone.* She held on. She focused.

After an hour of terrible contractions, her Alusi moved forward. She relaxed, retreated, and watched, letting her body do what it was made to do. Hours later, the child emerged. Najeeba could have sworn the child was shrieking even before it came out. So angry. From the moment the child was born, Najeeba understood that it would dislike surprises and have little patience. She cut the cord, tied the belly button, and pressed the child to her breast. A girl.

Najeeba cradled her and watched in horror as she, herself, bled and bled. Images of lying in the sand with semen seeping out of her kept trying to creep into her mind. Now that she was human again, she was no longer immune to these memories. She forced the memories away and focused on the angry child in her arms.

An hour later, as she sat weakly wondering if she would bleed to death, the blood slowed and then stopped. Holding the child, she slept. When she woke, she could stand. She felt as if her insides would fall out from between her legs but standing wasn't impossible. She took a close look at her child. She had Najeeba's thick lips and high cheekbones but she had the narrow straight nose of someone Najeeba didn't know.

And her eyes, oh, her eyes. They were that gold brown, *his* eyes. It was as if *he* were peering at her through the child. The baby's skin and hair color were the odd shade of the sand. Najeeba knew of this phenomenon, particular only to children conceived through violence. *Was it even spoken of in the Great Book?* She wasn't sure. She hadn't read much of it.

The Nuru people had yellow-brown skin, narrow noses, thin lips, and brown or black hair that was like a well-groomed horse's mane. The Okeke had dark brown skin, wide nostrils, thick lips, and thick black hair like the hide of a sheep. No one knows why *Ewu* children always look the way they do. They look neither Okeke nor Nuru, more like desert spirits. It would be months before the trademark freckles showed up on the child's cheeks. Najeeba gazed into her child's eyes. Then she pressed her lips to the baby's ear and spoke the child's name.

"Onyesonwu," Najeeba said again. It was right. She wanted to shout the question to the sky: "Who fears death?" But alas, Najeeba had no voice and could only whisper it. *One day, Onyesonwu will speak her name correctly*, she thought.

Najeeba slowly walked over to her capture station and connected its large water bag. She flipped it on. It made a loud *whoosh* and created the usual sudden coolness. Onyesonwu was jarred awake and started crying. Najeeba smiled. After washing Onyesonwu, she washed herself. Then she drank and ate, nursing Onyesonwu with some difficulty. The child didn't quite understand how to latch on. It was time to go. The birth blood would attract wild animals.

Over the months, Najeeba focused on Onyesonwu. And doing so forced her to care for herself. But there was more to it. *She glows like a star.*

She is my hope, Najeeba thought gazing at her child. Onyesonwu was noisy and fussy while awake, but she slept just as fiercely, giving Najeeba plenty of time to get things done and rest herself. These were peaceful days for mother and daughter.

When Onyesonwu grew sick with fever and none of Najeeba's remedies worked, it was time to find a healer. Onyesonwu was four months old. They had recently passed an Okeke town called Diliza. They had to go back. It would be the first time in over a year that Najeeba was around other people. The town's market was set on the outskirts of the town. Onyesonwu fussed and burned against her back. "Don't worry," Najeeba said as she walked down the sand dune.

Najeeba worked hard not to jump at every sound or whenever someone brushed against her arm. She bowed her head when anyone greeted her. There were pyramids of tomatoes, barrels of dates, piles of used capture stations, bottles of cooking oil, boxes of nails, items of a world that she and her daughter didn't belong to. She still had the money she'd taken when she left her home, and the currency was the same here. She was afraid to ask for directions, so it took her an hour to find a healer.

He was short with smooth skin. Under his small tent were brown, black, yellow, and red vials of liquids and powders, various bound stalks, and baskets of leaves. A stick of incense burned, sweetening the air. On her back, Onyesonwu peeped weakly.

"Good afternoon," the healer said bowing to Najeeba.

"My . . . my baby is sick," Najeeba cautiously said.

He scowled. "Please, speak up."

She patted her throat. He nodded, stepping closer. "How did you lose your . . ."

"Not for me," she said. "For my child."

She unwrapped Onyesonwu, holding her tightly in her arms as the healer stared. He stepped back and Najeeba almost wept. His reaction to her daughter was so much like her husband's reaction to her.

"Is she . . . ?"

"Yes," Najeeba said.

"You're nomads?"

"Yes."

"Alone?"

Najeeba pressed her lips together.

He looked behind her and then said, "Hurry. Let me see her." He inspected Onyesonwu, asking Najeeba what she had been eating, for she and her child weren't malnourished. He handed her a corked vial containing a pink substance. "Give her three drops every eight hours. She's strong, but if you don't give this to her, she will die."

Najeeba uncorked it and sniffed. It smelled sweet. Whatever it was, it was mixed with fresh palm tree sap. The medicine cost a third of the money she had. She gave Onyesonwu three drops. The baby sucked in the liquid and went back to sleep.

She spent the rest of her money on supplies. The dialect in the village was different, but she was still able to communicate in both Sipo and Okeke. As she frantically shopped, she started to accumulate an audience. Only determination kept her from running back into the desert right after buying the medicine. The baby needed bottles and clothes. Najeeba needed a compass and map and a new knife to cut meat. After buying a small bag of dates, she turned and found herself facing a wall of people. Mostly men, some old and some young. Most around the age of her husband. Here she was again. But this time, she was alone and the men threatening her were Okeke.

"What is it," she quietly asked. She could feel Onyesonwu fidgeting at her back.

"Whose child is that, Mama?" a young man of about eighteen asked.

She felt Onyesonwu fidget again and suddenly she was flush with rage. "I'm not your mama!" Najeeba snapped, wishing that her voice would function.

"Is that your child, woman?" an old man asked in a voice that sounded as if he hadn't drunk cool water in decades.

"Yes," she said. "She's *mine!* No one else's."

"Can't you speak?" a man asked. He looked at the man next to him. "She moves her mouth but no sound comes out. Ani has taken her filthy tongue."

"That baby is Nuru!" someone said.

"She's *mine*," Najeeba whispered as loudly as she could. Her vocal cords were straining and she could taste blood.

"Nuru concubine! *Tffya!* Go find your husband!"

"Slave!"

"*Ewu* carrier!"

To these people, the murder of Okekes in the West was more story than fact. She had traveled farther than she'd thought. These people didn't want to know the truth. So they watched as mother and child moved about the market. As they watched, they stopped and talked with friends, speaking ugly words that grew uglier the more they were exchanged. They grew angrier and agitated. They finally accosted Najeeba and her *Ewu* child. They grew bold and self-righteous. Finally, they struck.

When the first stone hit Najeeba's chest, she was too shocked to run. It hurt. It wasn't a warning. When the second hit her thigh, she had flashbacks of a year ago, when she died. When instead of stones, a man's body had slammed against her. When the third stone hit her on the cheek, she knew that if she didn't run, her daughter would die.

She ran as she should have run when the Nurus attacked that day. Stones hit her shoulder blades, neck, and legs. She heard Onyesonwu screeching and crying. She ran until she burst from the market into the safety of the desert. Only after scaling the third sand dune did she slow down. They probably thought they'd driven her to her death. As if woman and child couldn't survive alone in the desert.

Once safely away from Diliza, Najeeba unwrapped Onyesonwu. She gasped and sobbed. There was blood running from just above the child's eyebrow where a stone had hit her. The baby feebly rubbed at her face, smearing the blood. Onyesonwu continued to fight as Najeeba held her tiny hands back. The wound was shallow. That night, though Onyesonwu slept well, the medicine having broken her fever, Najeeba cried and cried.

For six years, she raised Onyesonwu alone in the desert. Onyesonwu grew into a strong feisty child. She loved the sand, winds, and desert creatures. Though Najeeba could only whisper, she laughed and smiled whenever Onyesonwu shouted. When Onyesonwu shouted the words Najeeba taught her, Najeeba kissed and hugged her. This was how Onyesonwu learned to use her voice without having ever heard one.

And a lovely voice Onyesonwu had. She learned to sing by listening to the wind. She often stood facing the wide open land and sang to it. Sometimes, if she sang in the evening, she attracted owls from far away. They'd land in the sand to listen. This was the first sign Najeeba had that her daughter was not just *Ewu* but very special, unusual.

In that sixth year, a realization came to Najeeba: Her daughter needed other people. In her heart, Najeeba knew that whatever this child would become, she could only become it within civilization. And so she used her map and compass and the stars to take her daughter there. What place sounded more promising for her sand colored daughter than Jwahir, which meant "Home of the Golden Lady"?

According to Jwahirian legend, seven hundred years ago there lived a giant Okeke woman made of gold. Her father took her to the fattening hut and weeks later she emerged fat and beautiful. She married a rich young man and they decided to move to a large town. However, along the way, because of her immense weight (she was very fat *and* made of gold), she grew tired, so tired that she had to lie down.

The Golden Lady couldn't get up, so this was where the couple had to settle. For this reason, the flattened land she left was called Jwahir and those who lived there prospered. It was built long ago by some of the first Okekes to flee the West. The ancestors of Jwahirians were of a special breed, indeed.

Najeeba prayed that she'd never have to tell her strange daughter the story of her conception. But Najeeba was a realist, too. Life was not easy.

I could have killed someone after my mother told me this story.

"I'm sorry," my mother said. "You're so young. But I promised myself that the minute *anything* began happening to you, I would tell you this. Knowing may be of some use to you. What happened to you today . . . in that tree . . . it's just the beginning, I think."

I was shaking and sweating. My throat felt raw as I spoke. "I . . . I remember that first day," I said, rubbing the sweat from my brow. "You chose that spot in the market to sell some cactus candy." I paused, frowning as it came back to me. "And that bread seller forced us to move. He shouted at you. And he looked at me like . . ." I touched and pressed the tiny scar on my forehead. *I'm going to burn my copy of the Great Book*, I thought. *It's the cause of all this.* I wanted to drop to my knees and beg Ani to burn the West to the ground.

I knew a little about sex. I was even a little curious about it . . . well, maybe more suspicious than curious. But I didn't know about *this*—sex as violence, violence that produced children . . . produced me, that happened to my mother. I stifled an urge to vomit, and then an urge to tear at my skin. I wanted to hug my mother but at the same time I didn't want to touch her. I was poison. I had no right. I couldn't quite bring myself to grasp what that . . . man, that monster, had done to her. Not at eleven years old.

The man in the photo, the only man I'd ever seen for the first six years of my life, wasn't my father. He wasn't even a good person. *Betraying bastard*, I thought, tears stinging my eyes. *If I ever find you, I'll cut off your penis.* I shuddered, thinking how I wanted to do worse to the man who'd raped my mother.

Up to this point, I'd thought I was Noah. Noahs had two Okeke parents, yet they were the color of sand. I'd ignored the fact that I didn't have the usual red eyes and sensitivity to sunshine. And that aside from their skin color, Noahs basically *looked* Okeke. I ignored the fact that other Noahs had no problem making friends with "normal looking" children. They weren't outcast as I was. And Noahs looked at me with the same fear and disgust as Okekes of a darker shade. Even to *them*, I was other. Why hadn't my mother burned that picture of her husband Idris? He'd betrayed her to protect his stupid honor. She'd told me he died . . . he *should* have died—been KILLED—violently!

"Does Papa know?" I hated the sound of my voice. *When I sing*, I wondered, *whose voice is she hearing?* My biological father could also sing sweetly.

"Yes."

Papa knew from the moment he saw me, I realized. *Everyone knew but me.*

"*Ewu*," I said slowly. "This is what it means?" I'd never asked.

"Born of pain," she said. "People believe the *Ewu*-born eventually become violent. They think that an act of violence can only beget more violence. I know this isn't true, as you should."

I looked at my mother. She seemed to know so much. "Mama," I said. "Has anything like what happened to me in the tree ever happened to you?"

"My dear, you think too hard," was all she said. "Come here." She stood up and wrapped me in her arms. We cried and sobbed and wept and bled tears. But when we were finished, all we could do was continue living.

Chapter 4

Eleventh Year Rite

YES, THE ELEVENTH YEAR OF MY LIFE WAS ROUGH.

My body developed early, so by this time I had breasts, my monthlies, and a womanly figure. I also had to deal with stupid leering and grabbing by both men and boys. Then came that rainy day I mysteriously ended up naked in the iroko tree and my mother being so shaken that she felt it time to tell me the repulsive truth of my origins. A week later came the time for my Eleventh Rite. Life rarely let up for me.

The Eleventh Rite is a two thousand-year-old-tradition held on the first day of rainy season. It involves the year's eleven-year-old girls. My mother felt the practice was primitive and useless. She didn't want me to have anything to do with it. In her village, the practice of the Eleventh Rite had been banned years before she was born. So I grew up sure that all the circumcising would happen to the other girls, girls *born* in Jwahir.

After a girl goes through her Eleventh Rite, she's worthy of being spoken to as an adult. Boys don't get this privilege until they're thirteen. So the ages between eleven and sixteen are happiest for a girl because she's both child and adult. Information about the rite wasn't withheld. There were plenty of books about the process in the school's book house. Still, no one was required or encouraged to read them.

So us girls knew that a piece of flesh was cut from between our legs and that circumcision didn't literally change who we were or make us better people. But we didn't know what that piece of flesh *did*. And because it was an old practice, no one really remembered *why* it was done. So the tradition was accepted, anticipated, and performed.

I didn't want to do it. No numbing medicine was used. That was part of the ritual. I had seen two freshly circumcised girls the previous year and I remembered how they walked. And I didn't like the idea of cutting off a part of my body. I didn't even like cutting my hair, thus my long braids. And I certainly wasn't one to do anything for the sake of tradition. I didn't come from that kind of background.

But as I sat on the floor staring into space, I knew something had changed in me last week when I ended up in that tree. Whatever it was caused a slight shake to my step that only I noticed. I'd heard more from my mother than the story of my conception. She'd said nothing about the hope she had in me. The hope that I would avenge her suffering. She hadn't been detailed about the rape, either. All of this was *between* her words.

I had many questions that couldn't be answered. But when it came to my Eleventh Year Rite, I knew what I had to do. That year there were only four of us who were eleven years old and girls. There were fifteen boys. The three girls in my group would no doubt tell everyone how I wasn't present at the rite. In Jwahir, to be uncircumcised past eleven brought bad luck and shame to your family. No one cared if you weren't born in Jwahir. You, the girl growing up in Jwahir, were expected to have it done.

I brought dishonor to my mother by existing. I brought scandal to Papa by entering his life. Where before he had been a respected and eligible widower, now people laughingly said he was bewitched by an Okeke woman from the bloody West, a woman who'd been used by a Nuru man. My parents carried enough shame.

On top of all this, at eleven, I still had hopes. I believed that I could be normal. That I could be *made* normal. The Eleventh Rite was old and it was respected. It was powerful. The rite would put a stop to the strangeness happening to me. The next day, before school, I went to the home of the Ada, the priestess who would perform the Eleventh Rite.

"Good morning, *Ada-m*," I respectfully said when she opened the door.

She met my eyes with a frown. She might have been a decade older than my mother, maybe two. I stood almost her height. Her long green dress was elegant and her short Afro was perfectly shaped. She smelled of incense. "What is it, *Ewu?*"

I winced at the word. "I'm sorry," I said, stepping back. "Am I disturbing you?"

"I'll decide that," she said, crossing her arms over her small chest. "Come in."

I stepped in, briefly noting that I'd be late for school. *I'm really going to do this,* I thought.

On the outside, her house was a small sand brick dwelling and inside it remained small. Yet somehow it was able to harbor a work of art that was gigantic in visual power. The mural that splashed over the walls was unfinished, but the room already looked as if it were submerged in one of the Seven Rivers. Painted near the door was a human-sized fish-man with a strikingly lifelike face. His ancient eyes were full of primordial wisdom.

Books told of huge bodies of water. But I'd never seen a drawing of one, let alone a giant colorful painting. *This can't really exist,* I thought. So much water. And in it were silvery insects, turtles with green flat legs and shells, water plants, gold, black, and red . . . fish. I stared around and around. The room smelled of wet paint. The Ada's hands were stained with it, too. I had interrupted her.

"You like it?" she asked.

"Never seen anything like it," I said quietly, staring.

"My favorite kind of reaction," she said, looking genuinely pleased.

I sat down and she sat across from me, waiting. "I . . . I'd like to put my name on the list, *Ada-m,*" I said. I bit my lip. To speak this request made it true, especially when spoken to this woman.

She nodded. "I wondered when you would come."

The Ada knew what was happening with everyone in Jwahir. She was the one who made sure the proper traditions were performed for deaths, births, menstrual celebrations, the party thrown when a boy's voice drops, the Eleventh Year Rite, the Thirteenth Year Rite, all of life's markers. She'd planned my parents' wedding and I'd hidden from her whenever she came by. I hoped she didn't remember me.

"I'll add your name. The list will be submitted to the Osugbo," she
said.

"Thank you," I said.

"Be here at two a.m. a week from today. Wear old clothes. Come
alone." She looked me over. "Your hair—unbraid it, brush it out and rebraid it loosely."

A week later, I snuck out of my bedroom window at twenty minutes to
two in the morning.

The door to the Ada's house was open when I arrived. I slowly stepped
inside. The living room was decorated with candles, all the furniture
cleared away. The Ada's mural, mostly finished, looked more alive than
ever in the candlelight.

The three other girls were already there. I quickly joined them. They
looked at me with surprise, and some relief. I was one more person to share
their fear. We didn't speak, not even a greeting, but we stood close together.

Besides the Ada, there were five other women present. One of them
was my great-aunt, Abeo Ogundimu. She'd never liked me. If she realized
I was here without the consent of Papa, her nephew, I'd be in real trouble.
I didn't know the other four women, but one of them was very old and
her presence demanded respect. I shivered with guilt, suddenly unsure of
whether I should be there.

I glanced at a small table in the center of the room. Set on it were
gauze, bottles of alcohol, iodine, four scalpels, and other items I didn't
recognize. My stomach rolled with nausea. A minute later, the Ada began.
They must have been waiting for me.

"We are the women of the Eleventh Rite," the Ada said. "We six guard
the crossroads between womanhood and girlhood. Only through us can
you move freely between the two. I am the Ada."

"I am Lady Abadie, the town healer," the short woman next to her
said. Her hands were pressed closely to her flowing yellow dress.

"I am Ochi Naka," another said. She was very dark skinned and had a
voluptuous figure that she showed off with her stylish purple dress. "Market seamstress."

"I am Zuni Whan," the other said. Under her loose blue midlevel dress, she wore pants, something women rarely wore in Jwahir. "Architect."

"I am Abeo Ogundimu," my great-aunt said with a smirk. "Mother of fifteen."

The women laughed. We all did. A mother to fifteen was a busy career indeed.

"And I am Nana the Wise," the imposing old old woman said, looking at each of us through her one good eye, her hunched back forever pushing her forward. My great-aunt was old, but she was young compared to this woman. Nana the Wise's voice was clear and dry. She held my eyes longer than she did the other girls'. "Now what are *your* names, so that we are well met?" she said.

"Luyu Chiki," the girl next to me said.

"Diti Goitsemedime."

"Binta Keita."

"Onyesonwu Ubaid-Ogundimu."

"This one," Nana the Wise said, pointing at me. I held my breath.

"Step forward," the Ada said.

I'd spent too much time mentally preparing for this day. All week, I'd had trouble eating, sleeping, fearing the pain and blood. By this point, I'd finally come to terms with it all. Now the old woman would bar my way.

Nana the Wise looked me up and down. Slowly she stepped around me, peering up with her one eye, like a tortoise from its shell. She grunted. "Unbraid that hair," she said. I was the only one with hair long enough to braid. Jwahir women wore their hair stylishly short, another difference between my mother's village and Jwahir. "This is her day. She must be unhindered."

I was flush with relief. As I undid my loose braid, the Ada spoke. "Who comes here untouched?"

Only I raised my hand. I heard the one named Luyu snicker. She quickly shut up when the Ada spoke again. "Who, Diti?"

Diti let out a tiny uncomfortable laugh. "A . . . schoolmate," she said quietly.

"His name?"

"Fanasi."

"Did you have intercourse?"

I quietly gasped. I couldn't imagine it. We were so young.

Diti shook her head and said, "No." The Ada moved on.

"Who, Luyu?" she asked.

When Luyu only stared back with defiant eyes, the Ada strode forward so quickly that I was sure she was going to slap Luyu across the face. Luyu didn't budge. She held her chin higher, daring the Ada. I was impressed. I noticed Luyu's clothes. They were made from the finest textiles. They were bright; they'd never been washed. Luyu came from money and she obviously didn't feel that she had to answer to even the Ada.

"I don't know his name," Luyu finally said.

"Nothing leaves this place," the Ada said. But I sensed a threat in her voice. Luyu must have, too.

"Wokike."

"Did you have intercourse?"

Luyu said nothing. Then she looked at the fish man on the wall and said, "Yes."

My jaw dropped.

"How often?"

"Many times."

"Why?"

Luyu glowered. "I don't know."

The Ada gave her a harsh look. "After tonight, you'll refrain until you're married. After tonight, you should know better." She moved on to Binta, who'd been crying the entire time. "Who?"

Binta's shoulders curled more. She cried harder.

"Binta, who?" the Ada asked again. Then she looked toward the five women and they moved in close to Binta, so close that Luyu, Diti, and I had to tilt our heads to see her. She was the smallest of the four of us. "You're safe here," the Ada said.

The other women touched Binta's shoulders, cheeks, neck, and softly chanted, "You are safe, you are safe, you are safe here."

Nana the Wise put her hand on Binta's cheek. "After tonight, all in this room will be bound," she said in her dry voice. "You, Diti, Onyesonwu, and Luyu will protect each other, even after marriage. And we, the Old

Ones, will protect you all. But truth is the only thing that will secure this bond tonight."

"Who?" the Ada asked for the third time.

Binta sunk to the floor and leaned her head against one of the women's thighs, "My father."

Luyu, Diti, and I gasped. The other women didn't seem surprised at all.

"Was there intercourse?" Nana the Wise asked, her face hardened.

"Yes," Binta whispered.

Several of the women cursed and sucked their teeth and muttered angrily. I shut my eyes and rubbed my temples. Binta's pain was like my mother's.

"How often?" Nana the Wise asked.

"Many times," Binta said, her voice growing stronger. Then she blurted, "I-I-I want to kill him." Then she clapped her hands over her mouth. "I'm sorry!" she said, her words muffled by her hands.

Nana the Wise removed Binta's hands. "You're safe here," she said. She looked disgusted and shook her head, "Now we can finally do something about it."

In fact, this group of women had known of Binta's father's behavior for a while. They were powerless to intervene until Binta went through her Eleventh Rite.

Binta vigorously shook her head. "No. They will take him away and . . ."

The women hissed and sucked their teeth. "Don't worry," Nana the Wise said. "We'll protect you and your happiness."

"My mother won't . . ."

"Shhh," Nana the Wise said. "You may still be a child but after tonight you'll also be an adult. Your words will finally matter."

The Ada and Nana the Wise barely glanced my way. No questions for me.

"Today," the Ada said to us all. "You'll become child and adult. You will be powerless and powerful. You will be ignored and heard. Do you accept?"

"Yes," we all said.

"You are not to scream," the healer said.

"You are not to kick," the seamstress said.

"You are to bleed," the architect said.

"Ani is great," my great-aunt said.

"You have already taken the first step into adulthood by leaving your homes and entering the dangerous night alone," the Ada said. "You'll each get a small sack of herbs, gauze, iodine, and body salts. You'll return home alone. In three nights, you're to take a long bath."

We were told to remove our clothing and handed pieces of red cloth to wrap around ourselves. Our tops would be taken to the back and burned. We'd each be given a new white shirt and veil, the symbols of our new adulthood. We were to wear our rapas home; they were symbols of our childhood.

Binta was first, her rite most urgent. Then Luyu, Diti, and then me. A red cloth was spread on the floor. Binta started crying again as she lay on it, her head on the red pillow. The lights were turned on which made what was about to happen that much scarier. *What am I doing?* I thought, watching Binta. *This is crazy! I don't have to do this! I should just run out the door, run home, slip into my bed, and pretend this never happened.* I took a step towards the door. I knew it wouldn't be locked. The rite was a girl's choice. Only in the past had girls been forced to do it. I took another step. No one was watching. All eyes were on Binta.

The room was warm and outside was like any other night. My parents were sleeping, as if it were any other night. But Binta was lying on a red cloth, her legs held apart by the healer and the architect. The Ada disinfected the scalpel and then heated it over a flame. She let it cool. Healers usually use a laserknife for surgery. They make the cleanest cuts and can instantly cauterize when necessary. I briefly wondered why the Ada was using a primitive scalpel instead.

"Hold your breath," the Ada said. "Don't scream."

Before Binta could finish taking in her breath, the Ada took the scalpel to her. She went for a small perturbing bit of dark rosy flesh near to top of Binta's *yeye*. When the scalpel sliced it, blood spurted. My stomach lurched. Binta didn't scream but she bit down on her lip so hard that blood dribbled from the side of her mouth. Her body jerked but the women held her.

The healer stanched the wound with ice wrapped in gauze. For a few moments everyone froze except Binta, who was breathing heavily. Then one of the other women helped her stand and move to the other side of the room. Binta sat down, her legs apart, holding the gauze in place, a stunned look on her face. It was Luyu's turn.

"I can't do this," Luyu started babbling. "I can't do this!" Still, she allowed herself to be held down by the healer and the architect. The seamstress and my great-aunt held her arms for good measure as the Ada took another scalpel and disinfected it. Luyu didn't scream but she made a sharp, "*peep*" Tears dribbled from her eyes as she fought with the pain. It was Diti's turn.

Diti lay down slowly and took a deep breath. Then she said something too quiet for me to hear. The minute the Ada brought the fresh scalpel to her flesh, Diti jumped up, blood oozing down her thighs. Her face was a mask of terror, as she tried to wordlessly scramble away. The women must have seen this reaction often because without a word, they grabbed her and quickly held her down. The Ada finished the cut, fast and clean.

It was my turn. I could barely keep my eyes open. The other girls' pain was swarming around me like wasps and biting flies. Tearing at me like cactus thorns.

"Come, Onyesonwu," the Ada said.

I was a trapped animal. Not trapped by the women, the house, or tradition. I was trapped by life. Like I had been a free spirit for millennia and then one day something snatched me up, something violent and angry and vengeful, and I was pulled into the body that I now resided in. Held at its mercy, by its rules. Then I thought of my mother. She'd stayed sane for me. She lived for me. I could do this for her.

I lay on the cloth trying to ignore the three other girls' eyes as they stared at my *Ewu* body. I could have slapped all three of them. I didn't deserve to suffer those scrutinizing stares during such a chilling moment. The healer and architect took my legs. The seamstress and my great-aunt held my arms. The Ada picked up the scalpel.

"Be calm," Nana the Wise said into my ear.

I felt the Ada part my *yeye's* lips. "Hold your breath," she said. "Don't scream."

Halfway through my breath, she cut. The pain was an explosion. I felt it in every part of my body and I almost blacked out. Then I was screaming. I didn't know that I was capable of such noise. Faintly, I felt other women holding me down. I was shocked that they hadn't let go and run off. I was still screaming when I realized that everything had fallen away. That I was in a place of periwinkle and yellow and mostly green.

I would have gasped with terror if I had a mouth to gasp with. I would have screamed some more, thrashed, scratched, spit. All I could think was that I had died . . . yet again. When I remained as I was, I calmed. I looked at myself. I was only a blue mist, like the fog that lingers after a fast, hard rainstorm. Around me I could see others now. Some were red, some green, some gold. Things focused and I could see the room, too. The girls and women. Each had her own colored mist. I didn't want to look at my body lying there.

Then I noticed it. Red and oval-shaped with a white oval in the center, like the giant eye of a jinni. It sizzled and hissed, the white part expanding, moving closer. It horrified me to my very core. *Must get out of here!* I thought. *Now! It sees me!* But I didn't know how to move. Move with what? I had no body. The red was bitter venom. The white was like the sun's worst heat. I started screaming and crying again. Then I was opening my eyes to a cup of water. Everyone's face broke into a smile.

"Oh, praise Ani," the Ada said.

I felt the pain and jumped, about to get up and run. I had to run. From that eye. I was so mixed up that for a moment, I was sure that what I'd just seen was causing the pain.

"Don't move," the healer said. She was pressing a piece of gauze-wrapped ice between my legs and I wasn't sure which hurt more, the pain from the cut or the ice's cold. My eyes shot around the room, searching. When my gaze fell on anything white or red my heart skipped a beat and my hands twitched.

After a few minutes, I began to relax. I told myself it was all just a pain-induced nightmare. I let my mouth fall open. The air dried my lower lip. I was now *ana m-bobi*. No more shame would befall my parents. Not because I was eleven and uncircumcised, at least. My relief lasted about one minute. It wasn't a nightmare at all. I knew this. And though I didn't know exactly what, I knew something terribly bad had just happened.

"When she cut you, you just went to sleep," Luyu said, as she lay on her back. She was looking at me with great respect. I frowned.

"Yeah, and you went all transparent!" Diti quickly said. She seemed to have recovered from her own shock.

"W-what?!" I said.

"Shhhh!" Luyu angrily hissed at Diti.

"She did!" Diti whispered.

I wanted to drag my nails across the floor. *What was all this?* I wondered. I could smell the stress on my skin. And I realized that I could smell that other smell, too. The one that I'd smelled for the first time during the tree incident.

"She should speak with Aro," the Ada told to Nana the Wise.

Nana the Wise only grunted, frowning at her. The Ada fearfully averted her eyes.

"Who's that?" I asked.

No one responded. None of the other women would look at me.

"Who's 'R O'?" I asked, turning to Diti, Luyu, and Binta.

The three of them shrugged. "Dunno," Luyu said.

When none of the women would elaborate on this R O, I dismissed their words. I had other things to worry about. Like that place of light and colors. Like the oval eye. Like the bleeding and stinging between my legs. Like telling my parents what I'd done.

The four of us lay there side by side in pain for a half hour. We were each given a belly chain made of thin delicate gold that we would wear forever. The elders raised their shirts above their bellies to show us theirs. "They've been blessed in the seventh of the Seven Rivers," the Ada said. "They'll live long after we've died."

We were also each given a stone to place underneath our tongues. This was called *talembe etanou*. My mother approved of this tradition, though its purpose had also long been forgotten. Hers was a very small, smooth orange stone. The stones vary with each Okeke group. Our stones were diamonds, a stone I'd never heard of. They looked like smooth ovals of ice. I held mine easily under my tongue. One was only to take it out when eating or sleeping. And one had to be careful at first not to swallow it. To do so was bad luck. Briefly I wondered how my mother hadn't swallowed hers when I was conceived.

"Eventually your mouth will make friends with it," Nana the Wise said.

The four of us dressed, putting on underwear with gauze pressed against our flesh and wrapping the white veils over our heads. We left together.

"We did well," Binta said, as we walked. She slurred her words a bit, because of her swollen mangled lower lip. We moved slowly, each step met with pain.

"Yes. None of us screamed," Luyu said. I frowned. I certainly had. "My mother said that in her group, five of the eight girls screamed."

"Onyesonwu thought it felt so good that she went to sleep," Diti said smiling.

"I-I thought I screamed," I said. I rubbed my forehead.

"No, you fainted dead away," Diti said. "Then you . . ."

"Diti, shut up. We don't talk about things like that!" Luyu hissed.

We were quiet for a moment, our walk to the road slowing even more. An owl hooted from nearby and a man on camelback trotted past us.

"We'll never tell, right?" Luyu said, looking at Binta and Diti. They both nodded. She turned to me with interested eyes. "So . . . what happened?"

I didn't really know any of them. But I could tell Diti liked to gossip. Luyu, too, though she tried to act as if she didn't. Binta was quiet but I wondered about her. I didn't trust them. "It was like I went to sleep," I lied. "What . . . what did you see?"

"You *did* go to sleep," Luyu said.

"You were like glass," Diti said with wide eyes. "I could see right through you."

"It only happened for a few seconds. Everyone was shocked but they didn't let go of you," Binta said. She touched her lip and winced.

I pulled my veil closer to my face.

"Has someone cursed you?" Luyu asked. "Maybe because you're . . ."

"I don't know," I quickly said.

We went our separate ways when we got to the road. Sneaking back into my room was easy enough. As I settled into my bed, I couldn't shake the feeling that something was still watching me.

The next morning, I pushed the covers off my legs and found that I'd bled through the gauze onto my bed. I'd started my monthly cycle a year ago, so the sight didn't bother me much. But the blood loss left me light-headed. I wrapped myself in my rapa and slowly walked into the kitchen. My parents were laughing at something Papa had said.

"Good morning, Onyesonwu," Papa said, still chuckling.

My mother's smile melted when she saw my face. "What's wrong?" she asked in her whispery voice.

"I-I'm all right," I said, not wanting to move from where I stood. "I just . . ."

I could feel the blood running down my leg. I needed fresh gauze. And some willow leaf tea for the pain. *And something for the nausea*, I thought just before I threw up all over the floor. My parents rushed over and helped me into a chair. They saw the blood when I sat down. My mother quietly left the room. Papa wiped the vomit on my lips with his hand. My mother returned with a towel.

"Onyesonwu, is it your monthly?" she asked, wiping my leg. I stopped her hand when she got to my upper thigh.

"No, Mama," I said, looking into her eyes. "It's not that."

Papa frowned. My mother was looking intensely at me. I braced myself. She slowly stood up. I didn't dare move when she slapped me hard across the face, my diamond stone almost flying from my mouth.

"Ah ah, wife!" Papa exclaimed, grabbing her hand. "Stop it! The child is hurt."

"Why?" she asked me. Then she looked at Papa, who still held her hands from striking me again. "She did it last night. She went and got circumcised," she said.

Papa looked at me shocked, but I also saw awe. The same look he'd given me when he saw me up in that tree.

"I did it for you, Mama!" I shouted.

She tried to snatch her hands from Papa so she could slap me again.

"Don't you blame me! Stupid idiot girl!" she said, when she couldn't pull her hands from him.

"I'm not blaming . . ." I could feel blood seeping from me, faster now. "Mama, Papa, I bring shame to you," I said, beginning to cry. "My existence is shame! Mama, I'm pain to you . . . since the day I was conceived."

"No, no," my mother said, shaking her head vigorously. "This was *not* why I told you." She looked at Papa. "See, Fadil! See why I didn't tell her all this time?"

Papa still held her hands, but now he looked as if he did it to hold himself up.

"*Every* girl here has it done," I said. "Papa, you're a well-loved blacksmith. Mama, you're his wife. You both have respect. I'm *Ewu*." I paused. "To not do it would bring *more* shame."

"Onyesonwu!" Papa said. "I *don't care* what people think! Haven't you learned that by now? Eh? You should have come to us. Insecurity is *no* reason to have it done!"

My heart ached but I still believed I'd made the right choice. He may have accepted my mother and me for what we were, but we didn't live in a vacuum.

"In my village, *no* woman was expected to be cut like that," my mother hissed. "What kind of barbaric . . ." She turned away from me. It was already done. She clapped her hands together and said. "My own daughter!" She rubbed her forehead as if doing so would smooth out her frown. She took my arm, "Get up."

I didn't go to school that day. Instead my mother helped me clean and pack my wound with fresh gauze. She made me a pain-relieving tea with willow leaves and sweet cactus pulp. All day, I lay in bed, reading. My mother took the day off to sit beside my bed, which made me a little uncomfortable. I didn't want her to see what I was reading. The day after my mother told me the story of my conception, I'd gone to the book house. Surprisingly, I found what I was looking for, a book on the Nuru language, the language of my biological father. I was teaching myself the basics. This would have seriously enraged my mother. So as she sat beside my bed, I hid the book inside another book as I read it.

All day, she stayed in that chair, unmoving, only getting up for brief meals or to relieve herself. Once, she went into her garden to Hold Conversation with Ani. I wondered what she told the Almighty and All-knowing Goddess. After all that had happened to her, I wondered what kind of relationship my mother could possibly have with Ani.

When my mother returned, as I read my Nuru language book and rolled my stone in my mouth, I wondered what she thought about as she sat there staring at the wall.

Chapter 5

The One Who is Calling

NONE OF THEM TOLD ANYONE. That was the first sign that our Eleventh Rite bond was true. And thus when I returned to school a week later, no one harassed me. All people knew was that I was now both adult and child. I was *ana m-bobi*. They had to at least give me that respect. Of course, we didn't say a word about Binta's sexual abuse, either. She later told us that the day after our rite, her father had to meet with the Osugbo elders.

"When he came home, afterwards, he looked . . . broken," Binta said. "I think they whipped him." They should have done more than that. Even back then I thought so. Binta's mother was also brought before the elders. Both of her parents were ordered to receive counseling from the Ada for three years, as were Binta and her siblings.

As my friendship with Binta, Luyu, and Diti bloomed, something else started. It began indirectly my second day back at school. I leaned against the school building as students around me played soccer and socialized. I was still sore but healing fast.

"Onyesonwu!" someone called. I jumped and nervously turned around, images of that red eye popping into my head. Luyu laughed as she and Binta slowly walked over to me. For a brief moment, we stared at each other. There was so much in that moment: judgment, fear, uncertainty.

"Good morning," I finally said.

"Good morning," Binta said, stepping forward to shake and release my hand with a snap between our fingers. "You just back today? We are."

"No," I said. "I came back yesterday."

"You look well," Luyu said, also giving me the friendship handshake.

"You too," I said.

There was an awkward pause. Then Binta said, "Everyone knows."

"Eh?" I said too loudly. "Knows? Knows what?"

"That we're *ana m-bobi*," Luyu said proudly. "*And* that none of us screamed."

"Oh," I said, relieved. "Where's Diti?"

"Hasn't left bed since that night," Luyu said with a laugh. "She's such a weakling."

"No, she's just taking advantage of missing school," Binta said. "Diti knows she's too pretty to need school, anyway."

"Must be nice," I grumbled, though I didn't like missing school.

"Oh!" Luyu said, her eyes growing wide. "Did you hear about the new student?"

I shook my head. Luyu and Diti looked at each other and laughed.

"What?" I said. "Didn't you two just get back today?"

"News travels fast," Diti said.

"For some of us, at least," Luyu said, smugly.

"Just tell me whatever you're going to tell me," I said, irritated.

"His name is Mwita," Luyu said, excitedly. "He arrived here while we were gone. No one knows where he's living or if he even *has* parents. Apparently he's really smart, but refuses to come to school. Four days ago, he came for one day and scoffed at the teachers, saying *he* could teach *them!* Not a great way to make a good first impression."

I shrugged. "Why should I care?"

Luyu smirked and cocked her head and said, "Because I hear he's *Ewu!*"

The rest of that day was a blur. In class, I searched for a face the color of a camel's hide with freckles like brown pepper, with eyes that weren't Noah. During midday break, I searched for him in the schoolyard. After school, while walking home with Binta and Luyu, I still looked around. I wanted to tell my mother about him when I got home but I decided not to. Would she really have wanted to know of another result of violence?

The next day was the same. I couldn't stop looking for him. Two days later, Diti returned to school. "My mother finally pushed me out of bed," Diti admitted. She made her voice severe. "'You aren't the first to go through this!' Plus she knew you all were back in school." Her eyes flicked toward me, then away, and I instantly understood that her parents didn't like me being in their daughter's rite group. As if I cared what her parents thought.

Regardless, it was now definitely the four of us. Any friends Luyu, Binta, and Diti had before were no longer important. I had no friends to drop. Most girls who went through their Eleventh Rite together, though they were "bound," didn't remain so afterward. But the change was natural for us. We already had secrets. And those were just the beginning.

None of us was the "leader," but Luyu was the one who liked to lead. She was fast and brazen. It turned out that there had been two other boys she'd had intercourse with. "Who is *the Ada?*" Luyu had spat. "I didn't have to tell her *everything*."

Binta always had her eyes downcast and spoke little when around others. Her father's abuse cut deep. But when she was with just us, she talked and smiled plenty. If Binta weren't born so full of life, I doubt she'd have survived her father's sickness.

Diti was the princess, the one who liked to lie around in bed all day while her servants brought her meals. She was plump and pretty and things typically fell right into her lap. When she was around, good things happened. A merchant selling bread would sell it to us at half price because he was in a hurry to get home. Or we'd be walking and a coconut tree would drop a coconut at Diti's feet. The Goddess Ani loved Diti. To be loved by Ani, what must that be like? I'm yet to know.

After school, we'd study at the iroko tree. At first, I was nervous about this. I was afraid the red and white creature I'd seen was linked to the iroko tree incident. Sitting under the tree felt like practically inviting the eye to come at me again. In time, as nothing happened, I relaxed a little. Sometimes I even went there alone, just to think.

I'm getting a little ahead of myself. Let me back up a bit.

It was eleven days after my Eleventh Rite, four days after I returned to school, three days after I realized I was bound to three girls my age, and a day after Diti returned to school that the other thing happened. I was slowly walking home. My wound was throbbing. The deep unprovoked pain seemed to happen twice a day.

"They'll still think you're evil," someone behind me said.

"Eh? What?" I said, slowly turning around. I froze.

It was like looking into a mirror when you've never seen your reflection. For the first time, I understood why people stopped, dropped things, and stared when they saw me. He was my skin tone, had my freckles, and his rough golden hair was shaved so close that it looked like a coat of sand. He might have been a little taller, maybe a few years older than me. Where my eyes were gold-brown like a desert cat's, his were a gray like a coyote's.

I instantly knew who he was, though I'd only seen him for a moment when I was in a disheveled state. Contrary to what Luyu told me, he'd been in Jwahir longer than the few days. He was the boy who saw me naked in the iroko tree. He'd told me to jump. It had been raining hard and he'd been holding a basket over his head but I knew it was him.

"You're . . ."

"So are you," he said.

"Yeah. I've never . . . I mean, I've heard of others."

"I've seen others," he said offhandedly.

"Where are you from?" we both asked at the same time.

We both said, "The West." Then we nodded. All *Ewu* were from the West.

"Are you all right?" he asked.

"Eh?"

"You're walking oddly," he said. I felt my face grow hot. He smiled again and shook his head. "I shouldn't be so bold." He paused. "But trust me, they *will* always see us as evil. Even if you have yourself . . . cut."

I frowned.

"Why would you have that done?" he asked. "You're not from here."

"But I *live* here," I said, defensively.

"So?"

"Who *are* you?" I said, irritated.

"Your name is Onyesonwu Ubaid-Ogundimu. You're the blacksmith's daughter."

I bit my lip, trying to remain irritated. But he'd referred to me as the blacksmith's daughter, not stepdaughter, and I wanted to smile at this. He smirked. "And you're the one who ends up naked in trees."

"Who are you?" I asked again. How strange we must have looked standing there on the side of the road.

"Mwita," he said.

"What's your last name?"

"I have no last name," he said, his voice growing cold.

"Oh . . . okay." I looked at his clothing. He wore typical boy attire, faded blue pants and a green shirt. His sandals were worn but made of leather. He carried a satchel of old schoolbooks. "Well . . . where do you live?" I asked.

The coolness thawed from his voice. "Don't worry about it."

"How come you don't come to school?"

"I'm in school," he said. "A better one than yours." He reached into his pocket and pulled out an envelope. "This is for your father. I was going to your home but you can take it to him." It was a palm fiber envelope stamped with the insignia of the Osugbo, a lizard in midstride. Each of its legs represented one of the elders.

"You live up the road past the ebony tree, right?" he asked, looking past me.

I nodded absentmindedly, still looking at the envelope.

"Okay," he said. Then he left. I stood there watching him walk away, barely aware of the fact that the throbbing between my legs had grown worse.

Chapter 6

Eshu

AFTER THAT DAY, it seemed I saw Mwita everywhere. He often came to our house with messages. And a few times I ran into him on his way to Papa's shop.

"How come you didn't tell me about him before?" I asked my parents one night during dinner. Papa was shoveling spiced rice into his mouth with his right hand. He sat back, chewing, his right hand resting over his food. My mother put another piece of goat meat on his plate.

"I thought you knew," he said at the same time that my mother said, "I didn't want to upset you." My parents knew so much back then. They should have also known that they couldn't shelter me forever. What was coming would come.

Mwita and I talked whenever we saw each other. Briefly. He was always in a hurry. "Where're you going?" I asked after he delivered yet another envelope from the elders to Papa. Papa was making a great table for the House of the Osugbo, and the engraved symbols on it had to be perfect. The envelope Mwita brought contained more drawings of the symbols.

"Somewhere else," Mwita said, smirking.

"Why're you always hurrying?" I said. "Come on. Just one thing?"

He turned to leave and then he turned back. "All right," he said. We sat on the steps to the house. After a minute he said, "If you spend enough time in the desert, you will hear it speak."

"Of course," I said. "It speaks loudest in wind."

"Right," Mwita said. "Butterflies understand the desert well. That's why they move this way and that. They're always Holding Conversation with the land. They talk as much as they listen. It's in the desert's language that you call the butterflies."

He lifted his chin, took a deep breath and breathed out. I knew the song. The desert sang it when all was well. In our nomad days, my mother and I would catch scarab beetles slowly flying by on days when the desert sang this song. Remove the hard shells and wings, dry the flesh in the sun, add spices—delicious. Mwita's song brought three butterflies—a tiny white one and two big black and yellow ones.

"Let me try," I said, excitedly. I thought about my first home. Then I opened my mouth and sang the desert's song of peace. I drew two hummingbirds who zipped around our heads before flying off. Mwita leaned away from me, shocked.

"You sing like . . . your voice is lovely," he said.

I looked away, pressing my lips together. My voice was a gift from an evil man.

"Some more," he said. "Sing some more."

I sang him a song I'd made up when I was happy and free and five years old. My memory of those times was fuzzy, but I clearly remembered the songs I sang.

It was like that each time with Mwita. He'd teach me a bit of simple sorcery and then be shocked by the ease with which I picked it up. He was the third to see it in me (my mother and Papa being the first and second), probably because he had it in him too. I wondered where he learned what he knew. Who were his parents? Where did he live? Mwita was so mysterious . . . and very handsome.

Binta, Diti, and Luyu first met him at school. He was waiting for me in the yard, something he'd never done. He wasn't surprised to see me come out of school with Binta, Diti, and Luyu. I'd told him much about them. Everyone was staring. I'm sure many stories were told that day about Mwita and me.

"Good afternoon," he said, politely nodding.

Luyu was grinning too widely.

"Mwita," I quickly said. "Meet Luyu, Diti, and Binta, my friends. Luyu, Diti, Binta, meet Mwita, my friend."

Diti snickered at this.

"So Onyesonwu is a good enough reason to come here?" Luyu asked.

"She's the only reason," he said.

My face felt hot, as the eyes of all four turned to me.

"Here," he said, giving me a book. "Thought I'd lost it but I didn't." It was a booklet on human anatomy. When we'd last spoken, he'd been bothered by how little I knew about the many muscles of the body.

"Thanks," I said, feeling annoyed at my friends' presence. I wanted to tell them again that Mwita and I were *just* friends. The only type of interaction Luyu and Diti had with boys was sexual or flirtatious.

Mwita gave me a look and I returned it with a look of agreement. After that, he only approached me when he thought I'd be alone. Most of the time he succeeded but sometimes he was forced to deal with my friends. He was fine.

I was always happy to see Mwita. But one day, months later, I was *ecstatic* to see him. *Relieved.* When I saw him coming up the road, an envelope in hand, I jumped up. I'd been sitting on the house steps staring into space, confused and angry, waiting for him. Something had happened.

"Mwita!" I screamed, breaking into a run. But when I got to him, all my words escaped me and I just stood there.

He took my hand. We sat down on the steps.

"I-I-I don't know," I babbled. I paused, a great sob welling up in my chest. "It couldn't have happened, Mwita. Then I wondered if this was what happened before. Something's been happening to me. Something's after me! I need to see a healer. I . . ."

"Just tell me what happened, Onyesonwu," he said, impatient.

"I'm *trying!*"

"Well, try harder."

I glared at him and he glared back, motioning his hand for me to get on with it.

"I was in the back, looking at my mother's garden," I said. "Everything was normal and . . . then everything went red. A thousand shades of it . . ."

I stopped. I couldn't tell him about how a giant red-eyed brown cobra slithered up to me and rose up to my face. And then how I was suddenly hit with a self-loathing so deep and profound that I started raising my hands to gouge out my own eyes! That I was then going to tear my own throat with my nails. *I am awful. I am evil. I am filth. I should not be!* The mantra was red and white in my mind as I'd stared in horror at the oval eye. I didn't tell him how a moment later an oily black vulture flew down from the sky, screamed and then pecked at the snake until it slithered away. How I snapped out of it just in time. I skipped all this.

"There was a vulture," I said. "Looking right at me. Close enough for me to see its eyes. I threw a rock at it and as it flew off, one of its feathers fell off. A long black one. I . . . went and picked it up. I was standing there wishing I could fly as it did. And then . . . I don't . . ."

"You changed," Mwita said. He was looking at me very closely.

"Yeah! I *became* the vulture. I swear to you! I'm not making this . . ."

"I believe you," Mwita said. "Finish."

"I . . . I had to hop out from underneath my clothes," I said holding my arms out. "I could hear *everything*. I could *see* . . . it looked as if the world had opened itself to me. I got scared. Then I was lying there, myself again, naked, my clothes next to me. My diamond wasn't in my mouth. I found it a few feet away and . . ." I sighed.

"You're an Eshu," he said.

"A what?" The word sounded like a sneeze.

"An Eshu. You can shape-shift, among other things. I knew this the day you changed into that sparrow and flew into the tree."

"What?" I screamed, leaning away from him.

"You know what you know, Onyesonwu," he said matter-of-factly.

"Why didn't you tell *me?*" I clenched my shaking fists.

"Eshus never believe what they are until they realize it on their own."

"So what do I do? What . . . how do you know all this?"

"Same way I know all the other things," he said.

"How's that?"

"It's long story," he said. "Listen, don't go telling your friends about this."

"I didn't plan to."

"Firsts are important. Sparrows are survivors. Vultures are noble birds."

"What's noble about eating dead things and stealing meat from chopping blocks?"

"Everything must eat."

"Mwita," I said. "You have to teach me more. I have to learn to protect myself."

"From what?"

Tears dribbled from my eyes. "I think something wants to kill me."

He paused, looked me in the eye and then said, "I'll never let that happen."

According to my mother, all things are fixed. To her there was a reason for everything from the massacres in the West to the love she found in the East. But the mind behind all things, I call it Fate, is harsh and cold. It's so logical that no one could call him or herself a better person if he or she bowed down to it. Fate is fixed like brittle crystal in the dark. Still, when it came to Mwita, I bow down to Fate and say thank you.

We met twice a week, after school. Mwita's lessons were exactly what I needed to hold back my fear of the red eye. I'm a fighter by nature and simply having tools to fight, no matter how inadequate, was enough to take the crippling edge off my anxiety. At least during those days.

Mwita himself was also a good distraction. He was well spoken, well dressed, and he carried himself with respect. And he didn't have the same type of outcast reputation I had. Luyu and Diti were envious of my time with him. They took pleasure in telling me about the rumors that he liked older married girls in their late teens. Girls who'd completed school and had more to offer intellectually.

No one could figure Mwita out. Some said that he was self-taught and lived with an old woman to whom he read books in exchange for a room and spending money. Some said he owned his own house. I didn't ask. I knew he wouldn't tell me. Still he *was Ewu* and so every so often, I'd hear people mention his "unhealthy" skin and "foul" odor and how no matter how many books he read, he'd only amount to something bad.

Chapter 7

Lessons Learned

I TOOK MY DIAMOND FROM MY MOUTH and handed it to Mwita, my heart beating fast. If a man touched my stone, he'd have the ability to do great harm or good to me. Though Mwita didn't respect Jwahir's traditions, he knew I did. So he was careful taking it.

It was a weekend morning. The sun had just come up. My parents were asleep. We were in the garden. I was exactly where I wanted to be.

"According to what I know, whatever you've turned into, you retain the knowledge of it forever," he said. "Does that feel right to you?"

I nodded. When I focused on the idea, I felt the vulture and the sparrow just below my skin.

"It's right there, under the surface," he said, slowly. "Feel the feather with your fingers. Rub it, knead it. Shut your eyes. Remember. Draw from it. Then *be* it."

The feather in my hand was smooth, delicate. I knew just where it would go. In the empty shaft on my wing. This time I was aware and in control. It wasn't like melting into a pool of something shapeless and then taking another shape. I was always something. My bones softly buckled and cracked and shrunk. It didn't hurt. My body's tissue was undulating and shifting. My mind changed focus. I was still me, but from a different perspective. I heard soft popping and sucking sounds and I smelled that rich smell that I only noticed during moments of oddness.

I flew high. My sense of touch was less, for my flesh was protected by feathers. But I saw all. My hearing was so sharp that I could hear the land breathing. When I returned, I was exhausted and moved to tears. All my senses buzzed, even after I changed back. I didn't care that I was naked. Mwita had to wrap me in my rapa as I cried on his shoulder. For the first time in my life, I could escape. When things felt too tight, too close, I could retreat to the sky. From up there, I could easily see the desert stretching far beyond Jwahir. I could fly so high that not even the oval eye could see me.

That afternoon, as we sat before my mother's garden, I told Mwita much about myself. I told him the story of my mother. I told him about the desert. I told him about how I'd gone somewhere else when I was circumcised. And I finally told him the details about the red eye. Mwita wasn't shocked even by this. That should have given me pause, but I was too enamored by him to care.

It was my idea to go to the desert. It was his idea to go that very night. It was my second time sneaking out of the house. We hiked across the sand for several miles. When we stopped, we made a fire. All around us was darkness. The desert hadn't changed since I'd left it six years ago. We were so at peace in cool quietness around us that we were speechless for the next ten minutes. Then Mwita poked at the fire and said, "I'm not like you. Not completely."

"Eh?" I said. "What do you mean?"

"I usually just let people think what they think," he said. "You were like that to me. Even after I got to know you. It's been over a year since I saw you in that tree."

"Just get to the point," I said impatiently.

"No," he snapped. "I'll say this the way I want to say it, Onyesonwu." He looked away from me, annoyed. "You need to learn to be quiet sometimes."

"No, I don't."

"Yes, you do."

I bit my lower lip, trying to keep quiet.

"I'm not completely like you," he finally said. "Just listen, okay?"

"Fine."

"Your mother . . . she was assaulted. My mother was not. Everyone believes an *Ewu* child is like you, that his or her mother was attacked by a Nuru man and he succeeded in impregnating her. Well, my mother fell in *love* with a Nuru man."

I scoffed. "This is not something to joke about."

"It happens," he insisted. "And, yes, we come out looking the same as children of . . . of rape. You shouldn't believe all that you hear and read."

"Okay," I softly said. "Go . . . go on."

"My aunt said that my mother worked for a Nuru family and their son used to talk to her in secret. They fell in love and a year later my mother was pregnant. When I was born, the news that I was *Ewu* got out. There'd been no attacks in the area, so people were perplexed as to how I came about. Soon the love between my parents was discovered. My aunt said that someone saw my mother and father together just after my birth, that my father had snuck into the tent. I'll never know if it was a Nuru or Okeke who betrayed us.

"A mob came and, again, I don't know if it was of Nurus or Okekes. They came for my mother with stones. They came for my father with fists. They forgot about me. My aunt, my father's sister, took me to safety. She and her husband kept me. My father's death seemed to absolve my existence.

"If one's father is Nuru, then the child is. So I was raised as a Nuru in my aunt and uncle's home. When I was six, my uncle had me become the apprentice of a sorcerer named Daib. I guess I should have been grateful. Daib was known for often going off on exhibitions. My uncle said he was once a military man. He knew literature, too. Owned many books . . . all of which would eventually be destroyed."

Mwita paused, frowning. I waited for him to continue.

"My uncle had to beg and pay Daib to teach me . . . because I was *Ewu*. I was there when my uncle begged him." Mwita looked disgusted. "On his hands and knees. Daib spat on him saying that he only did the favor because he knew my grandmother. My hatred of Daib fueled my learning. I was young but I hated like a middle-aged man at the end of his prime.

"My uncle had begged liked that, humiliated himself, for a reason. He wanted me to be able to protect myself. He knew my life would be rough. Life moved on, years passed somewhat pleasantly. Until I was eleven. Four years ago. The massacres started again in the cities and swiftly spread to our village.

"The Okeke fought back. And again, as they had been before, they were outnumbered and outarmed. But in my village, the Okeke people burned hot. They stormed our house, killing my aunt and uncle. I learned later that it was Daib and anyone associated with him that they were after. I said Daib had been in the military—well, there was more to it. He was, apparently, known for his cruelty. My aunt and uncle were killed because of him, because of me being taught by him.

"Daib had taught me how to make myself 'ignorable.' This was how I escaped. I ran into the desert, where I cowered for a day. The riots were eventually stamped out, every Okeke in the village killed. When I went to Daib's home, hoping to find his corpse, I found something else. In the middle of his half-burned house were the clothes he'd been wearing the last time I'd seen him, scattered on his floor as if he'd melted into thin air. And the window was open.

"I packed what I could and traveled east. I knew how I'd be treated. I hoped to find the Red People, a tribe of people who are neither Okeke nor Nuru, living somewhere in the desert in the middle of a giant sandstorm. It's said that the Red People know impossible juju. I was young and desperate. The Red People are just a myth.

"I made money along the way working idiotic bits of sorcery like making dolls dance and children levitate. People, Nuru and Okeke, are more comfortable with *Ewu* folk who play the fool, dance about, or do tricks, as long as you avoid eye contact and move on when you're done entertaining. It's only by chance that I ended up here."

When Mwita stopped talking, I just sat there. I wondered how far Mwita's village was from what was left of my mother's. "I'm sorry," I said. "I'm sorry for us all."

He shook his head. "Don't be. It's like saying that you're sorry that you exist."

"I am."

"*Don't* belittle your mother's trials and successes," Mwita said darkly.

I sucked my teeth and looked away, my arms around my chest.

"So you wish to not be here right now?" he asked.

I said nothing to this. *At least his father wasn't a beast,* I thought.

"Life isn't so simple," he said. He smiled. "Especially for Eshus."

"You're not Eshu."

"Well, for any of us, then."

Chapter 8

Lies

A YEAR AND HALF LATER, it was by chance that I heard the two boys talking as they walked by. They were about seventeen. One had a bruised face and a bandaged arm. I was reading a book under the iroko tree.

"You look like someone stepped on your head," the unhurt boy said.

"I know," the hurt boy said. "I can barely walk."

"I tell you, the man is evil, not a *true* sorcerer."

"Oh, Aro's a true sorcerer," the hurt boy said. "Evil, but true."

My ears pricked at the name briefly mentioned the night of my Eleventh Rite.

"That *Ewu* boy's the only one good enough to learn the Great Mystic Points, apparently," the hurt boy said, his eyes wide and wet. "Makes no sense. One's blood is supposed to be clean to . . ."

I got up and walked away, my thoughts clouded with rage. I angrily searched the market, the book house, I even went to my house. No Mwita. I didn't *know* where he *lived*. This angered me even more. As I left my house, I saw him coming up the road. I strode up to him and had to restrain myself from punching him in the face.

"Why didn't you tell me?" I shouted.

"Don't come at me like that," he grumbled when I got to him. "You know better."

I laughed bitterly. "I don't know anything about you."

"I mean it, Onyesonwu," he warned.

"I don't care what you mean," I shouted.

"What possesses you, woman?"

"What do you know about the Great Mystic Points? Eh?" I had no idea what these Mystic Points were but they were being held from me and I wanted to know them now. "And . . . and what of Aro? Why didn't . . ." I was so angry that I started choking on air. I stood there panting. "You've. . . .you're a liar!" I screeched. "How can I ever trust you?"

Mwita stepped back at this. I'd crossed a line. I kept shouting. "I had to overhear it from two boys! Two stupid inept common boys! I can't trust you ever again!"

"He *won't* teach you," Mwita bitterly said holding his arms out wide.

"What?" I said, my voice cracking. "Why?"

"You want to know? Fine, I'll tell you. I hope it makes you happy. He won't teach you because you're a girl, a *woman!*" He shouted at me. There were tears of rage in his eyes. He slapped his hand against my belly. "Because of what you carry here! You can bring life, and when you get old, that ability becomes something else even greater, more dangerous and unstable!"

"What?" I said again.

He laughed angrily and began walking away. "You push *too* hard," he said. "Ugh, you're not healthy for me."

"Don't walk away from me," I said.

He stopped. "Or you'll what?" He turned around. "Are you threatening me?"

"Maybe," I said. We stood like that. I don't remember if there were people around us. There must have been. People love a good argument. And one between two *Ewu* teenagers, one a boy and one a girl, was priceless.

"Onyesonwu," he said. "He won't teach you. You were born in the wrong body."

"Yeah, well I can change that," I said.

"No, you can't ever change *that.*"

No matter what I changed into, I could only become the female version of it. This was a rule of my ability that always seemed trivial to me. "He teaches you," I said.

He nodded. "And I've been teaching you what I know."

I cocked my head. "But . . . he doesn't teach you these . . . these Points, does he?"

Mwita didn't respond.

"Because you're *Ewu*, right?" I asked.

He still said nothing.

"Mwita . . ."

"What I teach you will have to be enough," he said.

"And if it's not?"

Mwita looked away.

I shook my head. "To omit information is lying."

"If I lie to you, it's only to protect you. You're my . . . You're special to me, Onyesonwu," he blurted, wiping some of his angry tears from his cheek. "Nobody, *nobody*, should be allowed to hurt you."

"Something's *been* trying to do just that!" I said. "That . . . that horrible red and white eye thing! It's evil! . . . I think it watches me in my sleep sometimes . . ."

"I *have* asked him," he said. "Okay? I asked him. I look at you and I know . . . I *know*. I told him about you. I told him after you ended up in that tree. I asked him again after you realized you were Eshu. He won't teach you."

"Did you tell him about the red eye?"

"Yes."

Silence.

"Then I'll ask him myself," I said flatly.

"Don't," he said.

"Let him reject me to my face," I said.

Anger flashed in Mwita's eyes and he stepped back from me. "I shouldn't love a girl like you," he said quietly through gritted teeth. Then he turned and walked away.

I waited until Mwita was far enough away. Then I stepped to the side of the road and concentrated. I didn't have the feather with me, so I had to calm myself first. The argument with Mwita left me shaking with emotion so it took several minutes to calm myself. By this time, Mwita was gone. But as I said, as a vulture, the world was open to me. I found him easily.

I followed him south from my house, through the palm tree farms at Jwahir's southern border. The hut he came to was sturdy but simple. Four goats roamed around it. Mwita went into a smaller hut beside the main one. Behind both huts opened the desert.

The next day, I walked there on foot, leaving my bedroom window open in case I returned as a vulture. A gate of cacti grew in front of Aro's hut. I boldly walked through the opening that was flanked by two tall cacti. I tried to avoid the thorns but one of them nicked my arm as I passed. *No matter,* I thought.

The main hut was large, made of stacked sand brick and adobe with a thatched roof. I could see Mwita nearby sitting against the only tree bold enough to grow near the hut. I smiled slyly to myself. If this was Aro's hut, I could sneak in before Mwita saw me.

A man strolled out before I could get halfway to the hut entrance. The first thing I noticed was the blue mist surrounding him. It disappeared as he came closer. He was about two decades older than my father. His head was closely shaved. His dark skin glistened in the dry heat. Several glass and quartz amulets rested over his white caftan. He walked slowly, looking me over. I didn't like him at all.

"What?" he said.

"Oh, um . . ." I stammered. "Are you Aro, the sorcerer?"

He glared at me.

I pushed on. "My name is Onyesonwu Ubaid-Ogundimu, daughter . . . stepdaughter of Fadil Ogundimu, daughter of Najeeba Ubaid-Ogundimu . . ."

"I know who you are," he said coolly. He brought a chewing stick from his pocket and stuck it in his mouth. "You're the girl the Ada says can become transparent and Mwita says can change into a sparrow."

I noticed he didn't mention me turning into a vulture.

"Things have been happening to me, yes," I said. "And I think I'm in danger. Something tried to kill me once, a year or so ago. This great oval red eye. It continues to watch me, I think. I need to protect myself. *Oga* Aro, I will become the best and greatest student you will ever have! I know it. I can feel it. I can . . . almost touch it."

I stopped talking, tears in my eyes. I didn't realize how determined I was until now. He was looking at me with such surprise that I wondered if I'd said something wrong. He didn't seem the type easily moved. His face returned to what I assumed was his usual demeanor. Behind him I saw Mwita coming, walking fast.

"You're full of fire," he said. "But I won't teach you." He motioned with his hand up and down, in reference to my body. "Your father was Nuru, a foul dirty people. The Great Mystic Points are an Okeke art only for the pure of spirit."

"B-but you teach Mwita," I said working hard to control my despair.

"Not the Mystic Points. What I teach him is limited. He's male. You're female. You can't measure up. Even in . . . the gentler skills."

"How can you say that?" I shouted, my diamond almost flying from my mouth.

"And furthermore, you're filthy with woman blood as we speak," he said. "How dare you come here in this state."

I only blinked, not knowing what he was talking about. Later I would realize he was referring to the fact that I was having my monthly. I had about a day to go, shedding mere drops of blood. He'd spoken as if I were awash in it.

He pointed at my waist, disgusted, "And *that* is only for your husband to see."

Again I was confused. Then I looked down and saw a glint of my belly chain hanging over my rapa. I quickly tucked it away.

"Let what haunts you do away with you. It's better that way," he said.

"Please," Mwita said, walking up. "Don't insult her, *Oga*. She's dear to me."

"Yes, you all stick together, I know," Aro said.

"I didn't tell her to come!" Mwita said firmly to Aro. "She listens to no one."

I stared at Mwita, astonished and insulted.

"I don't care who sent her," Aro said with a wave of his big hand.

Mwita looked down and I could have screamed. *He's like Aro's slave,* I thought. *Like an Okeke to a Nuru. But he was raised a Nuru. How backward!*

Aro walked away. I quickly turned and walked back toward the cactus gate.

"You brought this on yourself," Mwita growled, following me. "I told you not . . ."

"You didn't tell me *anything*," I said. I walked faster. "You *live* with him! He thinks that of people like us and you STAY IN HIS HOME! I'll bet you cook and clean for him! I'm surprised he even eats what you prepare!"

"It's *not* like that," Mwita said.

"It is!" I cried. We were through the cactus gate. "It's not bad enough that I'm *Ewu* and that that thing wants to get me! I had to be female too. That crazy man you live with loves and hates you but he just hates me! Everyone hates me!"

"Your parents and I don't hate you," he said. "Your friends don't hate you."

I wasn't listening to him. I was running. I ran until I was sure he wasn't following me. I dug up the memory of oily black feathers covering mighty wings, a powerful beak, a head carrying a brain that was intelligent in ways that only I and probably that goat's penis Aro understood. I flew high and far, thinking and thinking. And when I finally got home, I hopped through my bedroom window and changed myself to the thirteen- soon to be fourteen-year-old girl I was. I crawled naked into bed, drops of blood and all, and pulled the covers over myself.

Chapter 9

Nightmare

I STOPPED SPEAKING TO MWITA and he stopped coming to see me. Three weeks passed. I missed him but my fury toward him was stronger. Binta, Luyu, and Diti filled my extra time. One morning, while sulking in the schoolyard waiting for them, Luyu walked right past me. At first I thought she just hadn't seen me. Then I noticed she looked distraught. Her eyes were red and puffy, as if she'd been crying or hadn't gotten any sleep. I ran after her.

"Luyu?" I said. "Are you okay?"

She turned to me, her face blank. Then she smiled, looking more like herself.

"You look . . . tired," I said.

She laughed. "You're right. I slept terribly." Luyu and her loaded statements. This was definitely one of them. But I knew Luyu. When she wanted to tell you something, she told you in her own time. Binta and Diti came and Luyu moved away from me as the four of us sat down.

"It's a lovely day," Diti said.

"If you say so," Luyu grumbled.

"I wish I could be as happy as you always are, Diti," I said.

"You're just sulky because you and Mwita had a fight." Diti said.

"What? H-how do you know?" I sat up straight, frantic. If they knew about the fight, then they'd heard about what we were fighting about.

"We know *you*," Diti said. Luyu and Binta both grunted in agreement. "In the last two weeks we've seen twice as much of you."

"We aren't stupid," Binta said, biting into an egg sandwich she'd brought out of her satchel. It had been smashed between her books and looked very thin.

"So what happened?" Luyu said, as she rubbed her forehead.

I shrugged.

"Do your parents disapprove?" Binta asked. They crept in closer.

"Just leave the subject be," I snapped.

"Did you give him your virginity?" Luyu asked.

"Luyu!" I exclaimed.

"Just asking."

"Has your belly chain turned green?" Binta asked. She sounded almost desperate. "I hear that that's what happens if you have intercourse after your Eleventh Rite."

"I strongly doubt she had intercourse with him," Diti said, coolly.

Before going to bed, I sat down on the floor to meditate. It took great effort to calm myself. When I finished, my face was wet with sweat and tears. Whenever I meditated, not only did I sweat profusely (which was odd because normally I sweat very little), but I also always cried. Mwita said it was because I was so used to being under constant stress that when I let it all go, I literally cried with relief. I took a shower and said good night to my parents.

Once in bed, I fell asleep and dreamed of soothing sand. Dry, soft, untouched, and warm. I was wind rolling over its dunes. Then I moved across packed cracked lands. The leaves of stubborn trees and dry bushes sang as I passed. And then a dirt road, more roads, paved and dusty with sand, full of people traveling with heavy packs, scooters, camels, horses. The roads were black and smooth and shined as if they were sweating. The people walking on the roads carried little. They weren't travelers. They were near home. Along the road were shops and large buildings.

In Jwahir, people didn't Hold Conversation beside roads or in markets. And there were only a tiny handful of people who were light-skinned— none of them were Nurus. The wind had taken me far.

Most of the people here were Nuru. I tried to get a closer look. The more I tried, the more out of focus they became. All but one. His back was turned. I could hear him laughing from miles away. He was very tall, standing in the center of a group of Nuru men. He passionately spoke words I couldn't quite hear. His laugh vibrated in my head. He wore a blue caftan. He was turning to me . . . all I could see were his eyes. They were red with searing white undulating centers. They merged into one giant eye. Terror shot through my mind like poison. I perfectly understood the words I heard next.

Stop breathing, he growled. *STOP BREATHING!*

I jolted awake, unable to breathe. I threw off my covers, wheezing. I grasped my aching neck as I sat up. Each time I blinked, I could see that red eye behind my eyes. I wheezed harder and bent forward. Black spots clouded my vision. I admit, a part of me was relieved. Death was better than living in fear of that thing. As the seconds passed, my chest loosened. My throat let in puffs of air. I coughed. I waited, rubbing my aching throat. It was morning. Someone was in the kitchen frying breakfast.

Then the dream came back to me, every detail. I jumped up on shaky legs. I was halfway down the hallway when I stopped. I went right back to my room and stood at the mirror, staring at the angry bruises on my neck. I sat on the floor and held my head in my hands. The red oval eye belonged to a rapist, my biological father. And he'd just tried to throttle me in my sleep.

Chapter 10

Ndiichie

IF THE MAD PHOTOGRAPHER HADN'T ARRIVED, I'd have stayed in bed that whole day, too afraid to go outside. My mother came home that afternoon talking about him. She couldn't seem to sit down. "He was all dirty and windblown," she said. "He came to the market straight from the desert. Didn't even try to clean up first!"

She said he might have been in his twenties, but it was hard to tell because of all the matted hair on his face. Most of his teeth had fallen out, his eyes were yellow, and his sun-blackened skin was ashy from malnutrition and dirt. Who knows how he was able to survive traveling so far in his state of mind.

But what he bore was enough to cause all of Jwahir to panic. His digital photo album. He'd lost his camera long ago but he'd stored his photos on the palm-sized gadget. Photos from the West of dead, charred, mutilated Okeke people. Okeke women being raped. Okeke children with missing limbs and bloated bellies. Okeke men hanging from buildings or rotted to near-dust in the desert. Smashed-in babies' heads. Slashed bellies. Castrated men. Women whose breasts had been cut off.

"He's coming," the photographer had ranted, spittle flying from his cracked lips, as he let people look at his album. "He'll bring ten thousand men. None of you are safe. Pack your bags, flee, fly, fly you fools!"

One by one, group by group, he allowed people to click through his album. My mother went through the photos twice. She'd wept the entire time. People vomited, cried, screamed; nobody disputed what they saw. Eventually he was arrested. From what I heard, after giving him a large meal, a bath and haircut and supplies, he was politely asked to leave Jwahir. In any event, people were talking, news was spreading. He'd caused so much distress that a Ndi-ichie, Jwahir's most urgent type of public meeting, was called for that evening.

As soon Papa came home, the three of us left together.

"Are you okay?" he asked, kissing my mother and taking her hand.

"I'll live," she said.

"Ok. Let's go. Quickly," he said, picking up his pace. "Ndiichis rarely last more than five minutes."

The town square was already packed. A stage was set up and there were four seats on it. Minutes later, four people ascended the stairs. The crowd quieted. Only the babies in the audience continued conversing. I stood on my toes, excited to finally get a look at the Osugbo Elders I'd heard so much about. When I saw them, I realized I'd already met two of them. One wore a blue rapa with a matching top.

"That's Nana the Wise," Papa said into my ear. I just nodded. I didn't want to bring up my Eleventh Year Rite.

She slowly walked onstage and took her seat. After her came an old blind man using a wooden cane. He had to be helped up the stairs. Once seated, he looked over the crowd as if he could see us all for what we really were. Papa told me he was Dika the Seer. Then came Aro the Worker. I frowned deeply. How I disliked this man who denied me so much, who denied me. Apparently few knew he was a sorcerer because Papa described him as the one who structured the government.

"That man has created the fairest system Jwahir has ever had," he whispered.

The fourth was Oyo the Ponderer. He was short and thin with white puffs of hair on the sides of his head. His mustache was bushy and his salt-and-pepper beard long. Papa said he was known for his skepticism. If an idea got past Oyo, then it would work.

"Jwahir, kwenu!" all of the elders said, punching their fists in the air.

"Yah!" the crowd responded. Papa elbowed my mother and me to do the same.

"Jwahir, kwenu!"

"Yah!"

"Jwahir, kwenu!"

"Yah!"

"Good evening, Jwahir," Nana the Wise said standing up. "The photographer's name is Ababuo. He came from Gadi, one of the Seven Rivers cities. He has worked and traveled far to bring us news. We welcome and commend him."

She sat down. Oyo the Ponderer stood up and spoke. "I have considered probability, margin of error, unlikeness. Though the plight of our people in the West is tragic, it is unlikely that this hardship will affect us. Pray to Ani for better things. But there is no need to pack your things." He sat down. I looked across the crowd. People seemed persuaded by his words. I wasn't sure what I felt. *Is our safety really the point?* I wondered. Aro stood to speak. He was the only Osugbo elder who was not ancient. Still, I wondered about his age and his appearance. Maybe he was older than he looked.

"Abadou brings reality. Take it in, but don't panic. Are we all women here?" he asked. I scoffed and rolled my eyes.

"Panic won't do you any good," he continued. "If you want to learn how to wield a knife, Obi here will teach you." He motioned to a beefy man standing near the stage. "He can also train you to run long distances without getting tired. But we're a strong people. Fear is for the weak. Buck up. Live your lives."

He sat down. Dika the Seer slowly stood, using his cane. I had to strain to hear him speak. "What I see . . . yes, the journalist shows the truth, though his mind is unhinged by it," the seer said. "But faith! We must all have faith!"

He sat down. There was silence for a moment.

"That is all," Nana the Wise said.

Once the elders left the stage and the square, everyone began to speak at once. Discussions and agreements broke out about the photographer and his state of mind, his photos, and his journey. However, the Ndiichie had worked— people weren't panicked anymore. They were energetically pensive. My father joined in the discussion, my mother quietly listening.

"I'll meet you at home," I told them.

"Go ahead," my mother said, softly patting my cheek.

I had to work hard to get out of the square. I hated crowded places. I'd just emerged from the crowd when I spotted Mwita. He'd seen me first.

"Hi," I said.

"Good evening, Onyesonwu," he said.

And just like that the connection was made. We'd been friends, fighting, learning, laughing with each other, but in this moment, we realized we were in love. The realization was like flipping the power on. But my anger with him hadn't left me. I shifted from one foot to the other, mildly caring that a few people were looking at us. I started walking home and was relieved when he walked with me.

"How have you been?" he asked tentatively.

"How could you do that?" I asked.

"I told you not to go."

"Just because you tell me to do something doesn't mean I'll listen!"

"I should have made it so that you couldn't pass his cactuses," he mumbled.

"I'd have found a way through," I said. "It was my choice and you should have respected it. Instead you stood there telling Aro how it wasn't your fault that I'd come, trying to cover your own backside. I could have killed you."

"Precisely why he won't teach you! You act like a woman. You run on emotions. You're dangerous."

I had to work not to further prove Mwita's point. "You believe that?" I asked.

He looked away.

I wiped a tear from my eye, "Then we can't be . . ."

"No, I don't believe that," Mwita said. "You're irrational at times, more irrational than any woman or man. But it's not because of what's between your legs." He smiled and sarcastically said, "Besides, haven't you gone through your Eleventh Rite? Even the Nuru know that going through it will align a woman's intelligence with her emotions."

"I'm not joking," I said.

"You're different. Your passion is more than most," he said after a brief pause.

"Then why . . ."

"Aro *needed* to know that you came on your own volition. People who are driven by others . . . trust me, he'll never accept them. Come, we need to talk."

Once at my house, we sat on the back steps in front of my mother's garden.

"Does my papa know who Aro really is?"

"To an extent," he said. "Enough people know of him, those who want to know."

"Just not most."

"Right."

"Mostly men, I assume," I said.

"And some older boys."

"He teaches others, doesn't he?" I said, annoyed. "Other than you."

"He tries. There's a test you have to pass to learn the Mystic Points. You can only take it once. Failure is awful. The closer you get to passing, the more painful it is. The boys you overheard, they'd been tried. They all return home bruised and beaten. Their fathers think they've passed initiation as Aro's apprentice. In reality, they've failed. Aro teaches the boys some small things so the boys have skill at something."

"What are the Mystic Points anyway?"

He moved closer to me, close enough that I could hear his soft whisper. "I don't know." He smiled. "I know that one must be destined to learn them. Someone must ask for it to be so, for you to BE so."

"Mwita, I *have* to learn them," I said. "It's my father! I don't know how I . . ."

And that was when he leaned forward and kissed me. I forgot about my biological father. I forgot about the desert. I forgot about all my questions. It wasn't an innocent kiss. It was deep and wet. I was almost fourteen, he was maybe seventeen. We'd both lost our innocence years ago. I didn't think of my mother and the man who raped her as I always thought I would if I were ever intimate with a boy.

There was no hesitation in his hands working their way inside my shirt. I didn't stop him kneading my breasts. He didn't stop me from kissing his neck and unbuttoning his shirt. I ached between my legs, a sharp desperate ache. So sharp that my body jumped. Mwita pulled away. He quickly stood up. "I'll go," he said.

"No!" I said getting up. The pain was spreading all over my body now and I couldn't quite straighten myself.

"If I don't leave . . ." He reached forward and touched my belly chain that had come out as he'd fumbled with my top. Aro's words flew through my head. "That is for your husband to see," he'd said. I shivered. Mwita reached into his mouth and handed me my diamond. I smiled weakly as I took it and put it back under my tongue.

"I've unknowingly betrothed myself to you," I said.

"Who believes that myth?" he asked. "Too easy. I'll come see you in two days."

"Mwita," I breathed.

"It's best that you remain untouched . . . for now."

I sighed.

"Your parents will be home soon," he said. He lifted my shirt up and tenderly kissed my nipple. I shivered, the pain between my legs flaring. I squeezed them together. He looked at me, sadly, his hand still cupping my breast.

"It hurts," he said apologetically.

I nodded, my lips pressed together. It hurt so badly that areas of my vision were going dark. Tears ran down my face.

"You'll recover in a few minutes. I wish I had known you before you had it done," he said. "The scalpel that they use is treated by Aro. There's juju on it that makes it so that a woman feels pain whenever she is too aroused . . . until she's married."

Chapter 11

Luyu's Determination

AFTER HE LEFT, I went to my room and wept. It was all I could do to curb my fury. Now I understood why a scalpel was used instead of a laserknife. A scalpel, simpler in design, was much easier to bewitch. Aro. It was always Aro. For most of the night, I considered the many ways I could hurt that man.

I considered ripping the gold chain from my waist and spitting the stone in the garbage, but I couldn't bring myself to do it. Somewhere along the way, these two items had become part of my identity. I'd have felt so ashamed without them. I didn't sleep a wink that night. I was too angry at Aro and too afraid of another visit from my biological father in my sleep.

The next night, I slept only out of pure exhaustion. Thankfully, there was no red eye. By the time I met up with Binta and Diti after school the next day, I felt a little better.

"You know that photographer? I heard all his nails had fallen off," Diti said, playfully rolling her diamond in her mouth as she spoke.

"So?" I said, leaning against the school wall.

"So that's disgusting!" Binta snapped. "What kind of man is that?"

"Where's Luyu?" I asked, changing the subject.

Diti giggled. "She's probably with Kasie. Or Gwan."

"I swear, Luyu will fetch the highest bride price," Binta said.

Had any of these boys tried to touch Luyu? "What of Calculus?" I asked.

Calculus was Luyu's favorite. He was also the boy who scored highest in math class. All three of my friends had several suitors, Luyu having the most, then Diti. Binta refused to talk to any of hers. We were still chatting when Luyu came around the corner. There were dark circles under her eyes and she walked bent forward.

"Luyu!" Diti screamed. "What happened?!"

Binta started crying, grabbing Luyu's hand.

"Sit her down!" I shouted. Luyu's hands shook as they made and unmade fists. Then her face squeezed and she shrieked in pain.

"I'll go get someone," Binta said jumping up.

"No!" Luyu managed to say. "Don't!"

"What happened?" I said.

The three of us crouched around her. Luyu stared at me with wide hollow eyes. "You . . . you might know," she said to me. "Something's wrong with me. I think I'm cursed."

"What do you . . . ?"

"I was with Calculus." She paused. " . . . at the tree with the bushes around it."

We all nodded. It was where students went for privacy.

Luyu smiled despite herself. "I'm not like you three. Well, maybe Diti will understand." Binta reached into her satchel and handed Luyu a bottle of water. Luyu took a sip. Then she spoke with a rage I didn't know she was capable of. "I tried, but I enjoy it," she said. "I've always enjoyed it! Why shouldn't I?"

"Luyu what . . ." Diti began to say.

"Kissing, touching, intercourse," Luyu said, looking at Diti. "You know it. It's good. We learned that early." She looked at Binta. "It's good when it's *right*. I know that no man is to touch us now, and I *tried!*" I took her hand. She snatched it away.

"I've tried for three years. Then Gwan came one day and I let him kiss me. It was good but then it was bad. It . . . made me hurt! Who did this to me? No one can just . . ." she was breathing too heavily. "Soon we'll be eighteen, fully fledged adults! Why wait until marriage to enjoy what Ani gave me! Whatever the curse, I wanted to break it. I've been trying . . . Today it felt like I was going to die. Calculus refused to continue . . ." She looked beyond me, and screamed, "Look at him!"

We all turned to see Calculus standing behind the schoolyard fence. He quickly started walking away. "I'm not going to be the one who kills you!" he shouted.

"Ani will make your penis curl!" Luyu shouted.

"Luyu!" Diti screeched.

"I don't care," Luyu said, looking away.

"It'll pass," I said. "You'll feel better in a few minutes." It wasn't the first time I'd seen her like this. *That day she walked right past me looking sick,* I thought.

"I'll never feel better," she said.

"Is it a curse?" Binta asked me.

"I don't think so," I said, annoyed that they thought I knew all about curses.

"It is," Diti said. "Two years ago, I let Fanasi . . . touch me. We were kissing and . . . I hurt so badly that I started crying. He took offense and *still* won't speak to me."

"It's not a curse," Binta suddenly said. "It's Ani protecting us."

"From what?" Luyu snapped. "From enjoying boys? I don't want that kind of protection!"

"I *do!*" Binta retorted. "You don't know what's good for you. You're lucky that you aren't pregnant! Ani protected you. She protects me. My father . . ." She slapped her hand over her mouth.

"You father what?" Luyu asked, frowning.

I growled low in my throat. "Binta, speak," I said. "Ah, ah, Binta, what is this?"

"Did he try again?" Diti asked when Binta refused to speak. "He did, didn't he?"

"He couldn't do it because you were writhing in pain?" I asked.

"Ani protects me," Binta insisted, tears falling down her cheeks.

We were all silent.

"He-he understands now," Binta said. "He won't touch me anymore."

"I don't care," Luyu said. "He should be castrated like the other rapists."

"Shhh, don't say that," Binta whispered.

"I will say and do what I want!" Luyu shouted.

"No, you won't," I said, putting my arm around Binta. I chose my words carefully. "I think juju was worked on us at our Eleventh Rite. It's . . . probably broken with marriage." I looked hard at Luyu. "I think if you force intercourse, you'll die."

"It is broken with marriage," Diti said nodding. "My cousin always talks about how only a pure woman attracts a man pure enough to bring pleasure to the marriage bed. She says her husband is the purest man around . . . probably because he was the first who didn't bring her pain."

"Ugh," Luyu said, angrily. "We're tricked into thinking our husbands are gods."

On my way home, I ran into Mwita. He was reading at the iroko tree. I sat beside him and sighed loudly. He shut his book.

"Did you know that the Ada and Aro once loved each other?" he asked.

I raised my eyebrows. "What happened?"

Mwita leaned back. "When he first came here years ago, the Osugbo Society immediately called him to a meeting. The Seer must have seen that Aro was a sorcerer. Not long after, he was invited to work with Osugbo Elders. After he peacefully dealt with a disagreement between two of Jwahir's biggest traders, they asked him to become a full member. He's Jwahir's first not so elderly elder. Aro didn't look a day over forty. No one minded because Jwahir benefited from him. Do you know the House of Osugbo?"

I nodded.

"It was built with juju," Mwita said. "It was here before Jwahir was. Anyway, it has a way of making things . . . happen. One day, Nana the Wise asked Yere—that was the Ada's name when she was a young woman—to meet her there. Aro also happened to be there that day. They both took a wrong turn and came face-to-face. From the moment they met, they didn't like each other.

"Love is often mistaken for hate. But sometimes, people learn their mistake, as these two quickly did. Nana the Wise had set her eye on Yere as the next Ada. So Yere was asked often to come to the house for one reason or another. Aro spent almost all his time there. The House of Osugbo kept bringing them together, you see.

"Aro would ask, and then Yere would accept. He would speak, she would listen. She would wait and then he would come to her. They felt that they understood how things should always be. Yere was eventually appointed the Ada when the previous Ada passed away. Aro had established himself as the Worker. They complemented each other perfectly."

Mwita paused. "It was Aro who came up with the idea to put juju on the scalpel but it was the Ada who accepted. They felt they were doing something good for the girls."

I laughed bitterly and shook my head. "Does Nana the Wise know?"

"She knows. To her, it makes sense, too. She's old."

"Why didn't Aro and the Ada marry?"

Mwita smiled. "Did I say that they didn't?"

Chapter 12

A Vulture's Arrogance

THE SUN HAD JUST RISEN. I was perched in the tree, hunched forward.

I'd woken up fifteen minutes ago to see it before my bed. Staring at me. An insubstantial red sheet with an oval of white steam in the center. The eye hissed with anger and disappeared.

And that was when I spotted the shiny brown and black scorpion crawling up my bedclothes. The kind whose sting could kill. It would have reached my face in a matter of seconds had I not woken. I whipped up my covers, sending it flying. It landed with an almost metallic *plick!* I grabbed the nearest book and crushed the thing with it. I stamped on the book, over and over, until I stopped shaking. I was fuming as I threw off my clothes and flew out the window.

The vulture's natural angry look matched how I felt. From the tree, I watched the two boys walk through the cactus gate. I flew back to my bedroom and shifted back to myself. To remain a vulture for too long always left me feeling detached from what I could only define as being a human. As a vulture, I felt condescending when I looked at Jwahir, as if I knew greater places. All I wanted to do was ride the wind, search out carrion, and not return home. There is always a price for changing.

I'd changed into a few other creatures as well. I'd tried to catch a small lizard. I got its tail instead. I used this to change into one. This was surprisingly almost as easy as changing into a bird. I later read in an old book that reptiles and birds were closely related. There had even been a bird with scales millions of years ago. Still when I changed back, for days I found it extremely difficult to stay warm at night.

Using the wings of a fly, I changed into one. The process was awful—I felt as if I were imploding. And because my body changed so drastically, I couldn't feel nauseated. Imagine wanting to feel sick and not being able to. As a fly I was food-minded, fast, watchful. I had none of the complex emotions I had as a vulture. Most disturbing about being a fly was the sense of my mortality ending in a matter of days. To a fly, those days must have felt like a lifetime. To me, a human who'd changed into a fly, I was very aware of both the slowness and swiftness of time. When I changed back, I was relieved that I still looked and felt my age.

When I'd changed into a mouse my dominant emotion was fear. Fear of being crushed, eaten, found, starving. When I changed back, the residual paranoia was so strong that I couldn't leave my room for hours.

This day, I'd been a vulture for over half an hour and that sense of power was still with me when I returned to Aro's hut as myself. I knew those two boys. Stupid, annoying, privileged, boys. As a vulture, I'd heard one of them say that he'd rather be in bed sleeping the morning away. The other had laughed, agreeing. I gnashed my teeth as I walked up to the cactus gate for the second time in my life. As I passed, again one of the cactuses scratched me. *Show your worst*, I thought. I kept walking.

When I stepped around Aro's hut, there he was sitting on the ground in front of the two boys. Behind them, the desert spread out, wide and lovely. Tears of frustration wet my eyes. I needed what Aro could teach me. As my tears fell, Aro looked up me. I could have slapped myself. He didn't need to see my weakness. The two boys turned around and the blank, dumb, idiotic looks on their faces made me even angrier. Aro and I stared at each other. I wanted to pounce on him, tear at his throat, and gnash at his spirit.

"Get out of here," he said in a calm low voice.

The finality of his tone dashed away any hope I had. I turned and ran. I fled. But not from Jwahir. Not yet.

Chapter 13

Ani's Sunshine

THAT AFTERNOON, I banged on her door harder than I meant to. I was still wound up. At school, I'd been angrily quiet. Binta, Luyu, and Diti knew to give me space. I should have skipped school after going to Aro's hut that morning. But my parents were both at work and I didn't feel safe alone. After school, I went straight to the Ada's house.

She slowly opened the door and frowned. She was elegantly dressed as always. Her green rapa was tightly wrapped around her hips and legs and her matching top had shoulders so puffy that they wouldn't fit through the doorway if she stepped forward.

"You went again, didn't you?" she asked.

I was too agitated to wonder how she knew this. "He's a bastard," I snapped. She took my arm and pulled me in.

"I've watched you," she said, handing me a cup of hot tea and sitting across from me. "Since I planned your parent's wedding."

"So?" I snapped.

"Why'd you come here?"

"You have to help me. Aro has to teach me. Can you convince him? He's your husband." I sneered. "Or is that a lie, like the Eleventh Rite?"

She jumped up and slapped me hard with her open hand. The side of my face burned and I tasted blood in my mouth. She stood glaring down at me for a moment. She sat back down. "Drink your tea," she said. "It'll wash the blood away."

I took a sip, my hands almost dropping the cup. "I-I apologize," I mumbled.

"How old are you now?"

"Fifteen."

She nodded. "What did you think would happen by going to him?"

I sat there for a moment, afraid to speak. I glanced at the finished mural.

"You may speak," she said.

"I-I didn't think about it," I quietly said. "I just . . ." How could I explain it? Instead, I asked what I had come to ask. "He's your husband," I said. "You must know what he knows. That's the way between husband and wife. Please, can you teach me the Great Mystic Points?" I put on my most humble face. I must have looked half crazy.

"How did you learn about us?"

"Mwita told me."

She nodded and sucked her teeth loudly. "That one. I should paint him into my mural. I'll make him one of the fish men. He is strong, wise, and untrustworthy."

"We're very close," I said coldly. "And those who are close share secrets."

"Our marriage isn't a secret," she said. "Older folks know. They were all there."

"*Ada-m,* what happened? With you and Aro?"

"Aro is far older than he looks. He's wise and has only a handful of peers. Onyesonwu, if he wanted to, he could take your life and make everyone, including your mother, forget you existed. Be careful." She paused. "I knew all this from the moment I met him. That's why I hated him when we first met. No one should have that kind of power. But it seemed he kept finding me. Something connected whenever we argued.

"And as I got to know him, I realized he wasn't about power. He was older than that. Or so I thought. We married for love. He loved me because I calmed him and made him think more clearly. I loved him because, when I got beyond his arrogance, he was good to me and . . . well, I wanted to learn whatever he could teach me. My mother taught me to marry a man who could not only provide but also add to my knowledge. Our marriage should have been strong. For a while it was . . ." She paused. "We worked together where it was necessary. The Eleventh Rite juju helps a girl protect her honor. I myself know how difficult it is."

She paused and unconsciously looked at the front door, which was closed. "To make you *feel* better, Onyesonwu . . . I'll tell you a secret that not even Aro knows."

"Okay," I said. But I wasn't sure if I wanted to hear this at all.

"When I was fifteen, I loved a boy and he used it to have intercourse with me. I didn't really want to but he demanded it or else he'd stop speaking to me. It went like this for a month. Then he grew tired of me and stopped speaking to me anyway. I was heartbroken, but this was the least of my worries. I was pregnant. When I told my parents, my mother screamed and called me a disgrace and my father shouted and clutched at his heart. They sent me to live with my mother's sister and her husband. It was a month's journey by camelback. A town called Banza.

"I wasn't allowed to go outside until I gave birth. I was a skinny child and during the pregnancy I remained so, except for my belly. My uncle thought it was funny. He said that the boy I was carrying must have been a descendant of Jwahir's giant golden lady. If I smiled at all during this time, it was because of him.

"But most of that time, I was miserable. I paced around the house all day, craving the outdoors. And the weight of my body made me feel so alien. My aunt felt sorry for me, and one day she brought home some paint from the market, a paintbrush, and five bleached and dried palm fronds. I had never tried to paint before. I learned I could paint the sun and the trees, the outdoors. My aunt and uncle even sold some of my paintings in the market! Onyesonwu, I'm the mother of twins."

I gasped and said, "Ani has been good to you!"

"After carrying twins at fifteen, I wonder about that," she said. But she smiled. Twins are a strong sign of Ani's love. Twins are often paid to live in a town, too. If anything goes wrong, it is always said that if the twins weren't there things would have been worse. There were no twins that I knew of in Jwahir.

"I named the girl Fanta and the boy Nuumu," the Ada said. "When they were about a year old, I came back here. The babies stayed with my aunt and uncle. Banza was far enough that I couldn't go running there on a whim. My children should be in their thirties by now. They've never come to see me. Fanta and Nuumu." She paused. "So you see? Girls need to be protected from their own stupidity and not suffer the stupidity of boys. The juju forces her to put her foot down when she must."

But sometimes a girl is still forced, I thought, thinking of Binta.

"Aro wouldn't teach me a thing," she said. "I asked about the Mystic Points and he only laughed at me. I was fine with this but when I asked him about small things like helping the plants grow, keeping ants out of our kitchen, keeping the sand out of our computer, he was always too busy. He'd even place the Eleventh Rite juju on the scalpels when I was not around! It felt . . . *wrong*.

"You're right, Onyesonwu. There should be no secrets between a husband and wife. Aro is full of secrets and he gives no excuse for keeping them. I told him I was leaving. He asked me to stay. He shouted and threatened. I was a woman and he was a man, he said. True. By leaving him, I went against all that I was taught. It was harder than leaving my children.

"He bought me this house. He comes to me often. He's still my husband. He was the one who described the Lake of the Seven Rivers to me."

"Oh," I said.

"He's always given me inspiration to paint. But when it comes to those deeper things, he tells me nothing."

"Because you're a woman?" I asked hopelessly, my shoulder slumping.

"Yes."

"Please, *Ada-m*," I said. I considered getting on my knees, but then I thought of Mwita's uncle begging the sorcerer Daib. "Ask him to change his mind. At my Eleventh Rite, you yourself said that I should go see him."

She looked annoyed. "I was foolish and so is your request," she said. "Stop making a fool of yourself by going over there. He enjoys saying no."

I sipped my tea. "Oh," I said, suddenly realizing. "That fish man near the door. The one that is so old with the intense eyes. That's Aro, isn't it?"

"Of course it is," she said.

Chapter 14

The Storyteller

THE MAN JUGGLED LARGE BLUE STONE BALLS with one hand. He did it with such ease that I wondered if he was using juju. *He is a man, so it's possible,* I thought resentfully. It had been three months since Aro had rejected me that second time. I don't know how I got through those days. Who knew when my biological father would strike again?

Luyu, Binta, and Diti weren't so amazed by the juggler. It was a Rest Day. They were more interested in gossip.

"I hear Sihu was betrothed," Diti said.

"Her parents want to use the bride price to invest in their business," Luyu said. "Can you imagine being married at twelve?"

"Maybe," Binta said quietly, looking away.

"I could," Diti said. "And I wouldn't mind having a husband who is much older. He would take good care of me as he should."

"Your husband will be Fanasi," Luyu said.

Diti rolled her eyes, irritated. Fanasi still wouldn't speak to her.

Luyu laughed and said, "Just watch and see if I'm not right."

"I'm not watching for anything," Diti grumbled.

"*I* want to marry as soon as possible," Luyu said with a sly grin.

"*That's* not a reason to marry," Diti said.

"Says who?" Luyu asked. "People marry for lesser reasons."

"I don't want to marry at all," Binta mumbled.

Marriage was the last thing on my mind. Plus *Ewu* children weren't marriageable. I would be an insult to any family. And Mwita had no family to marry us. On top of all this I questioned what intercourse would be like if we *were* married. In school we were taught about female anatomy. We focused most on how to deliver a child if a healer was unavailable. We learned ways of preventing conception, though none of us could understand why anyone would want to. We'd learned how a man's penis worked. But we skipped the section on how a woman was aroused.

I read this chapter on my own and I learned that my Eleventh Rite took more from me than true intimacy. There is no word in Okeke for the flesh cut from me. The medical term, derived from English, was *clitoris*. It created much of a woman's pleasure during intercourse. *Why in Ani's name is this removed?* I wondered, perplexed. Who could I ask? The healer? She was there the night I was circumcised! I thought about the rich and electrifying feeling that Mwita always conjured up in me with a kiss, just before the pain came. I wondered if I'd been ruined. I didn't even *have* to have it done.

I tuned out Luyu and Diti's talk of marriage and watched the juggler throw his balls in the air, do a somersault, and catch them. I clapped and the juggler smiled at me. I smiled back. When he first saw me, he did a double take and then looked away. Now I was his most valuable audience member.

"The Okeke and the Nuru!" someone announced. I jumped. The woman was very very tall and strongly built. She wore a long white dress that was tight at the top to accentuate her ample bosom. Her voice easily cut through the market's noise.

"I bring news and stories from the West." She winked. "For those who wish to know, come back here when the sun sets." Then she dramatically whirled around and left the market square. She probably made this announcement every half hour.

"Pss, who wants to hear more bad news?" Luyu grumbled. "We've had enough with that photographer."

"I agree," Diti said. "Goodness. It's a Rest Day."

"Nothing can be done about the problems over there, anyway," Binta said.

That was all that my friends had to say on the matter. They forgot or simply overlooked me, who I was. *I'll just go with Mwita then*, I thought.

According to rumor, like the photographer, the storyteller was from the West. My mother didn't want to go. I understood. She was relaxing in Papa's arms on the couch. They were playing a game of Warri. As I prepared to leave, I felt a pang of loneliness.

"Will Mwita be there?" my mother asked.

"I hope so," I said. "He was supposed to be here tonight."

"Come right home, afterward," Papa said.

The town square was lit by palm oil lanterns. There were drums set in front of the iroko tree. Few people came. Most were older men. One of the younger men was Mwita. Even in the dim light, I could easily see him. He sat to the far left, leaning against the raffia fence that separated market booths from passersby. No one sat near him. I sat beside him and he put his arm around my waist.

"You were supposed to meet me at my house," I said.

"I had another engagement," he said, with a slight smile.

I paused, surprised. Then I said, "I don't care."

"You do."

"I don't."

"You think it's another woman."

"I don't care."

Of course I did.

A man with a shiny bald head sat down behind the drums. His hands produced a soft beat. Everyone stopped talking. "Good evening," the storyteller said, walking into the lantern light. People clapped. My eyes widened. A crab shell dangled from a chain around her neck. It was small and delicate. Its whiteness shone in the lantern light against her skin. It had to be from one of the Seven Rivers. In Jwahir, it would be priceless.

"I'm a poor woman," she said, looking out at her small crowd. She pointed to a calabash decorated with orange glass beads. "I got this in exchange for a story when I was in Gadi, an Okeke community beside the Fourth River. I've traveled that far, people. But the farther east I have come, the poorer I get. Fewer people want to hear my most potent stories and those are the ones I want to tell."

She sat down heavily and crossed her thick legs. She adjusted her expansive dress to fall over her knees. "I don't care for wealth, but please when you leave, put what you can in here, gold, iron, silver, salt chips, as long as it's worth more than sand," she said. "Something for something. Am I heard?"

We strongly answered, "Yes," "Gladly," "Whatever you need, woman."

She smiled broadly and motioned to the drummer. He started playing a louder but slower beat to draw us in. Mwita's arm held me tighter.

"You people are far from the conflict's center," she said, cocking her head conspiratorially. "That's reflected in the number of you here today. But you're all this town needs." The drummer's speed picked up. "Today I tell you a piece of the past, present, and future. I expect you to share it with your families and friends. Don't forget the children when they're old enough. This first story we know from the Great Book. We retell it to ourselves time and time again when the world doesn't make sense.

"Thousands of years ago, when this land was still made of sand and dry trees, Ani looked over her lands. She rubbed her dry throat. Then she made the Seven Rivers and had them all meet, making a deep lake. And from this lake she took a deep drink. 'One day,' she said, 'I'll produce sunshine. Right now, I'm not in the mood.' She turned over and slept. Behind her back, as she rested, the Okeke sprang from the sweet rivers.

"They were aggressive like the rushing rivers, forever wanting to move forward. As centuries passed, they spread over Ani's lands and created and used and changed and altered and spread and consumed and multiplied. They were everywhere. They built towers that they hoped would be high enough to prick Ani and get her attention. They built juju-working machines. They fought and invented among themselves. They bent and twisted Ani's sand, water, sky, and air, took her creatures and changed them.

"When Ani was rested enough to produce sunshine, she turned over. She was horrified by what she saw. She reared up, tall and impossible, furious. Then she reached into the stars and pulled a sun to the land. The Okeke people cowered. From the sun, Ani plucked the Nuru. She set them on her land. That same day, flowers realized they could bloom. Trees understood that they could grow. And Ani laid a curse on the Okeke.

"'*Slaves*,' Ani said.

"Under the new sun, most of what the Okeke built crumbled. We still have some of it, the computers, gadgets, items, objects in the sky that sometimes speak to us. The Nuru to this day point at the Okeke and say, *slave* and the Okeke must bow their heads in agreement. That is the past."

When the drumming slowed, several people, including Mwita, put money in the cup. I stayed where I was. I'd read the Great Book many times. I'd learned to read using this very story. By the time I could read it with ease, I also hated it.

"The news I bring from the West is fairly fresh," she said. "I was trained by my parents who were storytellers, as their parents were. My memory holds thousands of tales. I can tell you firsthand what it was like in Gadi, my village, when the slaughtering began. No one knew that it would burst the way it did. I was eight years old and I watched my family die. Then I fled.

"They killed my papa and brothers with machetes. I managed to hide in a closet for three days," she said, her voice dropping. "As I hid, in that room, Nuru men raped my mother repeatedly. They wanted to make an *Ewu* child." She glanced at Mwita and me. "As it happened, my mother's mind cracked and the stories she carried spilled out. As I cowered in the closet, I listened to her tell all the tales that had comforted me as a child. Tales that shook to the rhythm of the men forcefully entering her.

"When they finished, they took my mother. I never saw her again. I don't remember gathering my things and running, but I did. Eventually, I met others. They took me with them. That was many years ago. I have no children. My storyteller lineage will die with me. I can't bear the hands of a man on me."

She paused. "The killing continues. But there are few Okeke left where there used to be many. In a matter of decades, they'll have wiped us from their land. It was our land, too. So tell me, is it right that you dwell here content as this happens? You're safe here. Maybe. Maybe one day they'll change their minds and come East to finish what they started in the West. You can run from my stories and my words or . . ."

"Or what?" some man asked. "It's been written in the Great Book. We are what we are. We shouldn't have risen up in the first place! Let those who tried die for it!"

"Written by who?" she asked. "And my parents weren't involved in the movement. Nor was I."

I felt hot and angry. She'd only been telling the *story* of our so-called creation. She didn't believe it. What did this man think of Mwita and me? That we somehow deserved what we got? That Mwita's parents deserved death? That my mother deserved rape? Mwita rubbed my shoulders. If he hadn't been there, I'd have shouted at that man and whoever defended him. I was full of it—full of damage—as I would learn soon enough.

"I'm not finished," the storyteller said. The drummer beat a moderate beat. He was sweating but his eyes remained on her. It was easy to notice he was in love with her. And because of her past, his love was doomed. The closest he came to touching her was probably through the beat of his drum.

"As we were doomed in the past and are doomed in the present, we will be saved in the future," she said. "There's a prophecy by a Nuru Seer living on a tiny island in the Unnamed Lake. He says a Nuru man will come and force the Great Book's rewriting. He'll be very tall with a long beard. His mannerisms will be gentle, but he will be cunning and full of vigor and fury. A sorcerer. When he comes, there will be good change for Nuru *and* Okeke. When I left, there was an ongoing manhunt for this man. They were killing all tall Nuru men with beards and gentle mannerisms. All of these men have turned out to be healers, not rebels. So have faith, there is hope."

There was no applause but the storyteller's calabash quickly filled up. No one stayed to talk with her. No one even looked at her. As people walked into the evening, they were quiet and pensive, and they moved fast. I wanted to go home, too. Her stories had made me feel sick and guilty.

Mwita wanted to speak with her first. As we approached her, she smiled broadly. I stared at her crab shell. It looked like a spiral of hardened bread dough.

"Good evening, *Ewu* children. I give you my love and respect," she said, kindly.

"Thank you," Mwita said. "I'm Mwita and this is my companion, Onyesonwu. Your stories touched us."

Companion? I thought, tickled by the reference.

"The prophecy, where'd you hear of it?" Mwita asked.

"It's all the talk of the West, Mwita," she said with seriousness. "The Seer who spoke it viciously hates Okeke people. For him to say such a thing, it must be true."

"But why did he let the news out, then?" he asked.

"He's a Seer. A Seer can't lie. Withholding the truth is lying."

I wondered if that Seer also wanted to incite a manhunt. As Mwita walked me home, he seemed bothered.

"What?" I finally asked.

"I was just thinking about Aro," he said. "He must teach you."

"Why are you thinking that now?" I asked, annoyed.

"I've been thinking about it a lot lately. It's just not right, Onyesonwu," he said. "You're too . . . it's not right. I'll beg him today. Plead with him, even."

I saw Mwita the next day. When he didn't mention what happened when he'd "pled" with Aro, I knew I'd been rejected yet again.

Chapter 15

The House of Osugbo

THREE DAYS LATER, I went to see Nana the Wise in the House of Osugbo. It was either learn from her or leave Jwahir. Anything was better than just sitting there waiting for my biological father to try to kill me again. Because it was built with juju, the House of Osugbo had a way of making things happen. And those who governed Jwahir met and worked there, including Nana the Wise. It was worth a try.

I went in the morning, opting to walk right past school. I only felt a mild pang of guilt. Made of heavy yellow stone, the House of Osugbo was the tallest and widest building in Jwahir. Its walls were cool to the touch, even in the sun. Each slab of stone was decorated with symbols which I now knew were Nsibidi script. Mwita told me that Nsibidi wasn't just an ancient writing system. It was an ancient *magical* writing system.

"If you know Nsibidi, you can erase a man's ancestors by simply writing in the sand," he'd said. But that was as far as his knowledge went on the subject. Thus, all I could read was the writing above each of the four entrances:

THE HOUSE OF OSUGBO

As I approached, people walked around and past the House without a glance. Not one person went inside. It was as if it were invisible. *Weird,*

I thought. Each entrance's path was lined with small flowering cacti that reminded me of Aro's hut. The entranceways were doorless. I stepped onto one of its four paths and walked right up. I was sure someone would stop me, ask me what I was doing, and turn me away. Instead I walked right in, entering a long hallway lit by rose-colored lamps.

It was cool inside. Music played from somewhere, a playful guitar and drums. My sandals made crunching sounds on the stone floor from the sand I brought in. The sound echoed on the bare walls. I touched the wall on my left, which faced the inside of the building.

"It's true," I whispered, my hand on the lumpy brown surface. The House of Osugbo was built around a very fat baobab tree. *It must be so old,* I thought. I shivered. As I stood there, hand on the massive trunk, there was a burst of laughter. I jumped and started walking again. Ahead of me, two very old men came around the corner. They wore long caftans, one dark red, the other tan. Their smiles diminished when they saw me.

"Good morning, *Oga*. Good morning, *Oga*," I said.

"Do you know where you are, *Ewu* girl?" the one in red asked.

People always had to remind me of what I was. "My name is Onyesonwu."

"You aren't allowed here," he said. "This place is only for the old. Unless you're apprenticed, which *you* would never be."

With effort, I held my tongue.

"Why are you here, Onyesonwu?" the one in tan asked more kindly. "Efu is correct, you know. It's more for your safety than your insult."

"I just want to speak with Nana the Wise."

"We can take your message to her," the man in tan said.

I considered this. The air had taken on a nutty smell of monkey-bread fruit and I had a feeling that the House was observing me. It was frightening.

"Well," I said. "Can you . . ."

"Actually," the man in red named Efu said, smirking. "She should be in her chambers this morning as always. It should be okay if you go straight to her."

The two men exchanged a brief look. The man in tan looked uncomfortable. He looked away, "It is up to you."

I nervously looked down the hallway. "Which way do I go?"

After making the turn, I was to walk halfway down the hall, make a right, then make a left and go up some stairs. Those were Efu's directions. He might as well have laughed as he gave them. In the House of Osugbo, one doesn't choose where to go or what to do there. The House does. I learned this minutes later.

I followed their directions but I came to no stairs. On the outside, the House looked big but not nearly as big as it was on the inside. I passed halls and rooms. I didn't know there were so many old people in Jwahir. I heard several dialects of Okeke. Some rooms were full of books, but most had iron chairs with old people sitting in them.

I looked for the special bronze table my father had made for the House years ago. I frowned realizing that my father had probably been communicating mostly with Aro for that project. I didn't see the table anywhere. But I suspected all of the chairs were my father's work. Only he could make iron look like lace that way. As I passed, people took notice of me. Several of them scoffed or looked angry.

I found a tunnel made by the tree's roots. I leaned against one of them, frustrated. I cursed and slapped at the root. "This place is a bizarre labyrinth," I grumbled. I was wondering how I was going to find the exit when two young men with long black braided beards came up to me.

"Here she is, Kona," one of them said. He had a bag of dates. He popped one in his mouth. The other one laughed and leaned against the root next to me. They both might have been in their early twenties, though their beards made them look older.

"What are you doing here, Onyesonwu?" the one with the dates asked. He offered me one and I took it. I was starving.

"Why do you know my name?" I asked.

"Only Kona is allowed to answer questions with questions," he said. "I'm Titi. Apprentice to Dika the Seer. Kona is apprentice to Oyo the Ponderer. And you are lost." He handed me another date. They stood there watching me eat it.

"He's right," Titi said to Kona. Kona nodded.

"How long, do you think?" Kona asked.

"I'm not good enough to see that yet," Titi said. "I'll ask *Oga* Dika."

"Won't Mwita be angry with her, too?" Kona asked with a laugh.

I looked up, my attention caught. "Eh?"

"Nothing you won't know," Titi said.

"Is Mwita here?" I asked.

"Do you see him here?" Kona asked me.

"No," Titi said. "Not today, he isn't. Go and find Nana the Wise." He gave me another date.

"Can you show me where she is?" I asked.

"No," Titi said.

"Are you sure that's what you're here for?" Kona asked.

"We have to go," Titi said. "Don't worry, you won't be lost in here forever, beautiful *Ewu* girl." He handed me his bag of dates.

"You *are* welcome here," Kona said. It was the first nonquestion he'd said to me.

Then, as quickly as they came, they were on their way down the tunnel of roots. I ate a few dates and moved on. An hour later, I was still lost. I trudged down a hallway with windows too high for me to see out of. I didn't remember seeing windows from outside. I came to a stairway. It wound up in a stone spiral.

"Finally!" I said aloud. The stairway was very narrow and as I went up, I hoped I wouldn't meet anyone. I counted fifty-two steps and still no second floor. It was stuffy and hot. The lights on the wall were dim and orange. Ten stairs later, I heard footsteps and voices. I looked down. It was pointless to go back.

The voices grew louder. I saw their shadows and held my breath. Then I was face to face with Aro. I gasped and looked down, flattening against the wall. He said nothing to me as he squeezed by. His body was forced to press against mine. He smelled of smoke and flowers. He stamped on my foot as he passed. There were three men following him. None of them said "Excuse me." When they were gone, I sat down on the steps and wept. Titi was wrong. I wasn't welcome here at all, unless welcome meant being made a fool of. I wiped my hands on my dress, pulled myself up, and moved on.

The stairs finally ended at the start of another hallway. The first room I peeked into was Nana the Wise's. "Good, ah, afternoon," I said.

"Good afternoon," she said, leaning back in her wicker chair, a cup of tea in hand.

I took a cautious step back but my backside met a closed door. I turned around confused. When had I walked into the room?

"It's the way of the House," she said, peering at me with her one good eye.

"I think I hate this place," I mumbled.

"People hate what they don't understand," she said. "I was about to go out to the market for lunch but then my apprentice brought me this." She held up a container of pepper soup. She peeled off the top and put it on the wicker table beside her. "So here I am. I should have known to expect a visitor."

She motioned for me to sit on the floor and for a minute, I watched her eat her soup. It smelled wonderful. My stomach rumbled.

"How are your parents?" she asked.

"They're well," I said.

"Why have you come here?"

"I-I wanted to ask . . ." I tapered off.

She waited and ate.

"The . . . the Great Mystic Points," I finally said. "Please . . . you remember what happened to me at my Eleventh Rite, *Ada-m*." I searched her face but she only looked at me waiting for me to finish. "You're wise," I continued. "Wise as Aro, if not wiser."

"Don't compare us," she said gravely. "We're both old."

"I'm sorry," I quickly said. "But you know so much. You must know how much I need to know the Great Mystic Points."

"The work of mad men and women," she spat.

"Eh?"

She spooned out a large chunk of meat from her soup and ate it. "No, Onyesonwu, this is between you and Aro."

"But can't you . . ."

"No."

"Please?" I begged. "Please!"

"Even *if* I knew the Points, I wouldn't get between two spirits like yourselves."

I slumped back to the floor.

"Listen, *Ewu* girl," she said.

I looked up. "Please, *Ada-m*, don't call me that."

"And why not? Isn't that what you are?"

"I hate that word."

"*Ewu* or girl?"

"*Ewu*, of course."

"Is that not what you are?"

"No," I said. "Not in the way the word means."

She looked at her empty bowl and folded her hands. Her nails were short and thin, the tips of her index finger and thumb yellow. Nana the Wise was a smoker. "Some advice: Leave Aro alone, I beg. He's beyond you and he is stubborn."

I pursed my lips. Aro wasn't the only one who was stubborn.

"There may be another way to learn what you seek," she said. "The House is full of books. No one's read them all, so who knows what could be in them, eh?"

"But the people here don't . . ."

"We're old and wise. We can be stupid, too. Remember Titi's words." When my eyebrows rose with surprise, she said. "The walls are thin here. Come."

The room down the hall was small, but the walls were stacked with smelly, cracked, old books. "You're free to look here or in other rooms with books. Only the Osugbo elders have personal chambers. The rest of the House is everybody's. When you're ready to leave, you can."

She patted me on the head and left me there. I searched for two hours, going from room to room. There were books on birds who lived in places that didn't exist, how to have a good marriage with two wives who hated each other, the living habits of female termites, the biology of mythical giant flying lizards called *Kponyungo*, the herbs women should eat to en-large their breasts, the uses of palm oil. Intensified by my grumbling stom-ach, my anger grew with each useless book I pulled out. The annoyed, and often fearful, looks of elders didn't help.

The House was mocking me again. I could almost hear it laughing as it showed me stupid book after stupid book. When I pulled out a book full of provocatively posed naked women, I threw it to the floor and went looking for an exit. It took me an hour to find it. The door leading outside was plain and narrow, nothing like the elaborate entrances I saw from outside. I stumbled into the late afternoon sun and turned around. The entrance was one of the grand doors that I'd been seeing since I was six.

I spat and shook a fist at the House of Osugbo, not caring who saw. "Aggravating, pestilent, stupid, idiotic, horrible place," I shouted. "I will *never* set foot in you again!"

Chapter 16

Ewu

REJECTION.

Such things will quietly creep up on a person. Then one day, she finds herself ready to destroy everything. I lived with the threat of my biological father for five years. For three years, Aro rejected me, refused to help me. Twice to my face and numerous times to Mwita, maybe even to the Ada and Nana the Wise. I knew Aro was the only one who could answer my questions. This is why I didn't leave Jwahir after my experience in the House of Osugbo. Where would I have gone?

The previous day, Papa had been brought home on his brother's camel, complaining of chest pains. The healer was called. It had been a long night. This was why I'd cried all night. I kept thinking that if Aro had been teaching me, I could have made Papa well. Papa was too young and healthy to have heart problems.

My head felt squeezed. Everything sounded muffled. I dressed and snuck out of the house. I had only one plan: To get my way. I left the main road and stepped onto the path leading to Aro's hut. I heard the flap of wings. Above my head in a palm tree, a black vulture glowered down at me with probing eyes. I frowned and then froze with realization. I looked away, hoping to hide my thoughts. That vulture wasn't a vulture, as it hadn't been five years ago when I saw it. Oh, how Aro could not have known that I knew every aspect of him, as I knew every aspect of any creature I'd changed into. What a mistake that feather falling from his body had been for him.

This was why I felt such a rush of power whenever I changed into a vulture. I'd been changing into *Aro as a vulture*. Was this why it was so easy to learn from Mwita? But I already had the gift of the Eshu. I probed my mind for the Great Mystic Points. I could grasp at nothing. No matter. The vulture flew off. *Here I come,* I thought.

Finally, I arrived at Aro's hut. I felt a pang of hunger and the world around me grew vibrant. Clusters of bright light danced at the top of the hut and in the air. The monster came at me when I got to the cactus gate. A masquerade was guarding Aro's hut, a *real* one. It seemed this day Aro felt he needed protection. Masquerades commonly appear at celebrations. In these cases, they're just men dressed in elaborate raffia and cloth costumes dancing to the beat of a drum.

Tock tock tock went a small drum as the real masquerade rushed at me, spraying a wake of sand as tall as my house and wide as three camels. It shook its dusty colorful cloth and raffia skirts. Its wooden face was curled into a sneer. It danced violently, jabbing itself at me and then pulling back. I stood my ground, even as it slashed its needle-fingered hands an inch from my face.

When I didn't run, the spirit stopped and stood very still. We looked at each other, my head tilted up, its head tilted down. My angry eyes staring into its wooden ones. It made a clicking sound that resonated deep in my bones. I winced but didn't move. Three times it did this. On the third I felt something give inside of me, like a cracked knuckle. The masquerade turned and led me to Aro's hut. As it moved, it slowly faded away.

Aro stood on his hut's threshold giving me the kind of look a man would give a pregnant woman if he accidentally walked in on her in the bathroom defecating.

"*Oga* Aro," I said. "I've come to ask you to take me on as your student."

His nostrils flared as if he smelled something putrid.

"Please. I'm sixteen years old. You won't be sorry."

Still he didn't speak. My cheeks flushed and my eyes felt as if someone had poked a finger in them. "Aro," I said in a low voice. "You will teach me." Still he said nothing. "You *WILL* teach . . ." My diamond flew from my mouth. I shouted as loudly as I could, "TEACH ME! WHY WON'T YOU TEACH ME? WHAT'S WRONG WITH YOU? WHAT IS WRONG WITH *EVERYONE?*"

The desert quickly absorbed my yelling and that was it. I dropped to my knees. Simultaneously, I dropped into that place I'd been when I was circumcised. I did it without a thought. From far away I heard myself screaming, but this was of no concern to me. In this spirit place, I was the predator. On instinct, I flew at Aro. I knew how and where to attack him because I knew *him*. I was searing light determined to burn his very soul from inside out. I felt his shock.

I forgot my purpose in coming. I was tearing and clawing and burning. The smell of smoldering hair. The satisfying grunt of Aro in pain. And then I felt a hard kick in the chest. I opened my eyes. I was back in my physical body, flying backward. I landed hard, sliding back several more feet. The sand grated the skin from the palms of my hands and the backs of my ankles. My rapa untied, exposing my legs.

I lay on my back looking at the sky. For a moment, I had a vision that I couldn't have had. I was my mother, a hundred miles West, seventeen years ago. On my back. Waiting to die. My body, her body, was a knot of pain. Full of semen. But alive.

Then I was back in the sand. Nearby, one of his goats baaed, a chicken clucked. I was alive. *Protecting myself is a useless endeavor,* I thought. I had to somehow find the man who harmed my mother, the man who hunted me. I had to hunt him. *And when I find him,* I thought. *I'll kill him.* I sat up. Aro lay on the ground in front of his hut.

"I understand now," I said loudly. Somehow I saw my diamond. I picked it up and, without thinking or wiping off the sand, slipped it under my tongue. "You . . . you won't teach girls or women because you're *afraid* of us! Y-y-you fear our emotions." I giggled hysterically and then grew serious. "That is *not* a good enough reason!"

I stood up. Aro only groaned. Even half dead, he wouldn't speak to me.

"Damn your mother! Damn your entire bloodline!" I said. I turned to the side and spat. It was red with blood. "I'll die before I let you teach me!" Suddenly, I felt a painful hitch in my throat. I winced. Guilt had arrived. I hadn't wanted to kill him. I wanted him to teach me. Now the bridge was burned. I retied my rapa and walked home.

Mwita found him an hour later still lying where I'd left him. Mwita had run to the House of Osugbo to bring the elders. Because of the House's "thin walls," within hours news of what I'd done to Aro was all over Jwahir. My parents were in their room when I heard the knock on the door. I knew it was Mwita. I hesitated to open it. When I let him in, he grabbed my hand and pulled me to the back of the house. "What did you do, woman?" he hissed.

Before I could answer, he pushed me hard against the wall and held me there. "Shut up," he harshly whispered. "Aro may be dying." When I gasped, he nodded. "Yes, you feel that guilt. Why are you so *stupid?* What is *wrong* with you? You're a danger to yourself, to us all! Sometimes I wonder if you should take your own life!" He let go and stepped back. "How could you?"

I just stood there rubbing the small scar on my forehead.

"He's as close to a father as I will have," he said.

"How can you call that man your father?" I retorted.

"What do *you* know about *real* fathers?" he spat. "You've never had one! Just a caretaker." He turned to leave. "Do you know what they will do to us if he dies?" he asked over his shoulder. "They'll come after us. We'll go the way of my parents."

That night, at eleven o'clock, that red eye appeared. I looked at it defiantly, daring it to try something. It hovered above me for one minute, staring. Then it faded away. The same thing happened the next night. And the next. Rumors abounded. Luyu told me that Mwita and I were both suspected of beating Aro. "People say they saw you going there that morning," she said. "That you looked angry and ready to kill."

Papa was taking some days off work to recover from his own ailments and my mother didn't tell him a thing about what I'd done. My mother and her secrets. She was so good at keeping them. Thus, he knew nothing of the rumors, thankfully. But my mother did ask me if there was any truth to them.

"I'm not irrational," I told her. "Aro's more than people think he is."

People repeated it to each other: *Ewu* children are born from violence and so it's inevitable that they will become violent. Days passed. Aro remained ill. I readied myself for a witch hunt. *It'll happen the day Aro dies,* I thought. I packed a small satchel of things, the easier to run with. And so when Papa died five days later, people were already eying me with great suspicion.

Chapter 17

Full Circle

WE COME FULL CIRCLE. When I made my father's body breathe at his funeral, my reputation sank to new depths. After my mother took me home, Mwita made himself ignorable and eavesdropped on my family members.

"We should have stoned her to death after she tried to kill Aro."

"My daughter already has nightmares about her every night. Now this!"

"The faster she's ashes, the better."

At home, I slept more peacefully than I had in years. I woke to my body's miserable aching. It dawned on me: Papa was ashes. I curled up and wept. I felt as if I were breaking all over again. Grief took me into its dark muted place for several hours. Eventually it set me back down in my bed. I wiped my nose with my bed sheet and looked at my clothes. My mother had changed me out of my white dress into a blue rapa. I held my left hand up, the one that had meshed with Papa's body. There was a bit of crust between my index and middle finger.

"I could change to a vulture and fly away right now," I whispered. But if I stayed an animal for too long, I'd go mad. *Would that be so bad?* I wondered. *Mwita was right, I'm dangerous.* I decided to sneak out of the house come night, before people came for me. For the good of my mother, especially. She was a widow now. Her reputation was more important now than ever. There was a knock on the door.

"What do you want?" I said. The door swung open hitting the wall hard. I scrambled out of bed, ready to take on an angry mob. It was Aro. My mother stood behind him. She made eye contact with me and then walked away. He slammed the door behind him. There was a fresh-looking bruise above his eye. I knew that there were other bruises and scars hidden by his white funeral garments, injuries that were five days old.

"Do you have *any* idea what you did?"

"Why do you care?" I snapped.

"You don't *think!* You're unlearned and uncontrollable, like an animal." He sucked his teeth. "Let me see your hand."

I held my breath as he stepped closer. I didn't want him to touch me. He was Eshu, as I was. Someone with his skill would only need a cell of my skin to get even with me. But something made me sit still and allow him to take my hands. Guilt, grief, fatigue, you pick. He turned my hands this way and that, squeezed it, lightly ground my knuckles together. He let go, chuckling to himself and shaking his head.

"Okay, *sha*," he muttered to himself. "Onyesonwu, I will teach you."

"What?"

"I'll teach you the Great Mystic Points, if it is willed," he said. "You're a danger to us all if I don't. You're a danger to us all if I do, but at least I'll be your Master."

I couldn't help but smile. My smile faltered. "They may hunt me tonight."

"I'll make sure that that doesn't happen," he simply said. "I haven't died, so it shouldn't be difficult. It's your birth father you have to worry about. If you haven't guessed by now, he's a sorcerer as I am. If you hadn't idiotically gone through your Eleventh Rite, he wouldn't know of you yet. Thank *me* for protecting you all these years, otherwise you'd be long dead."

I frowned. Aro had been protecting me. It was a bitter pill to swallow. I considered asking him how but instead I asked, "Why does he want to kill me?"

"Because you're a failure," Aro said, smirking. "You were supposed to be a boy."

I winced.

"Now, I'd move you into my hut, but your mysterious mother needs you," he said. "And there's the problem of you and Mwita. During training, sexual contact will hinder you."

My cheeks felt hot and I looked away.

"By the way, it would have been selfish to run off and leave your mother," he said. He let his statement sit for a moment and I wondered if he could read my mind.

"I cannot," he said. "I just know your type."

"Why should I trust you?"

"Can't you defend yourself?" he said. "Don't you know me and therefore know what it takes to destroy me?"

"I do, but you now know me, too," I said. "You touched my hand."

A grin spread across his face. "So now we know each other. A good start."

"But you're the Master."

"So isn't it wise to become one, too? For your *own* sake?"

"Only if I can trust you to make me one."

"Yes, trust is earned, isn't it?" he said.

I thought about it. "Okay."

"Do you believe in Ani?"

"No," I said, matter-of-factly. Ani was supposed to be merciful and loving. Ani wouldn't have allowed me to exist. I'd never believed in Ani. She was just an expression I was used to using when I was surprised or angry.

"Some creator then?" he asked.

I nodded. "It is cold and logical."

"Are you willing to allow others the same right to their beliefs?"

"If their beliefs don't hurt others and, when I feel the need, I am allowed call them stupid in my mind, then yes."

"Do you believe it's your responsibility to leave this world in better shape than when you came into it?"

"Yes."

He paused, looking at me more intensely. "Is it better to give or receive?"

"They're the same," I said. "One can't exist without the other. But if you keep giving without receiving, you're a fool."

He chuckled at this. Then he asked, "Can you smell it?"

Immediately, I knew what he spoke of. "Yes," I said. "Strongly."

Fire, ice, iron, flesh, wood, and flowers. The sweat of life. Most of the time I forgot about the smell but I always became aware of it when strange things happened.

"Can you taste it?"

"Yes," I said. "If I try."

"Do you choose it?"

"No. It chose me long ago."

He nodded. "Then welcome." He walked to the door. Over his shoulder, he said, "And take that cursed stone from your mouth. It's meant to keep you grounded. It's useless to you."

Part II

Student

Chapter 18

A Welcome Visit to Aro's Hut

TWENTY-EIGHT DAYS PASSED before I decided to go to his hut. I was too afraid.

In those days, I couldn't sleep through a night. I'd wake to the dark, sure that someone was in the room with me, and it wasn't Papa or his first wife, Njeri the camel-racer. I'd have happily welcomed both of them. It was either the red eye about to kill me or Aro about to enact his revenge on me. Nevertheless, as Aro promised, no mob came after me. I even went back to school on the tenth day.

In his will, Papa left his shop to my mother and ordered Ji, his apprentice now graduated to Master, to run it. They would split the profits, 80 percent to my mother and 20 percent to Ji. It was a good deal for both, especially Ji who was from a poor family and now bore the title "Blacksmith Taught by the Great Fadil Ogundimu." In addition, my mother had her cactus candy and other vegetables. The Ada, Nana the Wise, and two of my mother's friends also came over each day to visit with her. My mother was okay.

Not once did Luyu, Diti, or Binta visit me and I vowed to never forgive them for this. Mwita didn't come, either. But his actions I understood. He was waiting for me to come to him, at Aro's hut. So for those four weeks, I was alone with my fear and loss. I returned to school because I needed the distraction.

I was treated like someone with a highly contagious disease. In the schoolyard, people moved away from me. They said nothing to me, mean or pleasant. What did Aro do to keep people from tearing me apart? Whatever it was, it didn't change my reputation of being the evil *Ewu* girl. Binta, Luyu, and Diti avoided me. They avoided eye contact as they walked away. They ignored my greetings. This made me so angry.

After a few days of this, it was time for a showdown. I spotted them standing in their usual place near the school wall. I boldly approached. Diti looked at my feet, Luyu looked to the side, and Binta stared at me. My confidence wavered. I was so aware of the brightness of my skin, the boldness of my freckles, especially the ones on my cheeks, the sandiness of the braids that reached down my back.

Luyu looked at Binta and hit her on the shoulder. Binta immediately looked away. I stood my ground. I at least wanted an argument. Binta started crying. Diti swatted irritably at a fly. Luyu looked me straight in the face with such intensity that I thought she was going to hit me. "Come," she said, glancing once around the schoolyard. She grabbed my hand. "Enough of this."

Diti and Binta followed close behind as we quickly walked down the road. We sat on the curb, Luyu on one side of me, Binta on the other, and Diti next to Luyu. We watched people and camels pass by.

"Why did you *do* it?" Diti suddenly asked.

"Shut up, Diti," Luyu said.

"I can ask whatever I want!" Diti said.

"Then ask properly," Luyu said. "We've done her wrong. We're not in the . . ."

Diti shook her head vigorously. "My mother said . . ."

"Did you even *try* to see her?" Luyu said. When she turned to me, she was crying. "Onyesonwu, what happened? I remember . . . when we were eleven, but . . . I don't . . ."

"Was it your father who made you to stay away from me?" I hissed at Luyu. "Does he not want his beautiful daughter being seen with her ugly evil friend anymore?"

Luyu shrank back from me. I'd hit it right on the nail.

"Sorry," I quickly said with a sigh.

"Is it evil?" Diti asked. "Can't you go to an Ani priestess and . . . ?"

"I'm not evil!" I shouted, waving my fists in the air. "Understand *that* about me, if not anything else." I gritted my teeth and pounded my fist against my chest, as Mwita often did when he was angry. "I am what I am but I am *not EVIL!*"

It felt like I was shouting to all of Jwahir. *Papa never felt I was evil,* I thought. I started sobbing, feeling the loss of him hit me again. Binta put her arm over my shoulder and hugged me close to her. "Okay," Binta whispered into my ear.

"Okay," Luyu said.

"All right," Diti said.

And that was how the tension broke between my friends and me. Just like that. Even at the moment, I felt it. Less weight. All four of us must have felt it.

But I still had to deal with my fear. And the only way to do that was to face it. I went a week later, during a Rest Day. I got up early, showered, made breakfast, dressed in my favorite blue dress, and wrapped a thick yellow veil over my head.

"Mama," I said, peeking into my parents' room. She was sprawled on the bed, for once, soundly asleep. I was sorry to wake her.

"Eh?" she said. Her eyes were clear. She hadn't been crying during the night.

"I made you some fried yam and egg stew and tea for breakfast."

She sat up and stretched. "Where are you going?"

"To Aro's hut, Mama."

She lay back down. "Good," she said. "Your father would approve."

"Do you think?" I asked, moving closer to the bed to hear my mother better.

"Aro fascinated your papa. All mysterious things did. Including you and me . . . though he didn't like the House of Osugbo much." We laughed. "Onyesonwu, your father loved you. And though he didn't know it as strongly as I do, he knew you were special."

"I-I should have told you and Papa about my feud with Aro," I said.

"Maybe. But we still wouldn't have been able to do anything."

I took my time. It was a cool morning. People were just coming out to do their morning chores. As I passed, no one greeted me. I thought about

Papa and my heart ached. In the last few days, my grief was so strong that I felt the world around me ripple as it did at his funeral. Whatever had happened at the funeral could happen again. This was part of my reason for finally going to Aro. I didn't want to hurt anyone else.

Mwita met me at the cactus gate. Before I could speak, he gathered me into his arms. "Welcome," he said. He hugged me until I relaxed and hugged him back.

"See," a voice said from behind us. We jumped away from each other. Aro stood behind the cactus gate, his arms crossed over his chest. He wore a long black caftan made of a light material. It fluttered around his bare feet in the cool morning breeze. "This is why you can't live here."

"I'm sorry," Mwita said.

"Sorry for what? You're a man and this woman is yours."

"I'm sorry," I said, looking at my feet, knowing that this was what he expected.

"You should be," he said. "Once we start, you're to keep him off of you. If you became pregnant while still learning, you could get us all killed."

"Yes, *Oga*," I said.

"You endure pain well, I gather," Aro said.

I nodded.

"That at least is good," he said. "Come through the gate."

As I passed through, one of the cactuses scratched my leg. I hissed with annoyance, jumping away. Aro chuckled. Mwita passed through behind me untouched. He headed for his hut. I followed Aro to his. Inside were a chair and a raffia sleeping mat. Other than a small scratched up calculator wordpad and a lizard on the wall, that was all there was. We walked through the back door to where the desert opened before us.

"Sit," he said, motioning to the raffia mats on the ground. He did the same.

We sat there looking at each other for a moment.

"You have tiger eyes," he said. "And those have been extinct for decades."

"You have old man's eyes," I said. "And old men don't have very long to live."

"I *am* old," he said, getting up. He went into his hut and returned with a cactus thorn between his teeth. He sat back down. Then he utterly shocked me.

"Onyesonwu, I'm sorry."

I blinked.

"I have been arrogant. I have been insecure. I have been a fool."

I said nothing. I wholly agreed.

"I was shocked that I was given a girl, a woman," he said. "But you'll be tall, so there is that. What do you know of the Great Mystic Points?"

"Nothing, *Oga*," I said. "Mwita couldn't tell me much because . . . *you* wouldn't teach him." I couldn't keep the anger from my voice. If he was admitting mistakes, I wanted him to admit all of them. Men like Aro will only admit wrongs once.

"I wouldn't teach Mwita because he didn't pass initiation," Aro said firmly. "Yes, he's *Ewu* and I was put off by that. You *Ewu* come to this world with soiled souls."

"No!" I said, pointing my finger in his face. "You can say that about me, but you can't say it about him. Didn't you bother to ask him about his life? His story?"

"Lower your finger, child," Aro said, his body going straight and stiff. "You're undisciplined, that's apparent. Do you want to learn discipline today? I can teach it well."

With effort, I calmed myself.

"I know his story," Aro said.

"Then you know he was made from love."

Aro's nostrils flared. "Regardless, I saw past his . . . mixed blood. I let him attempt initiation. You ask him what happened. All I will say is that, like all the others, he failed."

"Mwita said you wouldn't allow him to go through the initiation," I said.

"He lied," Aro said. "Ask him."

"I will," I said.

"There are few true sorcerers in these lands," he said. "And it's not by their choice that they become so. That's why we are plagued by death, pain, and rage. First, there is great grief, then someone who loves us demands that we become who we must become. Your mother most likely was the one who set you on this path. There is much to her, *sha*." He paused, seeming to consider this. "She must have demanded it the day you were conceived. Her demands obviously trumped your birth father's. If you had been a boy, he'd have had an ally instead of an enemy.

"The Great Mystic Points are a means to an end. Each sorcerer has his own end. But I can't teach you unless you pass initiation. Tomorrow. No child who's come to me has passed. They return home beaten, broken, ailing, sick."

"What happens during . . . initiation?" I asked.

"Your very being is tested. To learn the Points, you have to be the right person, that's all I can tell you. Have you thrown that diamond away?"

"Yes."

"You've been cut," he said. "That may be a problem. But it can't be helped now." He got up. "After the sun sets, no eating or drinking anything but water. Your monthly cycle is in two days. That may be a problem."

"How do you know when my . . . when it is?"

He only laughed. "It can't be helped. Tonight, before you sleep, meditate for an hour. Don't talk to your mother after sunset. But you may talk to Fadil, your father. Come here at five a.m. Make sure you bathe well and wear dark clothing."

I stared at him. How was I going to remember all those instructions?

"Go talk to Mwita. He'll repeat my directions if you need to hear them again."

I smelled burning sage as I approached Mwita's hut. He was sitting quietly on a wide mat meditating, his back to me. I stood in the doorway and looked around. So this was where he lived. Woven items hung on the walls and were piled around his hut. Baskets, mats, platters, and even a half-done wicker chair.

"Sit down," he said, without turning around.

I sat on the mat next to him, facing the hut's entrance.

"You never told me that you could weave," I said.

"Not important," he said.

"I would have liked to learn," I said.

He pulled his knees to his chest but said nothing.

"You haven't told me everything," I said.

"Do you expect me to?"

"When it's important."

"Important to whom?"

Mwita got up, stretched and leaned himself on the wall. "Have you eaten?"

"No."

"It's best if you eat heavily before the sun sets."

"What do you know about this initiation?"

"Why would I tell you about the greatest failure of my life?"

"That's not fair," I said, standing up. "I'm not asking you to humiliate yourself. Telling me what you went through was crucial."

"Why?" he said. "What good would it have done you?"

"It doesn't matter! You *lied* to me. There should be no secrets between us."

As he looked at me, I knew that Mwita was running through our relationship. He was searching for a truth or secret he could demand of me. He must have realized that I held nothing from him for he next said, "It'll only scare you."

I shook my head. "I'm more afraid of what I don't know."

"Fine. I almost died. I did . . . no, almost. The closer you come to completing the initiation, the closer you come to death. To be initiated is to die. I came . . . very close."

"What ha. . . ."

"It's different for everyone," he said. "There's pain, horror—absolute. I don't know why Aro even allows any of these local boys to try. That's his malicious side."

"When did you . . ."

"Not long after I came here," he said. He took a deep breath, looked hard at me and then shook his head. "No."

"Why? I'm to do this tomorrow, I want to know!"

"No," was all he said and that was the end of it. Mwita could walk through the palm tree farms in the dead of night. He'd done this several times after spending hours with me. Once when we were sitting in my mother's garden, a tarantula crept near my leg. He crushed it with his bare hand. But now, at the mention of his failed initiation, he looked utterly terrified.

Before I went home, Mwita reviewed my initiation requirements with me. I grew annoyed and asked him to write them down instead.

I knelt down beside my mother. She was in the garden, churning the soil around the plants with her hands. "How was it?" she asked.

"As much as I can expect from that crazy man," I said.

"You and Aro are too much alike." my mother said. She paused for a moment. "I talked to Nana the Wise today. She spoke of an initiation . . ." she trailed off as she searched my face. She saw what she needed to see. "When?"

"Tomorrow morning." I brought out the list. "There are all these things I have to do to prepare."

She read it and then said, "I'll make you a large early dinner. Chicken curry and cactus candy?"

I smiled broadly.

I took a long hot bath and for a while I was calm. But as the night wore on, my fear of the unknown returned. By midnight, the delicious meal I'd eaten was gurgling uneasily in my belly. *If I die during the initiation, Mama will be alone,* I thought. *Poor Mama.*

I didn't sleep. But for the first time since I was eleven years old, I wasn't afraid of seeing the red eye. The cocks started crowing around three a.m. I bathed again and dressed in a long maroon dress. I wasn't hungry and I felt a dull throb in my abdomen, both sure signs that my monthly was near. I didn't wake my mother before I left. She was probably already awake.

Chapter 19

The Man in Black

"PAPA, PLEASE GUIDE ME," I said as I walked. "Because I need guidance."

To be honest, I didn't think he was there. I had always believed that when people died, their spirits stayed close or sometimes came to visit. I still believed this, for it was this way with Papa's first wife, Njeri. I felt her often in the house. But I didn't feel Papa around me now. Only the cool breeze and the sounds of the crickets were with me.

Mwita and Aro were waiting for me in the back of Aro's hut. Aro handed me a cup of tea to drink. It was lukewarm and tasted like flowers. After drinking it, the mild crampiness that I'd been feeling disappeared.

"What happens now?" I asked.

"Walk into the desert," Aro said, wrapping his brown garments around him.

I turned to Mwita. "All that matters to you is what is ahead," Aro said.

"Go, Onyesonwu," Mwita mumbled.

Aro pushed me toward the desert. For the first time in my life, I was reluctant to go into it. The sun was just coming up. I started walking. Minutes passed. I began to hear my heart beat in my ears. *Something in the tea,* I thought. *A shaman's brew, maybe.* Whenever the breeze blew, I could distinctly hear sand grains clacking over each other. I clapped my hands over my ears. I kept walking. The breeze picked up, becoming a sand and dust filled wind.

"What is this?" I screamed, working to maintain my footing.

The sun was quickly blotted out. My mother and I had lived through three big sandstorms while we were nomads. We'd dug a hole and lain in it, using the tent to protect us. We were lucky not to be blown away or buried alive. Now here I was in such a storm with nothing between it and myself but my dress.

I decided to return to Aro's hut. But I couldn't see anything behind me. I shielded my face with my arm as I looked around. The whipping sand was drawing blood. Soon my eyelids were encrusted with sand, granules paining my eyes. I spit sand out only for more to fill my mouth.

Suddenly, the wind changed, moving behind me. It blew me toward a small orange light. When I got closer, I saw that it was a tent made of sheer blue material. There was a small fire burning inside.

"A fire in the middle of a sandstorm!" I shouted, laughing hysterically. My face and arms stung and my legs shook as I tried not to let the wind take me away.

I threw myself inside and was slapped with silence. Not even the tent's walls shuddered from the wind. Nothing held the tent down. The bottom of the tent was sand. I rolled to my side coughing. Through my stinging watery eyes, I saw the whitest man I'd ever seen. He wore a heavy black cloak with a hood that dropped over the top half of his face. But the bottom half I saw plainly. His wrinkly skin was white like milk.

"Onyesonwu," the man in black said very suddenly.

I jumped. There was something repulsive about him. I half expected him to scamper around the fire toward me with the speed and agility of a spider. But he remained seated, his long legs stretched before him. His sharp nails were grooved and yellow. He leaned back on one elbow. "Is that your name?"

"Yes," I said.

"You're the one Aro sends," he said, his wet pink flat lips bending into a smirk.

"Yes."

"Who sent you?"

"Aro."

"What are you then?"

"Excuse me?"

"What are you?"

"Human," I said.

"Is that all?"

"Eshu also."

"So are you human then?"

"Yes."

He reached into his robes and brought out a small blue jar. He shook it and set it down. "Aro calls me here and a female sits before me," he said. He flared his nostrils. "One who will bleed soon. Very very soon. This place is sacred, you know." He looked at me as if waiting for an answer. I was relieved when he picked up the container. He shook it and slammed it down. I wanted to rub my eyes they hurt so badly. He looked up at me with such anger that my heart jumped.

"You've been cut!" he said. "You can't climax! Who allowed this to happen?"

I stammered, "It was a . . . I wanted to please my. . . .I didn't. . . ."

"Shut up," he said. He paused and when he spoke his voice was cooler. "Maybe that can be helped," he said more to himself. He mumbled something and then said, "You may die today. I hope you're prepared. They won't find your body."

I thought of my mother and then pushed her image out of my mind.

The man in black threw the container's contents—bones. Tiny, fine bones, maybe from a lizard or some other small beast. They were bleached white and dry, several crumbling at the tips, revealing ancient porous marrow. They flew from the container and landed as if they would never move again. As if they were sure. My eyes felt heavy as I looked at the scattered bones. My eyes were drawn to them. He stared for a long time. Then he looked at me, his mouth a surprised O. I wished I could see his eyes. Then he masked his face with a more controlled look.

"This is normally where the pain starts. Where I get to listen to the boys scream," the man in black said. He paused, looking down at the bones. "But you," he smirked and nodded. "I must have *you* killed." He lifted his left hand and twisted his wrist. I felt a crack in my neck as my head turned itself all the way around. I grunted. All went dark.

I opened my eyes and instantly knew that I wasn't myself. The feeling was more peculiar than scary. I was a passenger in someone's head yet still able to feel sweat rolling down his face and the insect biting his skin. I tried to leave, but I had no body to leave with. My mind was stuck there. The eyes I looked through stared at a concrete wall.

He sat on a hard and cool block of concrete. There was no roof. Sunlight shined in, making the already hot room even more uncomfortable. I heard many people nearby but I couldn't tell exactly what they were saying. The person whose body I was in mumbled something and then laughed to . . . herself. The voice was a woman's.

"Let them come, then," she said. She looked down at herself and nervously rubbed her thighs. She wore a long coarse white dress. She was not as light-skinned as me but she was not dark like my mother either. I noticed her hands. I had only read about these in story tales. Tribal markings. This woman's hands were covered with them. The circles, swirls, and lines wove into complex designs snaking up her wrists.

She leaned her head back against the wall and closed her eyes in the sunshine and the world became red for a moment. Then someone grabbed her—us—with such roughness that I silently screamed. Her eyes flew open. She made no sound. She didn't fight. I desperately wanted to. Then thousands of people burst before us, all of them screaming, yelling, shouting, talking, pointing, laughing, glaring.

The people stayed back as if some invisible force kept them twenty feet from the hole we were being dragged to. Beside the hole was a pile of sand. The men dragged us to the hole and pushed us in. I felt the woman's whole body shudder as she hit the bottom. The ground was just higher than our shoulders. She looked around and I got a good view of the giant mob that was waiting for the execution.

Men shoveled dirt into the hole and soon we were buried to our neck. It was at this point that the woman's fear must have infected me because suddenly I was being torn in two. If I had a body, I'd have thought that a thousand men had one of my arms and a thousand had the other and both groups were pulling. From behind, I heard a man loudly say, "Who will throw the first stone at this problem?"

The first stone hit the back of our head. The pain was an explosion. Many more came after that. After a while, the pain of our head being stoned fell to the back and the sensation of being pulled apart came forward. I was screaming. I was dying. Someone threw another rock and I felt something break. I knew death the moment it touched me. As best I could, as nothing, I tried to hold myself together.

Mama. I was leaving her all alone. *I have to keep going,* I thought with despair. *Mama willed it to be so. She willed it!* I had too much left to do. I felt Papa catch and hold me. He smelled of hot iron and his grasp, as always, was strong. He held me for a long time in that spirit place where all was colorful light, sound, smell, and heat.

Papa held me close. The squeeze of a hug. Then he let go and was gone. Soon the world of the spirits, a place I would learn to call "the wilderness," began to melt and mix with a star-salted darkness. I could see the desert. There I was lying in it, half buried in the sand. A camel stood over me with a woman on its back. She wore a green shirt and pants and sat between the camel's two shaggy humps. I must have moved because suddenly the camel started. The woman calmed it with a pat.

Instinctively, I flew down and lay on my body. As I did so, the woman spoke.

"Do you know who I am?" she asked.

I tried to answer but I had no mouth, not yet.

"I'm Njeri." She looked up and grinned widely, the sides of her eyes creasing. "I *was* Fadil Ogundimu's wife." She was addressing someone else. She turned back to me and laughed. "Your papa has much to learn about the wilderness."

I wanted to smile.

"I know your kind. I was like you, though I wasn't given an opportunity to learn my gift. I could speak to camels. My mother went to see Aro. He refused me. I wouldn't have passed the initiation. But he could have taught me other useful things. Always walk your *own* path, Onyesonwu." She paused seeming to listen to someone. "Your father wishes you well."

As I watched her ride off, I felt myself change. I could suddenly feel the air against my skin and my heart beating. There was an odd feeling of being weighed down, as if a weight was attached to each part of me, weights that weren't so bothersome now but eventually would be. My mortality. I was exhausted. I ached all over, my legs, arms, my neck, and especially my head. I retreated into a restless, helpless sleep.

I woke to Mwita's humming as he rubbed oil into my skin. Staticky energy coated my body like a computer's monitor. His touch rubbed it away. He stopped when he realized I was awake. He pulled my rapa over my body. I grasped it weakly to my chest.

"You passed," he said. His voice was strange. It was strained with concern, but there was something else too.

"I know," I said. Then I turned my head and started crying. He didn't try to hold me and I was glad. *Why didn't she fight?* I thought. *I'd have fought even if it was hopeless. Anything to stay out of that hole a bit longer.*

I vividly remembered the sensation of having my forehead caved in by a large rock. It didn't hurt as much as it should have. It just felt like I was suddenly . . . exposed. A rock destroyed my nose, bloodied my ear, buried itself in my cheek. I was conscious through most of it. The woman was, too. I gagged. Nothing came out because my stomach was empty. I sat back and massaged my temples. Mwita handed me a warm towel to wipe and soothe my eyes. It was soaked in oil.

"What is this?" I asked in a hoarse voice. "It's not going to . . ."

"No," Mwita said. "That'll help get it out of your system. Wipe your face with it, too. I've rubbed it on the rest of you. You'll feel better soon."

"Where are we?" I asked, rubbing the oil on my eyes. It felt good.

"In my hut."

"Mwita, I died," I whispered.

"You had to."

"I was in a woman's head and I felt . . ."

"Don't think about it," he said, getting up. He picked up a plate of food sitting on his table. "Right now, you have to eat."

"I'm not hungry."

"Your mother made this," Mwita said.

"My mother?"

"She was here. Yesterday."

"Eh, but I didn't see her . . ."

"Two days have passed, Onyesonwu."

"Oh." I slowly sat up, took the plate from Mwita and ate. It was chicken curry and green beans. Within a few minutes, my plate was clean. I felt much better.

"Where's Aro?" I asked, rubbing the back and sides of my head.

"I don't know," Mwita sighed.

Then I understood what I had sensed in Mwita. It surprised me. I took his hand. If I didn't address this now, our friendship would die. Even back then, I knew that disregarded jealousy eventually turned poisonous.

"Mwita, don't feel that way," I said.

He pulled his hand away. "I don't know how to feel, Onyesonwu."

"Well, don't feel *that* way," I said, my voice hardening. "We've been through too much. And, besides, you're above that sort of thing."

"Am I?"

"Just because you were born a male does *not* make you more worthy than me." I harrumphed. "Don't act like Aro."

Mwita said nothing, but he wouldn't meet my eyes either.

I sighed. "Well, the way you feel won't stop me from . . ."

He pressed his hand over my mouth. "Enough talking," he whispered, his face close to mine. And then he moved over me; the oil on me made his motions smooth. My body ached and my head throbbed but for the first time in my life, I felt only pleasure. My Eleventh Rite juju was broken. I pulled Mwita closer. The sensation was so succulent that it brought tears to my eyes. It was so overwhelming that at some point, I stopped breathing. When Mwita noticed, he froze.

"Onyesonwu!" he said. "Breathe!"

Every part of my body was a sharp point of bliss. It was the most beautiful sensation I'd ever felt. When I only looked at him with bewildered eyes, he opened his mouth and breathed loudly to demonstrate. I began to see silvery red and blue explosions as my lungs demanded air. I had recently experienced death so it was easy for me to forget to breathe. I inhaled, my eyes locked on Mwita's. Then I exhaled.

"I'm sorry," he said. "I shouldn't have . . ."

"Finish," I breathed, pulling him to me, my head buzzing.

As our bodies met, fully, finally, throughout, Mwita reminded me to breathe. As he moved inside of me, he continued to remind me but by this time I wasn't listening. It was exquisite. Soon I was so hot that I was shaking. Minutes passed. The sensation began to feel earnest, then agitating. I couldn't release. I had been circumcised.

"Mwita," I said. We were both slick with sweat.

"Eh?" he said, out of breath.

"I . . . something's wrong with me. I . . ." I squeezed my face. "I can't."

He stopped moving and the terrible sensation in my loins decreased. He looked at me, beads of sweat dropping onto my chest. He surprised me with a smile. "Do something about it then, Eshu woman."

I blinked, realizing what he meant. I concentrated. He began to move inside of me again and immediately, it felt like I had released my very being. "Oooooooooooooooooh," I moaned. From far off I could hear Mwita laughing, as I fell into sleep with a sigh.

That tiny piece of flesh made all the difference. Growing it back hadn't been hard and it pleased me that for once in my life obtaining something of importance was easy.

Chapter 20

Men

I RETURNED HOME THAT DAY. The sun was just ambling into the sky and the air and sand were warming. My mother shouted my name when she saw me. She'd been sitting on the front steps waiting. There were bags under her eyes and her long braids needed rebraiding. It was the first time I'd ever heard my mother's voice go above a whisper. And the sound of it made my legs weak.

"Mama," I shouted back from up the road.

Around us the neighborhood went about its business. Everyone was so unaware of what my mother and I had gone through. People only glanced up with mild curiosity. Most likely the sound of my mother's voice was something talked about that night. Neither of us cared what they thought.

Aro didn't request my presence for a week. And in that week, I was plagued by nightmares. Over and over, night after night, I was stoned to death. I was haunted by someone else's demise. During the day, I was plagued by terrible headaches. When Binta, Diti, and Luyu came to my bedroom three days after my initiation, I was a blithering mess hiding under my covers weeping.

"What's wrong with you?" I heard Luyu ask. I threw the covers from over my head, shocked at hearing her voice. I saw Diti turn and leave.

"Are you all right? Is it your father?" Binta said, sitting on my bed beside me.

I wiped the snot from my nose. I was disoriented and my confusion caused me to think about my biological father instead of Papa. *Yes, he is my problem,* I thought. More tears dribbled down my face. I hadn't seen my friends in days. I'd left school two days before my initiation and I hadn't told them a thing. Diti returned and handed me a towel soaked with warm water.

"Your mother asked us to come," Luyu said.

Diti opened the curtains and pushed the window open. The room flooded with sunshine and fresh air. I wiped my face and blew my nose into the towel. Then I lay back, angry with my mother for asking them here. How was I supposed to explain my state to them? I had grown my clitoris back and I no longer carried my diamond in my mouth. My belly chain might as well have turned green.

For a while, they just sat there as I sniveled. If it weren't for them, I'd have let the snot run freely down my face and pool onto my covers. *What does it all matter?* I thought. My mood darkened and I reached for my bed sheet to pull it back over my head. *I'll just ignore them. Eventually they'll go away.*

"Onyesonwu, just tell us," Luyu said, softly. "We'll listen."

"We'll help you," Binta said. "Remember how the women helped me during our Eleventh Rite? If they hadn't helped me that night, I was going to kill him."

"Binta!" Diti exclaimed.

"Really?" Luyu said.

Binta had my full attention.

"Yes. I was going to poison him . . . that very next day," Binta said. "He gets drunk almost every evening. He smokes his pipe as he does it. He wouldn't have tasted it."

I wiped my face again. "My mother once said that fear is like a man who, once burned, is afraid of a glow worm," I said vaguely. I told them everything but the details of my initiation. From the day of my conception to the day I crawled into bed and didn't want to leave it. Their faces grew distant during the part about my mother's rape. I relished a little in forcing them to know the details. When I finished, they were so silent that I could hear the soft footsteps outside of the door. Moving down the hallway. My mother had listened to the whole thing.

"I can't believe you kept this from us all this time," Luyu finally said.

"You can really change into a bird?" Diti asked.

"Come on," Binta said pulling my arm. "We have to get you outside."

Luyu nodded and took my other arm. I tried to pull my arms away, "Why?"

"You need sunshine," Binta said.

"I'm . . . I'm not properly dressed," I said, yanking may arms away. I felt the tears coming back. Life was out there and death was, too. I feared both now. They pulled me from bed, unwrapped my night rapa and pulled a green dress over my head. We went outside and sat on the front steps of the house. The sun was warm on my face. There was no red haze blocking it, no sickly fuzzy mold growing on the ground, no smoke in the air, no looming death. After a while I quietly said, "Thank you."

"You look better," Binta said. "Sunshine heals. My mother says that you should open the curtains everyday because the sunlight kills the bacteria and such."

"You made your father breathe," Luyu said, her elbow on my knee.

"No," I said, grimly. "Papa had passed. I only made his body breathe."

"That was then," Luyu said.

I sucked my teeth and looked away, irritated.

"Oh," Diti said. Then she nodded. "Aro will teach her."

"Right," Luyu said. "She can do it already. She just doesn't know how."

"Eh?" Binta said, looking confused.

"Onyesonwu, do you know if you can do it?" Luyu asked.

"I don't know," I snapped.

"She can," Diti said. "And I think your mother is right. That's why she worked so hard to keep you alive. Mother's intuition. You're going to be famous."

I laughed at this. I suspected that I'd be more infamous than famous. "So you think my mother would've allowed us both to die out there in the desert if she didn't think I was so special?"

"Yes," Diti said looking serious.

"Or if you'd have come out a boy," Luyu added. "Your biological father is evil, and if you were a boy you would have been, too, I think. That's what he wanted."

Again we were quiet. Then Diti asked, "So will you stop going to school?"

I shrugged. "Probably."

"What was it like with Mwita?" Luyu asked, smirking.

It was as if speaking his name summoned him, for there he was coming up the road. Luyu and Diti snickered. Binta patted my shoulder. He wore light tan pants and a long matching caftan. His clothes matched his skin so well that he looked more like a spirit than a person. I'd always avoided wearing this color for this very reason.

"Good afternoon," he said.

"Not as good as it was for you and Onyesonwu a few nights ago, I hear," Luyu said under her breath. Diti and Binta giggled and Mwita looked at me.

"Good afternoon, Mwita," I said. "I-I've told them everything."

Mwita frowned. "You didn't ask me."

"Should I have?"

"You promised me secrecy."

He was right. "Sorry," I said.

Mwita looked at the three of them. "They can be trusted?" he asked me.

"Completely," Binta said.

"Onyesonwu is our Eleventh Rite mate, there should be no secrets between us, Mwita," Luyu said.

"I don't respect the Eleventh Rite," Mwita said.

Luyu bristled. Diti gasped, "How can you . . ."

Luyu held up a hand to silence Diti. She turned to Mwita with a hard face. "Just as we keep your secrets, we expect you to respect Onyesonwu as a woman of Jwahir. I don't care what kind of-of juju you're capable of."

Mwita rolled his eyes. "Done," he said. "Onyesonwu, how much did you . . ."

"Everything," I said. "If it weren't for them coming today, you'd have found me in my bed losing my . . . self."

"Okay," Mwita said, nodding. "Then you all have to understand that you're connected to her now. Not by some primitive rite, but by something real." Luyu rolled her eyes, Diti glowered at him, and Binta looked at Onyesonwu with surprise.

"Mwita, stop being such a camel's penis," I said, annoyed.

"Women always have to have companions," Mwita mused.

"And men always have false senses of entitlement," I said.

Mwita gave me a dark look and I gazed back. Then he took my hand and massaged it. "Aro wants you to come by tonight," he said. "It's time."

Chapter 21

Gadi

"YOU TOLD YOUR FRIENDS?" Aro asked. "Why?"

I rubbed my forehead. On the way to Aro's hut, I'd had one of my headaches and been forced to lean myself against a tree for fifteen minutes until it passed. The headache was mostly gone.

"They helped me, *Oga*. Then they asked so I told them," I said.

"You do understand that now they're part of it."

"Part of what?"

"You'll see."

I sighed. "I shouldn't have told them."

"Can't be helped now," Aro said. "So, answers. You will understand much tonight. But first, Onyesonwu, I have talked to Mwita about this and now I talk to you, though I wonder if I'm wasting my words. I know what you two did."

I felt my face grow hot.

"You possess both ugliness and beauty. Even to my eyes, you're confusing. Mwita can only see your beauty. So he can't help himself. But you can."

"*Oga*," I said trying to hold calm. "I'm no different from Mwita. We're both human, we should both make the effort."

"Don't deceive yourself."

"I'm not d . . ."

"And don't interrupt me."

"Then don't continue with these assumptions! If you're going to teach me, I don't want to hear any of that! I'll stop having intercourse with Mwita. Okay. I apologize. But he and I will both make the effort to refrain. Like two humans!" I was shouting now. "Flawed, imperfect creatures! That's what we *both* are, *Oga!* That's what we ALL are!"

He stood up. I didn't move, my heart pounding hard in my chest.

"Okay," Aro said with a smirk. "I will try."

"Good."

"However, you are never to speak to me as you just did. You're learning from me. I am your superior." He paused. "You may know and understand me, but if we came to blows again, I'd kill you first . . . easily and without hesitation." He sat back down. "You and Mwita are not to have intercourse. Not only will it disrupt your learning, but if you were to become pregnant, you'd risk a lot more than your own and the child's life.

"This happened to a woman long ago who was learning the Points. She was too early in her pregnancy for her Master be aware of it. When she attempted a simple exercise, the entire town was wiped out. Disappeared as if it never existed." Aro seemed satisfied with my shocked look. "You are now on the road to something very powerful but unstable. Have you seen your birth father's eye since you were initiated?"

"No," I said.

Aro nodded. "He won't even try to watch you now. That is how potent your path is. If you simply avoid meeting him face-to-face, you'll be safe." He paused. "Let's start. Where we begin is up to you. Ask me what you wish to know."

"I want to know the Great Mystic Points," I said.

"Build a foundation first. You know nothing about the Points, so you aren't even prepared to ask about them. To get the answers, you must have the right questions."

I thought for a moment, then I had my question. "Papa's first wife," I said. "Why didn't you teach her?"

"You wish me to apologize for my previous mistakes, too," he said.

I didn't but I said, "Yes. I do."

"Women are difficult," he said. "Njeri was like you. Wild and arrogant. Her mother was the same way." He sighed. "It was for the same reason I refused you. It was a mistake to refuse to teach her at least minor jujus. She'd have failed initiation."

I hoped Njeri heard his words. I believe she did. "Well . . . Okay. I guess, my next question is . . . Who was she?"

I wasn't surprised that Aro understood I was referring to the woman whose death the man in black had forced me to experience. "Ask Sola," he snapped.

"The man who initiated me?" I asked.

Aro nodded.

"Then who is Sola?"

"A sorcerer like me but older. He's had more time to gather, absorb and give."

"Why's his skin so white? Is he human?"

Aro laughed loudly at this, as if remembering a joke. "Yes," he said. "He throws the bones and reads your future. If you're worthy, he shows you death. You have to ride through death to pass, but riding through it doesn't mean you pass. That's decided afterward. Almost all who pass through death pass initiation. There are a few . . . like Mwita, who are denied for some reason."

"Why didn't Mwita pass?"

"I'm not sure. Neither is Sola."

"What of you, Aro? What was it like for you? What's your story?"

He looked at me in that way again, as if I wasn't worthy. He didn't know he did it. He couldn't control it. *My mother was right,* I thought. *All men bear stupidity.* I laugh at these thoughts now. If it were only so simple for women bear it too.

"Why do you look at me that way?" I snapped before I could stop myself.

He got up and walked toward the desert, a place that now also held a bit of mystery for me. I got up and followed. We walked until his hut was barely in sight.

"I'm from Gadi, a village on the fourth of the Seven Rivers," he said.

"That's where that storyteller was from," I said.

"Yes, but I'm much older than she," he said. "I knew it before the

Okeke started revolting. My parents were fishermen." He turned to me and smiled, "Shall I call my mother a fisherwoman? Does that suit you?"

I smiled back, "Yes, very much."

He harrumphed. "I'm the tenth of eleven children. All of us fished. My grandfather on my father's side was a sorcerer. He beat me the day he saw me change into a water weasel. I was ten years old. Then he taught me everything he knew. "

"I had been changing my shape since I was nine. The first time I did it, I'd been sitting at the river, a fishing stick in my hands, and a water weasel had come up to me. It grabbed me with its eyes. I remember nothing of those moments, only coming back to myself in the middle of the river. I'd have drowned if one of my sisters hadn't been in her boat nearby and seen me floundering."

"I went through initiation at thirteen. My grandfather knew so much but he was still a slave, as we all were. No, not all. Eventually I refused the fate set for me by the Great Book. One day, I saw my mother beaten bloody for laughing at a Nuru man who had tripped and fallen. I ran to help her but before I could get to her, my father grabbed and beat me so badly that I lost consciousness.

"When I came to, right there, I changed myself into an eagle and I flew away. I don't know how long I remained an eagle. Many years. When I finally decided to change back, I was no longer a boy. I became a man named Aro, who traveled and listened and watched. This is me. You see?"

I saw. But there were parts about himself that he was leaving out. Like his relationship with the Ada. "Your initiation," I said. "What did you . . ."

"I saw death, as you did. You'll recover, eventually, Onyesonwu. It was something you had to see. It happens to us all. We fear what we don't know."

"But that poor woman," I said.

"It happens to us all. Don't weep for her. She's reached the wilderness. Congratulate her instead."

"Wilderness?" I said.

"After death, the path leads there," he said. He smirked. "Sometimes before death, too. You were forced there the first time. The clitoris or penis, when put through that kind of trauma, will take sensitive ones there. This was why I was worried about you being circumcised. You must pass into the wilderness during initiation. Being Eshu saved you, for nothing taken from an Eshu's body is ever permanently gone until death."

We walked for a few minutes as I mulled over these things. I wanted to be away from him, to sit and think. Aro implied that I had grown my clitoris back during initiation and removed it afterward, for I'd had to grow it again with Mwita. I wondered why I'd done that, removed it again? Jwahir's customs were under my skin more than I realized.

"What happened to you that first day with the weasel?" I asked. "The day you almost drowned? Why does it happen like that?"

"I was visited. We all are."

"By who?"

Aro shrugged. "Whoever must visit us to show us how to do what we can do."

"Too much of this doesn't make complete sense. There are holes in . . ."

"What makes you think that you should understand it all?" he asked. "That's a lesson you have to learn, instead of being angry all the time. We'll never know exactly why we are, what we are, and so on. All you can do is follow your path all the way to the wilderness, and then you continue along because that's what must be."

We followed our own footsteps back to the hut. I was glad. I'd had enough for one day. Little did I know that this was the mildest day of them all. This day was nothing.

Chapter 22

Peace

IT'S A DAY THAT I'VE PULLED UP MANY TIMES in the last year to remind me that life is also good. It was a Rest Day. The Rain Fest lasts four days and during those days no one works. Sprinklers made from capture stations are set up all around the market. People can huddle under umbrellas, watch singing acrobats, and buy boiled yam and stew, curry soup, and palm wine.

This memorable day was on the first festival day, when not much was going on other than people hanging around and catching up with one another. My mother was spending the afternoon with the Ada and Nana the Wise.

I made myself a cup of tea and sat on the front steps to watch people pass by. I'd slept well for once. No nightmares, no headaches. The sun felt good on my face. My tea tasted strong and delicious. This day was just before I started learning the Points. When I was still capable of relaxing.

Across the road, a young couple showed off their new baby to some friends. Nearby, two old men concentrated on a game of Warri. On the side of the road, a girl and two boys drew pictures with colored sand. The girl looked as if she'd be eleven soon . . . I shook my head. No, I wasn't going to think about anything like that today. I looked up the road. I grinned. Mwita grinned back, his tan caftan blowing in the breeze. *Why does he insist on wearing that color?* I thought, though I kind of liked it. He sat beside me.

"How are you?" he said.

I shrugged. I didn't want to think about how I was. He touched one of my long braids, pushed it aside and kissed my cheek. "Some coconut sweets," he said, handing me the box tucked under his arm.

We sat there, close enough for our shoulders to touch, eating the soft square-shaped cakes. Mwita always smelled good, like mint and sage. His nails were always well trimmed. This was from his wealthy Nuru upbringing. Okeke men bathed several times a day but only the women took such care of their skin, nails, and hair.

Minutes later, Binta, Luyu, and Diti arrived on Luyu's camel. They were a whirl of brightly colored garments and perfumed oils. My friends. I was surprised that there wasn't a parade of men following their camel. But then again, Luyu liked to ride fast.

"You're early," I said. I hadn't been expecting them for another three hours.

"I had nothing better to do," Luyu shrugged, handing me two bottles of palm wine. "So I went to Diti's house and she had nothing better to do. Then we went to see Binta and she had nothing better to do. Do you have anything better to do?"

We all laughed. Mwita handed them the box of coconut sweets and they each happily took some. We played a game of Warri. By the end of the game, we were all nicely spirited from Luyu's wine. I sang some songs for them and they applauded. Luyu, Diti, and Binta had never heard me sing. They were amazed and, for once, I was proud. As the day progressed we moved inside. Well into the night, we talked about nothing much of substance. Insignificance. Wonderful unimportance.

See us here and remember it. We had all lost most of our innocence, certainly. In my, Mwita's, and Binta's case, all of it. But this day we were all happy and well. This would soon change. Dare I say that just after the Rain Festival, when I returned to Aro's hut, the rest of my story, though it spans over four years, begins to move very fast.

Chapter 23

Bushcraft

"BRICOLEUR, ONE WHO USES all that he has to do what he has to do," Aro said. "This is what you must become. We all have our own tools. One of yours is energy, that's why you anger so easily. A tool always begs to be used. The trick is to learn *how* to use it."

I took notes with a stick of sharpened charcoal on a piece of paper. At first, he'd demanded that I hold all lessons in my memory but I learn best by writing things down.

"Another of your tools is that you can change your shape. So already, you have tools to work two of the four Points. And now that I think of it, you have one to work the third. You can sing. Communication." He nodded, frowning to himself. "Yes, *sha*."

"We've come far for this, so listen." He paused. "And put down that charcoal stick, you're not allowed to write this down. You're not to *ever* teach this to anyone, unless he has passed his initiation, too."

"I won't," I nervously said.

Of course, by telling you all this, you see that I lied. Back then I spoke the truth. But much has happened since. Secrets mean less to me now. But I understand why these lessons can't be found anywhere, not even in the House of Osugbo—a place which I now knew had pushed me out by using its irritating tricks. It knew only Aro could teach me.

"Not even Mwita," he said.

"Okay."

Aro pushed back his long sleeves. "You've carried this knowledge, since you . . . have known me. That may help or it may not. We'll see."

I nodded.

"Everything is based on balance." He looked at me to make sure I was listening.

I nodded.

"The Golden Rule is to let the eagle and the hawk perch. Let the camel and the fox drink. All places operate off of this elastic but durable rule. Balance cannot be broken but it can be stretched. That's when things go wrong. Speak, so I know you hear me."

"Okay," I said. He wanted constant acknowledgment of my understanding.

"The Mystic Points are aspects of everything. A sorcerer can manipulate them with his tools to make things happen. It's not the 'magic' of children's stories. To work the Points is far beyond any juju."

"Okay," I said.

"But there's logic to it, pitiless calm logic. There is nothing that a man must believe that can't be seen or touched or sensed. We are not so dead to things around and within us, Onyesonwu. If you are paying attention, you can know."

"Okay," I said.

He paused. "This is difficult. I've never spoken this aloud. It is strange."

I waited.

"There are four points," he said loudly. "Okike, Alusi, Mmuo, Uwa."

"Okike?" I asked, before I could stop myself. "But . . ."

"Just names. The Great Book says that Okeke people were the first people on earth. The Mystic Points were known long before this wretched book existed. A sorcerer who *believed* he was a prophet wrote the Great Book. Names, names, names," he said with a wave of his hands. "They don't always equal up."

"Okay," I said.

"The Uwa Point represents the physical world, the body," Aro said. "Change, death, life, connection. You're Eshu. That is your tool to manipulate it with."

I nodded, frowning.

"The Mmuo Point is the wilderness," he said, moving his hand as if it traveled over ripples of water. "Your great energy allows you to glide through the wilderness while carrying the baggage of life. Life is very heavy. You've been to the wilderness twice. I suspect that there have been other times where you've stepped into it."

"But . . ."

"Don't interrupt," he said. "The Alusi point represents forces, deities, spirits, non-Uwa beings. The masquerade you met the day you came here was an Alusi. The wilderness is populated by them. The Uwa world is also ruled by Alusi. Silly magic men and fortune-tellers believe it is the other way around." He laughed dryly.

"Lastly, the Okike Point represents the Creator. This point cannot be touched. No tool can turn the back of the Creator toward what It has created." He spread his hands. "We call the sorcerer's toolbox that contains the sorcerer's tools Bushcraft." He stopped talking and waited. I took my cue to ask my questions.

"How can I . . . I was in the wilderness, did that mean I was dead?"

Aro just shrugged. "Words, names, words, names. They don't matter sometimes." He clapped his hands together and got up. "I'm going to teach you something that will make you sick. Mwita has a lesson with the healer today but that can't be helped. He'll be back soon enough to care for you if need be. Come. Let's go tend to my goats."

A black goat and a brown goat sat in the shade in the shed near Aro's hut. As we approached, the black goat stood up and turned around. We had a nice view of its anus opening up to push out tiny round black balls of feces. It made the place smell that much more strongly of goat, musky and pungent in the dry heat. I frowned and flared my nostrils, disgusted. I'd never liked the smell of goats, though I ate the meat.

"Ah, one has volunteered," Aro laughed. He led the black goat by its small horns around to the back of the hut. "Take it," he said, putting my hand to its horn. Then he went into his hut. I looked down at the goat as it tried to yank its head from me. When I turned around, Aro was coming out of the hut with a large knife.

I raised a hand to fend him off. He stepped around me, grabbed the goat's horn, turned its head, and slit its throat open. I was so prepared for combat that the goat's blood and its brays of shock and pain might as well have been my own. Before I knew what I was doing, I knelt beside the terrified animal, pressed my hand to its bleeding throat, and shut my eyes.

"Not yet!" he said, grabbing my arm and yanking me back. I sat back hard in the sand. *What just happened?* was all I could think as the goat bled to death before my eyes. Its eyes grew sleepy. It knelt down on its knobby knees, looking accusingly at Aro.

"Never seen anyone unlearned do that," Aro said to himself.

"Eh?" I said, out of breath, watching the goat's life fade. My hands itched.

Aro touched his chin. "And she'd have done it, too. I'm sure of it, *sha*."

"What . . ."

"Shhh," he said, still thinking.

The goat laid its head on its hoofs, closed its eyes, and did not move.

"Why did you . . ." I began.

"You remember what you did to your father?"

"Y-yes," I said.

"Do it now," he said. "This goat's *mmuo-a* is still around, confused. Bring it back and then mend the wound as you wanted to."

"But I don't know how," I said. "Before . . . I just did it."

"Then just do it again," he said, growing agitated. "What can I do with so much doubt, *sha*? Ah ah." He pulled me up and shoved me toward the goat's corpse. "Do it!"

I knelt down and rested my hand on its bloody neck. I shivered with revulsion, not from the dead goat, but the fact that it had died so recently. I froze. I *could* feel its *mmuo-a* moving around me. It was a light shifting in the air, a soft sandy sound nearby.

"It's running," I said softly.

"That's good," Aro said behind me, the frustration gone from his voice.

The poor thing was terrified and discombobulated. I looked at Aro. "Why did you kill it like that? That was cruel."

"What is it with you women?" Aro snapped. "Must everything make you cry?"

Anger flared in me and I could feel the ground beneath me grow warm.

Then it felt as if I knelt on hundreds of metal-bodied ants. They moved about underneath me, conducting something through me. I understood. I pulled it up from the ground and pushed it into my hands. More and more—there was an endless supply of it. I drew from my anger at Aro and from my own reserve of power. I drew from Aro's strength, too. I'd have also drawn from Mwita if he'd been there.

"Now," Aro said softly. "You see."

I saw.

"Control it this time," he said.

All my eyes saw was the goat's dead body. But its *mmuo-a* ran circles around me. I felt it right next to me, its hoof on my leg as it watched what I was doing. Beneath my hand, the cut to its neck was . . . churning. The cut's edges were knitting themselves up. The sight made me nauseated.

"Go," I told the *mmuo-a*. A minute later, I removed my hand, turned my head, and was violently sick. I didn't see the goat stand up and shake its head. I was vomiting too loudly to hear its cry of joy or feel it lay its head on my thigh in thanks. Aro helped me up. In the short walk to Mwita's hut, I vomited again. Much of it was filled with hay and grass. My breath tasted like the odor of live goat and that made me vomit again.

"Next time, it will be better," Aro said. "Soon, bringing back life will have little physical effect on you at all."

Mwita returned late. Aro wasn't a good caretaker. He made sure that I didn't choke on my own vomit but he had no soothing words. He wasn't that kind of man. Later that evening, Mwita shaved off the goat hairs growing on the back of my hand. He assured me that they wouldn't grow back but what did I care? I was too sick. He didn't ask me what had made me so ill. He knew from the day I started learning that there would be a part of me that he'd have no access to.

Mwita knew more than Jwahir's best healer. Even the House of Os-ugbo thought him worthy of its books, for Mwita consumed many medi-cal books he'd found there. Because he was such an expert on the human body, he was able to calm mine. But there were things I suffered from that came from the wilderness. He could do nothing about those. So I suffered much that night, but not as much as I could have.

This was how it was for three and half years. Knowledge, sacrifice, and headaches. Aro taught me how to converse with masquerades. This left me hearing voices and singing strange songs. The day I learned how to glide through the wilderness, I was ignorable for a week. My mother could barely see me. Several people probably thought I was dead after seeing what they thought was my ghost. Even after that, I was prone to moments of not being quite either there or here.

I learned to use my Eshu skills not only to change into other animals but to grow and change parts of my body. I realized that I could change my face a bit, altering my lips and cheekbones, and if I cut myself, I could heal the wound. Luyu, Binta, and Diti watched me as I learned. They feared for me. And sometimes they kept their distance, fearing for themselves.

Mwita grew closer to and more distant from me. He was my healer. He was my mate, for though we could not have intercourse, we could lie in each other's arms, kiss each other's lips, love each other dearly. Yet, he was barred from understanding what it was that was shaping me into something he both marveled at and envied.

My mother allowed what was to be. My biological father waited.

My mind evolved and thrived. But it was all for a reason. Fate was preparing for the next phase. After I tell you, you decide for yourself if I was ready for it.

Chapter 24

Onyesonwu in the Market

MAYBE IT WAS BECAUSE OF THE POSITION OF THE SUN. Or maybe the way that man inspected a yam. Or the way that woman considered a tomato. Or maybe it was those women laughing at me. Or that old man glaring at me. As if they all had little else to worry about. Or maybe it was the position of the sun, high in the sky, bright, sizzling.

Whatever it was, it got me thinking about my last lesson with Aro. The lesson was particularly infuriating. The purpose was for me to learn to see distant places. It was rainy season, so collecting rain water wasn't too hard. I took the water inside Aro's hut and concentrated on it, focusing hard on what I sought to see. The storyteller's news from years ago was on my mind.

I expected to see Okeke people slaving for Nurus. I expected to see Nuru people going about their business as if this were normal. I must have tuned in to the worst part of the West. The rainwater showed me ripped oozing flesh, bloody erect penises, sinew, intestines, fire, heaving chests, mewling bodies engaged in evil. Without thinking, my hand slapped the clay bowl away. It crashed against the wall, breaking in two.

"It's still happening!" I shouted at Aro who was outside tending to his goats.

"Did you think it stopped?" he said.

I *had*. At least for a while. Even I'd exercised *some* denial in order to live my life.

"It ebbs and flows," Aro said.

"But why?? What is . . ."

"No creature or beast is happy when enslaved," Aro said. "Nuru and Okeke try to live together, then they fight, then they try to live together, then they fight. Okeke numbers dwindle now. But you remember the prophecy that storyteller spoke of."

I nodded. The storyteller's words had stayed with me for years. In the West, she'd said, a Nuru seer prophesied that a Nuru sorcerer would come and change what was written.

"It will come to pass," Aro said.

I was walking through the market, rubbing my forehead, the sun beating down as if to provoke me, when the women laughed. I turned. It had come from within a group of young women. Women my age. Around twenty. From my old school. I knew them.

"Look at her," I heard one of them say. "Too ghastly to marry."

I felt it go snap inside me, in my mind. The last straw. I'd had enough. Enough of Jwahir, whose people were as bloated and complacent as the Golden Lady herself. "Is something wrong?" I loudly asked the women.

They looked at me as if *I* were disturbing *them*. "Lower your voice," one of them said. "Weren't you raised properly?"

"She was barely raised at all, remember?" one of the others said.

Several people paused in their transactions to listen. An old man glared at me.

"What is *with* you people?" I said, turning around to address all around me. "All this is unimportant! Can't you see?" I paused to catch my breath, actually hoping an audience would gather. "Yes, I am talking, come and listen. Let me answer *all* the questions you've all had about me for so long!" I laughed. The crowd was already larger than the meager gathering that came to hear the storyteller speak that night.

"Only a hundred miles away, Okeke people are being wiped away by the thousands!" I shouted, feeling my blood rise. "Yet here we all are, living in comfort. Jwahir turns her fat unmoving backside to it all. Maybe you even *hope* our people there will finally die off so you can stop hearing about it. Where is your *passion*?" I was crying now and still I stood alone. It had always been this way. This was why I decided to speak the words Aro had taught me. He'd warned me not to use these words. He said I wasn't remotely old enough to speak them. *I'll pry your cursed eyes open,* I thought as the words tumbled from my lips, smooth and easy as honey.

I won't tell you the words. Just know I spoke them. Then I flared my nostrils and drew on the anxiety, rage, guilt, and fear swarming around me. I had unknowingly done this at Papa's funeral and knowingly done it with the goat. I crossed over. *What will they see?* I wondered, suddenly afraid. *Well, it can't be helped now.* I dug deep into what made me me and took them into what my mother went through.

I should never have done this.

All of us were there, only eyes, watching. There were about forty of us and we were both my mother and the man who helped make me. The man who'd been watching me since I was eleven. We watched him get off his scooter and look around. We saw him see my mother. His face was veiled. His eyes were like a tiger's. Like mine.

We watched him ravage and destroy my mother. She was limp beneath him. She'd retreated into the wilderness and there she'd waited as she watched. She always watched. She had an Alusi in her. We felt the moment my mother's will broke. We felt her attacker's moment of doubt and disgust with himself. Then the rage that came from his people took him again, filling his body with unnatural strength.

I felt it inside me, too. Like a demon buried under my skin since my conception. A gift from my father, from his corrupted genetics. The potential and taste for amazing cruelty. It was in my bones, firm, stable, unmoving. Oh, I had to find and kill this man.

There was screaming from everywhere, from everyone. The Nuru men and their women, their skin like the day. And the Okeke women with skin like the night. The din was awful. Some of the men sobbed and laughed and praised Ani as they raped. Women called to Ani for help, a few of these women were Nuru. The sand was clumpy with blood and saliva and tears and semen.

I was so transfixed by the screaming that it took seconds for me to realize that it had started coming from the people in the market. I pulled in the vision as one folds up a map. Around me, people sobbed. A man fainted. Children ran in circles. *I didn't think about the children!* I realized. Someone grabbed my arm.

"What have you *done?*" Mwita shouted. He pulled me along at such a fast pace I couldn't immediately answer. People around us were too stunned and shaken to stop us.

"They *should* know!" I shouted, when I'd finally caught my breath. We'd left the market and started up the road.

"Just because we hurt doesn't mean others should!" Mwita said.

"It does!" I shouted. "We're all hurting whether we know it or not! It has to stop!"

"I know!" Mwita shouted back. "I know it more than you!"

"*Your* father didn't rape *your* mother to create you! What do *you* know?"

He stopped walking and grabbed my arm. "You're out of control!" he hissed. He threw down my arm. "*You* only know what you've seen!"

I just stood there. I was far too defiant and unwilling to own up to the stupidity of my comment and my lack of self-control.

"I will tell you," he said, lowering his voice.

"Tell me what?"

"Move," he said. "I'll tell you as we go. Too many eyes here." We walked for two minutes before he spoke. "You can be really stupid sometimes."

"So can . . ." I shut my mouth.

"You think you know the whole story, but you don't." He looked behind us and I looked too. No one was following us. Yet.

"Listen," he said. "It's true that I traveled east alone until I met Aro. But there was some time there, just after . . . When the Okeke and the Nuru were fighting and I turned myself ignorable to escape, I didn't know how to stay ignorable for long. Not yet. Only for a few minutes, really. You know how it is."

I did. It took me a month to sustain it for ten minutes. It required serious concentration. Mwita had been so young; I was surprised he was able to hold it at all.

"I made it out of the house, out of the village, away from the real fighting. But out in the desert, I was soon captured by Okeke rebels. They had machetes, bows and arrows, some guns. I was locked into a shack with Okeke children. We were to fight for the Okeke side. They killed anyone who tried to run away."

"That first day, I saw a girl raped by one of the men. The girls had it worse because they weren't just beaten into obeying, as we all were. They were raped, too. The next night, I saw a boy shot when he tried to escape. A week later, a group of us were forced to beat a boy to death because he'd tried to escape." He paused, flaring his nostrils. "I was *Ewu*, so they beat me more often and watched me more closely. Even with all the sorcery I knew, I was too afraid to attempt an escape.

"They showed us how to shoot arrows and use machetes. The few of us who showed that we had good eyes were taught to shoot guns. I was very good with guns. But twice I tried to kill myself with the one given to me. And twice I was beaten out of doing so. Months later, we were taken into the fighting against the Nuru, the race of people I was raised to live with as family.

"I killed many." Mwita sighed and continued, "One day, I got sick. We were camping in the desert. The men were digging mass graves for those who'd died in the night. There were so many, Onyesonwu. They threw me in with the bodies when they saw that I couldn't get up.

"I was buried alive. They moved on. After a few hours, the fever I was suffering from abated and I dug myself out. Immediately, I went looking for medicinal plants to cure myself. And that was how I was able to travel east. I'd spent two months with those rebels. If I hadn't looked dead, I'm sure I'd *be* dead. *Those* are your innocent Okeke 'victims.'"

We'd stopped walking.

"It's not as simple as you think," he said. "There is sickness on both sides. Be careful. Your father sees things in black and white, too. The Okeke bad, Nuru good."

"But it's the Nuru's fault," I said quietly. "If they hadn't treated the Okeke like trash, then the Okeke wouldn't be behaving like trash."

"Can't the Okeke *think* for themselves?" Mwita said. "They know best what it feels like to be enslaved yet look what they do to their own children! My aunt and uncle weren't murderers, Onyesonwu! They were *killed* by murderers!"

I was deeply ashamed.

"Come," he said, holding out his hand. I looked at it and noticed for the first time, a faint scar on his right index finger. *From the trigger of a hot gun?* I wondered.

A half hour later, I stood outside Aro's hut. I'd refused to go in.

"Then stay here," Mwita had said. "I'll tell him."

While Mwita and Aro talked, I was glad to be alone because . . . I was alone. I kicked the hut's wall with the heel of my foot and sat down. I scooped up some sand and let it run through my fingers. A black cricket hopped over my leg and a hawk screeched from somewhere in the sky. I looked to the west where the sun would set and the evening stars would rise. I took a deep deep breath and held my eyes wide open. I stayed very still. My eyes grew dry. My tears felt good when they came.

I stood up, took off my clothes, changed into a vulture and rode the late hot afternoon air into the sky.

I returned an hour later. I felt better, calmer. As I was putting my clothes on, Mwita poked his head from Aro's hut.

"Hurry up," he said.

"I will come when I please," I mumbled. I straightened out my clothes.

As the three of us talked, I found myself getting riled up again. "Who's going to stop it?" I asked. "It won't stop once the Nuru have killed all the Okeke in their so-called land, will it, Aro?"

"Doubtful," Aro said.

"Well, I've decided something. This prophecy will come true, and I want to be there when it does. I want to see him and I want to help him succeed at whatever it is he will do."

"And your other reason for going?" Aro asked.

"To kill my father," I said bluntly.

Aro nodded. "Well, you can't stay here anyway. I was able to stop the people from coming after you before but this time you dug your talon into a sore part of Jwahir's psyche. Plus your father is expecting you."

Mwita got up and without a word walked off. Aro and I watched him leave.

"Onyesonwu," Aro said, "it'll be a harsh journey. You have to be prepared for . . ."

I didn't hear the rest of what he said, for one of my headaches began to throb in my temples, increasing with each thump. Within seconds, it felt as it always eventually did, like stones hitting my head. It was the mixture of Mwita's leaving the hut, knowing I was to leave Jwahir, the images of violence still swirling around my mind, and the face of my biological father. All those things triggered my sudden suspicion.

I jumped up and stared at Aro. I was so pained, so flabbergasted, that for the second time in my life, I forgot how to breathe. My headache increased and everything tinted silvery red. The look on Aro's face scared me more. It was calm and patient.

"Open your mouth and take in air before you pass out," he said. "And sit down."

When I finally sat back down, I started sobbing. "It can't be, Aro!"

"All initiates have to see it," he said. He smiled sadly. "People fear the unknown. What better way to remove one's fear of death than to show it to him?"

I pressed my temples. "Why will they *hate* me so much?" Somehow I would end up being jailed and then stoned to death and many people would be very happy about it.

"You'll find out, won't you?" Aro said, solemnly. "Why spoil the surprise?"

I went to see Mwita. Aro had instructed me on several things, including when he thought I should leave. I had two days. Mwita sat on his bed, his back against the wall.

"You don't think, Onyesonwu," he said, looking blankly straight ahead.

"Did you know?" I asked. "Did you know that it was my own death that I saw?"

Mwita opened his mouth and then shut it.

"Did you?" I asked again.

He got up, took me in his arms and held me tightly. I closed my eyes. "Why'd he tell you?" he asked, his lips near my ear.

"Mwita, I forgot how to breathe. I was so stunned."

"He shouldn't have told you," he said.

"He didn't," I said. "I just . . . figured it out."

"He should have lied to you then," Mwita said.

We stood like this for some time. I inhaled Mwita's scent, noting that this was one of the last times I'd be able to do this. I held him back and grasped his hands.

"I'm coming with you," he said before I could say anything.

"No," I said. "I know the desert. I can change into a vulture when I must and . . ."

"I know it as well as you do, if not better. I know the West, too."

"Mwita, what did you see?" I asked, ignoring his words for a moment. "You saw . . . you saw yours, too, didn't you?"

"Onyesonwu, one's end is one's end and that's the end of it," he said. "You won't be going alone. Not even close. Go home. I'll come to you tomorrow afternoon."

I got home around midnight. My plans didn't surprise my mother. She'd heard about what I'd done at the market. All of Jwahir was buzzing about it. The gossip carried no details, only a hardened sentiment that I was evil and should be jailed.

"Mwita is coming with me, too, Mama," I said.

"Good," she said after a moment.

As I turned to go to my room, my mother sniffed. I turned around. "Mama, I . . ."

She held up a hand. "I'm human but I'm not stupid, Onyesonwu. Go and sleep."

I went back to her and gave her a long hug. She pushed me toward my room. "Go to bed," she said, wiping her eyes.

Surprisingly, I slept deeply for two hours. No nightmares. Later that night—or should I say morning—around four a.m, Luyu, Binta, and Diti showed up at my window. I helped them climb in my room. Once inside, the three of them just stood. I had to laugh. It was the most comical thing I'd seen all day.

"Are you all right?" Diti asked.

"What happened?" Binta asked. "We need to hear it from you."

I sat down on my bed. I didn't know where to start. I shrugged and sighed. Luyu sat beside me. I could smell scented oil and a hint of sweat. Luyu would normally never let the smell of sweat creep onto her skin. She stared at the side of my face for so long that I turned to her, irritated, "What?"

"I was there today, at the market," she said. "I saw . . . I saw it all." Tears welled up in her eyes. "Why didn't you tell me?" She looked down. "But you *have* told us, haven't you? Was that . . . your mother?"

"Yes," I said.

"Show us," Diti said quietly. "We want to . . . see, too."

I paused. "Okay." It wasn't as jarring for me the second time. I listened closely to the Nuru words he snarled at my mother but no matter how hard I tried, I couldn't understand them. Though I spoke some Nuru, my mother didn't and this vision was gathered from her experience. *Vile, vicious, cruel man,* I thought. *I'll take his breath away.* Afterwards, Binta and Diti remained stunned into silence. Luyu, however, only looked more tired.

"I'm leaving Jwahir," I said.

"I want to go with you, then," Binta suddenly said.

I quickly shook my head. "No. Only Mwita goes with me. You belong here."

"Please," she begged. "I want to see what's out there. This place, it . . . I have to get away from my Papa."

We all knew it. Even after the interventions, Binta's father still couldn't control himself. Though she tried to hide it, Binta was ill quite often. It was because of his abuse, because of the pain she endured from it. I frowned realizing something disturbing: If the pain came only when a woman was aroused, did that mean her father's touch aroused her? I shuddered. Poor Binta. On top of this, Binta was marked as "the girl who was so lovely even her father couldn't resist her." Mwita told me that there was already a growing competition for her among the young men because of this.

"I want to go, too," Luyu said. "I want to be a part of this."

"I don't even know what we're going to *do,*" I stammered. "I don't even . . ."

"I'll go, too," Diti said.

"But you're betrothed," Luyu said.

"Eh?" I said, looking at Diti.

"Last month, his father asked for her hand on his son's behalf," Luyu said.

"Whose father?" I asked.

"Fanasi's, of course," Luyu said.

Fanasi had been Diti's love since they were very young. He was the one who'd felt so insulted by Diti's cries of pain when he touched her that for years he refused to talk to her. I guess, it took those years for him to grow into a man and learn that he could take what he wanted.

"Diti, why didn't you tell me?" I asked.

She shrugged, "Didn't seem important, not to you. And maybe it's not, not now."

"Of course it is," I said.

"Well . . ." Diti said. "Would you be willing to speak to Fanasi?"

And that is how Mwita, Luyu, Binta, Diti, Fanasi, and I ended up in the main room the next day while my mother was at the market buying me supplies. Diti, Luyu, Binta, and I were nineteen. Mwita was twenty-two and Fanasi was twenty-one. All of us so naive, dabbling in what I would later realize was wishful thinking.

Fanasi had grown tall over the years. He stood half a head taller than Mwita and me, a full head taller than Luyu and Diti and even taller than Binta, the tiniest of us all. He was a broad-shouldered young man with smooth dark skin, piercing eyes, and powerful arms. He looked at me with great suspicion. Diti told him her plan. He'd looked at Diti then me and surprisingly said nothing. A good sign.

"I'm not what they say I am," I said.

"I know what Diti tells me," he said, in his low voice. "But only that."

"Will you come with us?" I asked.

Diti had insisted Fanasi was a free thinker. She said he'd been part of the storyteller's audience that day years ago. But he was also an Okeke man, so he didn't trust me. "My father owns a bread shop that I'm to inherit," he said.

I narrowed my eyes, wondering if his father was that mean man who had snapped at my mother when we'd first arrived in Jwahir. I wanted to shout at him, "Then the Nurus will come and tear you apart, rape your wife, and create another like me! You're a fool!" I could feel Mwita next to me willing me to keep quiet.

"Let her show you," Diti said softly. "Then you decide."

"I'll wait outside," Luyu said before Fanasi replied. She quickly got up. Binta followed close at her heels. Diti took Fanasi's hand and squeezed her eyes shut. Mwita simply stood next to me. I took us all to the past for the third time. Fanasi reacted with loud blubbering tears. Diti had to comfort him. Mwita touched my shoulder and left the room. As Fanasi calmed, his grief was replaced with anger. Raging anger. I smiled.

He pounded his large fist on his thigh. "How can this be! I . . . I didn't . . . I can't . . . !"

"Jwahir is much removed," I said.

"Onye," he said. He was the first to call me this. "I'm very sorry. Truly I am. People around here . . . we all have no idea!"

"It's okay," I said. "Will you come?"

He nodded. And then there were six.

Chapter 25

And So It Was Decided

WE WOULD LEAVE IN THREE HOURS. And because people knew this, they left me alone. Only their stares when I passed by showed their anxiousness for me to go, their anxiousness to forget again. I stood with Aro before the desert. From here, we'd go southwest around Jwahir and then due west. On foot, not on camel. I don't ride camels. When my mother and I were living in the desert I knew wild camels. They were noble creatures whose strength I'd refused exploit.

Aro and I walked up a sand dune. A strong breeze blew my braids back.

"Why does he want to see me?" I asked.

"You have to stop asking that question," Aro replied.

Again, the sandstorm came. This time, however, it wasn't so painful. Once in the tent, I sat down across from Sola. As before, his black hood covered his white face down to his narrow nose. Aro sat beside him and gave him a peculiar handshake that involved twining their fingers together.

"Good day, *Oga* Sola," I said.

"You've grown," Sola said in his papery voice.

"She belongs to Mwita," Aro said. He looked at me and added, "*If* she would belong to any man at all."

Sola nodded his approval. "So you know how this will end," Sola said.

"Yes," I said.

"Those that go with you," Sola said. "Do you understand that some of them may fall along the way?"

I was quiet. It had crossed my mind.

"And that all of this is your responsibility?" Aro added.

"Can it . . . be helped?" I asked Aro.

"Maybe," he said.

"What is it that I should do? How can I . . . find him?"

"Who?" Sola asked, cocking his head. "Your father?"

"No," I said. I suspected he and I would find each other. "The one the prophecy speaks of. Who is he?"

They were quiet for a moment. I sensed they were exchanging words without moving their lips. "Do so then, *sha*," Aro mumbled aloud. He looked drained.

"What do you know of this Nuru man?" Sola asked.

"All I know is that some Nuru Seer prophesized that a tall Nuru man who was a sorcerer would come and change things somehow, rewrite the book."

Sola nodded. "I know the Seer," Sola said. "You must forgive us all for our weaknesses, me, Aro, all of us old ones. We'll learn from this. Aro refused you because you were an *Ewu* female. I almost did the same. This Seer, Rana, guards a precious document. This was why he was given the prophecy. He was told something and couldn't accept it. His stupidity will give you a chance, I think."

I sighed and held up my hands. "I don't understand what you mean, *Oga*."

"Rana couldn't believe what he was told, apparently. He wasn't advised to look out for a Nuru man. It was an *Ewu* woman," he said. He laughed. "At least he was truthful about one thing, you *are* tall."

I walked home in a daze. I didn't want Mwita to walk with me. I cried the entire way. Who cares who saw me? I had less than an hour to be in Jwahir. When I walked in, my mother was waiting for me in the main room. She handed me her cup of tea as I sat beside her on the couch. The tea was very strong, exactly what I needed.

*   *   *

That's enough for today. In two days, I know what will happen here . . . maybe.

I can hope, can't I? What else can I have for myself and the child that grows inside me? Don't look so surprised.

Enough. I'm glad the guards let you in and I hope your fingers were fast enough. And if they snatch that computer from you and dash it to the ground, I hope your memory is good. I don't know if they'll let you back in here tomorrow.

You hear everyone out there? Already gathering to watch? They wait to stone to death the one who turned their small world upside down. Primitive. So much unlike Jwahir's people, who are so apathetic but so civilized.

Two guards right outside this cell have been listening. At least they've been trying to. Thankfully, they can't speak Okeke. If you're able to return here, if you're able to get past these arrogant, hateful, sad, confused bastards again, I'll tell you the rest. And when I'm finished, we'll both see what happens to me, no?

Don't worry about me and the cold here tonight. There are plenty of stones. so I have ways of staying warm. I have ways of staying alive, too. Protect that computer on your way out. If you don't return, I'll understand. You do what you can and the rest you leave in the cold arms of Fate. Take care.

Part III

Warrior

I had a bad night.

Yet another man will die because of me. Well, because of himself. He came into my cell this morning, before the sun came up. He hoped to make himself famous. I'm not like my mother in this regard. I couldn't just lie there. He was a Nuru man named after his father. He had a wife, five children, and was a talented river fisherman. He barged in here bold as an idiot. He never touched me. I am cruel. I put the ugliest vision in his mind and he ran out, silent as a ghost and sad as a broken Okeke slave.

I unplugged all the important circuits in his brain. He'll be fine for two days, too ashamed to speak of his attempted rape. And then he'll suddenly die. I don't pity his wife or his children. You make your bed, so you shall lie in it. A wife chooses her husband and even a child chooses her parents.

Anyway, I'm glad to see you, but why do you risk coming here? There's a reason with you, isn't there? No Nuru man would do this without a reason that goes beyond curiosity. You don't have to tell me. You don't have to tell me anything.

They'll stone me tomorrow. So today I'll give you the rest of my life. The child inside me, her name is Enuigwe; that is an old word for "the heavens," the home of all things, even the Okeke and Nuru. I tell this story to both you and her. She has to know her mother. She has to understand. And she has to be brave. Who fears death? I don't and neither will she. Type fast because I will speak that way.

Chapter 26

THE PAIN OF STONES AND RAGE FOR WHAT I had yet to do threatened to pull me underground. I felt the first throb as we passed the limits of Jwahir. We carried only the large packs on our backs and the ideas in our heads.

"Go straight west," Aro and Sola had instructed. The land soon opened before us, dunes with the occasional cluster of palm trees and patch of dry grass.

"So we just head that way?" Binta asked, squinting as she walked. She was extremely lighthearted for a girl who had poisoned her father mere hours ago. She told only me about putting the slow acting heart root extract in her father's morning tea. She'd watched him drink it and then snuck out of the house, not leaving even a note. By nightfall the man would be dead. "He had it coming," she'd whispered to me, with a grin. "But don't tell the others." I'd looked at her, shocked at her boldness, thinking, *Maybe she is up for this journey.*

"West, yes," Luyu said, rolling her *talembe etanou* around in her mouth. "Head that way for about, what? Four, five months?"

"Depends," I said, rubbing my temples.

"Well, however long it takes, we'll get there," Binta said.

"Camels would have been a thousand times faster," Luyu said yet again.

I rolled my eyes and looked behind us. Mwita and Fanasi strolled several feet back, silent and pensive.

"Each step I take is farther than I've ever been from home," Binta said. She laughed and ran ahead holding her arms out as if trying to fly, her pack bouncing against her back.

"At least one of us begins this journey happy," I mumbled.

For the rest of us, leaving was difficult. Fanasi's father turned out to be the bread maker who'd shouted at my mother and me on our first day in Jwahir. He and Fanasi's mother had come rushing to Aro's hut where we'd all gathered to leave. But they couldn't make it past Aro's gate. Fanasi and Diti had to walk out to them.

Fanasi's mother started loudly lamenting, "My son is being taken by a witch!" His father tried to intimidate his son into staying, threatening him with banishment and a possible beating. When Fanasi and Diti returned, Fanasi was so upset that he'd walked off to be alone. Diti had started weeping. She'd already been through this with her own parents earlier that day.

Luyu's parents also threatened her with banishment. But if there was one way to make Luyu do what you didn't want her to do, it was by threatening her. Luyu was always up for a fight. Still, after leaving, she grew quiet, too.

When Mwita had to say good-bye to Aro, I saw a new side of him. As the rest of us started walking into the desert, he froze. No words, no expression. "Come on," I said, taking his hand and trying to pull him along. He wouldn't move.

"Mwita," I said.

"Move on," Aro said. "Let me speak with my boy."

We walked a mile without Mwita. I refused to look back to see if he was coming. Soon, I heard footsteps not far behind. They grew closer and closer until there he was, walking beside me. His eyes were red. I knew to leave him alone for a while.

For me, leaving home was practically unbearable. Up to then, it had been inevitable. All the events of my life led me to this journey. Due west, no turns, no curves, a straight line. I wasn't meant to live my days as a Jwahir woman. But I wasn't prepared to leave my mother, either. We'd talked as we finished our cups of strong tea together. We hugged. I walked down the steps. Then I turned, ran back up, and threw myself into her arms. She held me, calm and silent.

"I can't leave you alone," I said.

"You will," she said in her whispery voice. She held me back. "Don't treat me like some weakling. You've come too far now. *Finish* it. And when you find . . ." She bared her teeth. "If you go for *no* other reason, go for *that* one. For what he did to me." She hadn't spoken directly about this since I was eleven. "You and I," she said. "We're one. No matter how far you go, it'll always be this way."

I left my mother. Well, first she left me. She simply turned and went inside the house and shut the door. When she didn't open it ten minutes later, I went to Aro's to join the others.

As I walked, I rubbed my throbbing temples and then the back of my head. The headaches, so soon after leaving Jwahir . . . it seemed too ominous. Two days later, the pain was at full blast. We had to stop for two days and for that first day, I wasn't even aware that we'd stopped. All that I know of this first day was what the others told me. While I was in my tent writhing in pain and shouting at phantoms, the others were nervous. Binta, Luyu, and Diti stayed at my side trying to calm me down. Mwita spent much of his time with Fanasi.

"She's had these before," he told Fanasi as they sat before a fire outside my tent. Mwita had made a rock fire—a pile of warmed rocks. It's simple juju. He said Fanasi had been so fascinated by it that he'd accidentally burned himself trying to get a feel for how the heat radiated from the softly glowing pile of stones.

"How can we make this kind of trip if she's so sick?" Fanasi asked.

"She isn't sick," Mwita said. He knew my headaches were linked to my death, but I hadn't told him the details.

"You can cure her, right?" Fanasi asked.

"I'll do my best."

By the next day, my headache receded. I hadn't eaten anything since we'd stopped. My hunger opened my brain to a strange clarity.

"You're up," Binta said, coming into my tent with a plate of smoked meat and bread. She grinned. "You look much better!"

"Still hurts but the pain is going back where it came from."

"Eat," Binta said. "I'll tell the others."

I smiled as she left whooping with joy. I looked myself over. I needed to bathe. I could nearly see the unwashed scent wafting off my body. The clarity I was experiencing made the world so crisp and clear. Every sound outside seemed right against my ear. I could hear a desert fox barking nearby and a hawk screeching. I could almost hear Mwita thinking as he came in.

"Onyesonwu," he said. His freckled cheeks were flushed red and his hazel eyes took in and judged my every detail. "You're better." He kissed me.

"We'll continue the day after tomorrow," I said.

"Are you sure?" he asked. "I know you. Your head still throbs."

"By the time we're ready to go, I'll have chased it away."

"Chased what, Onyesonwu?"

Our eyes met.

"Mwita, we have a long way to go," I said. "It's not important."

Late that night, I got up and went out for some fresh air. I had only eaten a bit of bread and drunk some water, wanting to maintain the strange clarity for a little longer. I found Mwita sitting on the ground behind our tent, facing the desert, his legs crossed. I walked up to him and paused. I turned to go back our tent.

"No," he said his back still to me. "Sit. You interrupted me just by coming close."

I smiled. "Sorry." I sat down. "You're getting good at that."

"Yeah. You're feeling better?"

"Much," I said.

He turned to look at me, eyeing my clothing.

"Not here," I said.

"Why not?"

"I'm still in training," I said.

"You'll always be in training. And we're out in the middle of nowhere."

He reached over and started to untie my rapa. I held his hand. "Mwita," I said. "We can't."

He softly took my hands and moved them away. I let him untie my rapa. The cool desert air felt wonderful against my skin. I glanced back to make sure everyone was still in their tents. We were some feet away, on a slight slope, and it was dark but it was still a risk. One I was willing to take. I let myself fall into the pure complete pleasure of his lips on my neck, nipples, belly. He laughed when I tried to remove his clothes.

"Not yet," he said, taking my hands.

"Oh, you just want my clothes off out here," I said.

"Maybe. I want to talk to you. You listen best when you're relaxed."

"I'm not relaxed at all," I said.

He smirked. "I know. My fault." He retied my rapa and I sat up. Without a word, we turned to the desert and allowed ourselves to fall into mediation. Once my body stopped screaming for Mwita, my blood stilled, my heart leveled, my skin cooled. I settled. I felt I could do anything, see anything, make anything happen, if only I didn't move. Mwita's voice was like a soft ripple on the stillest of waters.

"When we go back to our tent, Onyesonwu, don't worry about what will happen."

I digested this information and just nodded.

"It doesn't stop with what Aro taught you," he said.

"I know."

"Then stop being so afraid."

"Aro spoke of what happens when women sorcerers conceive before they finish training."

Mwita laughed softly and shook his head. "You already know how it will end. You've told me nothing about it, but somehow I doubt your full womb will cause the annihilation of an entire town the way Sanchi's did."

"Was that her name?"

"My first teacher, Daib, told me about her, too."

"And you don't fear that happening with me."

"Like I said, you know that's not how it ends. Plus, you're a far greater talent than Sanchi. You're twenty years old and you already can bring back the dead."

"Not all the time and not without consequence."

"Nothing's without consequence."

"And that's why I think we should avoid intercourse."

"But we won't."

I took my eyes from the blackness of the desert and set them on Mwita. In the faint light coming from the rock fire at the center of our tents, Mwita's yellow-skinned face glowed and his wolflike eyes twinkled.

"Have you ever wondered . . . what our baby would look like?" I asked.

"He or she would look like us," he said.

"What would that make him or her?"

"*Ewu,*" he said.

We were quiet for several minutes, calmness smoothing things out again.

"Leave the tent flap open for me," I said.

We grasped hands and slid them inches back, snapping each other's fingers loudly, the handshake of friendship. I stood up and unwrapped my rapa and let it fall to the ground as I looked down at him. I've turned into several types of animals over the years but my favorite will always be the vulture.

"It's night," Mwita said. "The air won't be as smooth."

My laughs were lost as my throat shifted and narrowed and my skin sprouted feathers. I was good at changing but each and every time was an effort. It is not something you just let happen. Your body knows how to do it, but you still have to *do* it. Nevertheless, as it is when one is good at something, I enjoyed the effort because in many ways the effort was effortless. I spread my wings and took to the sky. No one heard from me for an hour.

I flew into our tent and stood for a moment with my wings spread. Mwita was weaving a basket by candlelight. He always wove when he was worried.

"Luyu was looking for you," he said, putting his basket down. He threw me my rapa once I'd changed back.

"Eh? Why? It's late."

"I think she just wants to talk," he said. "She's been reading the Great Book."

"They all have."

"But she's starting to understand more."

I nodded again. Good. "I'll talk to her tomorrow."

I sat down beside him on our sleeping mat.

"Do you want me to go and wash first?" I asked.

"No."

"If I conceive, we're all . . ."

"Onyesonwu, there are times you have to take what is offered to you," he said. "There'll always be risk with us. *You* are a risk."

I leaned forward and kissed him. Then I kissed him again. And after that, nothing could have stopped us. Not even the end of the world.

Chapter 27

WE SLEPT IN LATE. And when I woke up, my headache was almost completely gone. I blinked at the sharpness of the world around me. My stomach growled.

"Onye," we heard Fanasi say from outside. "Can we come in?"

"Are you decent?" Luyu asked. Then she giggled and we heard her whisper, "He's probably ravaging her again." Then there were more giggles.

"Come in," I said, smiling. "But I stink. I need to wash."

They all piled in. It was a tight fit. After much giggling, grumbling (mainly from Mwita), and shifting, things quieted down. I took it as my cue to speak.

"I'm okay," I said. "The headaches are just something I have to learn to live with. I've . . . I've been having them since my initiation."

"She just needs to adjust to leaving home," Mwita added.

"We'll continue tomorrow," I said, taking Mwita's hand.

When everyone had piled out of my tent, I slowly sat up and yawned.

"You need to eat," Mwita said.

"Not yet," I said. "I want to do something first."

Still only wrapped in my rapa, with Mwita's help I stood. The world swam around me and then it settled. I felt a stone from far away hit the side of my head.

"Do you want me to go with you?" Mwita asked.

"Did you eat yesterday?"

"No," he said. "I'm not going to eat until you eat."

"So you think it's better if we're *both* weak."

"Are you weak?"

I smiled. "No."

"Then let's go."

The first time that I was able to glide into the wilderness on purpose was after going three days without food and drinking only water. I'd spent those days at Aro's hut and he made sure I wasn't idle. I cleaned his goats' hovel, washed his dishes, swept out his house, and cooked his meals. Each day I didn't eat, I worried more about encountering my father in the wilderness.

"He won't come after you now," Aro assured me. "I'm here, and you've been initiated. It's no longer so easy to reach you. Relax. When you're ready, you'll know."

I was taking a break next to his goats' hovel when clarity suddenly descended on me. It was hard to be around Aro's goats. They smelled more pungent than usual and their brown eyes seemed to see too deep into me. The one I had saved kept stepping up to me and staring. A moment later, I realized that they were waiting. The sensation started between my legs—a warm buzzing feeling. Then a numbness. When I looked at my abdomen, I almost screamed. It looked as if I'd begun to turn into clear jelly. Once I saw it, it quickly spread up and down the rest of me.

Fighting to stay calm, I stood up. Above me, all I saw were colors. Millions and millions of colors, but mainly green. They pooled, stacked, stretched, contracted, clustered, billowed. All this was juxtaposed against the world I knew. This was the wilderness. When I looked at the goats, I saw that they were prancing and baaing with joy. Their happy motions gave off puffs of rich blue that wafted toward me. I inhaled and it smelled . . . lovely. Then I realized this whole place smelled of many things, but of one thing in particular. That indescribable smell.

I stayed in the wilderness for a few more minutes. Then the goat that I had saved walked up and bit me. I felt like I dropped several feet and I hit the ground. Dazed, I walked back to Aro's hut where I found him waiting for me with a grand meal.

"Eat," was all he said.

Mwita and I left camp. The others watched us go without asking where we were going. About a third of a mile out, we sat down. It had only been a day and a half of fasting, yet the world around me had already shifted to that strange level of clarity.

"It's the traveling, I think," Mwita said.

"Have you done this before?" I asked.

"A long time ago," he said. "When . . . I was a boy. Just after I escaped from those Okeke soldiers."

"Oh. You starved?"

"For days."

I wanted to ask him what he saw but it wasn't the time. I looked out at the dry desert. Not a patch of grass. Aro told me that long ago, the land hadn't been like this. "Don't completely discount the Great Book," he said. "Something did happen to bring it all down. To change green to sand. These lands used to look a lot more like the wilderness."

Still, the Great Book, in my opinion, was mainly crafty lies and riddles. I shivered and the world shivered around me.

"You see that?" Mwita asked.

I nodded. "Any minute," I said, not really knowing what I was talking about but sure of it anyway. "Let me guide it."

"What else can I do?" Mwita said with a smile. "I have no idea how to guide a vision, lady sorceress in training."

"Just call me sorcerer," I said. "There's only one kind, man or woman. And we are always training." Then the world shivered again and I grabbed on. "Hurry, take it Mwita."

He looked at me confused and then did what it sounded like I wanted him to do. He took hold. "What . . . what is . . ."

"I don't know," I said.

It was as if the air beneath us solidified. Swift and strong, it took us at an impossible speed to a destination that only it knew. We moved far but we were also still. We were in two places at once or maybe in neither. As Aro always told me, you can't have all your questions answered. Who knows what Luyu, Binta, Fanasi, or Diti would have seen had they looked our way. According to the location of the sun, the vision moved mainly west, sometimes meandering northwest and then southwest in a manner that I can only describe as playful. Below, the desert flew by. Suddenly, I felt a terrible sense of foreboding. I'd once had a dream like this. It had shown me my biological father.

"We're in the towns now," Mwita said after a while. He sounded calm but he probably wasn't.

We moved too quickly over the bordering towns and villages for me to see much. But there was a smell of roasting meat and fire still in my nostrils.

"It's still happening," I said. Mwita nodded.

We rounded southwest where sandstone buildings were built close together, two sometimes three stories high. I didn't see one Okeke person. This was Nuru territory. If there were Okekes here, they were trusted slaves. The useful ones.

The roads were flat and paved. Palm trees, bushes, and other vegetation thrived here. It was not like Jwahir, where you had vegetation and trees that, though they lived, were dry and grew upward instead of outward. There was sand here but there were also patches of a strange darker-colored ground. Then I saw why. I'd never seen so much water. It was shaped like a giant dark blue snake. Hundreds of people could swim in it and it wouldn't matter.

"That's one of the Seven Rivers," Mwita said. "Maybe the third or fourth."

We slowed as we moved over it. I could see white fish swimming near the surface. I reached down and ran my hand in the water. It was cool. I held my hand to my lips. It tasted almost sweet, like rainwater. This wasn't capture station water forcibly pulled from the sky nor was it water from underground. This vision was truly something new. Mwita and I were both *here*. We could see each other. We could taste and feel. As we approached the other side of the river, Mwita looked worried.

"Onye," he said. "I've never . . . can people see us?"

"I don't know."

We passed some people in floating vehicles. Boats. No one seemed to see us though one woman looked around as if she felt something. Once over land, we picked up speed and flew up high over small villages until we reached a large town. It sat at the end of the river and the beginning of a huge body of water. Just beyond the buildings, I glimpsed . . . a field of green plants?

"You see that?" I asked.

"The body of water over there? That's the lake with no name."

"No, not that," I said.

We were taken between sandstone buildings where Nuru hawkers sold goods along the road. We passed over a small open restaurant. I smelled peppers, dried fish, rice, incense. An infant wailed from somewhere. A man and a woman argued. People bartered. I saw a few dark faces here—all were burdened with items and all of them walked quickly with purpose. Slaves.

The Nurus here weren't the wealthiest, but they weren't the poorest either. We came to a road blocked by a crowd standing before a wooden stage with orange flags hanging over the front. The vision took us to the front of the stage and set us down. It felt odd. First it was as if we sat on the ground, amid people's legs and feet. They absentmindedly moved aside for us, their attention focused on the people onstage. Then something raised us to a standing position. We looked around, terrified of being seen. Mwita pulled me close, slipping his arm firmly around my waist.

I looked right into the face of the Nuru man beside me. He looked into mine. We stared at each other. Standing inches shorter than Mwita and me, he looked about twenty, maybe a little older. He narrowed his eyes. Thankfully, the man onstage grabbed his attention.

"Who are you going to believe?" the man onstage shouted. Then he smiled and laughed, lowering his voice. "We're doing what must be done. We're following the Book. We have always been a pious loyal people. But what next?"

"Tell us! You know the answer!" someone shouted.

"When we've wiped them out, *what next?* We make the Great Book proud! We make Ani proud. We build an empire that is the most good of good!"

I felt sick. I knew who this was, just as you knew from the moment this vision took me. Slowly, I brought my eyes to his eyes, first taking in his tall broad-shouldered stature, the black beard that hung down his chest.

I didn't want to look. But I did. He saw me. His eyes grew wide. They flashed red for a second. He strode toward me.

"You!" Mwita shouted as he leaped onstage.

My biological father was still looking at me in shock when Mwita plowed into him. They went falling back and people in the crowd shouted and surged forward.

"Mwita!" I yelled. "What are you doing?"

Two guards were about to grab Mwita. They blocked my way. I scrambled onto the stage. I could have sworn I heard laughter. But before I could see, we were being pulled back. Mwita flew back to me right through the two men. My biological father pushed them aside. "When you're ready, Mwita, come find me. We'll finish this," he said. His nose bled but he was grinning. His eyes met mine. He pointed at me with a long narrow finger. "And you, girl, your days are numbered."

The crowd below us was in chaos, several fights breaking out. People pushed and shoved, rocking the stage on its foundation. Several men in yellow jumped onto the stage from the sides. They brutally kicked people off the stage. No one other than my biological father seemed to see us. He stood there a moment longer and then looked to his crowd and held up his hands smiling. Everyone immediately calmed. It was eerie.

We were moving backward fast. So fast that I couldn't speak or turn my head toward Mwita. We flew over the town, the river, another town. Everything was a blur until we were near camp. It was like a giant hand set us down right there in the sand. We sat there for several minutes breathing heavily. I glanced at Mwita. He had a large bruise rising on the side of his face.

"Mwita," I said, reaching to touch it.

He slapped my hand away and stood up, rage in his eyes. I moved away, suddenly very afraid of him.

"Be afraid," he said. There were tears in his eyes but his face was hard. He went back to camp. I watched him go into our tent and then I just sat there. There was a mild burst of pain in my forehead. My headache still lingered.

How did he know my biological father? I wondered. I couldn't understand it. *I* didn't look much like him. *And why was he about to beat me?*

The thought hurt more than the question. Of all the people in the world, my mother and Mwita were the two that I could fully trust to never ever hurt me. Now I had left my mother and Mwita . . . something in his brain had gone mad.

And then there was the question of what had literally happened. We'd *been* there. Mwita had delivered a blow and been delivered one in return. The people could see us, but what did they see? I scooped up a handful of sand and threw it.

Chapter 28

MWITA AND I KEPT OUR PROBLEMS QUIET. It was easy to do, for the next day Mwita took Fanasi with him to look for lizard eggs.

"The bread is getting stale. Ugh," Binta complained as she bit into a piece of the yellow flatbread. "I need some *real* food."

"Don't be such a princess," I said.

"I can't wait to reach a village," Binta said.

I shrugged. I wasn't looking forward to other villages or towns on the way. I had a scar on my forehead to show that people could be hostile. "We have to learn to live on the desert," I said. "We have a long long way to go."

"Yeah," Luyu said. "But we'll only find fresh men in the towns and villages. You and Diti may not mind staying away from them, but Binta and I have needs, too."

Diti grumbled something. I looked at her. "What's your problem?" I asked.

She only looked away.

"Onye," Binta said. "You said when you were little, you used to sing and owls would come. Can you still do that?"

"Maybe," I said. "I haven't tried it in a long time."

"Try it," Luyu said, perking up.

"If you want to hear singing, turn on Binta's musicplayer," I said.

"The batteries are low," Luyu said.

I chuckled. "It's solar, isn't it?"

"Come on. Stop being stingy," Luyu said.

"Really," Diti said in a low annoyed voice. "It's not all about you."

"I've never seen an owl up close," Binta said.

"I have," Luyu said. "My mother used to feed one every night outside her window. It was . . ." She grew quiet. We all did, thinking about our mothers.

I quickly started singing the song of the desert on a cool night. Owls are nocturnal. This was a song they'd like. As I sang, it filled me with joy, a rare emotion for me. The remnants of my headache finally left me. I stood up and raised my voice higher, spreading my arms and closing my eyes.

I heard the flap of wings. My friends gasped, giggled, and sighed. I opened my eyes and kept singing. One of the owls perched on Binta's tent. It was dark brown with large yellow eyes. Another owl landed on Luyu's tent. This one was tiny enough to fit into the palm of my hand. When I finished singing both owls hooted in appreciation and flew off. The large one left a dollop of feces on Binta's tent.

"There are consequences to everything," I laughed. Binta groaned with disgust.

That night, I lay in our tent waiting for Mwita. He was outside bathing with capture station water. He and Fanasi had returned with several lizard eggs, one tortoise—which none of us, not even Fanasi, could bring ourselves to kill and cook—and four desert hares that they'd killed in the desert. I suspected that Mwita used simple juju to catch the hares and find the lizard eggs. Mwita wasn't speaking to me, so I didn't know for sure.

As I lay there, my rapa tied around me, fear occupied my thoughts. I'd hoped this feeling was only temporary, a weird side-effect of the vision. I couldn't stop shaking. I was sure that he'd beat me this night, or even kill me. When he and Fanasi returned and showed us their catch, Mwita had looked me over. He kissed me lightly on the lips. Then he'd caught my eye. The rage I saw there was frightening. But I refused to avoid him.

I knew ways of defense using the Mystic Points. I could change into an animal ten times stronger than Mwita. I could drop into the wilderness where he could barely touch me. I could attack and tear at his very spirit as

I'd done to Aro when I was only sixteen. But I wasn't going to use any of that tonight. Mwita was all I had.

The tent flap opened. Mwita paused. I felt a flutter in my chest. He'd expected me to stay with Luyu or Binta. He *wanted* me to. I sat up. He wore only his pants made of the same material as my rapa. It was dark so I couldn't see his face clearly. He closed the tent flap and zipped it shut. I assured myself that I'd done nothing wrong. *If he kills me tonight, it won't be my fault,* I thought. *I can live with that.* But could I? If I was the one prophesied to make things right in the West, what good was I dead?

"Mwita," I said softly.

"You shouldn't be here," he said. "Not tonight, Onyesonwu."

"Why?" I asked, keeping my voice steady. "What's happened that . . ."

"Don't look at me," he said. "I see you." He shook his head, his shoulders curling.

I hesitated but then I moved forward and took him in my arms. He tensed up. I held him tight. "What *is* it?" I whispered, not wanting the others to hear. "Tell me!"

There was a long long pause and he frowned and glared at me. I didn't dare move.

"Lie down," he finally said. "Take this off and lie down."

I took off my rapa and he lay down beside me and took me in his arms. Something was so wrong with him. But I let him remember me. He ran his arms over my body, took my braids in his hands and inhaled, kissed and kissed and kissed. All this time, so many tears dropped on me that I was damp with them.

"Tie it back on," he said, sitting up and I did so.

He ran his hand over his rough hair. He'd shaved it when we left Jwahir but it was growing back, as was the hair on his face. Everything about Mwita was becoming rough.

"I heard you singing from all the way out there," he said, looking away. "We must have been miles away and I could still hear your voice. We saw a large bird fly by. I assumed it was going to you."

"I sang for Luyu, Binta, and Diti," I said. "They wanted to see owls."

"You should do it more," he said. "Your voice heals you. You look . . . better now."

"Mwita," I said. "Tell me what . . ."

"I'm *trying*. Shut up. Don't be so sure that you want to hear this, Onye."

I waited.

"I don't know what you will be," he said. "I've never heard of anyone doing what you did. We were really *there*. Look at my face. That's from his *fist!* I don't think you saw the villages on the borders of the Seven Rivers Kingdom, but I did. We passed over some rebel Okekes fighting Nurus. The Nuru outnumbered the Okeke a hundred to one. Okeke civilians were attacked, too. Everything was burning."

"I smelled the smoke," I said, quietly.

"Your vision protected you, but not me. I saw!" Mwita said, his eyes widening. "I don't know what kind of sorcery is at work here but you scare me. *All* of this does."

"Scares me too," I said carefully.

"You resemble your mother mostly, except in color and maybe the nose. You behave like her some . . . there're other things, too," he said. "But I can see it in the eyes now. You have his eyes."

"Yes," I said. "That's all we have in common." *And our ability to sing*, I thought.

"Your father was my teacher," he said. "He's Daib. I've told you about him. He's the reason my uncle and aunt, those who saved and raised me, were killed."

The news hit me as if my mother had slapped me, as if Aro had punched me, as if Mwita were strangling me. I hung my mouth open to breathe. *Both my own mother and the man I love have reason to hate me*, I thought helplessly. *All they need to do is look into my eyes*. I rubbed the back of my head expecting my headache to return but it didn't. Mwita brought his face up to mine. "How much of this did you know, Onye?"

I frowned not only at his question but at the way he asked it. "None, Mwita."

"This Sola you told me about, did he plan . . ."

"There's no plot against you, Mwita. Do you really believe I'm a false . . ."

"Daib is a powerful, *powerful* sorcerer," Mwita said. "He can bend time, he can make things appear that should never be there, he can make people think wrong things, and he has a heart full of the most evil stuff. I know him well," He brought his face even closer. "Even Aro couldn't keep Daib from killing you."

"Well, he did, somehow," I said.

Mwita sat back, frustrated. "Okay," he said after a while. "Okay. But . . . still, Onye, we're practically siblings."

I understood what he meant. My biological father, Daib, had been his first Master, his teacher. Though Daib hadn't allowed Mwita to attempt initiation, Mwita had been his student for years. And to be one's student of sorcery was a very close relationship—in many ways, closer than that of a parent. Aro, for all my conflict with him, was a second father to me—Papa being my first, *not* Daib. Aro had birthed me through another canal of life. I shivered and Mwita nodded.

"Daib would sing as he beat me," Mwita said. "My discipline and ability to learn so fast are because of your father's heavy hand. Whenever I did something wrong, or was too slow, or inaccurate, I would get to hear him sing. His voice always brought lizards and scarab beetles."

He looked deep into my eyes and I knew he was deciding. I took the moment to decide, too. To decide if *I* was being manipulated. If we all were. Since I was eleven, things had been happening to me, pushing me toward a specific path. It was easy to imagine that someone of great mystical power was manipulating my life. Except for one thing: the shocked and almost scared look on Daib's face when he saw me. Someone like Daib could never fake fear and ill preparedness. That look was real and true. No, Daib had as much control over all of this as I did.

That night Mwita would not let go of me, and I didn't need to hold onto him.

Chapter 29

THE NEXT DAY, we started off before dawn. West. Due west. We had a compass and we had the not too harsh sun. Luyu, Fanasi, Diti, and Binta started playing a guessing game. I wasn't in the mood, so I hung back. Mwita walked ahead of all of us. He hadn't spoken more than a "good morning" to me since we got up. Luyu left the guessing game to walk with me. "Stupid game," she said, hoisting her pack up.

"I agree," I said.

After a moment, she put her hand on my shoulder and stopped me. "So what's been going on with you two?"

I glanced at the others as they kept moving and shook my head.

She frowned, annoyed. "Don't keep me in the dark. I'm not moving another step until you tell me *something*."

"Suit yourself." I started walking.

She followed me. "Onye, I'm your friend. Let *me* in on some of this. You and Mwita will tear each other apart if you don't share some of the load. I'm sure Mwita confides some in Fanasi."

I looked at her.

"They talk," she said. "You see how they go off sometimes. You can talk to me."

It was probably true. The two were different, Fanasi traditional by upbringing and Mwita nontraditional by birth, but sometimes difference leads to sameness.

"I don't want Diti and Binta to know these things," I said after a moment.

"Of course," Luyu said.

"I . . ." Suddenly, I felt like crying. I swallowed. "I'm Aro's student."

"I know," she said frowning deeply "You were initiated and . . ."

"And . . . there are consequences to it," I said.

"The headaches," she said.

I nodded.

"We all know that," Luyu said.

"But it's not so simple. The headaches are because of something. They're . . . ghosts of the future." We'd stopped walking.

"Of what in the future?"

"How I die," I said. "Part of initiation is to face your own death."

"And how do you die?"

"I'm taken before a mob of Nurus, buried to my neck, and stoned to death."

Luyu flared her nostrils. "How . . . how old are you when it happens?"

"I don't know. I couldn't see my face."

"Your headaches, they feel like the stones thrown at your head?" she said.

I nodded.

"Oh, Ani," she said. She put her arm around me.

"There's one other thing," I said, after a moment. "The prophecy was wrong . . ."

"It will be an *Ewu* woman," Luyu said.

"How did . . ."

"I guessed. It makes more sense now." She chuckled. "I walk with a legend."

I smiled sadly. "Not yet."

Chapter 30

OVER THE NEXT FEW WEEKS, Mwita and I found it hard to talk to each other. But when we retired, we couldn't keep our hands off of each other. I was still afraid of getting pregnant but our physical needs were greater. There was such love between us, yet we couldn't speak. It was the only way. We tried to be quiet, but everyone heard us. Mwita and I were so wrapped up in ourselves during the night and then during the day in our dark thoughts, that this wasn't our concern. It was only when Diti accosted me one cold evening that I realized something was festering among us.

She'd kept her voice low but she looked ready to jump me. "What is *wrong* with you?" she said kneeling beside me.

I looked up from the stew of hare and cactus I was stirring, irritated by her tone. "You're invading my space, Diti."

She moved closer. "We all hear you two every night! You're like desert hares. If you don't watch yourself, there will be more than six of us arriving in the West. No one will take well to an *Ewu* baby of *Ewu* parents."

It took everything in my power not to smack her across the face with my wooden spoon. "Step away from me," I warned.

"No," she said but she looked afraid. "I'm-I'm sorry." She touched my shoulder and I looked at her hand. She took it away. "You don't have to flaunt it, Onye."

"What are you . . ."

"If you've mastered all this sorcery, why don't you cure us?" she said. "Or are you the only woman here allowed to enjoy intercourse?"

Before I could speak, Luyu came running. "Hey!" she said, pointing behind us. "Hey! What *is* that?"

We turned. Were my eyes deceiving me? A pack of sand-colored wild dogs were running so fast toward us that they kicked up a wake of dust. Flanking the dogs were two shaggy, single-humped camels and five gazelles with long spiraling horns. Above them flew seven hawks. "Leave everything!" I shouted. "Run!"

Diti, Fanasi, and Luyu took off, dragging a stunned Binta along.

"Mwita, come on!" I shouted, when he still hadn't come out of our tent where I knew he was napping. I unzipped the flap. He was still deep in sleep. "Mwita!" I screamed, the pounding of hooves drowning everything out.

His eyes cracked opened. They grew wide. He grabbed me to him as they came. We curled into each other as tightly as we could as the large beasts pounded throughout camp. The dogs went for my stew, dragging the pot away from the fire, despite the heat. The gazelles and camels rooted around in the tents. Mwita and I were silent as they stuck their heads into our tent and took what they wanted. One of the camels found my store of cactus candy. It stared at us as it munched the fruit with what only could have been pleasure. I cursed.

Another camel stuck its muzzle into a bucket and lapped up all the water. The hawks swooped down, snatching up the hare meat Diti and Binta were drying. When they finished, the united animals trotted off.

"Rule one of the rules of the desert," I said crawling out of the tent. "Never turn down a travel companion if it doesn't plan to eat you. I wonder how long those animals have been working together like that."

"Fanasi and I will have to go hunting tonight," Mwita said.

Luyu, Diti, Binta, and Fanasi came walking back looking angry.

"We should kill and eat all of them," Binta said.

"You attack one and they'll *all* attack you," I said.

We salvaged whatever food we could, which wasn't much. That evening, Fanasi, Mwita, and Luyu, who'd insisted on accompanying them, set out to hunt and gather. Diti avoided me by playing a game of Warri with

Binta. I warmed some water for a much needed bath. As I stood behind my tent in the dark and poured the warm water on myself, a fly bit me on the arm. Part of the rock fire's juju was to keep biting insects away but once in a while an insect snuck in. I smashed it on my ankle. It exploded into a smear of blood.

"Ugh," I said, washing it off. The bite was already turning bright red. The slightest slap or insect bite always turns my skin redder than normal. It was the same with Mwita. *Ewu* skin is sensitive in that way. I quickly finished washing.

That night, I noticed that Diti slept in Binta's tent. She and Fanasi could no longer sleep in each other's arms. It was that bad.

Chapter 31

I KNEW ABOUT THE TOWN HOURS before we got to it. While everyone slept, I had gone flying as a vulture. I flew for miles, riding the cool wind. I needed to think about Diti's request. I should have known how to break the Eleventh Rite juju. That was the most frustrating part of it. I couldn't think of a chant, combination of herbs, or use of objects that would work. Aro would have laughed at and insulted my slowness. But I didn't want to hurt my friends with a mistake.

The winds carried me west and that was how I happened across the town. I saw well-built sandstone buildings glowing with electric lights and cooking fires. A paved road ran through the town from south to north, disappearing in both directions into the darkness. The north was puckered with small hills and one large hill topped with a house lit brightly from within. When I got back to the camp, I woke Mwita and told him about the town.

"There shouldn't be a town here at all," he said, looking at the map.

I shrugged. "Maybe the map's too old."

"That town sounds established. The map can't be *that* old." He cursed. "I think we're off course. We need to find out the name. How far is it?"

"We'll get there by the end of the day."

Mwita nodded.

"We're not ready, Mwita."

"We just got robbed of all our food by a pack of animals," he said.

"You know how dangerous it can be." I touch the scar on my forehead. "We should go around it and never mention it. We can find food along the way."

"I hear you," he said. "I just don't agree with you."

I sucked my teeth and looked away.

"It's not right to keep them in the dark," he said.

"How much in the dark have you kept Fanasi?" I asked.

He cocked his head and smiled.

"Luyu suspects you," I said.

He nodded. "That girl has a sharp eye and ear." He leaned back on his elbows. "He asks questions. I answer them when I want to."

"What questions?"

"Have trust," he said. "And let go some. We're all involved."

We came within a mile of the town by the end of the day. Mwita collected stones for a rock fire. We washed and ate, and then sat before the fire and eventually grew quiet. Fanasi and Diti sat close to one another, but Diti kept pushing his arm from her waist. Luyu spoke first. "We don't have to go there. That's what's on all our minds, right?"

Mwita glanced at me.

"We've been traveling for weeks now," Luyu continued. "That's not long. I don't know how long it will take us to get to the . . . badness. We've all been saying about five months or so, but anything can happen along the way to delay us. So, I say we toughen up. Let's keep going."

"I want some real food," Binta angrily said. "Like fufu and egusi soup, pepper soup with real peppers instead of weird tasting spicy cactus! We'll eventually have to 'toughen up' anyway. In the morning, we should buy what we need and move on."

"I agree with Binta," Diti said. "No offense, everyone, but I wouldn't mind seeing some different faces, even for a few hours."

Fanasi glared at her. "We should keep going," he said. "There could be trouble there and we have no pressing need to risk it."

Luyu nodded vigorously at Fanasi and they smiled at each other. Diti moved away from Fanasi, mumbling something. He rolled his eyes.

"I wouldn't mind seeing a new town," Mwita said. I frowned at him. "But we'll have plenty of opportunity for that in the future," he continued. "And yes, it could be dangerous. Especially for Onye and me. Soon we'll be so far from home that the very air we breathe will be new. It's only going to get more dangerous . . . for us all. But I will say this, there is no town mentioned on my map here, so we're either off course or my map's wrong. I propose that Fanasi and I go to find out the town's name and then immediately return."

"Why you?" Diti asked. "You'll attract too much attention. Fanasi and I will go."

"You two don't seem to be getting along very well," I said.

Diti looked as if she wanted to bite me.

"Okay, then Luyu and Fanasi," Mwita said.

"I say we ALL go," Diti demanded.

"It would be stupid not to," Binta added.

They all looked at me. My vote, if for going, would mean a tie.

"I say we bypass the town."

"Of course you do," Diti hissed. "You're used to living like an animal in the sand. And *you* can let Mwita keep you warm at night."

I felt the blood rush to my face. I wondered how she'd become so stupid. I was used to Luyu, Diti, and Binta having, maybe not so much a respect, but a sort of fear of me. They were my friends and they loved me but there was something about me that made them shut up when it counted. "Diti," I carefully said. "You tread in dangerous . . ."

She jumped up, grabbed a handful of sand, and threw it in my face. I raised my hands just in time to protect my eyes. Mwita had taught me how to calm my emotions. Aro had taught me how to control and focus my emotions. I could feel anger and even fury but never would I blindly use what Aro had taught me. At least that was what he'd taught me. I was still in training. Without a thought and before Mwita could grab me, I launched myself at Diti, taking her square in the back as she turned to run. I only used physical strength to beat my friend. Aro and Mwita had taught me well.

She screamed and kept trying to scramble away but I held her tightly. I flipped her over. She screeched again, slapping me in the face. I slapped her back even harder. I grabbed her hands, sitting on her chest. I held them together with my right hand and then proceeded to slap her face back and forth with my left. "You vapid whore! You diseased goat's penis! You stupid idiotic breastless little girl. . . ."

Tears flew from my eyes. Around me, the world swam. Then Fanasi was pulling me off her as he shouted, "Stop it! Stop *it!*" My attention focused on him. He was taller and stronger but I too was tall and strong. Physically, we weren't so unevenly matched.

My rage coiled in my chest, preparing to strike again. I was sick of these sentiments coming out of even the people that I loved. All it took was getting them angry. This is what made my mother and Mwita different from everyone else, even Aro. In their deepest rage, no such insults ever came from their lips. Never.

Fanasi threw me to the ground. Mwita grabbed my arm before I could leap at Fanasi. He dragged me away. I let him. His touch had taken the spring from me. I needed Mwita on this journey so much.

"Get a hold of yourself," he said, looking down at me with disgust.

Still breathing heavily, I turned and spat sand from my mouth. "What if I don't want to?" I gasped. "What if that helps nothing?"

He knelt down before me. "Then you keep doing it," he said. He paused. "That is what will make you and me different. Different from the myth of the *Ewu*, different from those we'll face in the West. Control, thought, and *understanding*."

I spat out more sand and let him pull me to my feet. Fanasi took Diti to their tent. I could hear her sobbing and Fanasi speaking softly. Binta sat outside the tent, listening and looking sadly at her hands in her lap.

"You know why Diti is so angry," Luyu said, walking up to me.

"I don't care," I said, looking away. "There are more important things!"

"You should care, if you want us to get to where we're going," Luyu said angrily.

"Luyu," Mwita said. "The state of your clitoris is small in comparison." He motioned to his face. "Imagine being marked in this way. No matter where she and I go, that nonsense Diti spewed about Onyesonwu being used to "living like an animal," that kind of thought is on everyone's mind, Okeke or Nuru. We're as hated as the desert."

Luyu looked down and mumbled. "I know."

"Then act like it," Mwita snapped.

The rest of the day was tense. So tense that Fanasi and Luyu thought it better that they go into the town tomorrow morning. It wasn't the best time to leave me, Diti, and Binta alone with just Mwita there to break up a fight. But it was the best plan.

An hour passed. Diti and Binta stuck close together, washing and sewing clothes. Fanasi and Mwita sat in the center of the tents, to keep an eye on us crazy women. Mwita was giving Fanasi lessons in the Nuru language. He'd also offered to teach Diti, Binta, and Luyu. Only Luyu agreed to eventually learn. Luyu hadn't left my side since the fight.

"You have to practice," I said. We sat outside of my tent, facing the town. I was trying to teach her how to meditate.

"I don't think I'll ever be able to clear my mind of all thoughts," she said.

"That's what I used to think, too," I said. "Have you ever woken up and for a few seconds not known who you were?"

"Yeah," Luyu said. "That's always scared me."

"You don't remember because you're in a temporary state where you've cleared everything away and all that is left is you. Think of how you make yourself remember who you are when this happens."

"I remind myself of things," she said. "Like what I'm supposed to do that day or what I want to do."

I nodded. "Yes. You fill your head with thoughts. Here's something scary: If you don't recognize yourself, then who is the one who reminds you of who you are?"

Luyu stared blankly at me. She frowned. "Yeah, who is that?"

I smiled. "I couldn't sleep for a week after Mwita pointed that out to me."

"Any ideas about how to cure us of our forced chastity?" she asked after a moment.

"No."

We were quiet again.

"Sorry," Luyu said after a while. "I'm selfish."

I sighed. "No. You're not." I shook my head. "All these things are important."

"Onye, I'm sorry. I'm sorry for what Diti said. I'm sorry that your father . . ."

"I refuse to call him my father," I said looking at her.

"You're right. I'm sorry," Luyu carefully said. She paused. "He . . . he recorded it. He must have kept it."

I nodded. I didn't doubt that at all. Never had.

We ate dinner in silence and went to bed while the sun was still setting. Mwita watched me as I unbraided my long bushy hair. It was salted with sand from Diti's bout of stupidity. I planned to brush it out and braid it into a large thick long braid until I got a chance to rebraid it into the many tiny braids I preferred.

"Will you ever cut it?" Mwita asked, as I brushed.

"No," I said. "Don't cut yours either."

"We'll see," he said, he tugged at the hair on his face. "I do like this beard."

"Me, too," I said. "All wise men grow them."

I couldn't sleep. "You're used to living like an animal in the sand," Diti had said. Her words burned inside me like regurgitated bile. And then the way Binta had crept after her. Binta hadn't spoken to me since the fight. Delicately, I moved Mwita's arm from my waist and slipped away from him. I retied my rapa and left the tent. I could hear Luyu snoring in her tent and Fanasi's deep breathing in his. I heard nothing when I got to Diti and Binta's tent. I looked inside. They were gone. I cursed.

"Let's just leave our things here while we go get them," Luyu said.

I squatted near the cooling rocks, brooding. Had they really thought they could sneak away and be back before we missed them? Or maybe they hadn't intended to return at all. *Stupid, stupid idiot women,* I thought.

Fanasi stood with his back to us. Where I was angry, Fanasi was distraught. He'd given up so much for Diti and she didn't even take him along.

"Fanasi," I said, getting up. "We'll find her."

"It's still early," Mwita said. "We pack everything, including Diti and

Binta's things, and go find them. When we do, we move on, no matter the hour."

Fanasi insisted on carrying most of Diti's things, at least what she'd left. She'd taken her backpack and some small items. Mwita carried Binta's rolled-up tent. We used the light from the town to make our way over the low hills. As we walked, I sang softly to the breeze. I stopped singing. "Shh," I said, holding up a hand.

"What?" Luyu whispered.

"Just wait."

"I've got my palm-light handy," Mwita said.

"No, just wait." I paused. "We're being followed. No noise. Relax." I heard it again. Soft padding. Just behind me. "Mwita, your light," I said.

The moment he flipped it on, Luyu screeched and ran to me. She tripped over her feet and ran into me hard enough to knock me over. "It's . . . it's . . ." she babbled, scrambling over me as she looked back.

"Just wild camels," I said, pushing her off me and getting up.

"It licked my ear!" she shouted, rubbing vigorously at her very wet ear and hair.

"Yeah, that's because you sweat all the time and you need a bath," I said. "They like salt." There were three of them. The one closest to me grumbled low in its throat. Luyu cowered close to me. I couldn't fully blame her after the animal tribe attack we'd suffered.

"Hold the light up," I told Mwita.

They each had two large humps and their fur was thick and dusty. They were healthy. The one nearest to me gruffed some more and took three aggressive steps toward me. Luyu whooped and scrambled behind me. I stood my ground. My singing had attracted them.

"What do they want?" Fanasi said.

"Shh," I said. Slowly, Mwita moved in front of me. The camel approached him, bringing its soft face to his and sniffing. The other camels did the same. Mwita had just established his relationship with me to the camels and they understood—the male protects the female. He is the one to negotiate with. I admit it was good to have someone step in front of me for a change.

"They mean to travel with us a way," Mwita said.

"I figured that," I said.

"But look at them!" Luyu said. "They're filthy and . . . wild."

I heard Fanasi grunt agreement.

I scoffed. "And that's why I don't think we're ready to visit a town. When you're in the desert, you have to *be* in the desert. You accept sand in your clothes but not your hair. You don't mind bathing outside in the open. You leave a bucket of excess station water for other creatures who might want some. And when people, *any* kind of people, want to travel with you, you don't reject them unless they're cruel."

We continued on, this time with a trio of camels in tow. We reached the paved road before we reached the town. I stopped, experiencing mild déjà vu.

"I was six when I saw a paved road for the first time," I said. "I thought that giants had made them. Like the ones in the Great Book."

"Maybe they did," Mwita said, walking past me.

The camels didn't seem in the least bit curious about it. But once they were across, they stopped. We all walked several steps before realizing that they weren't coming. The camels groaned loudly as they sat down.

"Come on," I told them. "We're just going to find our companions."

The camels didn't budge.

"You think they sense something bad?" Mwita asked.

I shrugged. I loved camels but I didn't always understand their behavior.

"Maybe they'll wait for us," Fanasi said.

"I hope not," Luyu said.

"Maybe," Mwita said. He stepped up to the camel and when he did so, all three of them roared at him. He jumped back.

"Let's go," I said. "If they're not here when we get back, then so be it."

Chapter 32

AS I SAW WHEN I FLEW OVER IT THE NIGHT BEFORE, on one side of the town, the land was hilly. We entered on the flatter side where there were shops selling paintings, sculptures, bracelets, and blown glass along with the usual items.

"Onyesonwu, put your veil on," Mwita said. He'd wrapped his over his head, letting the thick green cloth fall low over his face.

"I hope they don't think we're sick," I said, doing the same with my yellow veil.

"As long as people stay away from us," Mwita said. When he saw the bothered look on my face, he said, "We'll say we're holy people."

We approached a cluster of large buildings. I glanced inside a window and saw bookcases.

"This must be their book house," I said to Luyu.

"Yeah, well, if it is, then they have two," she said.

The building to our left was also full of books.

"Ah ah," Mwita said quietly, his eyes wide. "There are people in there, even at this late hour. You think they're open to the public?"

The town was called Banza, a name that sounded vaguely familiar to me. And it was on Mwita's map. We were off course, having traveled northwest instead of due west.

"We need to pay closer attention," Mwita said, as we stood looking at his map.

"Easier said than done," Luyu said. "The walking gets so monotonous you drift off. I can see how it happened."

A few people looked at us with mild interest as they passed but that was all. I relaxed a little. Still, it was obvious that we weren't from here. Where our garments were long and flowing pants and dresses and veils, these people wore tighter clothes and cloth tied tightly over their heads.

The women wore silver rings in their noses and long tight half-dresses that flared at the bottom called skirts. They also wore shirts with no sleeves, showing their arms and shoulders. Most of the women's skirts, shirts, and headcloths were of clashing colors and prints. The men wore similarly close-fitting clashing pants and tight caftans. We searched for an hour and found ourselves at their central market. It was busy despite the fact that it was past ten p.m.

Banza was an Okeke town driven by art and culture. It wasn't old like Jwahir. Banza's wounds were fresh. As the years passed, Banza learned to use the bad to create the good. The town founders turned their pain into art, the making and selling of which became central to Banza's culture.

"Does this town sleep?" Luyu had asked.

"Their minds are too active," I said.

"I think everyone here is crazy," Mwita said.

We asked around about Diti and Binta. Well, Fanasi and Luyu did the asking. Mwita and I stood behind them, trying to hide our *Ewu* faces.

"Very pretty and dressed like holy women?" a man asked Fanasi. "I've seen them. They're around here somewhere."

"Stupid girls," a woman told Fanasi. Then she laughed. "They bought some of my palm wine. About ten men were following them." Apparently Diti and Binta were having a good time. We bought some bread, spices, soap, and dried meat. I asked Luyu to buy a sack of salt for me.

"What for?" she asked. "We have plenty."

"The camels, if they're still there," I said.

Luyu rolled her eyes. "Not likely."

"I know," I said. I also had Luyu buy two bunches of bitter leaf. Camels like bitter and salty things. Mwita had Fanasi buy me a blue rapa. And

Fanasi bought Diti a pick that was made from the bone of some sort of creature. Luyu bought something that sent shivers through my spine. I walked up just as she finished haggling with an old woman selling the tiny silver thing. The woman had a basket full of them.

"I'll sell it to you for that price only because I like you," the woman said.

"Thank you," Luyu replied with a grin.

"You're not from here, are you?" the woman asked.

"No," Luyu said. "We're from farther east. Jwahir."

The woman nodded. "Beautiful place, I hear. But you all wear so much cloth."

Luyu laughed.

"You know how to work a portable?" the woman asked.

Luyu shook her head. "Please, show me."

I watched as the women explained how to play the portable's audio file of the Great Book and make it tell the weather. But when she pressed a button on the bottom and the eye of a camera popped up, I had to ask, "What are you buying this for, Luyu?"

"In a minute," Luyu said, patting my cheek.

The old women shot me a distrustful look.

"Have you seen two girls dressed like us?" Luyu quickly asked the old woman.

The woman's eyes stayed on me a moment longer. "Is that one traveling with you?" she asked, motioning to me.

"Yes," Luyu said. She smiled at me. "This is my closest friend."

The woman's face darkened. "I'll pray to Ani for you, then. Both of you. I don't know about her, but you seem like a good clean girl."

"Please," Luyu pressed. "Where did you see these two girls?"

"I should have known. Those girls attracted men like magnets." She glared at me and looked as if she wanted to spit. I held her eyes. "Try the White Cloud Tavern."

"An old woman like that should know better," I mumbled to Luyu as we followed Fanasi and Mwita past the remaining market booths to the small building whose insides blazed with light.

"Forget her," Luyu said. She brought out her portable. "Here look." She pressed a button on the side and it beeped sweetly. She flipped it over and a tiny door on its bottom slid up to reveal a screen. "Map," Luyu said. The portable beeped again. "See look." She held it over the palm of her hand where it shined the white picture of a map. It rotated to maintain the proper direction each time she moved. If this map was accurate, and I believed it was, then it was far more detailed than the one Mwita had.

"See the orange line?" Luyu asked "The woman programmed it so that the map shows the way from Jwahir to the West if we'd gone straight west. We're about three miles off. And see here? You press this button and it starts tracking us. It'll beep when we start moving too far off course."

The line hit the Kingdom of the Seven Rivers, in particular a town on the fifth river called Durfa. I frowned. My mother's village was not far from there. Had she been aware of traveling so directly east? "Who do you think made the map?" I asked.

Luyu shrugged. "The lady didn't know."

"Well, I hope it wasn't a Nuru," I said. "Can you imagine if they had the exact location of so many Okeke towns?"

"They'll never leave their precious rivers," Luyu said. "Even to enslave, rape, and kill more Okekes."

I'm not so sure that's true, I thought.

We spotted them as soon as we entered the tavern. Binta sat on a young man's lap, a red glass of palm wine in hand, the top of her dress half open. The man was whispering in her ear, one hand pinching her exposed left nipple. Binta moved his hand away, then changed her mind and moved it back. Another man with a guitar passionately serenaded her. Yes, shy Binta. Diti sat in the middle of seven men who hung on her every word. She too had a glass of palm wine.

"We've come far and we'll go farther," Diti was saying, her words slurred. "We won't let our people keep dying. We're going to stop it. We're skilled in combat."

"You and what army?" a man said. They all laughed. "Do you two beautiful creatures even have a leader?"

Diti grinned, swaying slightly. "An ugly *Ewu* woman." Then she laughed hard.

"So two girls follow a prostitute west to save the Okeke people," one of the men laughed. "Ah ah, these Jwahir girls are even better than that big-breasted storyteller!"

"Diti!" Fanasi shouted, striding in.

She tried to stand and instead stumbled into the arms of one of the men. He helped her stand up, holding her out to Fanasi. "Is this one yours, then?" the man asked.

Fanasi took Diti's arm. "What are you doing?!"

"Having a good time!" she shouted, snatching her arm away.

"We were going to come back in the morning," Binta said, quickly pulling the top of her dress closed. I was so angry that I turned and walked out the door.

"Don't go far," Mwita said after me. He knew not to follow.

I stepped into the night, the breeze pushing my veil back right in front of a group of young men. They were smoking something that smelled like sweet fire. Brown cactus sap cigars. In Jwahir, these were deeply frowned upon. They loosen your morals, quicken your feet, and give you awful breath. I caught my veil and pulled it back up.

"Giant *Ewu* woman," the one closest to me said. He was the tallest of the four, standing almost at my height. "I've never seen you before."

"I've never been here before," I replied.

"Why are you hiding your face?" another asked, adjusting himself. His pants looked way too tight for his fat legs. All four of them stepped up to me, curious. The tall one who'd called me a giant leaned against the building beside me, putting himself between me and the tavern door.

"This is what I prefer to wear," I said.

"I thought *Ewu* women preferred to wear nothing at all." The one who said this wore his hair in long black braids. "That you and the sun are siblings."

"Come and give me entertainment," the tall one said, taking my arm. "You're the tallest woman I've ever seen."

I blinked, frowning. "What?"

"I'll pay you, of course," he said. "You don't need to ask. We know your trade."

"You can entertain me after him." This one looked no older than sixteen.

"I was here before both of you," the fat one said. "She entertains me first." He looked at me. "And I have more money."

"I'll tell your wife if you don't let me go first," the young one said.

"Tell her then," the fat one angrily barked.

In Jwahir, *Ewu* people were outcast. In Banza, *Ewu* women were prostitutes. It was no good wherever I went. "I'm a holy woman," I asserted, holding my voice steady. "I entertain no one. I am and will remain untouched."

"We respect that, lady," the tall one said. "It doesn't have to be intercourse. You can use your mouth and let us touch your breasts. We'll pay you well for . . ."

"Shut up," I snapped. "I'm not from here. I'm not a prostitute. Leave me be."

A series of unspoken words passed between them. They made eye contact with each other and their lips curled into mischievous smiles. Their hands left their pockets where their money was. *Oh Ani, protect me,* I thought.

They sprang at the same time. I fought, kicking one of them in the face, grabbing the testicles of another and squeezing as hard as I could. I just needed to make it to the door so the others could see me.

The tall one grabbed me. There was too much noise inside the tavern and the breath was knocked out of me before I could shout. I punched, scratched, and kicked. I was rewarded with grunts and curses as I made contact. But there were four of them. The one with the braids grabbed my thick braid and I fell backward. Then they started dragging me away from the door. Yes, even the young one. I anxiously looked around, holding my braid. There were other people nearby.

"Eh!" I shouted at a women just standing there staring. "Help! Help me, *o!*"

But she didn't. There were several people doing the same, just standing there watching. In this lovely town of art and culture, people did nothing when an *Ewu* women was dragged into a dark alley and raped.

This is what happened to my mother, I thought. *And Binta. And count-less other Okeke women. Women. The walking dead.* I began to get very very angry.

I was bricoleur, one who used what she had to do what she had to do, and so I did. I mentally opened my sorcerer Bushcraft bag and considered the Mystic Points. The Uwa point, the physical world. There was a slight breeze.

They held my face to the dirt, tore at my garments, and freed their penises. I concentrated. The wind increased. "There are consequences to shifting the weather," Aro had taught. "Even in small places." But I didn't care about that right now. When I'm truly angry, when I'm filled with violence, all things are easy and simple.

The men noticed the wind and let go of me. The boy yelled, the tall one stared, the fat one tried to dig a hole to crawl into, and the one with the braids pulled at his hair in terror. The wind pressed them to the ground. The most it did to me was blow my thick braid and loose garments about. I stood up, looking down at them. I gathered the wind, gray and black in my hands, and pressed it together, elongating it into a funnel. And I would thrust it into each man, as each had wanted to thrust his penis into me.

"Onyesonwu! Don't!" Mwita's voice was resonant, as if he'd thrown it at me.

I looked up. "See me!" I shouted. "See what they wanted to do to me!"

The wind kept Mwita back. "Remember," he shouted. "This is not what we are. No violence! It's what sets us apart!"

I began to tremble as my fury retreated and clarity set in. Without the blindness of rage, I clearly understood that I wanted to kill these men. They cowered on the ground. Terrified of me. I looked at the people who'd gathered. I looked at Binta, Luyu, Diti, and Fanasi all standing there. I refused to look at Mwita. I pointed the black roaring spear of wind at the youngest one.

"Onyesonwu," Mwita begged. "Trust me. Just *trust* me. Please!"

I pressed my lips together. Thinking of the first time I saw Mwita. When he'd told me to jump from the tree after I'd unknowingly turned into a bird. I hadn't been able to see his face, I didn't know who he was, but even then I trusted him. I threw the spear and it blasted a large hole beside the young one. Then the idea came to me. I changed myself. In the Great Book there is a most terrifying creature. It only speaks riddles and, in the stories, though it never kills, people fear it more than death.

I changed into a sphinx. My body was that of a giant robust desert cat but my head remained mine. It was the first time I used a shape I knew, altered its size, and kept a part of myself the same. The men looked up at me and screamed. They groveled lower to the ground. The onlookers also screamed, running in all directions.

"Next time you want to attack an *Ewu* woman, think of my name: Onyesonwu," I roared, whipping my thick tail at them. "And fear for your life."

"Onyesonwu?" one of the men asked, his eyes wide. "Eeee! The sorceress of Jwahir who can raise the dead? We're sorry! We're sorry!" He pressed his face to the dirt. The young one started crying. The other men gibbered apology.

"We didn't know."

"We smoked too much."

"Please!"

I frowned, changing back. "How do you know of me?"

"Travelers spoke of you, *Ada-m*," one man said.

Mwita stepped forward. "All of you, get out of here before I kill you myself!" He was trembling as I was. Once they ran off, Mwita ran to me. "Where are you hurt?"

I just stood there as Mwita pulled my clothes together and touched my face. The others quietly crowded around me.

"Excuse me," a woman said. She was about my age and, like many of the women, had a silver ring in her nose. She looked vaguely familiar.

"What?" I asked flatly.

The woman took a step back and I felt a deep satisfaction. "I . . . well, I wanted to . . . I want to apologize for . . . for that," she said.

"Why?" I frowned realizing where I'd seen her. "You stood there just like everyone else. I saw you."

She took another step back. I wanted to spit at her and then scratch her face off. Mwita held his arm more tightly around my waist. Luyu sucked her teeth loudly and mumbled something and I heard Fanasi say, "Let's go." Binta belched.

"I'm sorry," the woman said. "I didn't know you were Onyesonwu."

"So if I were any other *Ewu* woman, it would've been okay?"

"*Ewu* women are prostitutes," she said matter-of-factly. "They have a brothel in Hometown called the Goat Hair. Hometown is the residential part of Banza, where we all live. They come here from the West. You've never heard of Banza?"

"No," I said. I paused, sensing once again that I'd heard of Banza before. I sighed, disgusted by the place.

"I beg you. Go to the house on the hill," the woman said, looking at me and then at Mwita. "Please. This is not how I want you all to remember Banza."

"We don't care what you want," Mwita said.

The woman looked down and continued to beg. "Please. Onyesonwu is respected here. Go to the house on the hill. They can heal her wounds and . . ."

"*I* can heal her wounds," Mwita said.

"On the hill?" I asked, looking toward it.

The woman's face brightened. "Yes, at the top. They'll be so glad to see you."

Chapter 33

"WE DON'T HAVE TO DO THIS," Diti said.

"Shut up," I snapped. As far as I was concerned, what happened to me was as much her and Binta's fault as it was those men's.

We returned to the market. It was nearly one a.m. and people were finally starting to pack up their wares. Thankfully, a woman selling rapas was still open. News of what had happened traveled fast. By the time we got to the market, everyone knew who I was and what I'd done to the men who'd tried to "proposition" me for "entertainment."

The woman selling the rapas gave me a thick lovely multicolored rapa that was treated with weather gel so that it would remain cool in the heat. She refused my money, insisting she didn't want any trouble. She also gave me a matching top made from the same material. I put on the grand outfit and threw away my torn clothes. As was the style in Banza, both items fit closely, accentuating my breasts and hips.

How did these people know that I could bring things back to life? Diti, Luyu, and Binta may have guessed I had the potential to do so but they didn't know the details. I hadn't even told Mwita about that day I'd brought the goat back to life. Nor did I tell him about how Aro had me bring back a recently dead camel.

Afterward, Aro carried me into Mwita's hut. I was in a partial coma. The camel had been dead for an hour which meant I had a long way to chase and bring back its spirit. Mwita never told me what he said to Aro after he saw me or what he did to bring me back. But after I recovered, Mwita wouldn't speak to Aro for a month.

Since then, I'd brought a mouse, two birds, and one dog back to life. Each time was easier. With any of these instances, someone could have seen me, especially with the dog. I'd found it lying on the road. A little thing with brown fur. It was still warm, so there was no time to take it to a private place. I healed it right there. It got up, licked my hand, and ran, I presume, home. Then I went home and threw up dog hair and blood.

By the time we made it to the top of the highest hill, we were exhausted. The two-story house was large and plain. As we approached it, I smelled incense and heard someone singing.

"Holy people," Fanasi said.

Fanasi knocked on the door. The singing inside stopped and there were footsteps. The door opened. I remembered where I'd heard the name Banza as soon as I saw his face. Luyu, Binta, and Diti must have realized it as well for they gasped.

He was tall and dark-skinned, just like the Ada. This was half of the Ada's darkest secret. "They've never come to see me," she'd said.

"Fanta," I said. Oh, yes, I still remembered the Ada's twins' names. "Where's your sister Nuumu?"

He stared at me for a long moment. "Who are you?" he asked.

"My name is Onyesonwu," I said.

His eyes grew wide and without hesitation, he took my hand and pulled me in and said, "She's this way."

The woman who'd told us to go to the house on the hill was a selfish she-goat. She didn't direct us there out of compassion. As you know, twins bring good luck. Banza was small and flawed but it was relatively happy and prosperous. But now one of its twins was sick. Fanta led us through the main room that smelled like sweet bread and the children who'd eaten it here.

"We teach children here," Fanta said, briskly. "They love this place, but they love my sister more." He led us up a flight of stairs and down a hallway, stopping in front of a closed door painted with trees. A dense mythical forest. It was beautiful. Among the trees were eyes, some small, large, blue, brown, yellow. "Just her," he said to Mwita.

Mwita nodded. "We'll wait out here."

"There's a room down the hall," Fanta said. "See the one with the light on?"

Fanta and I watched them walk into the room. Mwita paused for a moment and met my eyes. I nodded. "Don't worry," I said.

"I'm not," Mwita said. "Fanta, come get me if you need to."

Entering the Ada's house was like walking into the bottom of a lake. Walking into the Ada's daughter's room was like entering a forest—a place I'd never seen even in my visions. Like the door, the walls were painted from ceiling to floor with trees, bushes, and plants. I frowned as I approached her bed. Something wasn't right with the way she was lying. I could hear her breathing: shallow, harsh, difficult.

"This is Onyesonwu the sorceress from the East, sister," Fanta said.

Her eyes widened and her breathing grew more labored.

"It's late," I said. "I'm sorry."

Nuumu waved a shaking hand. "My name," she wheezed." . . . is Nuumu."

I stepped closer. She looked as much like the Ada as her brother did. But something was very wrong with her. She looked as if she were in one place and her hips in another. She smiled at my scrutiny, wheezing loudly. "Come."

I understood when I got closer. Her spine was twisted. Twisted like a snake in midstride. She couldn't breathe well because her lungs were being crushed by the aggressive curvature of her spine.

"I. . . .wasn't always . . . like this," Nuumu said.

"Go and get Mwita," I told Fanta.

"Why?"

"He's a better healer than I," I snapped.

I turned to Nuumu after he had left. "We came to your town hours ago. We were looking for two of our companions. We found them in a tavern where four men tried to rape me because I am *Ewu*. A woman begged us to come here. We hoped for food, rest, and apologetic treatment. I didn't come to heal you."

"Did . . . I ask . . . you to heal me?"

"Not in so many words," I said. I rubbed my forehead. This was all mixed up. I was all mixed up.

"I . . . I'm sorr . . . y," Nuumu said. "We . . . all are born . . . with burdens. S . . . some of us . . . more than . . . others."

Mwita and Fanta came in. Mwita looked at the walls and then at Nuumu.

"This is Mwita," I said.

"May I?" Mwita asked Nuumu. She nodded. He helped her carefully sit up, listened to her chest, and looked at her back. "Can you feel your feet?"

"Yes."

"How long have you been like this?" he asked.

"Since . . . thirteen," she said. "But it has . . . gotten worse . . . with time."

"She's always had to walk with a cane," Fanta said. "People know her to be bent but only recently has she been confined to a bed."

"Scoliosis," Mwita said. "Curvature of the spine. It's hereditary, but that doesn't always explain it. Most common in girls, but boys get it, too. Nuumu, Have you always been slim?"

"Yes," she said

"It tends to affect the slimmer figured more severely," he said. "You breathe the way you do because your lungs are compressed."

I looked at Mwita and knew all I needed to know. She would die. Soon.

"I want to talk to Onyesonwu," he said, taking my hand and leading me out.

Once in the hallway, he softly told me, "She's doomed."

"Unless . . ."

"You don't know what the consequences will be," he said. "And who are these people anyway?" We stood there for a moment.

"You're the one always telling me to have faith," I said after a while. "You don't think we've been led here? Those are the *Ada's* children."

Mwita frowned and shook his head. "She never had any children with Aro."

I scoffed. "What do your eyes tell you? They look just like her. And she *did* have children. When she was fifteen, some stupid boy got her pregnant. She told me about it. Her parents sent her to Banza to have them. Twins."

I walked back in.

"Fanta, we have to bring her outside for this," I said.

He frowned at me. "What are you . . ."

"You know who I am," I said. "Don't ask questions. I can only do it outside."

Mwita and Fanasi helped, while Diti, Luyu, and Binta followed, afraid to ask what was happening. The sight of the twisted woman was enough to keep them quiet.

"Lay her here," I said, motioning next to a palm tree. "Right on the ground."

She groaned as they laid her down. I knelt beside her. I could feel it already.

"Step back," I said to everyone. To Nuumu I said, "This may hurt."

I began to pull it in, all the energy around me. It was good to have the others so close and so afraid. It was good to have her brother so concerned and full of love. It was good to have Mwita there, locked in on only my well-being. I took from all this. I gathered what I could from the sleeping town. There were brothers arguing nearby. There were five couples making love, one of them two women who loved and hated each other. There was an infant who'd just woken up hungry and whiny. *Can I do this?* I wondered. *I must.*

When I had enough, I used it to help me dig as much energy from the land as I could. There was always more to replace what I took. I felt the warmth rise into my body, into my hands. I placed them on Nuumu's chest. She screamed and I grunted, biting down on my lower lip, as I fought to keep my hands still. Her body began to slowly shift. I could feel her pain in my own spine. My eyes watered. *Hold on!* I thought. *Until it is done!* I felt my spine curve this way and that. My breath left me. And in that moment, a revelation came to me. *I know exactly how to break Diti, Luyu, and Binta's Eleventh Rite juju!* I shelved the knowledge in the back of my mind.

"Hold," I whispered to myself. If I removed my hands, a shock wave would burst from me and her spine would remain curved. My hands cooled. It was time to remove them. I was about to. Then Nuumu spoke to me. Not in voice. We didn't need that. We were connected as one body. It took great courage to admit what she admitted to herself, to me. I looked down at her. Her lips were dry, cracking, her eyes were bloodshot, her dark skin had lost its shine.

"I don't know how," I said, tears wetting my face. But I did. If I knew how to give life, I knew how to take it. I held her eyes a moment longer. And then I did it. I used my spirit hands to reach into her instead of the earth. *Green green green green!* was all I thought as I pulled the greenness from her. *Green!*

"What's she doing?" I heard Nuumu's brother scream. But he didn't come near us. I don't know what would have happened if he had. I pulled harder until I felt something snap and something else begin to tear. Her spirit finally gave. It shot from my hands into the air with a high-pitched scream of glee. Fanta started screaming again. This time he came running.

The sky was a swirl of colors, mostly green. The wilderness. Nuumu's spirit traveled straight up. I wondered when she would return. Sometimes they came back and sometimes they didn't. My father had left my mother and me for weeks before he returned to guide me during my initiation. Even then he didn't stay long. Without moving, I willed myself out of the wilderness back into the physical world just in time for Fanta's fist to connect with my chest, knocking me back. Mwita pulled Fanta back. My hand ripped from Nuumu's chest, leaving a dried mucusy hand print.

"You killed her!" Fanta screamed. He looked at Nuumu's body and sobbed so hard that I thought my body would shatter. Diti, Binta, and Luyu helped me sit back up.

"I could have healed her," I said, sobbing and shaking. "I could have."

"Then why didn't you!" Fanta shouted, tearing his arm away from Mwita.

"I am nothing," I cried. "I don't care what it would have done to me. What other purpose do I serve? I could have healed her!" My temples throbbed as phantom stones battered my head. Only my friends kept me from wallowing in the dirt, like the low thing I felt I was. Low like the gray beetles of disease and death in the Great Book that came for the young children of those who'd done terrible wrong.

"Then why didn't you?" Fanta asked again. He'd tired himself out and Mwita let him go. He draped himself over his limp and cooling sister.

"She wouldn't . . . she wouldn't *let* me," I whispered, rubbing my chest. "I should have healed her anyway but she didn't allow me to think to do it. It was her choice. That's all." My actions were an abomination to the natural order of things, though I understand now, weeks later, that this was for the best. The immediate consequence of my actions for me was an almost unbearable cloak of sorrow. I felt like scratching at my skin, gouging my eyes out, killing myself. I sobbed and sobbed, ashamed of my mother, disgusted with myself, wishing my biological father would finally erase my body, memory, and spirit. When it passed, it was like a black thick foul smelling veil lifted.

We all just sat there for several minutes, Fanta weeping over his sister, Mwita patting Fanta's shoulder, me lying spent in the dirt, and the rest staring. Slowly, Fanta lifted his head and looked at me with swollen eyes. "You are evil," he said. "May Ani curse all that you hold dear."

He did not ask us to leave. And though we didn't discuss it among ourselves, we decided to stay for one night. Mwita and Fanasi helped Fanta bring the body inside. Fanta started sobbing again when he saw that her spine was straight. All she'd had to do was let me let go. She'd have lived. I stayed as far from Fanta as possible. I also refused to go into the house. I'd rather sleep under the stars.

"No," I told Luyu, who'd wanted to sleep outside with me. "I need to be alone."

Binta and Diti cooked a large meal in the kitchen, while Luyu swept out the entire house. Mwita and Fanasi stayed with Fanta, afraid that he might try something rash. I could hear Mwita teaching them to chant. I wasn't sure if I heard Fanta's voice in the chanting but one didn't have to chant along to be affected by the chanting.

I unrolled my sleeping mat under a dry palm tree. Two doves were nestled in the tree's crown. They'd stared down at me with their orange eyes when I'd pointed a palm-light up the tree. Normally, I'd have been amused.

I moved my mat over. I didn't want to be bombarded with their feces all night. My body ached and my headache was back. Though it wasn't full blast, it was bad enough to force my thoughts to the West. What would I be by the time we got there? In the same night, I'd spared the lives of men who'd tried to rape me and taken the life of the Ada's daughter.

"Sometimes the good must die and the terrible must live," Aro had taught me. At the time, I'd scoffed at the idea and said, "Not if I can help it."

I rubbed my temples as a particularly hard phantom stone smashed the side of my head. I could almost hear my skull crumbling. I frowned. The crumbling sound wasn't in my head. Sandals on sand. I turned around. Fanta was standing there. I got to my feet, ready for a fight. He sat on my mat.

"Sit," he said.

"No," I said. "Mwita?" I called loudly.

"They know I'm out here."

I looked at the house. Mwita was watching from one of the upstairs windows. I sat beside Fanta. "I was telling the truth," I said when I couldn't take his silence anymore.

He nodded, scooping up a handful of sand and letting it sift between his fingers. From somewhere nearby came the loud *whoosh* of a capture station. Fanta sucked his teeth. "That man," he said. "People complain to him but he still acts disrespectfully. I don't know what he needs water for at this hour."

"Maybe he likes the attention," I said.

"Maybe," he said. We watched the thin white column extend to the sky.

"It's cold out here," he said. ". . . Why don't you come in?"

"Because you hate me," I said.

"How did she ask you?"

"She just did. No, not ask. To ask implies a choice."

He pressed his lips together, scooped up another handful of sand, and threw it.

"She told me once," he said. "Months ago, after she'd become bedridden. She said that she was ready to die. She thought this would make me feel better." He paused. "She said her body was . . ."

"Making her spirit suffer," I said finishing his sentence.

He looked at me. "She told you that?"

"It was like I was in her mind. She didn't have to tell me anything. She didn't feel I could cure her. She had to be free of her body."

"I . . . I was . . . Onye, I'm sorry. . . . For my words, my actions." He brought his legs to his chest and looked down. He was shaking, trying to hold in his grief.

"Don't do that," I said. "Let it out."

I held him as he fell apart. When he could speak, he was breathless like his sister. "My parents are dead. We aren't close with any relatives." He sighed. "I'm alone now." He looked at the sky. I thought about Nuumu's green spirit spiriting away with glee.

"Why didn't you two marry anyone?" I asked. "Didn't you want children?"

"Twins aren't expected to have normal lives," he said.

I frowned, thinking, *Says who?* Says tradition. Oh, how our traditions limit and outcast those of us who aren't normal.

"You're not. . . . you're not alone," I blurted. "We recognized you the moment we saw you. We knew your face. We knew your sister's face."

"Yes. How was that?" he asked, frowning.

"We know your mother."

"Did you meet her? Were you here years ago? I don't . . ."

"Listen," I said. I took a deep breath. "We *know* your mother. She's alive."

Fanta shook his head. "No, she's dead. She was bitten by a snake."

"Your mother was actually your great-aunt."

"What! But that . . . "He stopped and frowned. After a long moment, he said, "Nuumu knew. There was this tiny hole in the wall in the room we shared as children. We found a rolled up painting in there once, of a woman. On the back it said, 'To my son and daughter, with love.' We couldn't read the signature. We were about eight. I didn't care for it but Nuumu thought it meant something. She never showed it to our parents. Our mother wasn't a painter, neither was our father. That painting is what got Nuumu interested in painting. She was very good. Her work sold for high prices at the market . . ." He trailed off a baffled look on his face.

"Your mother is the Ada of Jwahir," I said. "She's highly respected and she paints all the time," I said. "Her name is Yere and she's married to Aro, the sorcerer who is my teacher. Do you want to hear more?"

"Yes! Of course!"

I smiled, glad to finally give him something good.

"When she was fifteen, a boy was interested in her . . ." I told him his mother's story and whatever else I knew of her. I left out the part about the Eleventh Rite juju she'd asked Aro to work on the girls.

We both slept well that night out there, Fanta's arms around me. I wondered how Mwita felt about this but some things are more important than a man's ego. In the morning, Mwita sent Diti and Luyu to the house of the Banza elders to give the news of Nuumu's death. The house would soon be full of mourners and people helping Fanta. It was time to go.

Fanta also planned to leave. After his sister's ceremony and crema-tion, he said he was going to sell his house and travel to Jwahir to find his mother. "There is nothing left for me here," he said. Without his twin, soon Banza would stop funding him. When a twin died, the remaining one was bad luck. We said good-bye to Fanta as the house filled up. Many of the people gave Mwita and me dirty looks and I feared for us. We'd come into town yesterday and now one of their precious twins was dead.

We took a different road down the hill. It led straight out of town. It also took us past the Goat Hair Brothel. It was a sight that I'll never forget. Though early in the day, the women were already out. They sat on the balcony of the three-story house. Their skin was bright and they wore clothes that made them even brighter. Mwita and I were much darker from traveling in the sun, so to my eyes, they practically glowed. They lounged on chairs and hung their delicate feet over the balcony. Some wore tops cut so low that their nipples showed.

"Where do you think their mothers are?" I asked Mwita.

"Or their fathers," he whispered.

"Mwita, I doubt any of them are like you," I said. "They have no fathers."

One of the girls waved. I waved back.

"They are kind of pretty, in their own way, maybe," I heard Diti say to Luyu.

"If you say so," Luyu said, doubtfully.

As we passed the last building, we heard a haunting rise of wailing voices. Banza's women had arrived at the house of their twins. Fanta would be well taken care of, at least for now. Once his sister was cremated, he would disappear into the night. I felt for Fanta. His other half had left him, had been happy to do so. But getting out of Banza was probably for the better. At its core, the town was good, but parts of it were festering. And now Fanta would be able to have a life instead of being an idea that gave other people selfish hope.

As we walked, that brothel not far behind us, I felt a wave of anger. To be something abnormal meant that you were to serve the normal. And if you refused, they hated you . . . and often the normal hated you even when you *did* serve them. Look at those *Ewu* girls and women. Look at Fanta and Nuumu. Look at Mwita and me.

Not for the last time I suspected that whatever I'd do in the West would be violent. Despite what Mwita said and believed. Look at how Mwita reacted to seeing Daib. It was reality. I was *Ewu*, who would listen to me without the threat of violence? Like those disgusting men outside the tavern. They hadn't heard me until they feared me.

Just before we came to the road, we met the three camels. To the left was a large pile of dung and it looked like one or two of them had gone and brought back clumps of dry grass to munch on. "You waited," I said smiling. Without thinking, I ran to the one that had threatened me and threw my arms around its shaggy dusty neck.

"What in the name of Ani are you doing?!" Fanasi shouted.

The camel groaned but welcomed my hug. I stepped back. The camel was large and probably female. I cocked my head. One of the other camels was not very big. A baby that soon wouldn't be. Possibly weaned recently. I wondered if the female would let us milk her. Camel milk had Vitamin C. My mother said she'd done this several times when I was very young.

"What should we call each of you?" I asked. "How about Sandi?" Mwita laughed and shook his head. Luyu was staring. Fanasi brought out the dagger he'd bought in Banza. Binta looked disgusted. And Diti looked annoyed.

"You're probably covered with lice, you know," Diti said. "I hope you're ready to cut off your lovely hair."

I scoffed. "Only domestic camels have that problem."

"That thing could have bitten your head off," Fanasi said, still holding his dagger.

"But it didn't," I said with a sigh. "Will you put that away?"

"No," he said.

The camels weren't stupid. They were watching each of us closely. It was only a matter of time now before one of the camels spit at or bit Fanasi. I turned back to the head camel. "I am Onyesonwu Ubaid-Ogundimu, born in the desert and raised in Jwahir. I'm twenty years old and a sorceress apprenticed to the sorcerer Aro and mentored by the sorcerer Sola. Mwita, tell it who you are."

He stepped up to them. "I'm Mwita, Onyesonwu's life companion."

Fanasi sucked his teeth loudly. "Why don't you just say you're her *husband?*"

"Because I'm *more* than that," Mwita said. Fanasi gave him a dirty look, mumbled something under his breath and proceeded to ignore everyone. Mwita turned back to the camel. "I was born in Mawu and raised in Durfa. I'm a pre-sorcerer. I wasn't allowed to pass initiation for . . . reasons." He glanced at me. "I'm also a healer, apprenticed to and passed by the healer Abadie."

The three camels just sat there and looked at both of us.

"Give it a hug," I said.

"What?" he asked.

Diti, Luyu and Binta giggled.

"Ani save us," Fanasi grumbled, rolling his eyes.

I pushed Mwita forward. He stood before the great beast. Then he held up his arms and slowly wrapped them around the camel's neck. The camel grunted softly. Mwita did the same to the other camels. They too seemed pleased by this gesture, grunting loudly and nudging Mwita hard enough to make him stumble.

Luyu stepped up. "I am Luyu Chiki, born and raised in Jwahir." She paused, glancing at me and then at the ground. "I . . . I have no title. I was apprenticed to no one. I travel to see what I can see and learn what I'm made of . . . and for." She slowly hugged the head camel. I smiled. She scampered behind me instead of hugging the others.

"They smell like sweat," she whispered. "Like a fat man's sweat!"

I laughed. "You see their humps? That's all fat. They don't need to eat for days."

I didn't look at Diti and Binta. The sight of them still made me want to spring at them and start slapping and slapping and slapping as I had before.

"I'm Binta Keita," she said loudly from where she was. "I left Jwahir, my home, to find a new life . . . I was marked. But I made it better and I'm not marked anymore!"

"I am Diti Goitsemedime," Diti said, also staying where she was. "And this is my husband Fanasi. We're from Jwahir. We're going west to do what we can do."

"I go to follow my wife," Fanasi added, looking bitterly at Diti.

We started southwest, using Luyu's map to get on course. It was hot and we had to walk covered by our veils. The camels led the way, moving in the right direction. This surprised everyone but Mwita and me. We traveled well into the night and when we made camp, we were too tired to cook anything. Within minutes, we'd all retired to our tents.

"How are you?" Mwita asked, pulling me close.

His words were like a key. All the emotion I'd held down suddenly felt ready to burst through my chest. I buried my head in his chest and wept. Minutes passed and my sorrow became fury. I felt a rush in my chest. I wanted so badly to kill my father. It would have been like killing a thousand of those men who attacked me. I would avenge my mother, I would avenge myself.

"Breathe," Mwita whispered.

I opened my mouth and inhaled his breath. He kissed me again and quietly, carefully, softly, he spoke the words that few women ever hear from a man. "*Ifunanya.*"

They're ancient words. They don't exist among any other group of people. There is no direct translation in Nuru, English, Sipo, or Vah. This word only has meaning when spoken by a man to the one he loves. A woman can't use the word unless she is barren. It is not juju. Not in the way that I know it. But the word has strength. It's wholly binding if it is true and the emotion reciprocated. This is not like the word "*love*." A man can tell a woman he loves her every day. *Ifunanya* is spoken only once in a man's life. *Ifu* means to "look into," "*n*" means "the," and *anya* means "eyes". The eyes *are* the window to the soul.

I could have died when he spoke this word because I'd never ever thought any man would speak it to me, not even Mwita. All the filth those men had heaped on me with their filthy actions and filthy words and filthy ideas, none of it mattered now. Mwita, Mwita, Mwita, again, Fate, I thank you.

Chapter 34

WE TRAVELED FOR TWO WEEKS before Mwita decided we should stop for a few days. Something more had happened in Banza. It started when we left Jwahir but now it was more pronounced. The group was splitting in multiple ways. There was a split between the men and the women. Mwita and Fanasi would often walk off together, where they'd talk for hours. But a divide between the sexes seemed normal. The split with Binta and Diti on one side and Luyu and me on the other was more problematic. And then there was the most problematic split between Fanasi and Diti.

I kept thinking about what Fanasi had said to the camels, how he'd come along mainly to follow Diti. I thought the vision I showed him of what was really happening in the West was his greater motivation to come. I'd forgotten that Fanasi and Diti had loved each other since childhood. They'd wanted to marry since they knew what marriage was. Fanasi had been heartbroken when he'd touched Diti and she'd screamed. For years, he pined away for her before finally gaining the courage to demand her hand in marriage.

He wasn't about to let her leave without him. But, by leaving Jwahir, Diti and Binta discovered life as free women. As the days passed, when Diti and Fanasi weren't bickering, they ignored each other. Diti permanently moved into Binta's tent and Binta didn't mind. Mwita and I could hear the two talking and giggling in hushed voices, sometimes well into the night.

I was sure that I could resolve things. That night, I built a rock fire and cooked up a large stew using two hares. Then I called a meeting. Once everyone was seated, I ladled out stew into chipped porcelain bowls, handing them to each, starting with Fanasi and Diti and ending with Mwita. I watched everyone eat for a while. I'd used salt, herbs, cactus cabbage, and camel milk. The stew was good.

"I've noticed tension," I finally said. There was only the sound of spoons hitting porcelain and slurping and chewing. "We've been traveling for three months. We're a long long way from home. And we're going to a bad place." I paused. "But the biggest problem right here, right now is with you two." I pointed at Fanasi and Diti. They looked at each other and then looked away. "We only survive because of each other," I continued. "That stew you enjoy is made with Sandi's milk."

"What?" Diti exclaimed.

"Ew!" Binta screeched. Fanasi cursed and put his bowl down. Mwita chuckled as he continued to eat. Luyu was looking doubtfully at her bowl.

"Anyway," I said. "You two say you're husband and wife yet you don't sleep in the same tent."

"She was the one who ran off," Fanasi suddenly said. "Behaving like an ugly *Ewu* prostitute in that tavern."

There it was again. I pressed my lips together, focusing on what I intended to say.

"Shut up," Diti snapped. "Men always think that when a woman enjoys herself, she *must* be a prostitute."

"Any of them could have had you!" Fanasi said.

"Maybe, but who did they go after instead?" Diti said, smiling devilishly at me.

"Oh, Ani help us," Binta moaned looking at me. I stood up.

"Come on then," Diti said, standing up. "I survived your other beating just fine."

"Eh!" Luyu exclaimed, putting herself between Diti and me. "What is wrong with you all?" Mwita merely sat and watched this time.

"What's wrong with *me?*" I said. "You ask what's wrong with *me?*" I laughed loudly. I didn't sit down.

"Diti, do you have something to say to Onye?" Luyu asked.

"Nothing," Diti said, looking away.

"*I know how to break it,*" I said loudly, barely able to breathe I was so angry. "I want to *help* you, you insipid blockhead! I realized how when I was healing Nuumu."

Diti only stared at me.

I took a deep breath. "Luyu, Binta, there is no one out here, but maybe in one of these villages or towns we pass through . . . I don't know. But I can break the juju." I turned and went to my tent. They would have to come to me.

Mwita came in an hour later with a bowl of stew. "How'll you do it?" he asked. I took it from him. I was ravenous but too proud to go out and take from the stew I'd made.

"They won't like it," I said, biting into a piece of meat. "But it'll work."

Mwita thought about it for a minute. Then he grinned.

"Yeah," I said.

"Luyu will let you but Binta and Diti . . . that's going to take some coaxing."

"Or the last of the palm wine," I said. "By now it's so fermented that they won't know their heads from their *yeyes* after two cups, *if* I agree to do it. Binta, maybe, but Diti . . . not without a thousand apologies." I eyed Mwita as he turned to leave the tent. "Make sure you tell that to Fanasi in my exact words," I said with a smirk.

"I planned to do just that."

Fanasi came to me that night. I had just settled in Mwita's arms after an hour of flight as a vulture. "I'm sorry to bother you," Fanasi said, crawling in.

I sat up, pulling my rapa closer to myself. Mwita draped our cover over my shoulders. I could barely see Fanasi in the glow of the rock fire from outside.

"Diti wants you to . . ."

"Then she has to come and ask," I said.

Fanasi frowned. "This isn't only about her, you know."

"It's about her first," I said. I paused for a moment and then sighed. "Tell her to come out and speak with me." I looked back at Mwita before exiting. He was shirtless and I was taking the cover. He waved a hand at me and said, "Just don't take too long."

Outside was even cooler. I wrapped the cover more tightly around myself and made for the dwindling rock fire. I raised my hand and swirled the air around it until it grew hot again. I waved some warm air toward my tent.

Fanasi placed a hand on my shoulder. "Hold your temper," he said. He went into Binta and Diti's tent.

"As long as she does," I mumbled. I stared at the glowing stones as Diti came out. Fanasi went into his tent and pulled the flap shut. As if Diti and I really had any privacy.

"Look," she said. "I just wanted . . ."

I held my hand up and shook my head. "Apology first. Otherwise, I'm going right back into my tent to sleep a long guilt-free sleep."

She frowned at me for too long. "I . . ."

"And wipe that look off your face," I said, cutting her off. "If I'm so disgusting to you, then you should've stayed home. You deserved your beating. You're stupid to provoke someone who can break you in half. I'm taller, bigger, and *much* angrier."

"I'm sorry!" Diti shouted.

I saw Luyu peak out of her tent.

"I . . . this journey," Diti said. "It's not what I expected. *I'm* not who I expected." She wiped her brow. It was hot now from the fire, suitable for the conversation. "I've never been outside of Jwahir. I'm used to good meals, fresh hot bread, and spiced chicken not stewed desert hare and *camel* milk! Camel milk is for infants and . . . infant *camels!*"

"You're not the only one here who's never left Jwahir, Diti," I said. "But you're the only one acting like an idiot."

"You showed us!" Diti said. "You showed us the West. *Who* could just sit there after seeing that? I couldn't just live my happy life with Fanasi. You changed all that."

"Oh, don't blame me!" I snapped. "None of you *dare* blame me! Blame yourselves for your ignorance and your complacency."

"You're right," Diti said quietly. "I . . . I don't know what's been happening to me." She shook her head. "I don't hate you. . . .but I hate what you are. I hate that whenever I look at you . . . It's hard for us, Onye. Eleven years of believing that *Ewu* people are dirty, lowly, violent people. Then we met you and then Mwita. Both of you are the strangest people we've ever met."

"Soon, you too will be viewed as low," I said. "Soon you'll understand how I feel *wherever* I go." But I was conflicted. Diti and Binta were going through something just as I was, as we all were. And I had to respect that. Despite it all. "You came out here to ask me something?"

Diti looked toward Fanasi's tent. "Take it off me. If you can. Will you?"

"You won't like what I have to do," I said. "I won't either."

Diti frowned. Her frown turned to a look of disgust. "No."

"Yes," I said.

"Ugh!"

"I know."

"Will it hurt in the same way?" she asked.

"I don't know. But when it comes to sorcery, you never get without giving."

Luyu came out of her tent. "Me, too," she said. "I don't care about you putting your hands on me. Anything to enjoy intercourse again. I don't have time for marriage."

Binta came scrambling out. "Me, too!" she said.

All I felt was doubt. "Okay," I said. "Tomorrow night."

"So you know exactly what to do?" Luyu asked.

"I think so," I said. "I mean, I've never done this before, obviously."

"What do you think you'll . . . do?" Luyu pressed.

I thought about it. "Well, something can't come from nothing. Even a bit of flesh. Once Aro pulled an insect's leg off, threw the leg aside, and said, 'make it walk again.' I was able to do it but I can't tell you how. There's a point where it goes from me doing something to something working through me and doing what's to be done."

I frowned considering this. When I healed it wasn't all me. If it wasn't all me, then who else was it? It was like that moment I told to Luyu, when you wake up and don't know who you are.

"Once I asked Aro what he thought happened when he healed and he said it had something to do with time," I said. "That you manipulate it to bring back the flesh." The three of them just stared at me. I shrugged and gave up explaining.

"Onye," Binta suddenly said. "I'm so so sorry. We shouldn't have gone there." She threw herself on me, knocking me over. "You shouldn't have been there!"

"It's okay," I said, trying to sit up. She still clung to me and now she was crying hard. I wrapped my arms around her, whispering, "It's okay. Binta. I'm okay." Her hair smelled like soap and scented oil. She'd braided her Afro into many small braids the day before we left Jwahir. Since then, the braids had grown out and still she hadn't undone them. I wondered if she'd decided to go dada. Two of the camels humphed from behind Luyu's tent where they were trying to rest.

"For goodness' sake," Fanasi said coming out of his tent, "Women."

Mwita came out of his tent, too. I noticed Luyu looking at his bare chest and I wasn't sure if it was out of the usual curiosity people had about the bodies of the *Ewu* or something more carnal.

"So it's decided then," Mwita said. "That's good."

"Indeed it is," Fanasi said cheerily.

Diti gave him a dirty look.

Chapter 35

I SPENT MOST OF THE NEXT DAY AS A VULTURE, soaring, relaxing. Then I returned to camp, dressed, and walked for about a mile to a place I had scoped out while flying. I sat under the palm tree, put my veil on my head, and pulled my hands into my garments for protection from the sun. I cleared my head of thought. I didn't move for three hours. I returned to the camp just before sunset. The camels greeted me first. They were drinking from a bag of water Mwita held for them. They nudged me with their soft wet muzzles. Sandi even licked my cheek, smelling and tasting the wind and sky on my skin.

Mwita kissed me. "Diti and Binta have made you a feast," he said.

I especially enjoyed the roasted desert hare. They were right to want me to eat. I needed my strength. Afterward, I took a bucket of water, went behind our tent, and washed thoroughly. As I poured water over my head, I heard Diti shout, "Don't!" I paused, listening. I couldn't quite hear over the sound of dripping water. I shivered and finished my bath. I dressed in a loose shirt and my old yellow rapa. By this time the sun had set completely. I could hear them all gathering. It was time.

"I've chosen a place," I said. "It's about a mile away. There's a tree. Mwita, Fanasi, you stay here. You'll see our fire." I met Mwita's eyes, hoping he understood my unspoken words: *Keep your ears open.*

I took a satchel full of stones and the four of us left. When we got to the tree, I dumped out the rocks and warmed them up until my joints loosened. The night was very cold. We'd come far enough for the weather to change. Though the days remained hot, the nights had become utterly frigid. It rarely got this cold at night in Jwahir.

"Who wants to go first?" I asked.

They looked at each other.

"Why not do it in the order of our rite?" Luyu said.

"Binta, you, then Diti?" I said.

"Let's do it the other way around this time," Binta insisted.

"Fine," Diti said. "I didn't come here to get scared." Her voice was shaking.

"Spit out your *talembe etanou* stones," I said.

"Why?" Luyu asked.

"I think they're charmed, too," I said. "But I'm not sure how."

Luyu spit hers in her hand and put it in a fold in her rapa. Diti spit hers into the dark. Binta hesitated. "Are you sure?" she asked.

I waved a hand at her. "Do what you like." She didn't spit hers out.

"All right," I said. "Ah, Diti, you have to . . ."

"I know," she said, taking her rapa off. Luyu and Binta both looked away.

I felt nauseated. Not out of fear but more from a deep sense of discomfort. She would have to spread her legs. But even worse, I had to also place my hands on the scar that was left from that swift cut nine years ago.

"You don't have to look like that," Diti said.

"How do you expect me to look?" I asked, annoyed.

"We'll just, ah, walk this way," Luyu suddenly said, taking Binta's hand and stepping away. "Call us when you're ready."

"Is the fire warm enough?" I asked Diti.

"Can you make it warmer?"

I did. "You're going to have to. . . . do what you did . . . before," I said, kneeling down beside the rocks. I looked at the sky as she lay down beside me and spread her legs. I took in a deep breath and lay my hands on her. I focused my mind immediately, ignoring the moist feel of my friend's *yeye*. I focused on pulling up handful after handful of what there was plenty of. I took strength from the fear and excitement of Luyu and

Binta nearby. I pulled from the restlessness of the camels, the mild worry of Mwita back at the camp, and the confused anxiety and excitement of Fanasi.

I could feel her scar but soon I could feel heat and a breeze pushing from behind me. Diti was whimpering. Then crying. Then screaming. I held on, my eyes closed, though I could feel the same burning, tearing, knitting between my legs. Her screams had to reach Mwita and Fanasi. I held on. The moment came. I took my hands away. Instinctively, I plunged my hands into the sand. I scrubbed them as if the sand were water. I used Diti's rapa to clean off my hands.

"It's done," I said in a husky voice. My hands were itchy. "How do you feel?"

She wiped the tears from her face and gave me a dirty look. "What did you do to me?" she said, her voice hoarse.

"Shut up," I snapped. "I told you it would hurt."

"You want me to see if it works?" she asked sarcastically.

"I don't care what you do," I said. "Go and get Luyu."

Once she was standing up, Diti seemed better. She looked down at me for a moment and then slowly walked away. I rubbed more sand on my itchy hands. "Everything has a consequence," I mumbled to myself.

All three of them screamed.

"Leave me here," I said when I finished with Binta. I was out of breath and sweating, still scrubbing my hands with the sand. I could smell all three of them on me and I was twitchy all over. I scrubbed harder. "Go back to the camp."

Neither they nor I needed to check if what I did worked. It had. I understood now that there was no reason to doubt myself with something so simple. "I can do much more," I said to myself. "But what would I suffer?" I laughed. My hands itched so badly that I wanted to place them on the hot rocks. I held them up in the fire light.

"Oh Ani, what did you make when you made me?" I whispered. My skin was chaffing. I picked at a small piece of skin. A swath of it the size of the entire back of my hand sloughed off. I dropped it on the sand. Right before my eyes, I saw the new skin begin to dry and chafe. It too would peel off. I grated it with sand. Layer after layer came off. The itching continued. There was a pile of skin on the ground and I was still peeling when Mwita spoke from behind me.

"Congratulations," he said, leaning against the palm tree, putting his arms around his chest. "You've made your friends happy."

"I . . . I can't make it stop," I said frantically.

Mwita frowned and looked more closely in the dim light. "Is that skin?" he asked. I nodded. He knelt beside me. "Let me see."

I shook my head, holding my hands behind my back. "No. It's awful."

"How do they feel?" he asked.

"Terrible. Hot, itchy."

"You need to eat," he said. He brought out a hunk of red cactus candy wrapped in a cloth. It was just the way I liked it, sticky and ripe.

"I'm not hungry," I said.

"It doesn't matter. All that skin requires energy and production from you, juju or not. You need to eat to replace it."

"I don't want to touch it. I don't want to touch anything with them."

He put the cactus candy aside. "Let me see, Onyesonwu."

I cursed and gave him my hands. It was always so humiliating. I would do something and I'd always need Mwita to put me back in order. As if I had no control of my abilities, my faculties, my body.

He looked at my hands for a long time. He touched the skin. Peeled some of it off, watched the new skin become old and peel again. He grasped my hands in his.

"They're hot," he said.

I envied him. I was the sorceress but he understood so much more than I. He wasn't allowed to learn the Mystic Points, yet he had sorcerer's ways.

"Okay," he said to himself after a while.

When he said nothing else, I asked, "Okay, what?"

"Shh," he said, reminding me of Aro. Sola, too. All three had a habit of listening to a voice or voices I couldn't hear. "Okay," he said again. This time he was speaking to me. "I can't heal this."

"What?"

"But you can."

"How?"

Mwita looked irritated. "You should know."

"Well, obviously I don't!" I snapped.

"You should," he said, laughing bitterly. "Ah, you should know how to do this. You have to *practice* more, Onye. Start teaching yourself."

"I know," I said, looking annoyed. "That's why I was saying we should be careful when we have intercourse. I'm not . . ."

"That chance is better taken," Mwita said. He paused, looking at the sky. "Only Ani knows why she made you a sorcerer instead of me."

"Mwita, just tell me what I should do," I said, rubbing my hands with sand.

"All you need to *do* is to wash your hands in the wilderness," he said. "You used your hands to manipulate time and flesh and now they're full of flesh and time. Take them to the wilderness where there is no time or flesh and it will stop." He got up. "Do it now so we can go back."

He was right, I hadn't been learning or practicing. Since we'd left, I'd only used my abilities when we needed them or when I needed them. I tried to drop into the wilderness. Nothing happened. I *was* unpracticed, and I had not fasted. I tried harder and still nothing happened. I calmed myself and focused inward. Letting my thoughts peel away, like the flesh on my hands. Gradually the world around me shifted and undulated. I watched the colors for a while as several pink hazes of color circled my head.

Then in the distance, I saw it, the red eye. I hadn't seen it since I was sixteen, since initiation. I quickly stood up. I was Eshu which meant I could shift into the bodies of other creatures and spirits. Here I was blue. Except my hands, which were a dull brown. I stared defiantly back at the eye.

"When you're ready," I said to him. Daib didn't reply. I pretended to ignore him. I held up my hands. Immediately they attracted several free happy spirits. Two pink ones and a green one passed through my hands. When I brought them down, my hands were a rich blue like the rest of me. I sat down and with relief came back to the physical world. I looked at my hands. They were still covered with peeling skin. But when I stripped the skin off, only stable rich skin was underneath. I looked at Mwita. He was sitting at the base of the tree, looking at the sky.

"Daib was watching me there," I said.

He turned around. "Oh, you're back." He paused. "Did he try anything?"

"No," I said. "He was just that red staring eye." I sighed. "My hands are better, though. But they're still a little warm, like they have a fever, and the skin is tender."

He held and looked them over. "I can help this," he said. "Let's go back."

When we got within range of the camp, we heard shouting. We walked faster.

"Is that all you think about, Fanasi?" Diti was yelling.

"What kind of wife are you? I didn't even say anything about . . ."

"I'm not staying with you tonight!" Diti screamed.

"Will you two just shut up!" Luyu shouted.

"What's going on?" I asked Binta, who was just standing there crying.

"Ask them," she sobbed.

Fanasi turned his back to me.

"None of your business," Diti grumbled, putting her arms around her chest.

I went to my tent, disgusted. Behind me, I heard Fanasi tell Diti, "I should never have come with you. I should have let you leave and been done with it."

"Did I ask you to come *for* me?" Diti said. "You're so selfish!"

I slapped aside my tent flap and crawled in. I wished that it had just been Mwita and me who'd left, that they'd all just stayed home. *What can they do when we get to the West, anyway?* I wondered. Mwita came in.

"It was supposed to make things better," I hissed.

"You can't fix everything," he said. He held out a bowl to me. "Here, eat."

"No," I said, putting it aside.

He gave me an angry look and left. We were all falling apart, all right. We'd been falling apart since we left but when I broke that juju, the cracks became more permanent. It wasn't my fault, I know, but back then I felt everything was. I was the chosen one.

It was all my fault.

Chapter 36

I FELL SICK THAT NIGHT. I was so angry and disappointed with all the bickering that I'd refused to eat anything and gone to sleep on an empty stomach. Mwita had been out most of the night, trying to talk sense into Fanasi. If he'd been there, he'd have forced me to eat before I slept. When he returned just before dawn, he found me curled into a tight ball, shivering and grumbling nonsense. He had to feed me spoonfuls of salt and then the broth from last night's stew. I couldn't even hold the spoon.

"Next time, don't be stubborn and thoughtless," he'd said angrily.

I was too weak to travel, but I was soon able to sit up and eat on my own. The camp was tense. Binta and Diti stayed in their tent. Fanasi and Mwita went off to talk. Luyu stayed with me. We lay in my tent practicing Nuru together.

"What think Diti's problem?" Luyu asked in very bad Nuru.

"She's stupid," I replied in Nuru.

"I. . . ." Luyu paused. In Okeke she asked, "How do you say *freedom* in Nuru?"

I told her.

She thought for a second and said in Nuru, "Think I . . . Diti taste freedom and now can't without."

"I think she's just stupid," I said again in Nuru.

Luyu switched to Okeke. "You saw how happy she was in that tavern.

Some of those men *were* lovely . . . None of us were ever allowed to be that free in Jwahir."

I laughed. "*You* were."

She laughed, too. "Because I learned to take what wasn't given to me."

Late that night as I lay beside Mwita, I was still thinking about Diti's stupidity. Mwita breathed softly, deep in sleep. I heard soft footsteps outside. I was used to the movement of the camels who often went out foraging at night or to mate. These footsteps were not big or many. I closed my eyes and listened harder. *Not a desert fox,* I thought. *Not gazelle.* I held my breath, listening harder. *Human.* The footsteps were going toward Fanasi's tent. I heard whispers. I relaxed. Diti had finally gotten some sense.

Of course I kept listening. Wouldn't you? I heard Fanasi whisper something. Then . . . I frowned. Listening closer. There was a sigh and then soft motion and a low groan. I almost woke Mwita up. I should have woken him up. This was bad. But what right did I have to stop Luyu from going into Fanasi's tent? I could hear their rhythmic breathing. They went on like this for over an hour. Eventually I drifted off, so who knew when Luyu returned to her tent.

We packed up our things before sunrise. Diti and Fanasi didn't speak to each other. Fanasi tried not to look at Luyu. Luyu acted completely normal. I laughed to myself as we started walking. Who knew there could be such theatrics in a small group in the middle of nowhere?

Chapter 37

BETWEEN DITI'S IGNORANT ARROGANCE, Luyu's boldness, and Fanasi's confused emotions, the next two weeks were far from boring. They were my distraction from darker thoughts. Luyu would set up her tent next to Fanasi's and sneak in there late at night every few days. They would both be exhausted come morning and spend the day not looking at each other. I must say, they put on a good act.

In the meantime, I practiced dropping into and gliding through the wilderness. Each time I did, I saw the red eye in the distance, watching me. I surprised Mwita by sneaking up on him as a desert fox. I cut and healed my skin over and over, until cutting and healing myself was easy. I even started a three-day fast, trying to evoke a traveling vision. If Daib wanted to spy on me, then I could spy on him.

"How come you didn't eat your breakfast?" Mwita asked.

"I'm trying for a vision. I think I can control it this time. I want to see what he's up to."

"It's a bad idea," he said, shaking his head. "He'll kill you." He left and returned with a plate of porridge. I ate, no questions asked.

I was preparing for what was to come. Still, I couldn't ignore the time bomb about go off in our camp. One evening, I went to Luyu, who was washing clothes in her bucket.

"We need to talk," I said.

"Talk, then," she said, wringing out her rapa.

I leaned closer, ignoring the drops of water that hit my face. "I know."

"Know what?"

"About you and Fanasi."

She froze, her hands deep in the bucket's water. "Just you?"

"As far as I know."

"How?"

"I heard."

"Oh, we're not loud like you and Mwita."

"Why are you doing this?" I said. "Don't you know what . . ."

"We both want it," Luyu said. "And it's not as if Diti cares."

"Then why all the secrecy?"

She didn't say anything.

"If Diti finds out . . ."

"She won't," Luyu snapped, looking hard at me.

"Oh, I'm not going to tell her. You will. Luyu, we're all as close as you can get without living on top of each other. Fanasi and Mwita talk. If Mwita doesn't know, he soon will. Or Diti or Binta will catch you. What if you get pregnant? There are only two men who could be the father here."

We looked at each other and then burst out laughing.

"How did we end up here?" I asked after we got ourselves under control.

"I don't know," she said. "He's wonderful, Onye. It might be because I'm older but oh, the way he makes me feel."

"Luyu, listen to yourself. This is Diti's husband."

She sucked her teeth and rolled her eyes. Later on that night, I briefly woke up to hear Luyu sneak into Fanasi's tent. Soon after they were at it again. This would only come to a bad end.

Chapter 38

WE CAME TO ANOTHER TOWN AND DECIDED to go in for supplies.

"Papa Shee? What kind of name is that?" Luyu asked. She was standing too close to Fanasi. Or maybe Fanasi was standing too close to her. He always seemed to be no more than a few steps away from her these days. They were getting lax.

"I remember this town," Mwita said. He didn't look as if the memory was a good one. He looked at Luyu's map as she held the portable over her hand. It was hard to see in the sunshine. "We're not far from the beginning of the Seven Rivers Kingdom. This is one of the last towns we'll encounter that won't be . . . hostile to Okekes."

Not far from us a caravan of people traveled to the town, too. Several times during the day, we'd heard the sound of scooters. Once, the camels had grown extremely agitated, roaring and shaking their dusty hides. They'd been behaving strangely of late. The previous night, the camels woke us up when they started roaring at each other. They'd remained kneeling but they looked angry. They were having an argument. When we got to the town, they refused to go any closer. We'd had to leave them a mile back while we went to the town's market.

"Let's make this fast," I said, pulling my veil over my head. Mwita did the same.

There were all styles of dress and I heard several dialects of Sipo and Okeke and, yes, even Nuru. There weren't many Nuru but there were enough. I couldn't help staring at them with their straight black hair and yellow-brown skin and narrow noses. No freckled cheeks or thick lips or strange colored eyes, like Mwita's and mine. I was a little confused. I'd never imagined Nurus walking among free Okekes in peace.

"Are those Nurus?" Binta said a bit too loudly. The woman with what was probably her teenage son glanced at Binta, frowned, and moved away. Luyu elbowed Binta to shut up.

"What do you think?" Mwita asked me, leaning toward my ear.

"Let's just get what we need and get out of here," I said. "Those men over there are looking at me."

"I know. Stay close." Mwita and I were both attracting an audience.

A sack of pumpkin seeds, bread, salt, a bottle of palm wine, a new metal bucket, we managed to buy almost all we needed before the trouble started. There were plenty of nomads, so it wasn't our style of dress or our way of speaking. It was what it always was. We were looking at dried meat when we heard the wild yell from behind. Mwita instinctively grabbed me and Luyu who stood on his other side.

"*Eeeeewuuuuuu,*" an Okeke man shouted in a deep deep voice. "*Eeeewuuuuuu!*"

His voice vibrated in my head in an unnatural way. He wore black pants and a long black caftan. Several brown and white eagle feathers were stuck in his long thick dada hair. His dark skin glistened with sweat or oil. The people around him moved aside.

"Make way for him," a man said.

"Make way," a woman shouted.

You know what happens next. You know it because you've heard me speak of a similar incident. I still had the scar on my forehead from it. Was this the same town? No, but it might as well have been. Not much had changed since my mother had had to run with me, an infant, from a crowd of people throwing stones.

I don't know when they started hurling stones at Mwita and me. I was too in the moment, staring at the wild man who could put his voice in my head. A stone hit me in the chest. I focused my responding anger on that man, that witch doctor who had the nerve to not recognize a true sorcerer. I attacked him in the same way I'd attacked Aro years ago. Ripping and tearing. I heard the crowd gasp and someone screamed. I stayed focused on the man who'd started it. He had no idea what was happening to him because he didn't know the Mystic Points. All he knew were children's jujus, baby tricks. Mwita could have done away with him without blinking.

"What are you doing?!" I heard Binta scream. This brought me back to myself. I fell to my knees. "Do you all know who this *is!*" Binta shouted at the crowd. Across from us, the witch doctor collapsed. The woman beside him shrieked.

"They've killed our priest!" a man shouted, spittle flying from his mouth.

I saw it sailing through the air. I was stunned. Who would have the audacity throw a brick at a girl so beautiful that her father couldn't resist her? With such perfect aim? The brick smashed into Binta's forehead. I could see the white. Her skull was caved in, brain tissue exposed. She fell. I screamed and ran for her. I wasn't close enough. The crowd burst into motion. People running, throwing more bricks, stones. A man came at me and I kicked him and grabbed his neck and began to squeeze. Then Mwita was pulling and dragging me.

"Binta!" I screamed. Even from where I was, I could see people kicking her fallen body and then I saw a man take another brick and . . . oh, it's too horrible to describe. I screamed the words I'd spoken back in Jwahir's market. But I didn't want to show these people the worst of the West. I wanted to show them darkness. They were all blind and that's what I made them. The entire town. Men, women, children. I took the very ability that they chose not to use. Mostly everyone went silent. Some clawed at their eyes. Some still reached around trying to inflict violence on whoever they could touch. Children whimpered. Some people shouted things like, "What is this evil?" or "Ani save me!"

Bastards. Let them stumble around in the darkness.

We scrambled through the confused blind people to Binta. She was dead. They'd smashed her skull, punctured her chest, crushed her neck and her legs. I knelt down and put my hands on her. I searched, I listened. "Binta!" I shouted. Several of those stupid blind people answered me as they stumbled toward my voice. I ignored them. "Where are you? Binta?" I listened some more for her confused terrified spirit. But she was gone.

"Where is she?" I shrieked, sweat pouring down my face. I kept searching.

She'd left. Why did she leave when she knew I could bring her back? I wonder if she understood that bringing her back and healing her would probably have killed me.

Eventually, Fanasi nudged me aside and picked her up, Mwita helping to take her weight. We left the town blind as they'd always been. You must have heard rumors of the famous Town of the Sightless. It's no legend. Go to Papa Shee. See for yourself.

When the camels saw us carrying Binta's body, they roared and stamped their feet. We set her down and they sat around her in a protective circle. The next few days were a muddled blur. I know we somehow managed to pull ourselves together enough to move away from Papa Shee. Sandi agreed to carry Binta's body. I know that at some point, we spent a day digging a six-foot hole in the sand. We used our pots and pans. We buried our beloved friend there in the desert. Luyu read a prayer from the electronic file of the Great Book in her portable. Then we each took turns to say something about Binta.

"You know," I said when it was my turn. "Before she left, she poisoned her father. Put heart root in his tea and watched him drink it. She set herself free before leaving home. Ah, Binta. When you return to these lands, you'll rule the world."

Everyone just looked at me, still in shock that she was dead.

My headaches returned after we buried her but what did I care? Binta had had the same fate, death by stoning. What made me so special? As we walked, I made it a habit of flying above and returning to everyone whenever we decided to stop. Sandi carried my things. All I could think about was the fact that Binta had never known the loving touch of a man. The closest she'd come was that night in the tavern in Banza, when she'd been so brazen. And then because of me, defending me, she died.

Chapter 39

THERE'S A STORY IN THE GREAT BOOK about a boy destined to be Suntown's greatest chief. You know the story well. It's a Nuru favorite, no? You all tell it to your children when they're too young to see how ugly the story is. You hope the girls will want to be like Tia the good young woman and the boys like Zoubeir the Great. In the Great Book, their story was one of triumph and sacrifice. It's meant to make you feel safe. It's supposed to remind you that great things will always be protected and people meant for greatness are meant for greatness. This is all a lie. Here's how the story really happened:

Tia and Zoubeir were born on the same day in the same town. Tia's birth was no secret and when she came out a girl, her birth was nothing special. The child of two peasants, she was given a warm bath, many kisses, a naming ceremony. She was the second child in her family, but the first child had been a healthy boy, so she was welcome.

Zoubeir, on the other hand, was born in secret. Eleven months earlier, the Suntown chief noticed a woman dancing at a party. That night he had her to himself. Even this chief, who had four wives, could not get enough of a woman like this, so he sought her out and had her over and over until she became pregnant. Then he told his soldiers to kill her. There was a rule that decreed that the first son born out of wedlock to the chief must succeed him. The chief's father had avoided this rule by marrying every woman he bedded. When he died, he had over three hundred wives.

However, his son, the current chief, was arrogant. If he wanted a woman, why should he have to marry her first? Honestly, was this chief not the stupidest man on earth? Why couldn't he be happy with what he had? Why couldn't he focus on things other than his carnal needs? He was the chief, no? He should have been busy. Anyway, this woman was three months pregnant when she outran the soldiers sent to kill her. Eventually, she came to a small town where she gave birth to a son she named Zoubeir.

On the day of Zoubeir's and Tia's births, the midwife ran back and forth between their mothers' huts. They were born at the exact same time, but the midwife chose to stay with Zoubeir's mother because she had a feeling that this woman's child was a boy and the other woman's child was a girl.

No one but Zoubeir and his mother knew who he was. But people did sense something about him. He grew tall like his mother and loud-mouthed like his father. Zoubeir was a natural leader. Even at a young age, his classmates happily obeyed him. Tia, on the other hand, lived a quiet, sad life. Her father often beat her. And as she grew older, she grew lovelier and her father began to have eyes for her too. So Tia grew the opposite of Zoubeir, short and silent.

The two knew each other, for they lived on the same street. From the day they saw each other, there was an odd chemistry. Not love at first sight. I wouldn't even call it love. Just chemistry. Zoubeir would share his meals with Tia if they found themselves walking home together from school. She would knit him shirts and weave him rings from colored palm fiber. Sometimes they would sit and read together. The only time Zoubeir was quiet and motionless was when he was with Tia.

When they were both sixteen, there came news that the chief of Suntown was very ill. Zoubeir's mother knew there'd be trouble. People liked to gossip and speculate when a potential power shift was involved. News of Zoubeir possibly being the chief's bastard son soon reached the ailing chief. If only Zoubeir had lowered his head a bit or kept a quieter profile, he could've peacefully returned to Suntown when the chief died. It would have been easy for him to claim the throne.

The soldiers came before Zoubeir's mother could warn him. When they found Zoubeir, he was sitting under a tree beside Tia. The soldiers were cowards. They hid yards away and one of them brought his gun up. Tia sensed something. And right at that moment, she looked up and spotted the men behind the trees. Then she just knew. *Not him,* she thought. *He is special. He will make things better for all of us.*

"Get down!" she screamed, throwing herself over him. Of course she caught the bullet and Zoubeir did not. Tia's life was snuffed out by five more bullets as Zoubeir hid behind her body. He pushed her off him and ran, swift like his long-legged mother seventeen years before. Once he was running, not even bullets could catch him.

You know how the story ends. He escaped and went on to become the greatest chief Suntown ever had. He never built a shrine or a temple or even a shack in the name of Tia. In the Great Book, her name is never mentioned again. He never mused about her or even asked where she was buried. Tia was a virgin. She was beautiful. She was poor. And she was a girl. It was her duty to sacrifice her life for his.

I've always disliked this story. And since Binta's death, I've come to hate it.

Chapter 40

HER DEATH KEPT LUYU FROM FANASI'S hut for two weeks. And then one late night, I heard them enjoying each other again.

"Mwita," I said as quietly as I could. I turned to face him. "Mwita, wake up."

"Mmm?" he said his eyes still closed.

"You hear?" I said.

He listened, then he nodded.

"You know who it is?"

He nodded.

"How long have you known?" I asked.

"What does it matter?"

I sighed.

"He's a man, Onye."

I frowned. "So? What about Diti?"

"What of her? I don't see her sneaking in there."

"It's not that simple. There's been enough pain."

"The pain has only just begun," Mwita said, growing serious. "Let Luyu and Fanasi find joy while they can." He took my braid in his hand.

"So if you and I have a fight," I said. "Would you . . ."

"It's different with us," he said.

We listened for a while longer and then I heard something else. I cursed. Mwita and I got to our feet. We crawled out just in time to see it happen. Diti pulled up her red rapa, clutching the knot on the side as she strode to Fanasi's tent. She walked swiftly. Too swiftly for me or Mwita to catch her and at least prevent her from seeing the full sight of Luyu, sweating and naked, straddling an equally sweating naked Fanasi. He was clutching Luyu as he sucked her nipple.

When Fanasi saw Diti over Luyu's shoulder, he was so shocked that he clamped his teeth down on Luyu's nipple. She screamed and Fanasi immediately released his teeth, terrified that he'd hurt Luyu and horrified that Diti was standing there watching. Diti's face contorted in a way that I'd never seen. Then she grabbed her face, digging her nails into her cheeks and let out a terrible shriek. The camels jumped up faster than I've ever seen any camel do and ran off.

"What . . . look at you! Binta's dead! I'm dead . . . We're all going to die and you do this?" Diti yelled. She fell to her knees sobbing. Fanasi carefully gave Luyu a rapa to cover herself, touching her breast briefly to see the damage that he did. He pulled a rapa around his waist and cautiously watched Diti as he climbed out of the tent. Luyu quickly followed. I gave her a dirty look. I helped Diti up and walked her away from everyone.

"How long?" Diti asked after a while.

"Weeks. Before . . . Papa Shee."

"Why didn't you tell me, eh?" She sat down in the sand and sobbed.

"This is life," I said. "It doesn't always go the way you think it will."

"Ugh! Did you see them? Did you *smell* them?" She stood up. "Let's go back."

"Wait a while," I said. "Calm yourself."

"I don't *want* to be calm. Did they look calm to you?" She flashed a look at me.

Seeing what she was thinking in her eyes, I held up my finger. "Hold your tongue," I said firmly. "Hold your blame, eh?" When things grew unbearable, she always blamed me. My temples throbbed. I stood up. Right in front of her, not caring what she saw, I changed into a vulture. I hopped from my clothes, looked up into Diti's shocked face, squawked at her, and flew off. A wind gusted in from the west. I rode it, exhilarated. It was so windy that for a moment, I wondered if a dust storm was coming.

I passed an owl. It was flying so fast southeast, fighting the wind, that it barely gave me a look. Below, I spotted the camels. I thought about flying down to greet them but it seemed they were having a private discussion. I flew for three hours. I never asked what exactly was said when Diti went back to everyone. I didn't care. I landed where I'd left my clothes, glad Diti didn't take them with her. They'd blown several yards away.

The first thing I noticed when I returned to camp was that only one of the camels was back. Sandi. "Where are the others?" I asked her. She only looked at me. Everyone else sat around the rock fire, except Mwita who was standing looking bothered. Diti's eyes were red and glassy. Luyu looked smug. Fanasi sat near Luyu, holding a wet cloth over the side of his face. I frowned.

"Have you all settled it?" I said.

"I am the witness," Mwita said. "Diti has spoken the words of divorce to Fanasi . . . after she tried to scratch his face off."

"If I were a man, you'd be dead," Diti growled at Fanasi.

"If you were a man, you wouldn't be in this situation," Fanasi shot back.

"Maybe . . . maybe I shouldn't have allowed any of you to come," I said. They all turned to me. "Maybe it should have been just Mwita and me, neither of us has anything to lose. But you all . . . Binta . . ."

"Yeah, well, it's too late, don't you think?" Diti snapped.

I pressed my lips together but I didn't look away.

"Diti . . ." Mwita said. He swallowed his words and looked away.

"What?" Diti snapped. "Go on, say what you wish to say for once."

"Shut up!" Mwita shouted above the moan of the wind. Diti gasped utterly shocked. "What is *wrong* with you?" Mwita said. "This man followed you . . . all the way out here! I have *no* idea why. You're a child. You're spoiled and coddled. His actions are nothing special to you! You have the nerve to *expect* them. Fine. But then you decide to reject him. You somehow even managed to throw other men in his face. And when he decided that he didn't want to be treated this way and accepted another strong beautiful woman, you start tearing at people's hair like some evil angry spirit . . ."

"*I* am the one who's been betrayed!" She glared at me as she said this.

"Yes, yes, we've been listening to you cry about betrayal for hours now. Look at what you've done to Fanasi's face. If his wounds get infected, you'll blame Onyesonwu or Luyu. So much stupid, *stupid* childish bickering. We're on a journey to the ugliest place on earth.

"We've tasted the ugliness. We *lost* Binta! You saw what they did to her. Maintain your perspective! Diti, if you want Fanasi and Fanasi wants you, go and have happy intercourse. Do it often and with passion and joy. Luyu, the same. If you want to enjoy Fanasi, do so for Ani's sake! Figure something out, while you still can!

"Onyesonwu was trying to *help* by breaking that juju. She suffered to *help* you. Be grateful! And fine, we are ugly to you; you were raised to think so. Your minds are split between seeing us as your friends and seeing us as unnatural. That's the way it is. But *learn to curb your tongues*. And *remember,* remember, remember why we're out here." He turned and walked away, breathing hard. None of us had anything to add.

That night, Diti slept alone, though I doubt she slept at all. And Luyu and Fanasi spent the first full but quiet night together in Fanasi's tent. And Mwita and I found comfort in each other's bodies well into the night. Come morning, the sun was blotted out by an approaching wall of sand.

Chapter 41

I WAS THE FIRST TO WAKE UP. When I crawled out of my tent, Sandi was standing there waiting for me. She groaned deep in her throat as I leaned close to her, inhaling the freshness of her fur. "You left your people to stay with us, didn't you?" I asked. I yawned and looked to the west. My stomach dropped. "Mwita! Come out here right *now!*"

He scrambled out and looked at the sky. "I should have known," he said. "I knew but I was distracted."

"We all were," I said.

We packed and secured our things, using our tents and rapas to protect our flesh. We tied our faces with cloth and tied our veils over our eyes. Then we dug down into the sand and huddled together with our backs to the wind, linking arms and hanging on to Sandi's fur. The sandstorm hit so hard that I couldn't tell which way the wind was moving. It was as if the storm settled on us from the sky.

The sand slapped and bit at our clothes. I'd wrapped Sandi's muzzle and eyes with thick rapa cloth but I worried about her hide. Beside me, Diti was weeping and Fanasi was trying to comfort her. Mwita and I leaned close to each other.

"Have you heard of the Red People?" Mwita said into my ear.

I shook my head.

"People of the sand. Only stories . . . they travel in a giant dust storm."
He shook his head. It was too noisy to speak.

An hour passed. The storm remained. My muscles began to cramp
from the strain of holding on. Noise, stinging wind, and no end in sight.
Storms didn't last nearly this long when I was with my mother. They came
fast and hard and left just as quickly. Yet another half hour passed.

Then, finally, the wind and the sand died. Just like that. We coughed
and cursed in the sudden silence. I rolled to the side, the exposed parts of
my skin raw and my muscles exhausted. Sandi groaned, slowly standing
up. She shook the sand from her hide, spraying sand about. We all weakly
complained. The sun shone down into the giant brown funnel of sand and
wind. The eye of the storm. It had to be miles wide.

They came from all around us, draped from head to toe in deep red
garments, as were their camels. All I could see were their eyes. One of them
came up to us on a camel. This person rode with a small child in front, a
toddler. The child giggled.

"Onyesonwu," the person said in rich voice. A woman.

I held my chin up. "I am." I slowly stood.

"Which of you is her husband, Mwita?" she asked in Sipo.

He didn't bother arguing with the title. "I am," Mwita said.

The child said something that could have been another language or
toddler-speak.

"Do you know who we are?" the woman asked.

"You're the Red People, the Vah. In the West, I heard many stories
about you all," Mwita said.

"You speak more like an easterner."

"I grew up in the West, then the East. We currently are heading back
West."

"Yes, so I've been told," the woman said, turning to me.

A man behind her spoke in a language I couldn't understand. The
woman responded and everyone else went into motion, moving away, getting off their camels, and bringing down their burdens. They took off their
veils. I saw why they were called the Red People. Their skin was red as
palm oil. Their reddish brown hair was shaved close, except for the young
children who wore their hair in large bushy dreadlocks.

The woman took off her veil. Unlike the others, she had a gold ring in her nose, two more in her ears, and one in her eyebrow. The toddler leaped off the camel with unexpected agility. The child threw off her veil, exposing her dreadlocks. I noticed that the little girl also had a gold ring in her eyebrow.

"Who are you?" the woman asked the others as she dismounted her camel.

"Fanasi."

"Diti."

"Luyu."

She nodded and looked at Sandi. She grinned. "I know you."

Sandi made a sound that I'd never heard before. A sort of purring guttural noise. She rubbed her muzzle against the woman's cheek and the woman chuckled. "You look well, too," she said.

"Who are you all?" Luyu asked. "Mwita knows of you, but I don't."

The woman looked Luyu up and down and Luyu looked back at her. I was reminded of the way she stood up to the Ada during our Eleventh Rite. Luyu had never respected authority.

"Luyu," the woman said. "I am Chieftess Sessa. That over there is the other one, Chief Usson." She motioned to a man equally adorned with rings standing beside his camel.

"Other what?" Luyu asked.

"You ask the wrong questions," Chieftess Sessa said. "You've met us at a good time. This is where we'll stay till the moon is pregnant." She looked at the wall of dust and grinned. "You're welcome to stay . . . if you like." She walked away, leaving us to decide. Around us, the Vah set up tents homier than ours. They were made from shiny stretched goatskin and were much bigger and higher. I saw capture stations, but not one computer.

"The next 'pregnant moon' is three weeks from now!" Luyu said.

"What is with these people?" Fanasi asked. "Why do they look like that? Like they eat, drink, and bathe in palm oil and cactus candy. It's bizarre."

Mwita sucked his teeth, annoyed.

"Who knows?" Luyu said. "What about their 'friend' the dust storm?"

"It travels with them," Mwita said.

"Why?"

He shrugged. "Why are they red?"

Luyu screeched and jumped as a white-brown sparrow hit her in the back of the head. The bird fell to the ground, righted itself and stood there confused.

"Leave it alone," Mwita said. "It'll be okay."

"I didn't plan to do anything else," Luyu said, staring at the bird.

"We can't stay here," Diti said.

"We have a choice?" I snapped. "Do *you* want to try getting through that storm?"

We set our tents up where we'd had them before the storm came. Except Luyu. She would stay with Fanasi.

For the first few hours, the Vah constructed their homes like the expert nomads they were. The sun was setting and the desert, even in the eye of the storm, was cooling down, but I refrained from building a rock fire. Who knew how these people reacted to juju?

We kept to ourselves and within ourselves we kept to ourselves more. Diti hid in her tent as did Fanasi and Luyu. Mwita and I, however, sat outside in front of ours, not wanting to look too antisocial. But while the Vah set up, even the children ignored us.

After dark, people began to socialize. I felt silly. Every tent I could see glowed with the light of a rock fire. Chieftess Sessa, Chief Usson, and an old man came to greet us. The old man's face was etched with the kind of wrinkles that come with age and wind. I wouldn't be surprised if there were grains of sand trapped forever inside those wrinkles. He looked at me with scrutiny. *He* made me more nervous than the angry-looking and silent Chief Usson.

"You can't look me in the eye, child?" the old man asked in a low gruff voice.

There was something about him that I found very agitating. Before I could respond, Chieftess Sessa said, "We came to invite you all to our settling feast."

"It's an invitation and an order," the old man said firmly.

Chieftess Sessa continued, "Wear your best clothes if you have any." She paused, motioning to the old man. "This is Ssaiku. You will undoubtedly come to know him well as the days pass. Welcome to Ssolu, our moving village."

Chief Usson gave all of us a prolonged angry glare and the old man Ssaiku eyed me and then Mwita before leaving our camp.

"These people are so strange," Fanasi said, when the three were gone.

"I don't have anything good to wear," Diti complained.

Luyu rolled her eyes.

"Must all their names start with *S* or have *S*'s in them? You'd think they were descendants of snakes," Fanasi said.

"That's the sound that travels best, the *ssss* sound. They live in all this noise from the dust storm, so it makes sense," Mwita said, going into our tent.

"Mwita, did you notice that old man?" I asked, joining him. "I can't recall his name."

"Ssaiku," Mwita said. "You should take note of him."

"Why? You think he'll be trouble?" I asked. "I don't like him at all."

"What about Chief Usson?" Mwita asked. "He looked pretty angry."

I shook my head, "He probably always frowns. It's that old man I don't like."

"That's because he's a sorcerer like you, Onye," Mwita said. He laughed bitterly to himself and grumbled something.

"Eh?" I said, frowning. "What did you say?"

He turned back to me and cocked his head. "How in Ani's name is it that I can tell and you can't?" He paused again. "How is it that . . ." He cursed and turned away.

"Mwita," I said loudly, taking his arm. He didn't pull it away, though I purposely pressed my nails into his flesh. "Finish your thought."

He brought his face close to mine. "*I* should be the sorcerer, *you* should be the healer. That's how it's always been between a man and woman."

"Well, it's *not* you," I hissed trying to keep my voice down. "You aren't the one whose mother in a wasteland of desperation asked all the powers of the earth to make her daughter a sorcerer. You aren't the one born from *rape*. You came from love, remember? *YOU* aren't the one the Nuru Seer prophesied would do something so drastic that she'll be *dragged out before a screaming crowd of Nurus, buried to her neck and stoned until she is dead!*"

He grabbed my shoulders, his left eye twitching. "What?" he whispered. "You . . ."

We stared at each other.

"That's . . . my fate," I said. I hadn't meant to tell him this way. Not at all. "Why would I *choose* that? I've been fighting from the day I was born. Yet you talk as if I took something precious from you."

"Hey, Onye?" Luyu called from her tent. "You should wear that rapa and top that woman gave you in Banza."

"That's a good idea," I called back, still facing Mwita.

I heard Fanasi playfully say, "Come here."

Luyu giggled.

Mwita left our tent. I poked my head out about to call him back. But he walked fast, passing people without greeting them, his head unveiled, his chin to his chest.

Those old beliefs about the worth and fate of men and women, that was the only thing that I didn't like about Mwita. Who was he to think he was entitled to be the center of things just because he was male? This had been a problem with us since we'd met. Again, I think of the story of Tia and Zoubeir. I despise that story.

Chapter 42

I WOKE UP TWO HOURS LATER WITH TEARS DRIED ON MY FACE. Music was playing from somewhere. "Get up," Luyu said, shaking me. "What's wrong with you?"

"Nothing," I muttered groggily. "Tired."

"It's time for the feast." She wore her best purple rapa and blue top. They were a little battered but she'd rebraided her cornrows into a spiral and put on earrings. She smelled of the scented oil she, Diti, and Binta used to drown themselves in back home. I bit my lip, thinking about Binta.

"You're not dressed!" Luyu said. "I'll get some water and a cloth. I don't know where these people bathe—there are always people around."

I slowly sat up, trying to shake off the deep sleep I'd been in. I touched my long braid. It was full of sand from the storm. I was unbraiding it when Luyu returned with a pot of warm water. "You're going to wear your hair down?" she asked.

"I might as well," I mumbled. "No time to wash it."

"Wake up," she said, lightly smacking my cheek. "This is going to be fun."

"Have you seen Mwita?"

"No," Luyu said.

I put on my outfit from Banza, fully aware that its many colors would attract attention that I wasn't in the mood for. I brushed out my thick long hair and used some of the warm water to get it to lie down. When I came out of my tent, Luyu was there to spray me with scented oil. "There," she said. "You look *and* smell lovely." But I noticed her eyes grace my face and sand-colored hair. The *Ewu*-born will always be *Ewu*.

Fanasi wore the brown pants and stained white shirt I saw him wear almost every day, but he'd shaved his face and head. This brought out his high cheekbones and long neck. Diti wore a blue rapa and top that I hadn't seen her wear before. Fanasi might have bought it for her in Banza. She'd combed out her large Afro and patted it into a perfect circle. I sucked my teeth when I noticed Fanasi fighting not to look at Diti and hungrily looking at Luyu. He was the most confused man I'd ever seen.

"Okay," Luyu said, leading the way. "Let's go."

As we walked, I wondered how long these people had been a nomadic tribe. My guess was a long, long time. Their tents were set up in a matter of hours and were no less comfortable than houses, even having floors made of the furry pelts of some sort of brown animal.

They carried their plants in large sacks of a type of fragrant substance called soil. And they all used minor juju to build fires, keep insects away, and so on. The Vah also had schools. The only thing they didn't have were many books. Too heavy. But they had a few for the sake of learning to read. Some of this I saw on the way to the feast. But most of it I learned during our stay.

It was a grand gathering, a large feast set up in the center. A band played guitars and sang. Everyone was dressed in their finest. The style was simple: red pants and shirts for men and combinations of red dresses for the women. Some of the women's dresses had beads woven into the hems and cuffs, others were cut to look jagged and so on.

By this time in my life, I saw myself through Mwita's eyes. I was beautiful. That is one of the greatest gifts Mwita gave me. I could never have seen myself as beautiful without his help. However, I knew that when I looked at these people, young, old, man, woman, child, with their red-brown skin, brown eyes, and graceful motions, they were the most beautiful people I'd ever seen. They moved like gazelles, even the old ones. And the men weren't shy. They made direct eye contact right away and smiled very easily. Beautiful, beautiful people.

"Welcome," a young man said, taking Diti's hand. She grinned very wide.

"Welcome," another young man said, pushing his way to Luyu.

The two of them were welcomed by several young men. Fanasi was welcomed by young women but he was too busy watching Diti and Luyu. When people simply nodded at me, keeping their distance, I wondered if even these isolated and protected people demonized the *Ewu*-born.

I was forced to throw this idea away when we got to our seats. There was Mwita, sitting beside a Vah woman. They were sitting too close for my liking. She said something to him and he smiled. Even sitting I could see that she had the longest legs I'd ever seen, long and muscled running legs like Zoubeir's mother in the old story. My heart flipped. Back home, I'd heard rumors about Mwita dealing with older women. I'd never really asked him if they were true but I suspected there was some truth to them. This woman was maybe thirty-five. And like all the other Vah people, she was stunning. She smiled at me, deep dimples piercing each cheek. When she stood, she was taller than me. Mwita stood up with her.

"Welcome, Onyesonwu," the woman said, tapping her chest. She looked me over. I looked her over, too. I felt the same sort of irritation that I felt with Ssaiku. This woman was also a sorcerer. *But she's apprenticed*, I realized I knew. *Ssaiku's apprentice*. She wore a dress with no sleeves, showing her muscled arms. It had a neckline that plunged low, showing off her large bosom. There were symbols etched into both of her biceps and on the swells of her breasts.

"Thank you," I said. Behind me, the others were welcomed and told to sit.

"I am Ting," she said.

Chief Usson stepped into the circle and the music immediately stopped.

"Now that our guests have arrived, let us settle," he said. Without his frown, Chief Usson was quite engaging. He had one of those voices that made people listen.

Ting took my hand. "Sit," she said. Her thumbnail brushed the palm of my hand. It was almost an inch long and sharp as a knife, the tip tinted bluish black. She sat beside me, Mwita on my other side.

"Please welcome our guests, Diti, Fanasi, Luyu, Mwita, and Onye-sonwu." Whispers flew through the gathering. "Yes, yes, we all know of this woman, the she-wizard, and her man." Chief Usson motioned for us to stand. Before so many eyes, I felt my face grow warm. *She-wizard?* I thought. *What kind of title is that?*

"Welcome," Chief Usson said grandiosely.

"Welcome," everyone else murmured. Then from somewhere some-one started hissing. The hiss spread through the crowd. I glanced at Ting, worried.

"It's all right," she said.

It was some sort of ritual. People smiled as they hissed. I relaxed. Chief-tess Sessa got up and stood next to Chief Usson. Together they recited some-thing in a language that I didn't know. The words had a lot of *S* and *Ah* sounds. Fanasi was right. If a snake could speak, it would sound like this. When they finished reciting, people jumped to their feet, cloths in hand.

"Take," a young boy said, handing all five of us similar cloths. The cloths were thin but stiff with proofing gel. The band began to play.

"Come," Ting said taking my hand and Mwita's. Two young men ap-proached Diti and another two Luyu, pulling them toward the giant ban-quet of food. Two women took Fanasi's hands, too. It was happy chaos, as people jostled and grabbed and filled their cloths with food. It seemed to be some sort of game, for there was a lot of laughter.

A woman pushed past me and accidentally brushed my arm. A tiny blue spark popped off me and the woman yelped, jumping away. Sev-eral other people paused to stare. The woman didn't seem angry but she wouldn't meet my eyes as she mumbled, "Sorry, Onyesonwu. Sorry," and hustled away from me.

I looked at Ting with wide eyes. "What . . ."

"Let me," Ting said, taking my cloth.

"No, I can . . ."

"Just wait here," she said firmly. "Do you eat meat?"

"Of course."

She nodded and went to the banquet with Mwita. While I waited, two men passed too close to me. Again there were tiny sparks and both men seemed to experience a brief jolt of pain.

"Sorry," I said holding my hands up.

"No," one of them said, backing away thinking I was going to touch him again. "We are sorry." It was both bizarre and annoying.

By the time we returned to our spot, Diti and Luyu had accumulated more men. All were so lovely that Luyu's face looked as if it would break from the size of her smile. A man with thick luscious lips was feeding Diti a cut of roasted rabbit. Fanasi was also surrounded. The women vied for his attention. He was so busy answering their thousands of questions that he couldn't eat or see what Diti and Luyu were doing.

Though none sat with Mwita, several women, young and old, openly stared at him, and even made way for him at the banquet. Every man stopped and greeted him warmly, some even shaking his hand. Men and boys only stole glances at me when they thought I wasn't looking. And the women and girls openly avoided me. But there was one who couldn't resist.

"That's Eyess," Ting said smiling, as the toddler came running to me and tried to take my hand. I tried to yank it away before she could touch me but she was too fast. She snatched my hand, almost making me drop my cloth of food. Large sparks popped. But she only laughed. The little girl who'd been riding with Chieftess Sessa seemed to be immune to whatever afflicted me. She said something to me in the Vah language.

"She does not know Ssufi, Eyess," Ting told her. "Speak in Sipo or Okeke."

"You look strange," the little girl said in Okeke.

I laughed. "I know."

"I like it," she said. "Is your mother a camel?"

"No, my mother is human."

"Then why does your camel tell me she takes care of you?"

"Eyess can hear them," Ting explained. "She was born with the ability. That's why she talks so well for a three-year-old. She's been talking all her life to everything."

Something caught the little girl's eye. "Be back!" she said running off.

"Whose is she?" I asked.

"Chieftess Sessa and Chief Usson's," Ting said.

"So Chieftess Sessa and Chief Usson are married, then?"

"Goodness no," Ting said. "Two chiefs can't be married. That is Chieftess Sessa's husband there." She motioned to a man handing Eyess a small bundle of food. The little girl grabbed the food, kissed his knees, and disappeared again among people's legs.

"Oh," I said.

"That's Chief Usson's wife." She pointed to a plump woman sitting with some other women. We sat down and unrolled our food. Mwita was already eating. He seemed to have picked up the way of the Vah when it came to eating because he was shoveling food into his mouth with his hands and eating with his mouth open. I unrolled my cloth and looked at what Ting had gathered. Everything was mixed together and the sight of it made me lose my appetite. I've never liked my food to mix. I picked at a piece of fried lizard egg as I pushed a slice of green cactus aside with my finger.

"So where is . . . your Master? Doesn't he eat?" I asked after a while.

"Do you eat?" she said, looking at my still full cloth.

"I'm not very hungry."

"Mwita seems comfortable."

We both looked at him. He'd finished everything in his cloth and was getting up for more. He met my eyes. "Do you want me to get you something?" he asked.

I shook my head. Eyess came and plopped herself beside me. She grinned and unrolled her meal and started eating ravenously.

"So is it true?" Ting asked.

"What?"

"Mwita won't tell me anything. He says to ask you," she said. "Rumor had it that you blanketed a town in a black mist after they tried to harm you. That you turned their water to bile. And you're really a ghost sent to the lands to wash away our evils."

I laughed, "Where did you hear all this?"

"Travelers," she said. "In towns some of us visit for supplies. On the wind."

"Everyone knows," Eyess added.

"What do you think, Ting?" I asked.

"I think it's nonsense . . . most of it." She winked.

"Ting, why can't people touch me here?" I smiled. "Other than you and Eyess?"

"Don't take offense," she said, looking away.

I continued looking at her, waiting for her to say more. When she didn't, I just shrugged. I wasn't offended. Not really. "What are those?" I asked to change the subject. I pointed at the markings on her biceps and the swells of her breasts. The ones on her breasts were circles with a series of loops and swirls inside them. On her left bicep was what looked like the shadow of some sort of bird of prey. On the right was a cross surrounded by tiny circles and squares.

"Can't you read Vai, Bassa, Menda, and Nsibidi?" she asked.

I shook my head. "I know of Nsibidi. A building in Jwahir is decorated with it."

"The House of Osugbo," she said, nodding. "Ssaiku told me of it. Those aren't decorations. You'd know if you'd been apprenticed longer."

"Well, that couldn't be helped, could it?" I said, annoyed.

"Guess not," she said. "I gave these markings to myself. Writing scripts are my center."

"Center?"

"What I'm most gifted at," she said. "It becomes clearest around when you hit thirty. I can't tell you exactly what my markings mean, not in words. They changed my life, each in their own needed way. This one here is a vulture, I can tell you that." She met my eyes as she gnawed on a rabbit bone.

I decided to change the subject. "So how long have you been in training?"

The band started playing a song that Eyess apparently loved. She jumped up and ran to the musicians, weaving around people with that gazellelike nimbleness. When she got to the band, she started gleefully dancing. Ting and I watched for a moment, smiling.

"Since I was eight years old," Ting said turning to me.

"You passed your initiation that young?" I asked

She nodded.

"So you know how you . . ."

"I'll die an old satisfied woman, not far from here," she said.

Envy is a painful emotion.

"I'm sorry," she said. "I don't mean to gloat."

"I know," I said, my voice strained.

"Fate is cold and cruel."

I nodded.

"Your fate is in the West, I know. Ssaiku knows more," she said. "He usually doesn't come to the feast. I'll take you to him when you and Mwita are finished."

Mwita returned carrying three cloths. He handed me one. I unrolled it. In it was roasted rabbit. He handed me another full of cactus candy. I smiled at him.

"Always," he said, sitting down beside me, his shoulder touching mine.

"Ah, you are strange," Ting said, when I began to eat.

"You haven't seen anything yet," I said, my mouth full.

She looked from me to Mwita and then narrowed her eyes. "So you haven't completed training?"

I shook my head, refusing to meet her eyes.

"Don't worry about your camp," Mwita finally said.

"How can I be sure?" she asked. "Ssaiku won't even allow me to be alone with a man. You both must know about the woman who . . ."

"We know," we both said.

After eating, we left Diti, Luyu, and Fanasi behind. They didn't notice. Ssaiku's tent was large and airy. It was made from a material that was black but let the breeze right in. He sat on a wicker chair, a tiny book in his hands. "Ting, bring them palm wine," he said, putting his book down. "Mwita, wasn't I right?" he asked, motioning for us to sit.

"Very," he replied, going to the tent's corner and getting two round sitting mats. "It was indeed the most delicious meal I've ever had."

I looked at Mwita and frowned, sitting on the mat Mwita set down for me.

"You'll sleep well tonight," Ssaiku said.

"We thank you for your hospitality," Mwita said.

"As I already told you, it's the least we can do."

Ting returned managing glasses of palm wine on a tray. She handed the first to Ssaiku, then to Mwita and then to me. She only touched the glasses with her right hand. I almost laughed. Ting was the last person I'd have taken to be so traditional. But then again, Ssaiku was her Master and if he was anything like Aro, he expected this. She sat beside me, a small smile on her face as if anticipating an interesting discussion.

"Look at me, Onyesonwu," he said. "I want a good look at your face."

"Why?" I asked, but I looked at him. He didn't answer. I withstood his inspection.

"You usually braid your hair?" he asked.

I nodded.

"Stop," he said. "Tie it with a piece of palm fiber or string, but no more braiding from this point on." He sat back. "You're both so strange to look at. I know Nuru and I know Okeke. The *Ewu*-born make no sense to my eyes. Eh, Ani is testing me again."

Ting snickered, and Ssaiku gave her a sharp look.

"I'm sorry, *Ogasse*," she said, still smiling. "You're doing it again."

Ssaiku looked very annoyed. Ting wasn't frightened by this. As I've said, one's Master has a closer relationship to an apprentice than the apprentice's father. If there is no push and pull, no testing of nerves on both sides, it wouldn't be a true apprenticeship.

"You told me to tell you whenever you do it, *Ogasse*," Ting continued.

Ssaiku took a deep breath. "My student is right," he finally said. "Understand, I never believed the one I was to teach would be this long-legged . . . girl. But it was written. Since then I promised to taper my assumptions. There's never been an *Ewu* sorcerer. But it has been asked. So it's not because Ani is testing us that it's so, it is merely so."

"Well said," Ting said, pleased.

"What makes sense is no longer necessarily what should be," Mwita said, finishing his palm wine and looking at me. I fought hard not to roll my eyes.

"Right. Mwita, you understand me best here," Ssaiku said. "Now, it's no accident that you're here. I was told to find and take you in. I'm a sorcerer who's much much older than he looks. I come from a long line of chosen keepers, the keepers of this moving village, Ssolu. I maintain the dust storm that protects it."

"You're maintaining it right now?" I asked.

"It's simply juju for me, as it will be for Ting," he said. "Now, as I said, I was told to find you. There's a part of your training that you must complete. You'll need help."

I frowned. "Who . . . who told you to find me?"

"Sola," he said.

My eyes widened. Sola, the white-skinned man in black whom I'd met twice in the dust storm. I could still hear his words that first time we met for my initiation, "I must have *you* killed." Then he'd shown me my death.

I shuddered. "You *know* him?" I asked.

"Of course."

It had never occurred to me that they were all connected. All the old ones. I thought about how the last time I'd met with Sola, just before leaving Jwahir, Aro sat beside him instead of me, as if Sola were his brother and I, Aro's daughter. "What about Aro?" I asked.

"I know Aro well. Have known him a long, long time."

"Did he speak of me?" I asked. My heart quickened.

"No. He didn't mention you. He is your Master?"

"Yes," I said, disappointed. I hadn't realized how much I missed Aro.

"Ah, it becomes clear now," he said, nodding. "I was having trouble putting my finger on what it was." He looked at Mwita. Ting looked at Mwita too, as if trying to see what her Master had just realized. "And *you* are his other child," Ssaiku said.

"I guess you can say that," Mwita said. "But I was apprenticed to another before."

"Aro didn't ask anything about us? Say anything?" I asked, confused.

"No." There was a flutter in the room as a large brown parrot flew into the tent and landed on a chair. It squawked and shook its head.

"Dizzy birds," Ting said. "They're always falling into Ssolu."

"Go back to the celebration," Ssaiku told us. "Enjoy yourselves. In ten days, the women will Hold Conversation with Ani. Onyesonwu, you will go with them."

I almost laughed. I hadn't Held Conversation with Ani since I was a child. I didn't believe in Ani. I held in my cynicism, though. It really didn't matter. When we got back to the celebration, things were just heating up. The band was playing a song that everyone knew the words to. Eyess danced for everyone as she sang loudly. I think I'd have been like her if I hadn't been born an outcast.

"What do you think will happen?" Mwita asked me as we stood among all the singing people. I glimpsed Luyu standing on the other side of the circle with two men. Both had their arms around her waist. I didn't see Diti or Fanasi.

"No idea," I said. "I was about to ask you the same thing, since naturally you should know everything."

He sighed loudly and rolled his eyes. "You don't listen," he said.

"Onyesonwu!" Eyess shouted. I jumped at the sound of my name. Everyone turned. "Come sing with us!"

I smiled embarrassed, shaking my head and putting up my hands. "It's okay," I said backing away. "I-I don't know any of your songs."

"Please come sing," Eyess begged.

"Why don't you sing one of your own songs then," Mwita said loudly.

I glared at him and he smiled smugly.

"Yes!" Eyess exclaimed. "Sing for us!"

Everyone quieted as she led me to the circle's center. People avoided touching me as I passed. I stood there, aware of all eyes on me.

"Sing us a song from your home," Eyess said.

"I was raised in Jwahir," I said, when I realized I couldn't sneak away. "But I'm from the desert. That's my home." I paused. "I sing this to the land when it is content."

I opened my mouth, closed my eyes, and sang the song that I'd learned from the desert when I was three years old. Everyone oohed and ahhed when the brown parrot I'd seen in Ssaiku's tent came and landed on my shoulder. I kept singing. The sweet sound and vibration coming from my throat radiated through the rest of my body. It smoothed away my anxieties and sadness. For the moment. When I finished, everyone was silent.

Then people started hissing and clapping praise. The noise startled the bird on my shoulder and it flew away. Eyess threw her arms around my leg, looking up at me with admiration. Sparks flew from her arms and several people jumped back, muttering mild exclamations. The musicians started playing again, and I quickly left the center of the circle.

"Beautiful," people said as I passed.

"I'll sleep well tonight!"

"Ani blesses you a thousand times."

If they touched me they experienced pain, yet they heaped praise on me like I was their chief's long lost daughter.

"Oh!" Eyess exclaimed, hearing the band start a tune she couldn't resist. She ran back to the circle where she wiggled a dance that made everyone laugh. Mwita put his arm around my waist. It never felt so good.

"That was . . . fun," I said as we walked back to our tent.

"Works every time," Mwita said. He touched my bushy hair. "This hair."

"I know," I said. "I'm going to use a long piece of palm fiber and loop it around all the way to the bottom. That won't be too different from braiding it."

"It's not that," he said. I waited but he didn't say more, which was fine. He didn't have to. I felt it, too. I'd felt it as soon as Ssaiku told me what he wanted me to do. Like I was all . . . charged up. Something was going to happen when I went on that retreat.

When we got to our camp, we found only Fanasi. He was sitting before the dwindling rock fire, staring at the glowing stone. A bottle of palm wine sat between his legs.

"Where is . . ."

"I have no idea, Onye," he said, slurring his words. "Both have deserted me."

Mwita patted him on the shoulder and went into our tent. I sat beside Fanasi. He reeked of palm wine. "They'll be back, I'm sure," I said.

"You and Mwita," he said after a while. "You're the true thing. I'll never have that. Just wanted Diti, some land, babies. Look at me now. My father would spit."

"They'll come back," I said, again.

"I can't have them both," he said. "And looks like I can't have even one. Stupid. Shouldn't have come here. I want to go home."

I looked at him, irritated. "This place is full of beautiful women who will eagerly have you," I said, getting up. "Go find and bed one and stop sulking."

Mwita was in our tent lying on his back when I entered. "Good advice," he said. "All he needs is another woman to mess up his head even more."

I sucked my teeth. "He shouldn't have chosen Luyu," I snapped. "Didn't I say this? Luyu likes *men,* not one man. This couldn't have been more predictable."

"You blame him now? Diti refused him even after the juju was broken."

"What do you mean 'even after'? Do you know what the pain from that juju is like? It's horrible! And we've been raised to feel that it's wrong to open our legs, even when we want to. We weren't brought up to be free as . . . as *you* were." I paused. "When you were with all those older women, women like Ting, who criticized you?"

Mwita narrowed his eyes at me. "That very first time, you would have happily opened your legs to me if it weren't for that juju. There were no Jwahir rules for women holding *you* back."

"Don't change the subject."

Mwita laughed.

"Did you have intercourse with Ting?"

"What?"

"I know you and I think I know her."

Mwita only shook his head, lying back down, and putting his hands behind his head. I took off my celebration clothes and wrapped myself in my old yellow rapa. I was leaving the tent when I felt a tug at my rapa, almost pulling the thing off.

"Wait," Mwita said. "Where are you going?"

"To wash," I said. We'd set up Luyu's tent as a place to bathe. We didn't have the heart to use Binta's.

"Did you do it?" I finally asked. "With those other women before me?"

"Why does it matter?"

"It just does. Did you?"

"You're not the first woman I've had intercourse with."

I sighed. I'd known. It made no difference. My worry was about Ting. "Where did you go when you left here?" I asked.

"For a walk. People welcomed me into their homes. A group of men sat me down and wanted to know all about us and our travels. I told them some things, not all. I met Ting and she took me to Ssaiku's tent where we all talked." He paused. "Ting is, like everyone else here, beautiful, but the poor woman might as well have the Eleventh Rite juju on her. She's not allowed intimacy. And . . . Onye you know the word I have spoken to you."

Ifunanya.

"It applies to soul *and* body," Mwita said, yanking on my rapa again, pulling it below my breasts. I pulled it up.

"I'm sorry," I said.

"You should be," Mwita said. He waved his hand. "Go and wash."

Chapter 43

NEITHER DITI NOR LUYU RETURNED THAT NIGHT. Fanasi sat all night staring into what was left of the rock fire. He was still there when I got up the next morning to brew some tea. "Fanasi," I said. My voice startled him. Maybe he was sleeping with his eyes open. "Go sleep."

"They haven't returned," he said.

"They're fine. Go sleep."

He stumbled to his tent where he crawled in and stopped moving, his legs still sticking out. I was in the bath tent, halfway through rinsing soap from my body, when I heard one of them return. I paused.

"Glad you could make it back," I heard Mwita say.

"Oh, stop," I heard Diti say.

Silence.

"Don't try and make me feel guilty," Diti added.

"When have I ever said that you shouldn't enjoy yourself?" Mwita asked.

Diti grunted. "Has he been here all night?"

"He waited for both of you all night," Mwita said. "He just went to sleep."

"For both of us?" she scoffed.

"Diti . . ."

I heard her go back to her tent. "Leave me be. I'm tired."

"Suit yourself," Mwita said.

Luyu returned three hours later. Diti was sleeping off whatever it was she was sleeping off, probably a combination of intercourse and palm wine. Luyu looked refreshed, escorted by a man about our age. "Good morning," she said.

"Afternoon," I corrected her. I'd spent the morning in meditation. Mwita had gone off somewhere. I presumed it was to find either Ssaiku or Ting.

"This is Ssun," she said.

"Good afternoon," I said.

"Welcome," he said. "Last night, your singing, it gave me good dreams."

"When you finally *went* to sleep," Luyu added. They grinned at each other.

"He was waiting up for you," I said, motioning to Fanasi.

"Is that Diti's husband?" Ssun asked, cocking his head, trying to see him.

I almost laughed.

"I hope he didn't mind that my brother took Diti from him for a night," he said.

"Maybe a little," Luyu said.

I frowned. *What kind of norms and rules do these people have?* I wondered. Everyone seemed to be having intercourse with everyone. Even Eyess wasn't of Chieftess Sessa's husband's blood. While Luyu and Ssun talked, I quietly walked over to Fanasi and kicked one of his legs hard. He groaned and rolled over.

"Eh, what is it?" he said. "I was sleeping nicely."

Luyu gave me a very dirty look. I smiled at her.

"Fanasi," Ssun said, walking over to him. "I had your Luyu for the night. She tells me that you may take offense."

Fanasi quickly got to his feet. He swayed a little but at full height, he was taller and more imposing than Ssun. Instinctively Ssun stepped back. Diti peeked out of her tent, a smile on her face.

"Take her as long as you want," Fanasi said.

"Ssun," I said. I was about to reach out and take his hand but then thought better of it. "It was nice to have your acquaintance. Come." I walked with him away from our camp. He maintained his distance of a few inches from me. "Have my brother and I caused trouble?" he asked.

"Nothing that wasn't there already," I said.

"In Ssolu, we follow our urges. I'm sorry, we've neglected to consider that you all aren't from here."

"It's all right," I said. "You may have set things back in order with us."

That evening, Luyu moved back into her tent and we were forced to use Binta's tent for bathing.

Those days leading up to the retreat were the worst for the five of us. Diti, Luyu, and Fanasi refused to speak to one another. And both Luyu and Diti continually disappeared during afternoons and evenings.

Fanasi befriended a few men and spent evenings with them talking, drinking, feeding the camels, and especially cooking bread. I didn't know Fanasi was such a good baker. I should have. He was a bread maker's son. Fanasi made several types of bread and soon women were asking for his bread and to be taught how to make it. But when in our camp, he kept to himself. I wondered what was on his mind. I wondered about all three of them. On the surface they seemed okay but it was only Luyu who I felt really *was* okay.

Living with the Vah people was odd. Aside from no one touching me, I loved these people. I was welcome here. And I got to know names and personalities. There was a couple living in a tent near us, Ssaqua and Essop, who had five children, two of whom had different fathers. Ssaqua and Essop were a lively couple who argued and discussed every issue. They called Mwita and me often to settle disputes. One of the arguments they called me to settle was over whether the desert had more areas of hardpan or sand dunes.

"Who could answer that?" I said. "No one's been everywhere. Even our maps are limited and out of date. And who's to say everything *is* desert."

"Ha!" said Essop, poking his wife in the belly. "See, I was right! I win!"

Children in the village of Ssolu ran amok, in a good way. They were always somewhere helping or learning from someone. Everyone welcomed them. Even the very young ones. As long as a baby could walk, he or she was everyone's responsibility. I once saw a child of about two get fed by her mother and then run off to explore. Hours later, I saw her sitting to lunch with another family on the other side of the village. Then that evening, I found her with Ssaqua and Essop and two of their children, eating dinner!

Of course, Eyess visited me often. We shared many meals together. She liked my cooking, saying that I used "so much spice." It was nice having a little shadow, but she always grew annoyed when Mwita came and took some of my attention from her.

What made Ssolu most comfortable for me was what made them different from any society I knew. Everyone here could build a rock fire. They just knew how to do it. And when I'd sung, people had been pleased and amused when the bird landed on my shoulder. The idea of my singing having such a calming effect on them didn't bother them.

The Vah weren't sorcerers. Only Ssaiku and Ting knew the Mystic Points. But juju was part of their way of life. It was so normal that they felt no need to ever fully understand it. I never asked them if they knew these minor jujus instinctively or had been taught. It seemed a rude question, like asking how one learned to control his urine.

My mother had been like the Vah in how she accepted the unanswerable and the mystical. But when we got to Jwahir, to civilization, it had become something to hide. In Jwahir, it was only acceptable for elders like Aro, the Ada, or Nana the Wise to know juju. For anyone else juju was an abomination.

What would I have been like if I grew up here? I wondered. They had no issue with *Ewu* people. They embraced Mwita like one of their own. They gave him hugs and handshakes, patted him on the back, let their children hang around him. He was wholly welcome.

Yet, they could not touch *me*. Even in Jwahir people would brush against me in the market. When I was young, people were always tugging at or feeling my hair and I'd had my share of fights with other children. This was the only issue I had with the people of the nomadic town of Ssolu.

Chapter 44

WHEN I AM NOT MOVING TOWARD MY FATE, it comes to me. Those days leading up to the retreat were really the beginning of the process Ssaiku hinted at. We'd only been with the Red People for three short days. Four days until the retreat. Not nearly enough time to unwind.

Still, I woke up relaxed, content, rested. Mwita's arm was around my waist. Outside I could hear the drone of Ssaiku's storm. Over the noise I could hear people chatting as they started the day, the *maa* of goats, and the sound of a baby crying. I sighed. Ssolu was like home in so many ways.

I closed my eyes thinking of my mother. She'd be outside the house tending to her garden. Maybe she'd visit the Ada later on or stop by my father's shop to see how Ji was getting along. I missed her so much. I missed not having to . . . travel. I sat up and pushed my long hair back. The palm fiber I'd used to tie it had come undone. My hands automatically started braiding it as I usually did when it felt in the way. Then I remembered Ssaiku's words about how I was to keep my hair unbraided. "Ridiculous," I muttered looking for the fiber.

"What?" Mwita mumbled, his face to the mat.

"I just lost my . . ."

A tiny white head with a small red wattle hanging from its beak was peeking into our tent. It whistled softly. I laughed. A guinea fowl. In Ssolu, the plump docile birds roamed about as freely as the children and they knew never to go near the storm. I wrapped my rapa around myself and sat up. I froze. I smelled that strange smell, the one that always came when something magical was happening. The bird pulled its head out of my tent.

"Mwita," I whispered.

He quickly got up, wrapped his rapa around his waist and grasped my hand. He seemed to smell it, too. Or at least, he sensed something was odd.

"Onye!" Diti shouted from outside. "You better come out here!"

"Do it slowly," Luyu said. They both sounded several yards from our tent.

I sniffed the air, the strange otherworldly aroma filling my nose. I didn't want to leave the tent but Mwita pushed me, pressing close behind. "Go on," he whispered. "Face whatever it is. It's all you can do."

I frowned, shoving back. "I don't *have* to do anything."

"Don't be a coward," Mwita snapped.

"Or what?"

"It's not what we left home for," he said. "Remember?"

I sucked my teeth, fear pressing my lungs. "I don't know what I left home for anymore. And I don't know what's out there. . . .waiting for me."

Mwita scoffed. "You know what you have to do."

I wasn't sure which of my thoughts he was responding to.

"Go on," he said, pushing me again.

I kept thinking about the retreat, how something would happen there. Our tent was security—in it was Mwita and our few belongings, it was a shield from the world. *Oh Ani, I want to stay in here,* I thought. But then the image of Binta popped into my mind. My heart pounded harder. I moved forward. When I pushed the flap aside and crawled out, I almost bumped right into it. I looked up, up, and up.

It stood directly before our tent, tall as a middle-aged tree. Wide as three tents. A masquerade, a spirit from the wilderness. Unlike the violent needle-clawed one that had guarded Aro's hut the day I attacked him, this one stood still as a stone. It was made of tightly packed dead wet leaves and thousands of protruding metal spikes. It had a wooden head with a frowning face carved into it. Thick white smoke dribbled from the top. This smoke was what was producing the smell. Around it strutted about ten guinea fowl. They looked up at it every so often, heads tilted, softly whistling questioningly. Two sat on its right and one on its left. *A monster that attracts cute harmless birds,* I thought. *What next?*

The masquerade stared down at me as I slowly stood up, Mwita right behind me. Yards away were Diti and Fanasi and a growing crowd of on-lookers. Fanasi had an arm around Diti's waist as Diti clasped him for dear life. A terrified Luyu was hiding behind her tent directly to my right. I wanted to laugh. Luyu stayed, Diti and Fanasi cowered.

"What do you think it wants?" Luyu loudly whispered as if the creature weren't right there. She crept closer. "Maybe if we give it what it wants it'll go away."

Depends on what it wants, I thought.

Suddenly the creature began descending to the ground, its raffia body packing upon itself. The guinea fowl sitting beside it moved a foot to the side before sitting back down. The masquerade stopped descending. It was sitting. I sat down before it. Mwita sat behind me. Luyu stayed close, too. She didn't have a magical bone in her body and this made her bravery in the face of the mysterious that much more amazing.

With its head closer to the ground, the strange-smelling smoke around us grew thick. My lungs hitched and I worked hard not to cough. That would have been rude, I knew. Several of the guinea fowl actually *did* cough. The masquerade didn't seem to care. I glanced at Luyu and nod-ded. She nodded back. "Tell them all to step away," I told her.

Without a hint of questioning, she went to the people. "She says to get back," Luyu said.

"That is a masquerade," a woman blankly replied.

"I don't know what it is," Luyu said. "But . . ."

"It's come to speak with her," a man said. "We just want to watch."

Luyu turned to me. At least now I knew what it wanted. The Red People continued to amaze me with their instinctive knowledge of the mystical. "Move back, anyway," I said flatly. "It's a private talk."

They moved to a seemingly safe distance. I saw Fanasi and Diti push into the crowd and disappear. Then it was speaking to me.

Onyesonwu, it said. *Mwita.* The voice came from every part of it, creeping from its body like its smoke. Traveling in all directions. The guinea fowl stopped their soft whistling and the ones who were standing all sat down. *I greet you,* it said. *I greet your ancestors, spirits and chis.* As it spoke, the wilderness sprung up around us. I wondered if Mwita could see it. Brilliant colors, undulating tubules extending from the physical ground. They looked like trees if there were trees in the wilderness. Wilderness trees.

I glanced around for the eye of my father. I could see its glow but it was blocked by the bulk of the masquerade. This was the only hint that I could trust this powerful masquerade creature. "We greet you, *Oga,*" Mwita and I said.

"Hold out your hand, Onyesonwu."

I turned to Mwita. His eyes were narrow and intense, his jaw clenched, his lips pressed, his nostrils flared, his eyebrows furrowed. He suddenly stood up. "What will you do?" he asked it.

Sit down, Mwita, it said. *You cannot take her place. You cannot save her. You have your own role to play.* Mwita sat down. Just like that, it had read his mind, leaped over his questions and arguments, and addressed the exact issue that was at the center of Mwita's heart. *Touch her if you must but do not interfere,* it said.

Mwita grasped my shoulder. Into my ear he whispered, "I will go with whatever you wish to do." I heard the pleading in his voice. Pleading for me to refuse. To act. To flee. I thought of my Eleventh Rite when I had a similar option. If I'd fled my father wouldn't have seen me so soon. I wouldn't be here. But I *was* here. And no matter what, something was going to happen in four days when I went on that retreat. Fate is cold. It is brittle.

Slowly, I held my hand out. I kept my eyes open. Mwita grasped my shoulder tightly and pressed closer. I don't know what I expected but I wasn't prepared for what happened next. Its layer of wet leaves all lifted at the same time exposing its many needles. It leaned away from me and then whipped forward with a soft *whisp!* I flinched back and blinked. When I opened my eyes I saw that I was covered with drops of water and . . . the masquerade's needles.

My entire face, arms, chest, belly, legs. The needles had even somehow found their way to my back! Only the parts of me covered by Mwita's body were needle-free. Mwita shouted, wanting to touch me and not touch me. "Are you . . ." He jumped up, looking at me, then at the needles. "What is . . . Onye? What . . . ?"

I whimpered as I stared at myself, on the verge of screaming, surprised I was still conscious and felt okay. I looked like a pincushion! Why wasn't I bleeding? Where was the pain? And why had it told me to hold out my hand if it was going to do this? Was that some kind of cruel joke?

The masquerade started laughing. A deep guttural guffaw that shook its wet leaves. Yes, it was the creature's idea of a joke.

It got up, sprinkling us with moisture and smoke. It turned and began to walk away, toward Ssaiku's tent as it dribbled its trail of wilderness smoke. The guinea fowl followed single file. Several people followed, too. Someone brought a flute, someone else a small drum. They played for the masquerade as it walked, still laughing.

When we could no longer see it, Mwita and I stared at each other.

"You *feel* . . . okay?" he asked.

I was starting to feel . . . odd. Unwell. But I didn't want to scare him. "I'm fine."

After a few moments, we both smiled and laughed. A needle fell out. Mwita pointed at it and laughed harder, which made me laugh harder. More needles fell out. Luyu came running. She screamed when she saw me up close. Mwita and I laughed even harder. I was shedding needles now.

"What's wrong with you two?" Luyu asked, calming down when she saw the needles falling out. "What did that thing do to you?"

I shook my head still chuckling. "Don't know."

"Was it . . ." she knelt down to look at the remaining needles on my back. "Was that a real masquerade?"

I nodded, feeling a wave of nausea pass over me. I sighed and sat back. When Luyu tried to touch one of the remaining needles protruding from my cheek, a spark the size of a kola nut popped from me. She jumped back holding her hand, hissing with pain.

Now I was outcast from everyone but Mwita.

Chapter 45

BY THE NEXT DAY, I was woefully sick. The sight of food, even simple curried goat, turned my stomach. And when I did manage to get the food into my mouth, it tasted metallic and produced sparks against my teeth, a very unpleasant sensation. I could only comfortably drink water and eat bits of plain bread. Two days later I was still ill.

The masquerade had introduced something into my body. Those needles were infected with poison. Or was it medicine? Or maybe both. Or neither. Poison or medicine implies that it has something to do with me. As opposed to me being part of a larger plan.

Not only was I constantly nauseated, unable to eat, and nearly allergic to everyone except Mwita (it turned out that I wasn't allergic to Ssaiku and Ting, either) but every so often I'd be washed with a terrible hyperawareness. I'd be able to hear a fly breathe or see a grain of sand tumble to the ground like a boulder. I'd suddenly have hawklike strength, vision or I could nearly smell everyone's mortality. Mortality smelled muddy and wet and I reeked of it.

I knew what this hunger-induced clarity was. It was a stronger version of what had brought Mwita and me face-to-face with my father months ago. But I was going to control it this time. I *had* to; if I couldn't then maybe I *was* dangerous. To add to my issues, the wilderness kept trying to invade my space.

"I'm alive," I muttered as I walked on the outskirts of Ssolu. "So leave me be." But the wilderness would not, of course. I looked around, my heart beating fast. I wanted to laugh. My heart was pounding while I had one foot in the spirit world and the other in the physical world. Absurd. I was part blue energy and part physical body. Half alive and half something else. It was the fifth time this had happened, and as I did before, I turned to look into the angry eye of my father. I spat at him, ignoring the shiver of apprehension I felt whenever I saw him. He was always there watching, waiting . . . but for what?

I was standing near a family's tent. A mother, a father, and two boys and three girls. Or maybe some of the children were from other parents. Maybe the two "parents" were lovers or friends. You never knew with the Vah. But a family was a family and I envied what I saw and again missed my mother.

They were having dinner. I could smell the okra soup and fufu as if it were right in my face. I could see the glint in the man's eye as he looked at the woman and I knew he craved her but did not love her. I could almost feel the roughness of the children's long dreadlocks. If any of them looked toward me what would they see? Maybe a version of me that looked molded from water. Maybe nothing. I leaned against the blue energy of a wilderness tree to shield myself from my father's fiery gaze. The tree felt soft and cool. I sank down, waiting until I passed fully back into the physical world.

As soon as I shut my eyes, something grabbed me. My entire body went numb as two of the wilderness tree's branches wrapped tightly around my left arm and neck. I clawed at the one around my neck and yanked. I wheezed painfully as it held tighter. The branch was so strong.

But I was stronger. Much stronger. As rage flew through me, my blue energy blazed. I snatched the branch from my neck and ripped it off. The tree screamed a high-pitched shriek but that didn't stop me. I tore the other branch from my arm and snatched up and tore the one trying to get at my leg. Then I stood up nearly ready to roar, fists balled, legs slightly bent, eyes wide. I was going to tear the entire tree apart . . . and that was when the wilderness retreated from me. The moment my being and body settled fully in the physical world, all the strength left me. I sat down hard on the ground, panting quietly, afraid to touch my sore neck.

One of the little girls eating dinner with the family turned. She saw me and waved. I weakly waved back, trying to smile. I slowly stood up, pretending that nothing had just happened. "You want to eat with us?" she asked in her innocent little-girl voice. Now they were all looking at me and beckoning.

I smiled and shook my head. "Thank you but I'm not hungry," I said, moving on as quickly as my stricken body could take me. Those people seemed so normal, pure, untainted. There was no way I'd sit at their table.

When I got back to my tent, Fanasi was sitting in front of his tent sulking. I wasn't in the mood, so I didn't bother asking him what was wrong. But it was obvious. Diti and Luyu were nowhere to be found. Neither was Mwita, and as I lay down in my tent I was glad he wasn't there. I didn't want him to know I was so . . . ill. I didn't want *anyone* to know. The Vah already treated me as if I were afflicted with something. And in a way I was. I couldn't go near any of them without causing sparks and a shot of sharp pain. I felt like enough of an outcast without announcing that on top of all that I wasn't feeling well either.

I told Luyu everything. But only because she happened to be the one to come into my tent an hour later, when I was half in the wilderness and half in the physical world again. I was too exhausted to do anything but sit there. When the wilderness finally retreated, there she was at my tent's opening staring at me.

I expected her to crawl right back out but again Luyu surprised me. She crawled in, sat down, and just gazed at me. I lay back and waited for her questions.

"So what is that?" she finally asked.

"What?" I sighed.

"You were like . . . water," she said. "Made of solid water . . . but water if it was like stone but water."

I chuckled. "Was I?"

She nodded, "Just like what happened that day during our Eleventh Rite." She cocked her head. "Is that when you go into the . . . world of the dead?"

"Not dead, the wilderness," I said. "The spirit world."

"But you can't be alive there," she said. "So it's the world of the dead."

"I . . ." I sighed again and recited one of Aro's lessons. "Just because something is not alive, does not mean it is dead. You have to be alive first to be dead." I closed my eyes and lay back. "The wilderness is someplace else. Neither of flesh nor time."

"So why'd it happen during our rite?" she asked.

I laughed. "It's a long story."

"Onye, what's wrong with you?" she asked after a moment. "You haven't looked right since . . . since that masquerade did that thing to you." She moved closer when I didn't answer. "Remember what we talked about way back when we first left home?"

I only looked at her.

"We agreed to share the load, you and I," she said. She took my hand and a large spark popped off it. A look of pain crossed her face as she slowly put my hand down. She smiled at me but didn't try to take my hand again. "Talk. Tell me."

I looked away, suppressing the urge to cry. I didn't want to burden anyone with any of it. I turned to her, noting dark brown skin, flawless even after all we'd been through. Her thick lips pressed firmly together. Her large almond-shaped eyes looked deep into mine, never flinching. I sat up. "Okay," I said. "Come walk with me."

We strolled along the outskirts of Ssolu, in the half mile between the storm and the last of the tents. Only groups of livestock congregated here. The guinea fowl and chickens kept their distance. So among camels and goats, I talked and Luyu listened.

"You should tell Mwita," she said when I finished. I had to stop and bend forward as a wave of hunger-induced fatigue passed over me.

"I don't want to . . ."

"It's not only about you," she said. She stepped forward about to help me up. She quickly stepped back. "Are you all right?"

"No."

"Can I . . ."

"No." Slowly, I straightened up. "Go ahead. Say what you were going to say."

"Well, something is . . ." She paused, looking me in the eye. "A few days, you have this retreat. I think, well, you probably already know."

I nodded. "Something is going to happen but I don't know what."

"Mwita can make it better, I think," she said.

"Maybe," I muttered.

It dropped right at my feet. A yellow lizard with a large scaly head. It flipped onto its feet and began to slowly walk away. I laughed to myself, assuming it had been swept up by the storm and thrown into Ssolu like so many other creatures. All I wanted to do was sit on the sandy ground and watch it go.

Another strange wave of hyperawareness blew over me. I glanced at Luyu. She was watching me closely. I could see every cell on her face.

"You see that?" I asked. I feebly pointed at the lizard as it turned to face us. I wanted to shift Luyu's attention. She was about to run off to get Mwita; I just knew it.

Luyu frowned. "See what?"

I shook my head, my eye following the lizard. I sank to the sand. I was so weak.

Another wave of awareness blew over me, and I heard a soft moan. I wasn't sure if it came from me or the wilderness springing up around me again. There was a wilderness tree right beside Luyu. Then things flickered and became only the physical world again. I wanted to vomit.

"Stay where you are. I'm going to get Mwita," Luyu said. "You just went all transparent again."

I was too weak to respond. The lizard was slowly walking up to me, and I focused on it as Luyu ran off.

"Let her go," a voice said. It was a female voice but low and strong like a man's. It was coming from the approaching lizard. Something about the voice was vaguely familiar.

"I didn't intend to stop her," I said with a weak laugh. "Who are you?" I wondered if I was imagining the voice. I knew I wasn't. I was suffering from an illness passed on to me by a great spirit of the wilderness. It had come to me to do just that. Then it had gone and met with Ssaiku, Ting later told me. Nothing that happened to me after my encounter with the masquerade would be a figment of my imagination.

"You've come far," it said, ignoring my question. "I'll take you farther."

"Are you really here?" I asked.

"Very much so."

"Will you bring me back?"

"Could anyone take you from Mwita?"

"No," I said. "Where will you take me?" I was just talking now. Not really interested in the answers. I needed something to keep me calm as the lizard began to grow and change colors.

"I will take you where you need to go," she said, her voice becoming more sonorous and full as she grew. It began to sound like three of the same voice in one. "I'll show you what you need to see, Onyesonwu."

So she knew me. I narrowed my eyes. "What do you know of my fate?" I asked.

"I know what you know."

"What of my biological father?"

"That he is an evil, evil man."

I forgot the rest of my questions. I forgot everything. Before me stood what I could only call a *Kponyungo*, a firespitter. The size of four camels, it was the brilliant color of every shade of fire. Its body was wiry and strong like a snake's, its large round head carried long coiling horns and a magnificent jaw full of sharp teeth. Its eyes were like small suns. It sweat a thin smoke and smelled like roasting sand and steam.

When my mother and I were nomads, during the hottest parts of the day we'd sit in our tent and she'd tell me stories about these creatures. "*Kponyungo* like to befriend travelers," she said. "They come to life during the hottest part of the day just like now. They rise from the salt of long dead oceans. If one befriends you, you will never be alone."

My mother was one of the only people I knew who spoke of oceans as if they'd truly existed. She always told me stories about them when something scared me, like the sight of a rotting camel or when the sky grew too cloudy. To her, *Kponyungo* were kind, majestic beings. But oftentimes, encountering something in real life is not the same as encountering it in stories. Like now.

I had no words. I knew it was here. Standing before me, as everyone in Ssolu went about their business a half mile away. Passersby may have noticed me standing there staring but they wouldn't have stopped. I was untouchable to them, I was strange, a sorceress, even if they did like me. Could they see the *Kponyungo* standing before me? Maybe. Maybe not. If they could, maybe it was custom to leave me to my fate.

I felt a now familiar sensation, a sort of detachment and then deep mobility. I was going "away" again. This time it was happening close to a town of people, without Mwita at my side. I was all alone and this creature was taking me. As I floated upward, the *Kponyungo* flew beside me. I could feel its heat.

"A creature like myself is not so different from a bird," she said in her strange voice. "Change yourself."

Could I change myself when I was "traveling" like this? I'd never considered it. But she was correct. I'd changed myself into a lizard once and it was not so different from changing into a sparrow or even a vulture. I reached out to touch the *Kponyungo*'s rough skin. I quickly pulled my hand back, suddenly afraid.

"Go ahead," she said.

"Are you . . . are you hot?"

"Find out," she said. Her face didn't express it but I knew she was amused. I slowly reached out and touched a scale. I actually heard and smelled my skin sizzle.

"Ah!" I yelped, shaking my hand. Still, she took me higher and higher. We were fifty feet above Ssolu now. "Am I . . . ?" I looked at my hand. It didn't look burned, nor did it hurt as much as it should have.

"You are you even when in wilderness," she said. "But your own abilities and mine protect us."

"Can I die like this?"

"Yes, in a way," she said. "But you won't," she said at the same time that I said, "But I won't."

"Okay," I mumbled. I reached out again. This time I endured the pain, the sound and smell of my skin burning. I cracked off one of her scales. Smoke rose from my hand and I wanted to scream but even through the smoke I could see that I was unharmed.

Because we were ascending higher and higher, it was hard to concentrate. Still, with the scale in hand, changing into a *Kponyungo* was only mildly difficult. I stretched my new sleek body, enjoying the heat of my-self. I resisted the strong urge to swiftly fly downward, burrow deep into the sand, and heat my body so intensely that the sand melted into glass. I laughed to myself. Even if I'd wanted to, I could not. I wasn't the one controlling this journey, the *Kponyungo* was. I wondered if this was also why I couldn't grow my body as big as hers. I could only stretch to about three-fourths her size.

"Well done," she said when I finished. "Now let me take you to a place you have never seen before."

We zoomed toward the storm wall and plunged into it. We came out the other side in less than a second. The position of the sun told me that we were flying west. We flew in a half circle and headed east. "There is Papa Shee," she said, a minute later.

I barely glanced at that evil place where the people had brutally taken Binta's life and would forever suffer blindness. Generation after genera-tion. I'd cursed Papa Shee and all who were born in it. I cursed it again as we passed.

"There is your Jwahir," she said.

I tried to slow down so I could see, but she pulled me along. I saw nothing more than a blur of distant buildings. Still, even as we passed it in the blink of an eye, I could feel my home calling to me, trying to draw me back. My mother. Aro. Nana the Wise. The Ada. Had her son Fanta arrived in Jwahir to surprise her yet?

The *Kponyungo* and I flew over vast lands; the dryness I had always known. Sand. Hardpan. Stunted trees. Dry dead grass. We moved too fast for me to spot the occasional camel, sand fox, hawk we must have passed over. I wondered where we were going. And I wondered if I should be afraid. It was impossible to tell how much time was passing or how far we were going. I felt no hunger or thirst. No need to urinate or defecate. No need to sleep. I was no longer human, no longer a physical beast.

I glanced at her eyes every so often. She was a giant lizard of heat and light. But she was more, too. I just had a feeling. Who was she? She'd glance back at me, as if she knew what I was wondering. But she said nothing.

A long time and a long distance later, the land below suddenly changed.

The trees we passed were taller here. We flew faster. So fast that all I could see was light brown. Then darker brown. Then . . . green.

"Behold," she said, finally slowing down.

Greeeeen! As I'd never seen it. As I'd never *imagined* it. This made the field of green I'd seen when I'd gone "away" with Mwita that first time seem tiny. From horizon to horizon the ground was alive with dense high leafy trees. *Is this even possible?* I wondered. *Does this place really exist?*

I met the *Kponyungo*'s eyes and they glowed a deeper orange-yellow. "It does," she said.

My chest ached, but it was a good ache. It was an ache of . . . home. This place was too far to ever get to. But maybe someday it would not be. Maybe someday. It's vastness made the violence and hatred between the Okeke and Nuru seem small. On and on this place went. We flew low enough to touch the treetops. I caressed the leaf of a strange palm tree.

A large eaglelike bird flew up from a nearby tree. Another tree blooming with large bright pink flowers was crowded with large blue and yellow butterflies. In other treetops sat furry beasts with long arms and curious eyes. They watched us fly by. A breeze sent ripples in the treetops like wind on a puddle of water. It made a whispering sound that I will never forget. So much green, alive and heavy with water!

She stopped us and we hovered above a large wide tree. I smiled. An iroko tree. Just like the one I'd found myself in the first time my Eshu abilities manifested and I'd changed into a sparrow. This tree was also fruiting its bitter-smelling fruit. We landed on one of its large branches. Somehow, it bore our weight.

A family of those furry beasts sat on the far side of the tree's top staring at us, unmoving. It was almost comical. What must they have understood with their eyes? Had they ever seen two giant wiry lizards that glowed like the sun and smelled of smoke and steam? Doubtful.

"I will send you back in a moment," she said, ignoring the furry monkeylike creatures, which still had not moved. "For now, take this place in, hold it close to you. Remember it."

What I remember most about it was the deep sense of hope it placed in my heart. If a forest, a true vast forest, still existed someplace, even if it was very very far away, then all would not end badly. It meant there was life *outside* the Great Book. It was like being blessed, cleansed.

Nevertheless, when the *Kponyungo* returned me to Ssolu, after I'd made my body human again, I had to work hard to remember any of this. As soon as I was back in my own skin, the sickness descended upon me like a thousand scorpions sent by my father.

Chapter 46

BUT IT HAD NOTHING TO DO WITH MY FATHER and every-thing to do with the masquerade's visit. Or so the sorcerer Ssaiku said. When I returned to myself after my visit to the green place, Ssaiku, Ting, and Mwita were waiting for me. We were in my tent. Incense was burning, Ssaiku was humming some forlorn tune and Mwita was staring at me. As soon as I lay atop my body, he smiled and nodded and said, "She's back."

I smiled back at him but then immediately cringed as I realized that every muscle in my body was clenching.

"Drink this," Mwita said, holding a cup to my lips. Whatever it was caused my muscles to relax within a minute. Only when Mwita and I were alone did I tell him all that I had seen. I never got to hear what he thought of it all because as soon as I finished telling the story, I slipped into the wilderness, which to him meant I nearly disappeared. When I slipped back into the physical world, I returned again to painfully cramped muscles.

It wasn't the type of illness that made you vomit, burn with fever, or suffer bouts of diarrhea. It was spiritual. Food repulsed me. The wilderness and the physical world battled for prominence around me. My awareness fluctuated between heightened and dulled. I mostly stayed in my tent the rest of those days before the retreat.

Fanasi and Diti peeked into my tent every so often. Fanasi brought me bread that I didn't eat. Diti tried to start conversations with me that

I couldn't finish. They looked like mice waiting for the right moment to flee. The sight of the masquerade must have really made it clear that I was not just a sorceress but also connected to mysterious and dangerous forces.

Luyu stayed with me whenever Mwita could not. She sat with me when I disappeared and when I reappeared in the same place, she'd still be there. She'd look terrified but she'd still be there. She didn't ask me any questions and when we talked, she'd tell me about the men she bedded or other mundane things. She was the only one who could make me laugh.

Chapter 47

THE MORNING OF THE TENTH DAY, Mwita had to wake me. I hadn't been able to fall asleep until the last hour. I was still unable to eat and too hungry to sleep. Mwita did his best to exhaust me. Even in my state, his touch was more soothing than food or water. Still, I couldn't stop thinking about how many people would die if I conceived. Nor could I get it out of my head that something bad was going to happen when I went on the retreat.

"I hear them singing," Mwita said. "They've already gathered."

"Mmm," I said, my eyes still closed. I had been listening to them for over an hour now. Their song reminded me of my mother. She sang this song often, though she refused to go with the Jwahir women to Hold Conversation. "She hasn't gone since I was conceived," I mumbled, opening my eyes. "Why should I ever go?"

"Get up," Mwita said softly, kissing my bare shoulder. He got up, wrapped his green rapa around his waist and went outside. He returned with a cup of water. He reached into my pile of clothes and grabbed my blue top.

"Wear this," he said. "And . . ." He found a blue rapa. "And this."

I pushed myself up, the cover falling off me. As the cool air touched my body, awareness flooded over me. I wanted to sob. I wrapped the blue rapa around myself. He handed me the water. "Be strong," he said. "Get up."

When I stepped out, I was shocked to see Diti, Luyu, and Fanasi sitting there, fully dressed, and eating fresh bread. The smell of the bread made my stomach growl. "We were beginning to think you two were too . . . exhausted to go," Luyu said with a wink.

"You mean you were in camp to hear it?" I asked.

Fanasi bitterly laughed. Diti looked away.

"I got in late but yes," Luyu said with a smirk.

By the time I'd washed and dressed, the group of women was walking out. They moved slowly. It was easy to catch up with them. No one seemed to mind Mwita and Fanasi, who were the only men in the group. Ting was there, too. "To represent Ssaiku," she said. I noticed a quick look pass between her and Mwita.

It wasn't a long walk to the edge of the dust storm on the west side, about a mile and a half. But we walked at such a slow pace that it took nearly an hour. We sang songs to Ani, some that I knew, many that I didn't. By the time we stopped, I was dizzy from hunger and glad to sit down. It was windy, noisy, and a little scary. You could see where the wind turned to storm, only a few yards away.

"Let her hair go," Ting told Mwita. He took the twine of palm fiber off my hair and it blew about. Everyone was quiet now. Praying. Many knelt, their heads to the sand. Diti, Luyu, and Fanasi remained standing, staring at the dust storm. Luyu and Diti came from families that only occasionally prayed to Ani. Their mothers had never gone on retreats and neither had they. I couldn't keep my mind off my own mother and how it all happened to her, how she'd been praying like these women when the scooters came. Ting was behind me. I felt her do something to my neck. I was too weak to stop her. "What are you doing?" I asked.

She leaned close to my ear. "It's a mixture of palm oil, the tears of a dying old woman, the tears of an infant, menstrual blood, the milk of a man, the skin from the foot of a tortoise, and sand."

I shivered, repulsed.

"You don't know Nsibidi," she said. "It is a written juju. To mark anything with it is to enact change; it speaks directly with the spirit. I've marked you with a symbol of the crossroads where all your selves will meet. Kneel forward. Ask it of Ani. She'll give it."

"I don't believe in Ani," I said.

"Kneel and pray anyway," she said, pushing me forward.

I pressed my forehead to the sand, the sound of the wind in my ears. Minutes passed. *I'm so hungry,* I thought. I began to feel something holding me down. I turned my head and stared into the sky. I saw the sun set, come back up and then set again. A long time passed, that's what matters.

Suddenly, I dropped into the sand. It swallowed me like the mouth of a beast. The last thing I remember before the world exploded was a girl saying, "It's okay, Mwita. She's releasing. We've been waiting for this since she got here."

Every part of me that was me. My tall *Ewu* body. My short temper. My impulsive mind. My memories. My past. My future. My death. My life. My spirit. My fate. My failure. All of me was destroyed. I was dead, broken, scattered, and absorbed. It was a thousand times worse than when I first changed into a bird. I remember nothing because I was nothing.

Then I was something.

I could feel it. I was being put back together, bit by bit. What was doing this? No, it was not Ani. It was not a goddess. It was cold, if it could be cold. And brittle, if it could be brittle. Logical. Controlled. Dare I say that it was the Creator? It Who Cannot Be Touched? Who doesn't *care* to be touched? The fourth point that no sorcerer could ever consider? No, I can't say that because that is the deepest blasphemy. Or at least that's what Aro would say.

But my spirit and body were utterly completely obliterated . . . was this not what Aro said would happen to any creature who encountered the Creator? As It reassembled me, It arranged me in a new order. An order that made more sense. I remember the moment the last piece of me was returned.

"Ahhhhhhhhhhhhhhhhhh," I breathed. Relief, my first emotion. Again, I am reminded of that time in the iroko tree. When my head was like a house. Back then it was as if some of that house's doors were cracking open—doors of steel, wood, stone. This time all of those doors *and* windows were blown out.

I was dropping again. I hit the ground hard. Wind on my skin. I was freezing. I was wet. *Who am I?* I wondered. I didn't open my eyes. I couldn't remember how to. Something hit my head. And something else. Instinctively, I opened my eyes. I was in a tent.

"How can she be dead?" Diti was screaming. "What happened?"

Then it all slammed into me. Who I was, why I was, how I was, when I was. I shut my eyes.

"Don't touch her," Ssaiku said. "Mwita, speak to her. She's coming back. Help her complete her journey."

A pause. "Onyesonwu." His voice sounded strange. "Come back. You were gone for seven days. Then you fell from the sky, like one of Ani's missing children in the Great Book. If you live again, open your eyes, woman."

I opened my eyes. I was lying on my back. My body hurt. He took my hand. I grasped his. More came in that moment. More of who I now was. I smiled, and then I laughed.

This was a moment of madness and arrogance that I cannot say was only my fault. The power and ability that I realized was a part of me now was overwhelming. I was stronger and more in control than I ever imagined I could be. And so as soon as I returned, I was off again. I hadn't eaten in seven days. My mind was clear. I was so so strong. I thought of where I wanted to go. I went there. One minute I was on that mat in the tent, the next I was flying, as myself, as my blue spirit.

I was going after my father.

I flew right through the sandstorm. I felt its stinging touch. I burst through its wall into the hot sun. Morning. I flew over miles of sand, villages, dunes, a town, dry trees, and more dunes. I flew over a small field of green, but I was too focused to care. Into Durfa. Straight to a large house with a blue door. Through the door and up to a room that smelled of flowers, incense, and dusty books.

He was at a desk, his back to me. I dropped deeper into the wilderness. I had done it to Aro when he'd refused me one too many times. And I'd done it to the witch doctor in Papa Shee. This time I was even stronger. I knew where to tear and bite and destroy, where to attack. Layered over his turned back, I could see his spirit. It was a deep blue, like mine. This startled me for a moment, but it didn't stop me.

I pounced the way a starved tiger must have long ago when it found its prey. I was too eager to realize that though his back was turned, his spirit wasn't. He had been waiting. Aro had never told me how it felt when I'd attacked him. The witch doctor in Papa Shee had simply died, no physical markings on him when he fell over. Now, in this moment with my father, I learned what it was like.

It was the kind of pain that death wouldn't stop. My father put it to me in full force. He sang as he tore, gorged, stabbed, and twisted at parts of me that I didn't know were there. He sat at his desk, his back turned. He sang in Nuru but I couldn't hear the words. I am like my mother, but not completely. I cannot hear and remember as I suffer.

Something in me kicked in. A survival instinct, a responsibility and a memory. *This isn't how I end,* I thought. Immediately, I pulled what remained of me away. As I retreated, my father stood and turned around. He looked into what were my eyes and grabbed what was my arm. I tried to pull away. He was too strong. He turned the palm of my right hand over and dug his thumbnail into it, etching some sort of symbol there. He let go and said, "Go back and die in the sands you arose from."

I traveled backward for what felt like forever, sobbing, pained, fading. As I approached the wall of dust, the world grew bright with spirits and the desert sprouted those strange colorful wilderness trees. I faded completely and remember nothing.

Mwita later told me that I died a second time. That I turned transparent and then completely disappeared. When I reappeared in the same place, I was flesh again, my body bleeding all over, my garments soaked with blood. He couldn't wake me. For three minutes, I had no pulse. He blew air into my chest and used kind juju. When none of this worked, he sat there, waiting.

During the third minute, I started breathing. Mwita shooed everyone out of the tent and asked two girls walking by to bring him a bucket of warmed water. He bathed me from head to toe, rinsing away the blood, bandaging wounds, rubbing circulation into my flesh and sending me good thoughts. "We have to talk," he'd said over and over. "Wake up."

I awoke two days later to see Mwita sitting beside me humming to himself as he wove a basket. I slowly sat up. I looked at Mwita and couldn't recall who he was. *I like him,* I thought. *What is he?* My body ached. I groaned. My stomach rumbled.

"You wouldn't eat," Mwita said, putting his basket down. "But you would drink. Otherwise, you'd be dead . . . again."

I know him, I thought. Then as if whispered by the winds outside I heard the word he'd spoken to me, *Ifunanya.* "Mwita?" I said.

"The one and only," he said coming over to me. Despite my body's pains and the restriction of bandages on my legs and torso, I threw my arms around him.

"Binta," I said into Mwita's shoulder. "Ah! Daib!" I clung to Mwita more tightly, clenching my eyes shut. "The man is no man! He . . ." Memories began to flood my senses. My journey to the West, seeing his face, his spirit. The *pain!* Defeat. My heart sank. I had failed.

"Shh," he said.

"He should have killed me," I whispered. Even after being recreated by Ani, I still couldn't take him down.

"No," Mwita said, taking my face in his hands. I tried to pull my shameful face away but he held me there. Then he kissed me long and full. The voice in my head that was screaming failure and defeat quieted, though it did not stop its mantra. Mwita pulled away and we stared into each other's eyes.

"My hand," I whispered. I held it up. The symbol was of a worm coiled around itself. It was black and crusty and hurt when I tried to close my hand into a fist. *Failure,* the voice in my head whispered. *Defeat. Death.*

"Didn't notice that," Mwita said, frowning as he held it closer to his face. When he touched it with his index finger, he pulled his hand back, hissing.

"What?" I said weakly.

"It's like it's charged. Like sticking my finger into an electrical socket," he said rubbing his hand. "My hand's numb."

"He put it there," I said.

"Daib?"

I nodded. Mwita's face darkened. "You feel all right otherwise?"

"Look at me," I said, not wanting him to look at me at all. "How could I feel . . ."

"Why'd you do that?" he asked, unable to further contain himself.

"Because I . . ."

"You weren't even happy to be alive. You weren't even relieved that you would see us again! Ah, your name truly fits you, *o!*"

What could I say to that? I hadn't thought about it. It was instinct. *And yet you failed,* the voice in my head whispered.

Ssaiku came in. He was dressed as if he'd been traveling, wearing a long caftan and pants fully draped with a long green thick cloth robe. The moment he saw that I was awake, his solemn face warmed. He spread his hands grandiosely. "Heeeeey, she awakens to grace us with her magnificence. Welcome back. We missed you."

I tried to smile. Mwita scoffed.

"Mwita, how does she look?" Ssaiku asked. "Report."

"She's . . . pretty beaten up. She's healed most of the open wounds but she can't heal everything with her Eshu skills. Must have something to do with how they were inflicted. A lot of deep bruises. Looks like something raked at her chest. She has burns on her back . . . at least that's what they manifest themselves as. She has a sprained ankle and wrist. No broken bones. From what she's told me happened, I suspect it will hurt for her to breathe. And when her monthly comes, that too will be painful."

Ssaiku nodded and Mwita continued.

"I've treated everything with three different salves. She should stay off the ankle and avoid the wrist for a few days. She'll have to eat a diet of desert hare livers for a week when her monthlies begin because her blood will be very heavy. Her monthlies will come tonight, because of the trauma. I've already had Ting ask some women to gather the livers and make a stew."

I noticed for the first time how utterly exhausted Mwita looked. "There's one thing," Mwita said. He took my right hand and turned the palm up. "This."

Ssaiku took my hand, looking closely at the marking. He sucked his teeth, disgusted. "Ah, *he* put this on her."

"H-how did you know it was . . . him?" I asked.

"Where else would you have gone in such a hurry?" he asked. He stood up.

"What is it?" Mwita asked.

"Ting may know," he said. "At two years old the girl could read Okeke, Vah, and Sipo. She'll be able to read this." He patted Mwita on the shoulder. "I wish we had someone like you here. To be so well versed in the physical and spiritual is a rare gift."

Mwita shook his head. "Not so knowledgeable in the spiritual, *Oga*," he said.

Ssaiku chuckled, patting Mwita's shoulder again. "I'll be back," he said. "Mwita, get some rest. She lives. Now go treat yourself as if you do, too."

Seconds after Ssaiku left, Diti, Luyu, and Fanasi came running in. Diti screamed, planting a kiss on my forehead. Luyu burst into tears and Fanasi just stood there staring.

"Ani is great!" Diti blubbered. "She must love you so much."

I could have laughed at this sentiment.

"We love you, too," Luyu said.

Without a word, Fanasi turned and left the tent. On his way out, he almost bumped into Ting. She skirted around him and came right to me. "Let me see," she said, pushing Luyu and Diti aside.

"What?" Luyu said, trying to see over Ting's shoulder.

"Shh," Ting scolded, taking my hand. "I need silence." She brought her face to my palm and stared for a long time. She touched the symbol and yanked her hand away hissing, glancing at Mwita.

"What is it?" Mwita and I asked at the same time.

"An Nsibidi symbol. Barely. Very very old, though," Ting said. "It means 'slow and cruel poison.' Look, the lines have already begun. They'll travel up her arm to her heart and squeeze it dead."

Mwita and I looked closely at my hand. The branded symbol was black as ever but now there were tiny filaments growing from the edges. "What about agu root and penicillin mold?" Mwita asked. "If it behaves like an infection maybe . . ."

"You know better, Mwita," Ting said. "This is juju." She paused. "Onye, try to change yourself."

Even with all my injuries, the idea was enticing. I could feel it. I wouldn't be able to change into more creatures than I could before, but I could become, for example, a vulture and never risk losing myself no matter how long I stayed one. Shifted myself. It came smoothly, easy . . . until I got to the hand marked with the symbol. It wouldn't change. I tried harder. How I must have looked to Diti and Luyu, especially Luyu who had never seen me change.

I hopped around my fallen bandages, all vulture except for a wing that was a hand. I squawked angrily, jumping out of my clothes. I couldn't fly with one hand. I fought a claustrophobic panic and tried another shape, a snake. My tail was a hand. I couldn't even turn myself partly into a mouse. I tried an owl, a hawk, a desert fox. The more shapes I tried, the hotter my hand grew. I gave up, changing back to myself. My hand gave off a foul smelling smoke. I covered myself with my rapa

"Don't try anything else," Ting said quickly. "We don't know the consequences. We have twenty-four hours, I suspect. Give me two to consult with Ssaiku." She got up.

"Twenty-four hours before what?" I asked.

"Before it kills you," Ting said, hurrying away.

I shuddered with hatred. "Whether I live or die, I'll destroy that man." *You will fail again,* the voice in my head whispered.

"Look what happened to you when you tried," Mwita reminded me.

"I wasn't thinking," I said. "Next time, I . . ."

"You're right. You weren't thinking," he said. "Luyu, Diti, go and bring her something to eat."

They jumped up, glad to have something to do.

"Don't mix anything together," he said.

"We know," Luyu said. "You're not her only friend."

"How come I can do it?" I asked Mwita, once they'd left. "Aro never mentioned anything like this traveling ability."

Mwita sighed, letting go of his anger at me. "I think I know why," Mwita surprised me by saying.

"Huh?" I said. "Really?"

"It's not the time," he said.

"I have twenty-four hours to live," I said angrily. "When do you plan to tell me?"

"In twenty-five," he said.

Chapter 48

TING TOOK THREE HOURS TO RETURN. In this time, the poison lines lengthened by three inches and my hand had begun to itch horribly. Chief Usson and Chieftess Sessa stopped in with their daughter Eyess. Eyess jumped into my lap. I hid my pain and let her plant a big kiss on my lips. "You will never die!" she exclaimed.

Other people came to wish me well, bringing food and oils. They gave me tight hugs and shook my hand, the one without the symbol, of course. Yes, now that I had "released" whatever had built up in me, yet was slowly being poisoned by something my biological father had inflicted on me, I was no longer untouchable. They also brought tiny human figurines made from sand. If you held these to your ear, you heard soft sweet music.

What had happened when I first died was starting to really set in. The world around me was more vibrant. Whenever Mwita touched me, I shivered. And when people hugged me, I could hear their hearts beating. An old man hugged me and his heart sounded full of wind. I had a strong urge to touch him. I could heal him without suffering much, but I heeded Ting's warnings to not try anything. It was so hard to sit still. *Yet even with all these tools, Daib still lives and I am dying,* I thought.

"Give it a few more hours," Mwita said. "If you get up now, you won't be doing yourself any good."

"Well, we'll have to risk that," Ssaiku said, walking in. Behind him,

Ting entered followed by, judging from their attire, the town's Ani priestess and priest.

"I may be able to stop the poison," Ting said.

Mwita and I grabbed hands. Then he yanked his away. "Ah, I hate that thing," he said glaring at my symboled hand.

"Sorry," I said.

"It won't be easy," Ting said. "And whatever happens will be permanent."

Suddenly, I wanted to scream with laughter. When she said *permanent*, it clicked. I understood a part of the puzzle. When I had been my future self in that concrete jail cell awaiting execution, I'd looked down at my hands. They'd been covered with tribal symbols . . . Nsibidi.

"You'll be the one to do it, no?" I asked Ting.

She nodded. "I'll be overseen by Ssaiku. The priest and priestess will pray during the process. Words to battle words." She paused. "Your father is *very* powerful."

"He's not my father," I said.

She patted my shoulder. "He is. But he could not have raised you."

To prepare for the process, I had to take a cleansing bath. Mwita procured a large palm fiber bathtub. It was treated with weather gel and was thus as good as any metal or stone tub. Mwita and several others gathered capture station water, boiled it, and poured it into the bath for me. My wounds stung as I slowly got into the steaming water. The symbol on my hand itched so vigorously that I had to fight the urge to tear at my hand's skin.

"How long do I have to stay in here?" I moaned. The water smelled sweet with the herbs Ting had given me.

"Thirty more minutes," Mwita said.

When I got out of the bath, my body was red with heat. I looked down at the three deep scratches on my chest. Right between my breasts. As if Daib had wanted to remind Mwita of his presence. *If I survive,* I thought.

I hated Daib.

When Mwita and I returned to Ssaiku's tent, everyone was ready. The priest and priestess were already begging Ani. I felt annoyed, thinking about the Creator who'd recreated me and the fact that Ani was a weak human idea. I held my tongue remembering the Golden Rule of Bush-craft: Let the eagle and the hawk perch. Ssaiku closed the tent flap behind us and ran his hand over it. Instantly, all noise from outside ceased. Ting sat on a mat, a bowl of very black paste beside her. There were two mats with symbols drawn on them.

"Sit there," Ting said. "Onye, you are not to get up until it is done."

It was like sitting on hot skittering metal spiders. I wanted to scream and if it weren't for Mwita, I would have.

"It's the symbols. They're alive as anything else," Ting said. "Give me your hand." She looked closely. "It spreads. *Ogasse*, I need two hours of protection."

"You will have it," Ssaiku replied.

"Protection from what?" I asked.

"Infection," Ting said. "When I mark you."

"If I can't do it any longer, I will speak up," Ssaiku said. "I've warned everyone already. I think some of them will welcome the time to explore a bit without the storm."

Ssaiku couldn't protect me and maintain the sandstorm at the same time.

"This will hurt," Ting said. She paused, looking nervous. "If it works, you'll never be able to heal with your right hand again."

"What?" I screeched.

"You'll have to always use your left hand to heal," Ting said. "I-I don't know what will happen if you use your right. It's full of his hate." She took Mwita's hand. "Hold her," she said.

Mwita put his left arm around my waist and put his right hand on my shoulder. He kissed my ear. I braced myself. I'd already been through so much. But I held steady. Ting took my right hand and poked the back of my hand using her long sharp thumbnail. There was a fiery eruption of pain. I cried out, at the same time, forcing myself to focus on her face. She dipped her nail in the paste and started drawing.

It was as if Ting fell into a trance and was taken over by someone else. She smiled as she worked, enjoying every loop and swirl, every line, ignoring my grunts and heavy breathing. Sweat beaded and fell down her forehead. The tent began to smell like burned flowers as smoke rose from my hand. Then there was the itching. The symbol was fighting back.

She turned my palm up and began to draw near the symbol. I looked down and was horrified. It quivered, coiled, and moved slowly away from her drawings. It was disgusting. But there was nowhere for it to escape. As the drawings closed in around it, it began to fade. Every surface of my hand was covered. Daib's symbol disappeared. She drew the final symbol over the spot where it had been, a circle with a dot in its center. Ting's eyes cleared and she sat back.

"Ssaiku?" Ting asked, wiping her face with the back of her hand.

He didn't respond. He had his eyes shut tightly. His face was strained and he was sweating profusely, dark patches in the armpits of his caftan.

The itching started on my left hand. Ting cursed under her breath when she saw the panic on my face. The priest and priestess paused in their prayers.

"Has it worked?" the priestess asked.

Ting turned up my left hand. The symbol was there now. "It's jumped, like a spider," she said. "Give me three minutes. Mwita, get me palm wine."

He quickly got up and brought the bottle and a glass to Ting. She grabbed the bottle and drank deeply from it. Her hands were shaking. "Evil man," she whispered, taking another swig. "This thing he put on you . . . eh, you can't understand." She took my hand. "Mwita, hold her tightly. Don't let her run. I have to chase it away now."

She started drawing again. I gritted my teeth. When she'd chased and trapped the symbol in the center of my palm, it did something that made me want to jump up and tear out of that tent like my life depended on it. It sunk deep into my hand and then emitted such an electrical shock that for a moment, I couldn't control my muscles. All of the nerves on my body flared. I screamed.

"Hold her," Ting said, grasping my hand with all her strength, her eyes wide as she drew. Mwita held me down as I bucked and shrieked. Somehow, Ting managed to complete that last circle. The symbol, repelled, jumped from my hand and landed with a *clack* on the floor. It sprouted many black legs and ran.

"Priest!" Ssaiku shouted, as he sat down hard on the floor and sighed with extreme fatigue. The tent flap fell open on its own. The noise from outside came tumbling in.

The priest leaped forward and ran after the symbol. Skipping this way and that. Finally, *Smack!* He stamped his sandal on it hard. When he removed his foot, only a smudge of charcoal was left. "Ha!" Ssaiku triumphantly exclaimed, still breathing heavily. Ting sat back, exhausted. I lay there panting on the floor, the mat underneath me still feeling like metal spiders. I rolled off it and stared at the ceiling.

"Try to change your hand," Ting said.

I was able to change it into a vulture's wing. However, instead of just black feathers, it was speckled with black and red ones. I laughed and lay back on the floor.

Chapter 49

MWITA AND I SPENT THE NIGHT IN SSAIKU'S TENT. Ssaiku had an important meeting and wouldn't be back until the morning.

"What about the sandstorm?" Mwita asked Ting. "Is it still . . ."

"Listen for yourself," she said. I could hear the distant roar of the wind. "He can control it when he travels. That's nothing for him. I think people had a good time while the storm was down, though. I'm always telling him that he should do that once in a while." She moved to leave. "Someone will bring you both a large meal."

"Oh, I couldn't eat anything," I moaned.

"You must eat too, Mwita." She looked at me. "The last time he ate was the last time you ate, Onye."

I looked at Mwita shocked. He only shrugged. "I was busy," he said.

We fell asleep minutes after Ting left. It was past midnight when Luyu woke us. "Ting said you have to eat," she said, lightly smacking my cheek again. She'd spread out a gigantic meal of roast rabbit, a large bowl of stewed rabbit livers, cactus candy, curried stew, a bottle of palm wine, hot tea, and something I hadn't eaten since I was in the desert with my mother.

"Where did they find aku?" Mwita asked, taking one of the fried insects and popping it in his mouth. I grinned, doing the same.

Luyu shrugged. "A bunch of women handed me all these plates but that one bothers me. It looks like . . ."

"It is," I said. "Aku are termites. You fry them in palm oil."

"Ugh," Luyu said.

Mwita and I ate ravenously. He made sure I ate all the rabbit liver stew.

"It was stupid to eat that much," I moaned, when we finally stopped eating.

"Maybe, but it's a good risk to take," he said.

Luyu sat with her legs stretched out as she watched us and sipped a glass of palm wine. I lay out on the floor. "Where are Diti and Fanasi?" I asked.

Luyu shrugged. "Around, I guess." She crawled to me. "Let me see your hands."

I held them out. They were like one of the Ada's works of art. The drawings were perfect. Perfect circles, straight lines, graceful ebbs and flows. My hands were like the pages of some ancient book. The symbols on my right hand were smaller and closer together than the ones on my left. More urgent. I flexed my right hand. It didn't hurt. No pain meant no infection. I smiled, very very glad.

"I could look at them all day," Mwita said.

"But this hand is useless," I said, making a fist with my right hand. "Or should I say dangerous."

"So when do you think we'll be, well, moving on?" Luyu asked.

"Luyu, I can barely walk," I said.

"But you'll be able to soon enough. I know you," she said. "I'm in no hurry really. It's nice here. But in a way I am. I . . . I was talking to some men. They told me things, about how it is in the West." She paused. "I know something has happened to you." She took a deep breath and steadied herself. "I pray, I pray to Ani, I swear to Ani, that you better be the real thing. You have to be the one prophesied." She paused, looking with wide eyes at Mwita, then me. "I'm sorry! I didn't mean . . ."

"It's all right," I said. "I've told him."

Mwita cocked his head, eyeing me. "You told her before telling me?"

"It doesn't matter," Luyu said. "What matters is that it has to be true because what's happening over there, what waits for you to put an end to it, is of the oldest evil. I used to think it was the Nurus. They were born ugly and superior . . . but, it's deeper than humans." She wiped her eyes. "We can't stay here too long. We have things to do!"

Mwita took Luyu's hand and squeezed it. "I couldn't have said it better myself."

Ssaiku's tent was warm and comfortable. There were empty plates around us. We were alive. We were where we needed to be in that moment. I pushed aside my growing doubts and reached forward and took Mwita's and Luyu's hands and, with our heads down, we instinctively shared a prayer.

Then Luyu let go of our hands. "I'm going to go . . . socialize. If you need me come to the tent of Ssun and Yaoss." She smirked. "Call out before entering."

I soon fell into a warm black recharging sleep. I woke up with sun in my eyes as it shined through the tent's flap. My body ached a hello. Mwita's arm was clamped around me. He was softly snoring. When I tried to move it, he held me tighter. I yawned and brought up my right hand. I held it in the sunshine and willed it to sprout feathers. With great great ease, it did. I turned to Mwita and met his open eyes.

"Has it been twenty-five hours yet?" I asked.

"Can you wait another hour?" he asked, reaching between my legs. He was disappointed when his fingers came away bloody. My monthly had arrived. As if from the realization, the womb pain descended on me, and I suddenly felt nauseated.

"Lie down," Mwita said, jumping up and wrapping his waist with his rapa. He left and came back with a bundle of clothes and a fresh rapa.

"Here," he said and placed a tiny dried leaf in my mouth. "One of the women gave me a small sack of it."

It was bitter but I managed to chew and swallow it. I got up, took care of myself, and then lay back down. My nausea was already decreasing. Mwita poured me a glass of the remaining palm wine. It was sour but my body welcomed it.

"Better?"

I nodded. "Now tell me a story."

"Before I say anything, note that we've *both* been keeping secrets," Mwita said.

"I know," I said.

"Okay." He paused, pulling at his short beard. "You can travel the way you do because you have the ability to *alu*. You're . . ."

"*Alu?*" I said. The word had a familiar sound to it. "You mean like Alusi?"

"Just listen, Onyesonwu."

"How long have you known?" I asked, frantic.

"Known what? You don't even know what you're asking."

I frowned but held my mouth shut, looking at my hands. *So going "away" was called alu,* I thought.

"Your mother is close to the Ada," Mwita said.

I frowned. "So?"

Mwita took my shoulders. "Onyesonwu, be quiet. Let me talk. You listen."

"Just . . ."

"Shh," he said.

I sighed, putting my hands over my face.

"Your mother is close to the Ada," he calmly said. "They talk. The Ada is Aro's wife. They talk. And you know what Aro is to me. We talk. This is how I know about your mother. It's good that it happened this way because now I can tell *you*."

"Why didn't you tell me before?" I asked. "Why didn't my mother tell me?"

"Onyesonwu?"

"Talk faster, then," I said.

"I've thought about it," he said, ignoring me. "Your mother knew exactly what she was doing when she asked that you be a sorceress once you were born and a girl. It was her revenge." He looked down at me. "Your mother can travel within, she can *alu*. The word for the mythical creature we know of as the Alusi comes from the actual sorcerer's term 'to *alu*,' to 'travel within.' She . . ."

I held up a hand. "Wait," I said. My heart pounded hard. It all fell into place. I thought about the *Kponyungo* that had taken me *alu*. Its voice had sounded familiar but I didn't know why. This was because it was my mother's, a voice I'd never really heard. *She loved Kponyungos*, I thought. *How did I not know?* "The *Kponyungo* was my mother?" I whispered to myself.

Mwita nodded. Another thought occurred to me: *Maybe that's why I couldn't make myself the same size as her when she took me* alu. *Maybe, when* alu *one can't outgrow her own parent.*

"So I get the ability from her?"

"Right," he said. "And . . . this may have caused . . ." He shook his head. "No, that's not the right way to put it."

"Don't make it easy," I insisted. "Just tell me. Tell me everything."

"I don't want to hurt you," he said quietly.

I scoffed. "If you haven't noticed, I can take pain fairly well."

"Okay," he said. "Well, the fact is your mother would have passed initiation. This is what Aro believes after talking to both your mother and the Ada. It has something to do with your grandmother. Do you know anything about your grandparents?"

"Not much," I said, rubbing my face. What he was telling me felt so unreal, yet it made sense. "Nothing like that."

"Well, that's what Aro believes," he said. "You know how you felt when you met Ting and Ssaiku, that repellence and attraction? There is always energy between your kind." He paused. "It's why your mother chose to live when she realized she was carrying you. It's part of why you and your mother are so close. And it's probably why Daib chose your mother to impregnate. Your mother can become two beings, herself and an Alusi— she can split herself.

"Aro didn't tell you because he didn't think you needed more surprises. Plus you hadn't shown any hint of going *alu* back then. I don't think he'd have ever imagined you'd have the ability so strong."

I sat back, my mouth hanging open.

"While I'm telling you all this," Mwita said. "I might as well tell you the rest of what I know about your mother."

I wish it was my mother who told me what Mwita went on to tell me. I'd have loved to hear it from her. But my mother has always been full of secrets. It was that Alusi side, I guess. Even when she showed me the green place, she preferred to do it without me knowing it was her. My mother never told me much about her childhood, either.

All I really knew was that she was close to her brothers and her father, Xabief. Not so much her mother, Sa'eeda. My mother's people were Salt People. Their main business was selling salt extracted from a giant pit that used to be a salt water lake. My mother's people were the only ones who knew how to get to it. Her father used to take her and her older brothers along on the two-week journey to collect and bring back salt. She loved the road and she couldn't bear to be away from her father for so long.

According to Mwita, my mother's mother, Sa'eeda, was also a free spirit. And though she loved her children, motherhood was not easy for her. To have all her children out of the house for those months suited her well. And it suited her husband well, too, for fatherhood came easily to him and he loved and understood his wife.

On the Salt Road, my mother learned to love the desert, the roads, the open air. She used to drink milky tea and have loud raucous conversations with her brothers and father. But there was more to these trips. Wherever she was out there in the desert, her father would encourage her to fast.

"Why?" she'd asked the first time.

"You'll see," her father had replied.

I wondered if maybe she even met a *Kponyungo* here, too, as it rose out of the salt beds.

I closed my eyes as Mwita told me these things that my mother had told the Ada and never told me.

"So she had perfect control of this even back then?" I asked.

"Even Aro looked envious when he told me about how many places your mother has traveled to," Mwita said. "Especially the forests."

"Oh, Mwita, it was so beautiful."

"I can't even imagine," Mwita said. "So much life. Your mother . . . how all that must have touched her."

"Mama is . . . I never knew," I whispered. "But who asked for it to be so with her? If she would have passed initiation, someone had to ask for it to be so."

Mwita shrugged. "My guess is that it was her father."

"Something terrible must have happened for him to have asked."

"Maybe." He took my hand. "One last thing. When we left Jwahir, Aro was considering taking on your mother as his student."

"What?" I sat up. The healing cuts on my chest and the bruises on my legs throbbed.

"And you know she'll say yes." Mwita said.

Chapter 50

ALL MORNING I FELT STRANGE IN MY SKIN. My body ached horribly from Daib's evil thrashing. I was full of doubt about my own abilities and purpose. My monthly made my womb hot as a rock fire stone. My hands were covered in juju drawings. My right hand was dangerous. My mother was more than I'd imagined and what she was was in me. And the same with my biological father. But life never stops.

"I'll be back soon," Mwita said. "Can you manage?"

"I can," I said. I felt awful but I wanted some time alone, too.

Minutes later, as I was slowly stretching my legs, Luyu came running in.

"They've gone!" she screeched.

"Eh?" I said.

"They left when the sandstorm stopped," Luyu babbled. "They took Sandi."

"Stop, wait, who?!"

"Diti, Fanasi," Luyu cried. "All their things are gone. I found this."

The letter was written in Diti's squiggly handwriting on a piece of torn white cloth.

My friend Onyesonwu,
I love you very much but I do not want to be a part of this. Since
Binta was killed, I've felt this way. Neither does Fanasi. The storm has

stopped and we take it as a sign to flee. We don't wish to die as Binta did. Fanasi and I have realized our love. And Luyu, yes, we have consummated our marriage. We'll return to Jwahir, Ani willing, and have the life we are meant to have. Onye, thank you. This journey has changed us forever, for the better. We simply wish to live, not die like Binta. We'll take news of you back to Jwahir. And we hope to hear great stories about you. Mwita, take care of Onye.

Your friends,
Diti and Fanasi.

"Sandi felt they needed her more than we did," I whispered, tears dribbling down my face. "The sweet camel. She doesn't like either of them much."

I looked up at Luyu. "I'm with you to the end," she said. "That's why I came." She paused. "And that's why Binta came."

Ting rushed in. "Ssaiku's back," she said. "You're dressed? Good." She ducked out. A moment later, she returned with Ssaiku and a nervous looking Mwita. He was followed by someone draped in black robes. My legs went weak.

Chapter 51

LUYU SLIPPED OUT AS SOLA CEREMONIOUSLY SWEPT IN. He was much taller than I'd have expected him to be. The only two times I'd seen him, during my initiation and just before leaving Jwahir, he'd been sitting. Now, he seemed to tower over even me. I couldn't tell because of his long heavy robes but I think he was long-legged like Ting, for she too looked much shorter when sitting.

"Onyesonwu, get us palm wine," Sola ordered, sitting down.

"Just outside," Ssaiku said. "You'll see it."

I was glad to have a reason to get out of there. Diti and Fanasi were gone. Over a day away. They had Sandi with them but I wasn't sure if even she could keep them alive. If one of them got sick . . . I pushed the thought from my mind. Whether they lived or died, they were gone. I refused to wonder if I would ever see them again.

The palm wine was next to Ssaiku's camels, packed with other supplies. I pulled out two of the green bottles. When I reentered the tent, Ting got up to get glasses. "Follow my lead," she mumbled, moving past me. She handed a glass to Sola and then I poured, then Ssaiku, then Mwita. Then she held a glass out and I poured for her and then myself. We sat on mats in a circle, our legs crossed. Mwita on my left, Ting on my right, and Ssaiku and Sola across from us. For too long, we all sat drinking and staring at each other. Sola took very small sips of his wine.

As before, his robe's hood came over his head to hide the upper part of his face.

"Let me see your hands," Sola finally said in his dry thin voice. He took my left hand and hesitated slightly before taking my right. He ran the pad of his thumb over my symboled skin, holding his yellow nail up so as not to scratch me. "Your student is gifted," he told Ssaiku.

"You knew it before I did," Ssaiku said.

Sola smiled, his teeth were white and perfect. "True. I knew Ting before she was even born." He looked at me, "Tell me how it happened."

"Huh?" I said confused. "Oh . . . well, we were out there near the edge of the storm and . . ." I paused. "*Oga* Sola, may I ask you one question first?"

"You may ask two, since you've just asked one."

"Why didn't Aro come?"

"Why do you care?"

"He's my Master and I . . ."

"Why not ask why your mother could not come? That is more logical, no?"

I didn't know what to say to this.

"Aro doesn't have that ability," Sola said. "He cannot quickly cover distance. That's not his center. His skills lie elsewhere. So buck up. Stop whining. Tell me about your silly actions." He snapped his dry fingers for me to get on with it.

I frowned. It's difficult to tell something to someone who's already deemed it silly. I told them everything I remembered, except my suspicions about it being the actual Creator who brought me back the first time.

"How long have you known that Daib was your father?" Sola asked.

"Months now," I said. "Mwita and I . . . something happened. We've met him before. It's the third time I've traveled like this."

"The first time, I was the one who attacked him," Mwita said. "The man is . . . was my Master."

"What?" Ssaiku said loudly. "How can that be?"

"*Sha,*" Sola whispered. "So it comes together now." He chuckled. "These two share the same 'father.' One is Daib's biological offspring and the other is his student. It's a sort of metaphorical incest. What isn't immoral about these two?" He chuckled again.

Ting was looking at Mwita and me with wide fascinated eyes.

"What has Daib become?" Mwita asked. "I spent years with him. He's as ambitious as he is powerful. A man like that *always* grows."

"He's grown like a cancer, a tumor," Sola said. "He is like palm wine to the Palm Wine Drunkard in the Great Book, except that the intoxication Daib creates causes men to do unnatural violence. Nuru and Okeke are so like their ancestors. If I could wipe this land of you all and let the Red People roam and multiply, I would."

I wondered, what people Sola was of and if they were any better than the Okeke or Nuru. I strongly doubted it. Even the Red People weren't perfect.

"Let me tell you both about your . . . 'father,'" Sola said. "He is the one who will bring death to your precious East. He gathers thousands of men still crazed from the ease of wiping out so many Okekes in the West. He's convinced them that greatness lies in spreading. Daib the Military Giant. Mothers and fathers name their firstborn sons after him. He is also a powerful sorcerer. He is serious bad news.

"His words aren't bravado. He *will* succeed and his followers *will* see the fruits of their labor. First he'll finish off the few Okeke rebels left. Before they die, they too will be corrupted. They'll die evil. Mwita can tell us how it is already happening, no?

"Some of these villages are valuable. Some have been allowed to manage crops like corn and palm trees. The Okeke managers of these crops have gathered a little power for their good work. They will lose it all dying or fleeing. Daib does this as we speak. Gradually, Okekes will be fully wiped from the kingdom. The only ones kept will be the most broken slaves. Very soon, it could be two weeks, maybe less, Daib will start leading the Nuru military east to seek and destroy the exiles.

"It will, quite simply, be a revolution. I've seen it in the bones. Once it starts, once those groups of armed Nuru boys and men leave their kingdom, you won't be able to stop it. You'll be too late."

As if I could stop it regardless, I thought. Hadn't I just nearly gotten myself killed trying?

Sola looked at Ssaiku. "You all seem to have the right idea in these parts. Keep moving and hiding."

Ssaiku frowned at the insult but said nothing. Ting looked angry.

"I know much about Daib," Sola said, pinching his chin. "Should I tell you?"

"Yes," Mwita said in a strained voice.

"He was born in the Seven Rivers town of Durfa to a woman named Bisi. The woman was Nuru but she was born dada, imagine that. Unheard of. Had hair so long that by the time she was eighteen it was dragging on the ground. She was a creative soul, so she liked to decorate her dreadlocks with glass beads. She was tall like a giraffe and loud like a lion. She was always shouting about how women were treated badly.

"It is because of Bisi that women in Durfa now receive educations. She started that school that everyone wants to be in. In secret, she helped many Okekes escape during a rash of Okeke riots. She was one of the very few who rejected the Great Book. She lived up to the dreadlocks on her head. The dada-born are usually free thinkers.

"No one knows who the father was, for no one ever really saw Bisi with one particular man. It is rumored that she had many many lovers but it's also rumored that she had none. Regardless, one day her belly started growing. Daib was born during a normal day. There was no great storm or crash of lightning or burning corncob in the sky. I know all of this because this man was and always will be my student."

I jumped as if kicked in the spine. Next to me Mwita cursed loudly.

"Bisi brought him to me when he was ten. I suspect she was able to contact me because she was born with tracking abilities. I never asked her. I also suspect that when she gave birth to him, she must have been thinking deeply about the state of the Seven Rivers Kingdom. It must have disgusted her. And she wished with all her heart that her son would make a change. She asked for him to be a sorcerer.

"Anyway, she told me that she'd seen him change into an eagle, that goats would follow and obey him. Small things like that. Daib and I had an immediate connection. The moment I saw him, I knew he'd be my student. For twenty years, he was my child, my son. I will not go into the details. Just know that it was right and then it went wrong. So you must see it now. Your father, Mwita's Master, and my student," Sola said. Then he sang, "Three is the magic number. Yes it is. It's the magic number." He smirked, "I knew Daib's mother well. She had lovely hips and a mischievous smile."

I shivered at the thought of him bedding my grandmother. Again I wondered just how human Sola was. "So what am I to do, *Oga* Sola?" I asked.

"Rewrite the Great Book," he said. "Don't you know that?"

"But how do I *do* that, *Oga* Sola? The idea doesn't even make sense! And you say we only have two weeks? You can't rewrite a book that is already written and known by thousands of people. And it's not even the book that is making people behave this way."

"Are you sure about that?" Sola coldly asked. "Have you *read* it?"

"Of course I have, *Oga*," I said.

"Then you have understood the images of light and dark? Beauty and ugliness? Clean and dirty? Good and evil? Night and day? Okeke and Nuru? See?"

I nodded, but I felt I needed to look at the book again to further connect the dots. Maybe I could find the something I needed to take down my father.

"No," he said. "Leave the book now. You know what you have to do. You just haven't brought it forward in your mind yet. That's why he was able to humiliate you the way he did. You better figure it out soon, though. My only advice is this: Mwita, keep her from going *alu*. It'll take her right to Daib again. He'll kill her swiftly now. The only reason he didn't before was because he wanted her to suffer. Whatever happens between her and Daib *must* happen on its own time, not *alu* time."

"But how do I stop her?" Mwita asked. "When she goes, she just goes."

"You're the one she belongs to, figure it out," Sola said.

Ting elbowed me to keep my mouth shut.

Sola pursed his lips. "Now, woman, you've jumped an important hurdle. You've been unlocked. Many envy what we can do but if they knew what it took to be what we are, few would want to join the ranks." He looked at Mwita. "Few." He looked at Ting. "This woman here has trained for nearly thirty years. You, Onyesonwu, haven't even gotten a decade in. You're a baby, yet you have this task. Beware of your ignorance.

"Ting knew her center early. It is in these juju scripts. You, I suspect, will focus on your Eshu side, changing and traveling. But you lack control. No one can help you with that." He snapped his fingers and seemed to whisper to someone. Then he said, "We're through with this palaver." He smiled broadly. "I'm not hungry but I want to taste Vah cuisine, Ssaiku. And where are your town's old women? Bring them, bring them!"

He laughed raucously and so did Ssaiku. Even Mwita looked amused.

"Onyesonwu, Ting, go to Chieftess Sessa's tent and bring us the food she has prepared," Ssaiku said. "And tell those who wait there that their company is eagerly requested."

Ting and I quickly left the tent. I didn't care how much my body protested at the fast movement, I'd have done anything to get out of there. Once outside, we walked slowly as I tried to hide my slight limp.

"I think they wish to speak with Mwita alone," Ting said.

"Right,' I said.

"I know," Ting said. "They're old and have the same problem. But it's changing."

I grunted.

"Sola laughed at me when I first came to him . . . until he threw his bones and got the shock of his life," Ting said. "Then Sola had to convince Ssaiku about me."

"How did you . . . find Sola?"

"Woke up one day, knew what I wanted and where to find him, and found him. I was only eight." She shrugged. "You should have seen his face when I entered his tent. Like I was a pile of rotten goat feces."

"I think I know the look. He's so white. Is he . . . is he human?"

"Who knows," she said laughing.

"Do . . . do you think when the time comes that I'll know what to do? As you did?"

"You'll find out soon." She looked at my ankle. "Maybe you should go sit down. I'll bring the food."

I shook my head. "I'm okay. You just hold the heavier plates."

Mwita, Ting, and I didn't eat with Sola and Ssaiku. I was relieved. Sola didn't look up once the food was set before him. Heaps of everything, even egusi soup, something I hadn't had since we'd left Jwahir. The three of us made a quick exit as soon as the two started to eat and talk about the breasts and backgrounds of the old women who were soon to arrive.

It took us nearly a half hour to get back to our campsite because of my ankle. I refused to lean on Mwita or Ting. When we got there we found Luyu sitting alone. She'd unbraided and brushed out her Afro. Even in her sorrow, she was lovely. I froze, looking at Mwita, who was looking at the two spaces where Diti and Fanasi's tents had been. A look of complete and utter disgust passed over his face. "You can*not* be serious," he said. "They *left?*"

Luyu nodded.

"When?! During the . . . when Ting was saving Onyesonwu's life? They *left?*"

"I found out, right after you left," I said. "Then Sola came . . ."

"How could he?" Mwita shouted. "He knew . . . I told him so much . . . and he still ran off? Because of *Diti?* That *girl?*"

"Mwita!" Luyu exclaimed getting up. Ting chuckled.

"You don't know," Mwita said. "You've just been having intercourse with him, with men, you and Diti, like rabbits."

"*Eh!*" Luyu exclaimed. "It takes a woman *and* man to . . ."

"He and I spoke like brothers," he said, ignoring her. "He said he understood."

"Maybe he did," I said. "But that doesn't make him the same as you."

"He had nightmares about the killings, the torture, the rapes. He said he had a duty. That change was worth dying for. Now he runs off because of a woman?"

"Wouldn't you?" I said.

He looked me square in the face, his eyes wet and red. "No."

"You came because of me."

"Don't bring us into this," he said. "*You're* tied to it, you'll die in it. I'll die for you. This isn't only about us."

I froze. "Mwita, what do you mean . . ."

"No," Ting spoke up. "Hold your tongue. All of you. Stop this."

Ting took my cheeks in her warm hands. "Listen to me," she said. As I looked into her brown eyes, tears fell fast from mine. "Enough answers. This isn't the time, Onye. You're exhausted, you're overwhelmed. Rest.

Leave it alone." She turned to Mwita. "There are three of you left. It's right. Let it go."

Somehow I slept that night. Mwita's body was pressed to mine and my belly was full from the small feast Ting brought us. Still, it was in this sleep that the dreams started. Of Mwita flying away. The dream was of Mwita and me on a small island with a small house. All around us was so much water. The ground was soft with it and covered with tiny green water plants. Mwita sprouted wings with brown feathers. Without even a kiss, he flew away, never looking back.

Chapter 52

WE LEFT SSOLU IN THE DEEPEST PART OF NIGHT. Chieftess Sessa, Chief Usson, Ssaiku, and Ting accompanied us.

"You'll have an hour, so move quickly," Ssaiku said, as we passed all the tents for the last time. "If you're caught when I resume the storm, bear down and keep moving."

I heard the sound of small feet. "Eyess!" Chieftess Sessa hissed. "Go back to bed!"

"But Mommy, she's leaving!" Eyess shouted in tears. Her loud voice woke several people in nearby tents. Ting cursed to herself.

"Go back to bed, everyone, please," Chief Usson said.

People came out anyway. "Can't we say good-bye, chief?" a man asked. Chief Usson sighed and reluctantly assented. More whispering and gathering. Within a minute, there was a large crowd.

"We know where they're going," a woman said. "Let us at least see them off."

"We've enjoyed having Onyesonwu here," another woman said. "Strange as she is."

Everyone laughed. More people gathered, their bare feet whispering over the sand.

"We've enjoyed her beautiful friend Luyu, too," a man said. Several men agreed and everyone laughed again. Someone lit sticks of incense.

After several moments, as if someone had given a cue, they all began to sing in Vah. The song sounded like a chorus of snakes and it carried easily over the noise of the storm. They didn't smile as they sang. I shivered.

Eyess held my leg tightly. She sobbed and eventually buried her face in my hip. If I weren't carrying a burden on my back, I'd have picked her up. I put my hand on her back and pressed her to me. When the song ended, Chieftess Sessa had to tear Eyess from my leg. She allowed her to give me a hug and a slobbery kiss on the neck before sending her along, then Chieftess Sessa gave each of us a kiss on the cheek. Chief Usson shook Mwita's hand and kissed Luyu and me on the forehead. Ssaiku and Ting walked us to the edge of the storm.

"Watch closely," Ssaiku told Ting as we stood before it. "It's different when you're close to it. Everyone, kneel down."

He raised his hands and turned his palms to the storm. He spoke something in Vah and turned his hands downward. The ground shuddered as he pressed the storm's strength to the ground. Ssaiku's hands strained and I could see the muscles in his neck flexing underneath his wrinkles. All the sand in the air dropped. The sound reminded me of the sounds the Vah people make so often when they speak their language. *Sssssssss.* We covered our faces from all the dust. Ssaiku pushed forward. A wind blew it all away, clearing the air. The night sky was full of stars. I'd gotten so used to the constant background noise of the storm that the silence was profound.

Ssaiku turned to Ting, "Instead of using words as I did, you'll write into the air."

"I know," she said.

"Learn it again," he said. "And again." He looked at Mwita and took his hand. "Take care of Onyesonwu."

"Always," Mwita said.

He turned to Luyu. "Ting tells me about you. In many ways, you're like a man in your bravery and your . . . other appetites. Again, I wonder if Ani is testing me by showing me a woman like you. Do you understand what you move into?"

"Very much so," Luyu said.

"Then watch over these two. They need you," he said.

"I know," Luyu said. "And thank you." She looked at Ting. "Thank you *both* and I also thank your village. For everything." She shook hands with Ssaiku and gave Ting a tight hug. Then Ting went to Mwita and gave him a hug and a kiss on the cheek. Neither Ting nor Ssaiku hugged or even touched me.

"Beware of your hands," Ting told me. "And be aware of them." She paused, her eyes filling with tears. She shook her head and stepped back.

"You know the way," Ssaiku said. "Don't stop going until you get there."

We were over a mile away when the sandstorm whipped up behind us. It churned and rolled like a living cloud clawing at the clear sky. We sorcerers are certainly a powerful sort. The ferocity and power of that storm only proved this more. Mwita, Luyu, and I turned west and started walking.

"We're near water," Mwita said.

Once the sun was up, I pulled my veil lower over my face. Mwita and Luyu did the same. The heat was stifling, but it was a different kind of heat. Heavier, more humid. Mwita was right. There was water close by.

Over the next few days, we started wearing our veils all the time to stay cool. But the nights were comfortable. None of us spoke much. Our minds were too heavy. This gave me the time and silence to really mull over all that had happened in Ssolu.

I'd died, been remade, and then brought back. My hands continued to look strange to me, covered in dark black symbols and always bearing the faint scent of burned flowers. When Mwita and Luyu were asleep, I'd sneak out, change into a vulture, and ride the air. It was the only way I kept the darkness of doubt at bay.

As a vulture, the vulture that was Aro, my mind was singular, sharp, and confident. I knew that if I focused and was audacious I could defeat Daib. I understood that I was extremely powerful now, that I could do more than the impossible. But as Onyesonwu the Ewu Sorceress shaped by Ani herself, all I could think about was the thrashing Daib had given me. I'd been no match for him even in my remade state. I should have been dead. And the more the days passed, the more I just wanted to crawl into a cave and give up. Little did I know that I'd soon get my chance to do just that.

Chapter 53

FOUR DAYS AFTER LEAVING SSOLU, the land was still cracked, dry and bleached. The only animals we saw were the occasional beetle on the ground and passing hawk in the sky. Thankfully, for the time being, we had enough food so that we didn't have to eat beetle or hawk. The oddly humid heat made everything hazy and dreamlike.

"Look at that," Luyu said. She was leading the way, her portable in hand to keep us on track.

I'd been walking with my head down, deep in my gloomy thoughts about Daib and the death I was voluntarily heading toward. I looked up and squinted. From afar, they looked like tall skinny giants having a meeting.

"What is that?" I asked.

"We'll soon see," Mwita said.

It was a cluster of dead trees. They were a half mile off from the straight line we were making to the Seven Rivers Kingdom. It was the middle of the day and we needed the shade so we went to the trees. Up close they were even stranger. Not only were they each as wide as a house, they felt like stone not wood. Luyu knocked on a brown-gray trunk as I spread my mat in the shade of another tree's base.

"So solid," Luyu said.

"I know this place," Mwita said with a sigh.

"Really?" Luyu asked. "How?"

But Mwita just shook his head and ambled off.

"He's moody today," Luyu said, sitting beside me on my mat.

I shrugged. "He probably came through here when he fled the West," I said.

"Oh," Luyu said, looking in his direction. I hadn't told her much about Mwita's past. Somehow I didn't think Mwita wanted me telling anyone about the murder of his parents, his humiliating apprenticeship under Daib, or his child soldier days.

"I can't imagine how he must feel coming back here," I said.

After a peaceful two hours of rest, we continued on. It came about five hours later. And it came with a vengeance. Dark gray clouds curdled and surged in the sky.

"This can't be happening," Mwita muttered as we stared west. It was heading east, right at us. Not a sandstorm. An ungwa storm, a dangerous storm of terrible lightning and thunder and intermittent deluges of rain. We'd been lucky so far as it was the dry season when we left Jwahir and these storms only happened during the brief rainy season. We'd been traveling for a little less than five months. In Jwahir, this was right on time. I guess it was the same here, too. To be caught out in an ungwa storm was to risk death by lightning strike.

These were the only times that my mother and I were in danger during our nomad days. My mother said it was only by Ani's will that we survived the ten ungwa storms we encountered.

This one wasn't far and it was coming fast. All around us was flat dry land. Not a dead tree in sight, not that trees would help. We'd have been in even more danger if this storm had caught us at those stone trees. The wind picked up, nearly blowing my veil off. We had about a half hour.

"I . . . I know a place we could take shelter," Mwita suddenly said.

"Where?" I asked.

He paused. "A cave. Not far from here." He plucked Luyu's portable from her hand and pressed a button on the side of it for light. The clouds had just snuffed out the sun. Though it was about three p.m., it looked like late dusk. "About ten minutes . . . if we run."

"Okay, which way?" Luyu screeched. "Why are we . . ."

"Or we could try to outrun it," he suddenly said. "We could head northwest and . . ."

"Are you *crazy?*" I snapped. "We can't outrun an ungwa storm!"

He muttered something that I couldn't hear because of the rumble of thunder.

"What?"

He frowned at me. A stroke of lightning cracked the sky. We all looked up.

"Which way to your cave?" I demanded.

Still he said nothing. Luyu looked about to explode. Each second we stood there brought us closer to death by lightning strike.

"I . . . I don't think we should go there," he said after a moment.

"So we should stay out here and *die?*" I shouted. "Do you know what will . . ."

"Yes!" he snapped. "I've been through it, too! But the shelter . . . that place isn't right, it . . ."

"Mwita," Luyu said. "Let's go, there's no time for this. We'll deal with whatever's there." She looked fearfully at the sky. "We don't have a choice."

I eyed him closely. It was rare to see fear in Mwita but there it was.

"So you can push me toward a masquerade riddled with needles and demand that I face my fear but you can't face a stupid cave?" I shouted waving my arms about. "You'd rather get us all killed? I thought you were the man and *I* was the woman."

My words bit deep but I didn't care. It started to rain along with the lightning and thunder. He pointed a finger in my face and I looked fiercely back at him. Luyu screeched at an especially loud crash of thunder. She pressed close behind me.

"You go too far," he said.

"I can go much farther!" I shouted, angry tears falling from my eyes and mixing with the rain.

In the middle of nowhere, an ungwa storm about to set upon us, we stood glaring at each other. He snatched my hand and began to pull me along. Over his shoulder he bellowed, "Luyu?"

"I'm right behind you!"

We didn't run. I didn't care. I wasn't afraid—I was too angry. Mwita pulled me along at a steady pace, Luyu held my shoulder, her head down. I don't know how he could see his way in the heavy rain.

We weren't struck. It wasn't Ani's will, I guess. Or maybe it was our will. It took fifteen minutes. When we got to the large granite formation with the cave yawning at the base, we stopped. Luyu and I instantly knew why Mwita didn't want to come here.

The rain was coming down hard causing streams of water to drape the cave's opening but with each stroke of lightning you could see them clearly. They swung in the storm's wind. The bodies of two human beings hanging at the cave's opening. Bodies so old that they were dried and shriveled from the heat and sun, more bone than flesh.

"How long have they been there?" I whispered. Neither Luyu or Mwita heard me.

There was a loud blast as lightning struck the ground not far behind us. A strong wind shoved us toward the cave. Mwita led the way but he didn't let go of my hand. I had demanded that we go into the cave so we were all going.

The water falling over the entrance flowed down on my head and shoulders as we entered. My attention was focused on the swinging bodies to my right. They had been a woman and man, at least according to the sun-bleached raggedy clothes. The woman wore a long dress and veil and the man a caftan and pants. You couldn't tell if they were Okeke, Nuru, or anything else. They hung from thick ropes looped around copper rings embedded in the cave's ceiling. We had to press against the side of the cave's entrance to avoid touching them. Inside was too dark to see the cave's depth.

"The cave isn't that deep," Mwita said, pushing some rocks together. I helped, trying to ignore the cave's tangy, almost metallic scent. We needed to get a nice big rock fire, more for light than warmth. Luyu just stood there staring at the two dead people. I didn't bother asking her to help. Both Mwita and I had experienced our own deaths. Luyu had not.

"Mwita," I said quietly.

He shot me a heated look.

I defiantly endured it, mumbling, "I stand by what I said."

"Of course you do," he said.

"You have to face your own fears, too," I said. "And you were going to get us killed."

After a moment, his face softened. "Okay." He said. He paused, then said. "I'd never get either of you killed. I just needed a moment to think." He began to turn away but I took his hand and turned him back to me. "Were they there when you . . ."

"Yes," Mwita said, avoiding my eyes. "They were much . . . fresher back then, though."

So these people had been hanging here for more than a decade. I wanted to ask if he knew what they had done. I wanted to ask him many things but it wasn't the time.

"Luyu," he said minutes later, after he and I had made a nice pile of stones. "Come over here. Stop staring at them."

Slowly she turned as if coming out of a trance. Her face was wet. "Sit down," Mwita said. I walked over and took her hand.

"We should bury them," she said as I sat her before the pile of cool stones.

"I tried that," Mwita said. "I don't know how they were put up there but they can't be pulled down and their bones won't fall down." He looked at me and I understood. Juju kept them up there. Who had they been?

"We're not even going to try?" she said. "I mean, that's just rope and you were here, what, as a kid? They should come right down."

Mwita ignored her as he got the rock fire going. What its light illuminated was enough to drag Luyu's attention from the dead bodies. I was already feeling unease, now I just wanted to run out into the rain and chance the lightning. In the back of the cave, half covered with sand that had swept in over the years, were possibly hundreds of computers, monitors, portables, and e-books. Now I knew where the metallic smell came from.

The ancient monitors were a half inch thick, not even close to the monitors you saw used today that were much thinner, and most were smashed or cracked. The desktop computers were too large to hold with one hand. Old and amazingly ancient things packed in a cave in the middle of nowhere and long forgotten. I looked at Mwita, appalled.

The Great Book spoke of such places, caves full of computers. They were put here by terrified Okekes trying to escape Ani's wrath when she turned back to the world and saw the havoc the Okeke had created. This was just before she brought the Nuru from the stars to enslave the Okeke . . . or so the book said. Did this mean that parts of the Great Book were true? Had the Okeke really crammed technology away in caves to hide them from an angry goddess?

"This place is haunted," Luyu whispered.

"Exactly," Mwita said.

There was nothing I could say. We were in a tomb of humans, machines, and ideas while a deadly storm raged outside.

"How did you find this place?" I asked. "How'd you end up here?"

"And how did you remember the way so well?" Luyu added.

He went over to the swinging bodies. Luyu and I joined him. "Look up there," he said, pointing at the copper rings. "Who would drive those into stone like that?" He sighed. "I'll never know what happened or who these people were. When I came, it must have been just after they were hung. They still had . . . flesh. I'd say they were about the age we are now."

"Okeke or Nuru?" Luyu asked. I noted how she didn't consider the fact that they could have been Ewu or Red People.

"Nuru," he said. He looked at the bodies. "I can't believe they're still here . . . but then again, I can."

After a moment he said, "I came across this cave days after I escaped the Okeke rebels, after they'd left me for dead." He pointed to his left. "I sat against that wall and ate my medicinal plants and prayed to Ani that they would work."

Luyu looked like she was dying to know Mwita's story of what he meant by left for dead. Thankfully, she had the tact not to ask. The best way to deal with a moody Mwita was to let him talk.

"I was half out of my mind, really," he continued. He reached out and actually touched the leg of the dead man. I shuddered. "I'd lost the only family I knew. I'd lost my Master, terrible person though he was. I'd seen terrible things while forced to fight for the Okeke, done terrible things. I was *Ewu*. And I was only eleven years old.

"I had supplies. Food and water. I wasn't starving or dying of thirst and I knew how to find food. It was the heat that drove me in here. They were both very dead but they didn't smell . . ." He stepped over to the woman. "She was covered with white crablike spiders, except for her face and hands," he continued. "They were climbing over each other but if you stared long enough, which I did, you could see that they were following a pattern around her body. I remember the fingertips of her hands were blue. Like she'd dipped them in indigo."

He paused, again. "Even back then, I understood that the spiders were protecting her. The pattern they moved in reminded me of one of the few Nsibidi symbols Daib taught me. The symbol for ownership. I think I stood there for about twenty minutes just staring. All I could think of were my parents, whom I'd never known. They hadn't been hung but they'd been executed . . . for creating me. As I stood there, slowly, the spiders began to drop off her and move to the sides of the cave. When they'd all dropped off, they just remained there. Like they were waiting for me to do something.

"I tried everything. I tried to yank the bodies down. I tried to cut the rope. I tried burning it. Burning their bodies by making a huge fire under them. I even tried using juju. When nothing worked, I just walked past them, sat with my back to the computers and wept. After a while, the spiders . . . they crawled back on her. I stayed there two days pretending I didn't see the bodies and the spiders on the woman. I got stronger, got better, and then I left."

"What about the man?" Luyu asked. "Was there anything peculiar about him?"

Mwita shook his head, his hand still on the dusty leg of the dead man. "You don't need to know about all that."

Silence. I wanted to ask and I'm sure Luyu did too. Know all about what?

"So you think they were sorcerers?" she asked.

He nodded. "And their killers obviously were, too" He paused, frowning. "Now they are just bones." He suddenly grabbed the man's leg and gave a great yank. The rope groaned and dust puffed from the corpse, but that was it. The near-skeleton stayed intact. I wondered where the woman's spiders had gone.

*   *   *

A blanket of doom, sadness and despair settled on me that night, getting heavier the more the rain and lightning soaked and blasted the land. Luyu chose a spot on the other side of the cave as far from the bodies and the computers as possible. Mwita had built her a small rock fire. I wasn't sure if she wanted privacy or she wanted to give us privacy, but it worked either way.

Mwita and I lay on our mat underneath his rapa, our clothes folded beside us. The rock fire provided more than enough warmth but it wasn't warmth or intercourse that I needed. For once, I didn't mind how tightly he grasped me as he slept. I didn't like being in that cave. I could hear the heavy spatter of rain outside, the boom of thunder, the creaking of the bodies as they swung in the storm's wind.

Both Mwita and Luyu slept, despite it all. We were all exhausted. I didn't sleep a wink, though I had my eyes closed. Even with Mwita's and the large rock fire's warmth, I shivered. The facts flew about my mind like bats: There was no way that I could take down my father. I was going to get the three of us killed. *He was waiting for me,* I thought, remembering his turned back when I went after him.

"Onyesonwu," I heard Mwita say.

I didn't feel like responding. I didn't want to open my mouth or my eyes. I didn't want to breathe air or speak. I just wanted to wallow in my misery.

"Onyesonwu," he softly repeated, his arm tightening. "Open your eyes. But don't move."

His words sent a shock of adrenaline through me. My mind focused. My body stopped shivering. I opened my eyes. Maybe it was my misery or a need to prove myself but when I looked into the many eyes of the hundreds of white spiders crowded before me, along with a deep fear, I felt . . . ready. One of the spiders in front slowly raised a leg and kept it there.

"So they *are* still here," I said, not moving.

We were both quiet, seeming to read each other's minds. We were listening to see if Luyu was awake. But the storm was too noisy.

"They're all over me," he said, his voice wavered just a little. "My back, legs, back of my neck . . ." Every part of him that was not touching me.

"Mwita," I said softly. "What was it about the man that you didn't tell us?"

He didn't answer immediately. I started to feel very very afraid. "He was covered with spider bites," Mwita said. "His face was twisted with pain." I wondered if they had started biting the man before the man's murderers had strung him up.

My cheek was pressed to the mat. The spider still had its leg raised. A thousand things flew through my mind. I suspected that they wanted Mwita. I would *never* let them have him. The spider with its leg up was waiting. Well, I was waiting, too.

It brought its leg down. I felt them behind me, rushing over Mwita. I saw them coming at me from the front. I could smell them, a fermented odor, like strong palm wine. Even with the storm's noise, I could clearly hear the tap of their many legs. Since when did spider legs on sand sound so loud? Like metal clacking on metal? That was all I needed to know. For the first time, I used my new control of my abilities and pulled the wilderness around me and leaped up.

In the wilderness and the physical world, they looked like spiders, but in the wilderness they were much larger and made of white smoke. They passed through each other as they tried to crowd my blue form. I did to them what I did to Aro the day that he refused to teach me one too many times. I scratched, ripped, shredded, dismembered. I became a beast. I tore those creatures apart.

I slammed a foot back in the physical world, crushing a bunch of fleeing spiders, and caught Mwita's wide eyes. He was still on the mat, naked and covered with defiant white spiders. Around him, hundreds of spider corpses littered the cave floor. If even one bit him, I would seek out and kill every single one of these creatures and then hunt them down in the spirit world and destroy them again. Every single one.

I glanced in Luyu's direction. She was standing up, on the other side of her fire. I shook my head, she nodded. Good. Outside, lightning flashed. My state of mind was so sharp now. I was not the Onyesonwu you sit here speaking with. I cannot imagine what I must have looked like in the fire light, stark naked, angry, wild, the one I loved, threatened. *They think I'd let them take Mwita rather than risking Mwita's death*, I thought. I grinned evilly.

Lightning flashed again, the thunder came a second later. It rained harder. The smell of ozone was strong. You could feel the charge in the air. I waited, I willed it, as I repeated my name in my mind like a mantra. The lightning crashed down right outside the cave with a great *BOOM!* A blast of flame pounded the ground. I leaped at Mwita, grabbed his leg, and pulled up what the storm threw down. I sent it into Mwita. Every spider on him popped like a palm kernel in a fire. The smell of burning feathers filled the cave.

The spiders that lived skittered into the flame at the entrance of the cave. I will never know if this was a mass suicide or a decision to return to whence they came. I had retreated from the wilderness entirely the moment that lightning struck, so I did not see if they'd returned there.

"Mwita?" I whispered, ignoring the spider carcasses lying beside him. My body was drenched with sweat yet I shivered with cold. Luyu ran over and threw a rapa over us.

"I'm fine," he said, caressing my cheek.

"I guided it," I said.

"I know," he said with a laugh. "I didn't feel a thing."

"What were those?" Luyu asked.

"I have no idea," I said.

Something caught Mwita's eye. I turned in the direction he was staring. Luyu did, too. "Oh," she said.

The bodies had fallen, the ropes holding them singed by the blast. And now the dry remains burned bright. The mysterious executed sorcerer and sorceress finally got the funeral pyre they deserved.

The storm was still going when morning came. The only way we knew it was morning was by checking the time on Luyu's portable. While Luyu boiled some rice to mix with some dried goat meat and spices, Mwita used a pan to dig a grave on the side of the cave. He insisted on doing it alone.

I walked over to the electronics at the back of the cave. We'd avoided these items more than the corpses. They were the old devices of a doomed people. After what had happened last night, I was in the mood to look doom in the face.

"What are you doing?" Luyu asked, as she turned the rice. "Haven't you had enough . . ."

"Leave her," Mwita said, pausing in his digging. "One of us should look."

Luyu shrugged. "Okay. I know I'm not going near that cursed junk."

I chuckled to myself. I understood her sentiment and I think Mwita probably felt the same way. But me, well, this was a page right out of the Great Book. If I was going to somehow rewrite it then it made sense for me to look.

The tinny smell of old wiring and dead motherboards was stronger up close. There were scattered keys from keyboards and pieces of thin plastic in the sand from broken screens and casings. Some of the computers had designs on the outside—faded butterflies, loops and swirls, geometric shapes. Most were a uniform black.

A device that looked like a small very thin black book caught my eye. It was wedged between two computers and when I pulled it out, I was surprised to see that it had a screen when I opened it up. It looked beaten up but, unlike the other items, not old. It was about the size of the palm of my hand. The back of it was made of an extremely hard substance that looked oddly like a black leaf. The screen was unscratched.

All the buttons on the front were blank, the words rubbed off long ago. I touched a button. Nothing happened. I touched another and the thing made a sound like water. "Oh!" I exclaimed, almost dropping it.

The screen lit up showing a place of plants, trees, and bushes. I gasped softly. *Just like the place my mother showed me*, I thought. *The place of hope.* My chest swelled and I sat down right there beside the pile of decaying useless hardware from another time.

The image rolled and moved, like someone was walking and I was looking through her eyes. Through its tiny speakers came the sound of birds and insects singing and grasses, plants, and leaves being stepped on and pushed aside. Then the title slowly came up from the bottom of the screen and I understood that this was a large portable with a book on it. The book's title was *The Forbidden Greeny Jungle Field Guide*, written by some group calling themselves The Great Explorers of Knowledge and Adventure Organization.

Suddenly the image froze and the sound stopped. I pressed more buttons but nothing helped. It switched itself off and no matter how many times I pressed the buttons, nothing more happened.

No matter. I threw it aside. I straightened up. I smiled. Hours later, the sky smiled too. The storm had finally passed. We left the cave before dawn.

Over the next two days of travel, the land grew hillier. The ground became a mix of sand and patches of a sort of dry grass. Here we found lizards and jackrabbits to eat, and just in time, as our dried meat was running out. We came across fat-trunked trees I couldn't name and more and more palm trees. The climate remained cold at night and relatively warm during the day. And thankfully, we came across no more ungwa storms. Of course, there are worse things.

Chapter 54

THERE IS A PORTION OF THE GREAT BOOK that most versions exclude. The Lost Papers. Aro had a copy of them. The Lost Papers go into detail about how the Okeke, during their centuries festering in the darkness, were mad scientists. The Lost Papers discuss how they invented the old technologies like computers, capture stations, and portables. They invented ways to duplicate themselves and keep themselves young until they died. They made food grow on dead land, they cured all diseases. In the darkness, the amazing Okeke brimmed with wild creativity.

Okeke familiar with the Lost Papers are embarrassed by them. Nurus like to cite them whenever they want to point out how fundamentally flawed Okeke are. During the dark times, the Okeke may have been problematic, but now they were worse off.

A sad miserable unthinking lot, I thought, as we approached the first of many villages just before the border of the Seven Rivers Kingdom. I could understand how they felt. Only a few days ago I had felt the same way. Hopeless beyond hopeless. If we had not found that cave of corpses, spiders, and moldering computers, I probably would have wanted to join them.

These villages consisted of Okeke who were too afraid to fight or flee. They were shifty-eyed people who'd be easily exterminated when my father came east with his army. They walked with their heads down, afraid of their own shadows. They grew sad limp onions and tomatoes in soil brought from the riverside. In the front and back of their clay brick huts, they cultivated a waxy maroon plant which they dried and smoked to make themselves forget. It made their eyes red, their teeth brown, their skin smell like feces, and had no nutritional value. Of course, of all things, this weed grew easily in the ground here.

The children had large bellies and stunned faces. Mangy dogs trotted about looking as pathetic as the people; we saw one making a meal of its feces. And once in a while, when the wind shifted, I could hear screaming in the distance. These villages had no names. It was sickening.

Everyone, even the children, wore a dangling earring with black and blue beads in the upper part of their left ear. It was the only hint of culture and beauty that these people possessed.

We got past the first cluster of huts unnoticed. Around us, Okeke people dully trudged about, argued, slept in the roads, or wept. We saw men with missing limbs, some of them lay against huts, the wounds festering. Near death, or dead. I saw a pregnant woman laughing hysterically to herself as she sat in front of her hut pushing dirt into a mound. My hands itched and I felt jittery.

"How do you feel, Onyesonwu?" Mwita asked, as soon as we were past the last hut. A half mile away was another village.

"The urge isn't so strong here," I said. "I don't think these people want healing."

"Can't we go around these places?" Luyu asked.

I just shook my head, offering no explanation. I didn't have one. The next group of huts was in the same condition. Sad, sad people. But this place was at the bottom of a hill and we were in full view as we walked down it. As we passed the first hut an old woman with many unhealed cuts on her face stopped and stared at me. She looked at Mwita and her face pulled into a wide toothless grin. Then the woman's grin decreased. "But where are the rest of you?" she asked.

We looked at each other.

"You," the woman said pointing at me. I backed away. "You cover your face but I know. Oh, I know." The she turned and shouted. "Ooooonyesonwuuuuuuuu!"

I stepped back and crouched, ready to fight. Mwita grabbed and pulled me to him. Luyu ran in front of me, pulling out a knife. They came running from everywhere. Dark faces. Wounded souls. Wearing raggedy rapas and torn pants. As they gathered so did the smell of blood, urine, pus, and sweat.

"She is here, *o!*"

"The girl who will end the slaughter?"

"The woman whispered the truth," the old woman continued. "Come and see, come and see! Oooooooonyesonwuuuuuuu!!! *Ewu, Ewu, Ewu!*"

We were surrounded.

"Take it off," the old woman said, standing before me. "Let us see your face."

I glanced at Mwita. His face told me nothing. My hands itched. I removed my veil and a gasp flew through the crowd. "*Ewu, Ewu, Ewu!*" they chanted. A group of men to my right lurched forward.

"Ah ah!" the old woman shouted, holding them back. "We aren't finished yet! The General should be afraid now! Ha! His match is here!"

"That one there," a woman said, moving forward, pointing at Mwita. The side of her face was swollen and she was very pregnant. "He's her husband. Isn't that what the woman said? That Onyesonwu would come and we would see the truest love? What can be truer than two *Ewu* who can love each other? Who are *able* to love?"

"Shut up, Nuru concubine, whore ready to burst with human rot," a man suddenly spat. "We should hang you and cut out the evil growing in you!"

People quieted. Then several shouted agreement and the crowd lurched this way and that.

I pushed Mwita and Luyu aside and stepped toward the voice. Everyone in front of me jumped back, including the old woman. "Who just spoke!" I shouted. "Come up here. Show yourself!"

Silence. But he was pushed forward. A man of about thirty, maybe older, maybe younger. I couldn't tell because half his face was destroyed. He looked me up and down. "You're an Okeke woman's curse. May Ani help your mother by taking your life."

My entire body tightened. Mwita grabbed my hand. "Control your-self," he said into my ear.

I swallowed my instinct to tear off what remained of the man's head. My voice shook as I spoke. "What's your story?"

"I come from over there," he said, pointing west. "They're at it again and this time they'll finish us. Five of them raped my wife. Then they slit me up like this. Instead of finishing me off, they let me and my wife go. Laughing, they said they'll catch up with me soon enough. Later I learned my wife was carrying one of them. One of *you*. I killed her and the evil thing growing inside her. The thing in her looked wrong even in death."

He stepped closer. "We are nothing in the face of the General. Listen to me everyone," he said raising his hands high and turning to the crowd. "We are at the end of our days. Look at us now, looking to this spawn of evil to save us! We should . . ."

I snatched my arm from Mwita, grabbed the man's hand with my left hand and held tight. He fought, gnashed his teeth, cursed. Not once did he try to hurt me, though. I concentrated on what I was feeling. This was not the same as when I brought things back to life. I was taking and taking and taking, as a worm eats away rotten flesh from a rotting but alive leg. It felt itchy, painful, and . . . amazing.

"Move . . . everyone . . . back," I muttered through gritted teeth.

"Back, back! Move!" Mwita shouted, pushing people.

Luyu did the same. "If you value your lives!" she shouted. "Move back!"

I relaxed my body, kneeling down as the man crumbled to the ground. Then I let go and held my breath. When nothing happened, I let it out. "Mwita," I said weakly, holding out my arm. He helped me stand. The people crowded back in to look at the man. A woman knelt beside him and touched his healed face. He sat up.

Silence.

"See how Oduwu can smile now?" a woman said. "I've never seen him smile."

More whispers as Oduwu slowly stood up. He looked at me and whispered, "Thank you." A man let Oduwu lean on him and they began to walk away.

"She's come," someone else said. "And the General will run." Everyone started cheering.

They crowded around me and I gave what I could. If I had tried to heal so many people, men, women, children, of disease, anguish, fear, wounds . . . if I had tried even a fraction of what I did now before what happened with the Red People, I'd have died. Every single one who came to me in those hours, I made better. Yes, I was a different woman from the one who struck the people of Papa Shee blind. But I will *never* regret what I did to those people because of what they did to Binta.

Mwita concocted herbal medicines for people and checked pregnant women's bellies to make sure all was well. Even Luyu helped, sitting with the healed and telling stories of our journey. These people were quite prepared to spread the word of the Sorceress Onyesonwu, the Healer Mwita and the Lovely Luyu of the Eastern Exiles.

A man ran up to me as we left. He was whole but limped severely as he walked. He didn't ask me to heal him. I didn't offer. "That way," he said, pointing west. "If you are that woman, they have started again in the corn villages. Gadi is next, the way it looks."

We camped in a patch of dry naked land not far from Gadi.

"They said an Okeke woman who never ate but looked well fed has been going around 'whispering the news,'" Luyu said, as we sat in the dark. "She predicts an *Ewu* sorceress will end their suffering." It was cold but we didn't want to attract attention by building a rock fire. "They said she spoke softly and had a strange dialect."

"My mother!" I said. I paused. "They'd have killed us, otherwise." My mother was going *alu,* sending herself here and telling the Okeke about me, to expect me and be glad. Aro truly was teaching her, then.

We were silent for a moment, thinking about this. From nearby an owl hooted.

"They're so wounded," Luyu said. "But can you blame them?"

"Yes," Mwita said.

I agreed with Mwita.

"They kept talking about the General," Luyu said. "They said he's the one behind all this, at least in the last ten years. They call him the Council's Broom because he is in charge of cleaning out the Okeke."

"How successful he's been since I was his student," Mwita said bitterly. "I don't even understand why he took me on if he would do something like this."

"People change," Luyu said.

Mwita shook his head. "He's always hated anything Okeke."

"Maybe his hate wasn't so big back then," Luyu said.

"It was big enough, years before, to rape my mother," I said. "The way they . . . never got tired. Daib must have worked some sort of juju on them all."

"Look at the Vah people," Luyu said. "They're a people who openly embrace juju. Eyess was born into a community that thought this way, so though she won't ever be a sorcerer, she doesn't fear sorcery. Now see Daib, born and raised in Durfa where all he sees and learns are that the Okeke are slaves and should be treated worse than camels."

"No," I said, shaking my head. "What of his mother, Bisi? She was born and raised in Durfa, too. Yet, she helped Okeke people escape."

"That's true," Luyu said frowning. "And he *was* taught by Sola."

"Some people are just born evil," Mwita said.

"But he wasn't always that way," Luyu said. "Remember what Sola said?"

"I don't care about any of this," Mwita said, his hands becoming tight fists. "All that matters is what he is *now* and the *fact* that he needs to be stopped."

Luyu and I had to agree with that.

That night I again had the dream of being on that island and watching Mwita fly away. I woke up and looked at him sleeping beside me. I patted his face until he woke up. I didn't have to ask him for what I wanted. He gave it with pleasure.

In the morning, when I came out of our tent, I almost fell over all the baskets. Baskets of deformed tomatoes, grainy salt, a bottle of perfume, oils, boiled lizard eggs, and other things. "They gave what they could,"

Luyu said. Someone must have given an eye pencil, for she'd lined her eyes with bright blue and penciled in a blue mole on her cheek. She'd also put on two green beaded bracelets, one for each wrist. I picked up the bottle of oil and sniffed it. It smelled strongly of cactus flowers. I rubbed some on my neck and went to our capture station. I flipped it on.

"I hope this doesn't attract anyone," I said.

"It probably will," Luyu said. "But everyone around here, maybe even in the Seven Rivers towns, knows about what you did yesterday. One version or another."

I nodded, watching the bag fill with cool water. "Is that a bad thing?"

Luyu shrugged. "It's the least of our worries. Plus your mother already got the ball rolling."

Chapter 55

THE KINGDOM OF THE SEVEN RIVERS and its seven large towns, Chassa, Durfa, Suntown, Sahara, Ronsi, Wa-wa, and Zin, very poetic names for such a corrupted place. Each hugs a river and all the rivers meet in the center to make a large lake, like a spider with a missing limb. The lake had no name because no one knew what lived at its bottom. Back in Jwahir, no one would believe such a body of water was possible. Durfa, my father's town, sits closest to this mysterious lake. According to Luyu's map, it was the first Seven Rivers town we'd intersect.

The borders of the kingdom were not blocked off by walls or juju, nor were they definite. You knew you were in it when you were in it. You became immediately aware of the scrutiny, the eyes. Not by soldiers or any of that sort, but by the Nuru people. Officials patrolled the area, but the people policed themselves.

There once were small Okeke villages between the towns and along the rivers. When we got there, these villages were nearly empty. The few remaining Okeke were being driven out. On the west side of the Seven Rivers, all these villages had been taken over. The slow exodus was on the eastern side, just east of Chassa and Durfa, the two wealthiest, most prestigious towns. These towns ironically had the greatest need for Okeke labor. With the Okeke gone, Nuru laborers from the poorer towns like Zin and Ronsi would do the work.

We heard what was happening before we saw it because we had to walk up a hill. Gadi, the village of Aro's birth, was being destroyed. We peaked above the dry grass and saw terrible things. To our right, a woman was fighting two Nuru men who kicked her and tore at her garments. The same thing was happening to the left. There was a loud crack and an Okeke man running by fell. A Nuru and Okeke man rolled on the ground fighting. It was the Nurus in control of things here. That was clear.

We looked at each other, eyes wide, nostrils flared, mouths open.

We dropped all that we carried and ran into the chaos. Yes, even Luyu. There are gaps in my memory of what happened next. I remember Mwita running and a Nuru man pointing a gun at his back. I threw myself on the man. He dropped his gun. He tried to get ahold of me. I kicked back, pushing myself into the wilderness like it was the water. I could see him swiping at where my own body had been. Mwita ran off. I leaped after him, still in the wilderness. So that man, who would have killed Mwita, I did not kill.

Mwita and I had discussed how we would never flat out succumb to the violence people, Nuru and Okeke alike, believed *Ewu* were prone to by nature. Here, we went against all of that. We became exactly what people believed we were. But our reasons for using violence were not rooted in being *Ewu*. And Luyu shared that same purpose. She was a pure Okeke woman of the most docile blood according to the Great Book.

I remember giving my clothes to Mwita and then changing and shifting into things, growing claws and tiger's teeth. I remember weaving between the physical world and the wilderness as if they were land and water. I knocked men off women, their penises still erect and slick with blood and wetness. I fought men with knives and guns. There were many Nuru soldiers and few Okeke ones, I fought both, helping whoever was unarmed. I took bullets into myself, expelled them, and moved on. I closed up my own stab and bite wounds. I smelled blood, sweat, semen, saliva, tears, urine, feces, sand, and smoke with the nostrils of various beasts. That is the little I remember.

We didn't stop what was happening there but we allowed several Okeke to escape. And I pushed to the ground and healed as many Nuru people as I could subdue. Those men then cowered in corners, appalled at what they'd done only moments ago. In a few minutes, they would begin to help the wounded, Nuru and Okeke. They would put out the fires. Then they would try to stop those other Nurus who were happily killing Okekes. And then these healed Nurus would be killed by their own blood-crazed people.

When I came back to myself I was pulling Luyu into a hut. Its thatch roof was burning. Moments later, Mwita threw himself in with us. He gave me my clothes and I quickly dressed. Both he and Luyu carried guns. Not far ahead, it continued—the screaming, fighting, killing. Breathing heavily, we looked at each other.

"We can't stop this," Mwita finally said.

"We have to stop this," Luyu said at the same time.

I closed my eyes and sighed.

From nearby a man shouted and another man screamed. The fire on the roof above us was spreading. "Once we find Daib, I think we'll know what to do," I said.

From then on, we snuck about. It was hard to do. The Nurus had suppressed the weak rebellion and now they were simply torturing people. The screeching mixed with the laughter and grunts of the torturers made my stomach turn. But somehow we got past it all and found ourselves faced with a spectacular sight.

Just behind the last group of huts were tall green stalks of corn. Hundreds and hundreds of them, a whole field of them. It was nothing nearly as breathtaking as the place my mother had shown me but it was still amazing to my desert-born eyes. My mother grew corn when we were in the desert and there were gardens of it in Jwahir but never this much. A breeze sent a whisper through the plants. It was a lovely sound. It sounded like peace, growth, bounty, and that hint of hope. Each plant was heavy with perfect ears of corn, ready to harvest. What an opportune time for the Nurus swoop in. The planning of General Daib, no doubt.

We'd left all of our travel things behind. Luckily, Luyu kept her portable in her pocket. We used its map to make our way through the cornfield. Durfa was on the other side. We moved quickly and stopped only once to yank and eat some corn. After walking for a half hour, we heard voices. We dropped down.

"I'll go see," I said, shrugging my clothes off.

Mwita took my arm. "Be careful," he said. "It'll be hard to locate us in this field."

"Put my rapa on top of the stalks," I said. I quickly changed into a vulture and flew off. The cornfield was huge but it was easy to locate the source of the voices. Less than a half mile away, in the middle of the cornfield was a hut.

I landed as quietly as I could on the edge of its thatch roof. I counted eight Okeke men in tattered clothes. Two had long black oily guns strapped to their backs.

"We should still go," one was saying.

"Those *aren't* our orders," another insisted, looking frustrated.

I took off, flying high to get the lay of the land. The cornfield was flanked by the towns of Durfa on the west side, Gadi on the east, and the lake with no name on the south. I saw what I wanted to make sure of when I flew higher. No more hills. From here on, the land was flat.

With the rapa on the top of the corn stalks, it was easy to find Luyu and Mwita. "Rebels," I told them as I put my clothes back on. "Not far. Maybe they can tell us where to find Daib."

Mwita looked at Luyu. Then back at me with a worried look.

"What?" Luyu asked.

"We should try to get there ourselves," he said to me, ignoring Luyu's question. "I trust rebels as much as I trust Nurus."

"Oh," I said, remembering Mwita's experience with Okeke rebels. "Right. I . . . wasn't thinking."

"What about me?" Luyu said. "I could . . ."

"No," he said. "Too dangerous. We can do things, but you. . . ."

"I have a gun," she said.

"They have two," I said. "And they know how to use theirs."

We stood there thinking.

"I don't want to kill anyone if we don't have to," Mwita said, sighing. He rubbed his sweaty face. Then suddenly, he threw his gun into the cornfield. "I hate killing. I'd rather die than keep doing it."

"But this is about more than you or any of us," Luyu said, looking appalled. She moved to retrieve it.

"Leave it," Mwita said firmly.

She froze. Then she threw her gun away, too.

"How about this," I said. "Mwita, we make ourselves ignorable. That way Luyu can approach them and if they try anything, we have the element of surprise. Tell them . . . tell them that you, bring good news of the coming of Onyesonwu, something like that. If they're rebels then they must still have *some* hope."

We slowly approached the hut, Mwita on Luyu's left and me on Luyu's right. I remember the look on Luyu's face. Her jaw was set, her dark skin glistened with sweat, there were droplets of blood on her cheeks. Her Afro was lopsided. She looked so different from the girl she was back in Jwahir. But one thing about her was the same—her audacity.

Some sat on stools or on the ground, three of them playing a game of Warri. Others stood or leaned against the hut. They'd all used red paste to draw stripes on their faces. None of them looked over thirty. When they saw Luyu, the two with the guns immediately pointed them at her. She didn't flinch.

"Eh, who is this?" a soldier asked in a low voice, standing up from the game of Warri. He pulled a dull-looking blade from his pocket. "Duty, *ta!* Don't shoot," he said, holding up a hand. He looked past Luyu. "Check around the hut." All but one of the gun-toting soldiers ran off into the cornfield. He kept his gun pointed at Luyu. The head soldier looked her up and down. "How many are with you?"

"I bring you good news."

"We'll see," he said.

"My name is Luyu," she said, holding his eyes. "I'm from Jwahir. Have you heard of the Sorcerer Onyesonwu?"

"I have," the head soldier said with a nod.

"She's here with me. So is her companion, Mwita," Luyu said. "We've just come from that village over there." She pointed behind her. When she moved, the man holding the gun flinched.

"Is it lost?" the head soldier asked.

"Yes," Luyu said.

"Where is she then? Where is he?"

Some of the men were returning now and saying that it was clear.

"Will you harm us?" Luyu asked.

He looked Luyu in the eye. "No." His restraint broke and a tear fell from his eye. "We'd *never* harm you." He held out a hand and quietly said, "Down." The soldier lowered his gun. Mwita and I showed ourselves. Four of the men shouted and ran off, one of them fainted, and three of them dropped to their knees.

"Whatever you need," the head soldier said.

Only three of them would speak to us: the leader of the group, whose name was Anai, and two soldiers named Bunk and Tamer. The others kept their distance.

"Ten days ago, they started again and this time whole armies are amassing in Durfa," Anai said. He turned and spat. "Another push. Maybe the last. My wife, children, mother-in-law, I finally sent them east."

I'd built a normal fire and we were roasting ears of corn.

"But you haven't seen any actual armies pass?" Luyu asked.

Anai shook his head. "We were told to wait here. We haven't heard anything from anyone in two days."

"I don't think you will be hearing from anyone," Mwita said.

Anai nodded. "How did you all escape?"

"Luck," Luyu said. Anai didn't press the issue.

"How'd you traveled so far without camels?" Bunk asked.

"We had camels for a time but they were wild and had their own plans," I said.

"Eh?" he said.

Anai and Tamer chuckled. "Strange," Anai said. "You're strange people."

"I think we've been traveling for five months," Mwita said.

"I applaud you," Anai said patting Mwita's shoulder. "All this way, leading two women at that."

Luyu and I looked at each other, rolled our eyes but said nothing.

"You seem healthy," Bunk said. "You're blessed."

"We are," Mwita said. "We are."

"What do you know of the General?" I asked.

Several of the men nearby listening to our conversation looked at me, fearful.

"Wicked man," Bunk said. "It's almost night. Don't speak of him."

"He's just a man," Tamer said, looking annoyed. "What do you want to know?"

"Where can we find him?" I asked.

"Eh! Are you mad?" Bunk said, horrified.

"Why do you want to know?" Anai asked, frowning and leaning forward.

"Don't ask what you really don't want to know," Mwita said.

"Please, just tell us where we can find him," I said.

"No one knows where the General lives or if he even has a home in this world," Anai said. "But he has a building that he works from. It's never guarded. He needs no protection." He paused for emphasis. "It's a plain building. Go to the Conversation Space—it's a large open space in the center of Durfa—his building is on the north side. The front door is blue." He stood up. "We move tomorrow to Gadi, orders or no orders. Stay with us tonight. We'll protect you. Durfa is close to here. Just through the corn."

"We can just walk in?" Luyu asked. "Or will people attack us?"

"You two, no," Anai said, motion to Mwita and me. "They'll see your *Ewu* faces and kill you in seconds. Unless you make yourselves . . . invisible again." He turned to Luyu. "We can give *you* all you need tomorrow to move about in Durfa with the least trouble."

Chapter 56

THEY INSISTED ON GIVING US THE HUT FOR THE NIGHT. Even the soldiers who refused to speak to us agreed to sleep outside. With guards, we felt safe enough to actually sleep. Well, Luyu slept. She was snoring seconds after curling up on the floor. Mwita and I didn't sleep for two reasons. The first reason happened soon after I lay down. I was thinking about Daib. *All it'll take is his death,* I kept thinking. *Cut off the snake's head.*

Just as Mwita stretched out beside me and put his arm around my waist, I started lifting. I moved through his arm, my body insubstantial. "Eh?" he exclaimed, shocked. "Oh, no, you don't!" He reached out and wrapped his arm around my waist and shoved me down. I lifted again, my mind focused on Daib. Then, with a loud grunt, he pushed me back to the floor, back into my body. I snapped out of my angry trance.

"How . . ." I breathed. Daib would've killed me. It would have all ended just like that. "You're not a sorcerer," I said. "How can you . . ."

"What is *wrong* with you!" he exclaimed, working hard to keep his voice at a whisper. "Remember what Sola said!"

"I didn't mean to."

We stared at each other both generally appalled at things we weren't even sure of.

"What kind of pair are we?" Mwita mumbled, rolling on his back.

"I don't know," I said. I sat up. "But how did you do that? You're not . . ."

"I don't know or care," he said, irritated. "Stop reminding me of what I'm not."

I sucked my teeth loudly and turned away from him. Outside I heard one of the soldiers whisper and the other chuckle to himself.

"I'm . . . I'm sorry," I said. I paused. "Thank you. Again, you saved me."

I heard him sigh. He rolled me over to face him. "That's what I'm here for," he said. "To save you."

I took his face and brought it to mine. It was like a hunger that neither of us could satiate. By the time the sun was coming up my nipples were raw from Mwita's lips, there were scratch marks on Mwita's back and bite marks on his neck. We ached sweetly. And all of it energized instead of tired us. He held me close and looked deep into my eyes. "I wish we had more time. I'm not finished with you," he said smiling.

"I'm not finished with you either," I said, grinning.

"A nice house," he said. "Out in the desert, away from everything. Two floors, lots of windows. No electricity. Four children. Three boys, one girl."

"Only one girl?"

"She'll be more trouble than all three boys combined, trust me," Mwita said.

There were footsteps outside the hut. A face peeked in. I pulled my rapa more tightly around me. "Just checking," the soldier said. Mwita drew a rapa around his waist and went out to speak with the soldier. I lay there staring at the scorched black ceiling that in the dim predawn light looked like an abyss.

Mwita came back in. "They need to do something to Luyu before we go," he said.

"Do what?" Luyu groggily said, just waking up.

"Nothing serious," Mwita said. "Get dressed."

Mwita stood behind Anai who knelt in front of a fire holding a metal poker in the flames. The others were packing up. I took and squeezed Luyu's hand. A soft breeze made the corn stalks lean west.

"What is that?" Luyu asked.

"Come and sit down," Mwita said.

Luyu pulled me with her. Mwita handed us each a small plate of bread, roasted corn, and something I hadn't had since we'd left Jwahir: roasted chicken. It was bland but delicious. When we finished eating, two of the soldiers who refused to speak to us took our plates.

"Okeke are slaves here, you know this," Anai said. "We live freely but we have to answer to any Nuru. Most of us spend the day working for Nurus and some of the night working for ourselves." He laughed to himself. "Though we obviously look different from the Nuru, they feel it important to mark us." He picked up the thin red hot poker.

"Ah, no!" Luyu exclaimed.

"What!" I said. "Is it really necessary?"

"It is," Mwita calmly said.

"The sooner you do it, the less time you have to think about it," Anai told Luyu.

Bunk held up a tiny metal hoop with a chain of black and blue beads. "This used to be mine," he said.

Luyu glanced at the poker and took a deep breath. "Okay, do it! Do it!" She painfully squeezed my hand.

"Relax," I whispered.

"I can't. I can't!" But she stayed still. Anai moved quickly, sticking the sharp poker into the cartilage at the top of her right ear. Luyu made a high pitched peeping sound but that was it. I almost laughed. It was the same reaction she'd had during her Eleventh Rite circumcision.

Anai inserted the earring. Mwita gave her a leaf to eat. "Chew it," he said. We watched as she chewed, her face contorted with pain. "Are you all right?" Mwita asked.

"Think I'm going to be . . ." She turned to the side and threw up.

Chapter 57

OUR GOOD-BYES WERE QUICK.

"We've changed our plan," Anai told us. "We're going around Gadi. There is nothing there for us. Then we're going to wait."

"For what?" Mwita asked.

"News of you three," Anai said.

And with that we parted. They went east, and we went west, to my father's town, Durfa. We started down the row of lush green corn.

"How does it look?" Luyu asked, tilting her head toward me to show her earring.

"It actually looks nice on you," I said.

Mwita sucked his teeth but said nothing, walking a few steps ahead. We had nothing but the clothes on our bodies and Luyu's portable. It felt good, almost liberating. Our clothes were dirty with dust. Anai said Okeke walked about in dirty ragged clothes, so this would help Luyu blend in.

Where the corn ended, a black paved road busy with people, camels, and scooters began. So many scooters. The rebels said that in the Seven Rivers towns they called them *okada*. Some of the okada had female passengers but I saw none with women drivers; in Jwahir it was the same. Across the road, Durfa began. The buildings were sturdy and old like the House of Osugbo but nowhere near as alive.

"What if someone asks me to work for them," Luyu said. We still hid in the corn.

"Then say you will and just keep walking," I said. "If they insist, then you have no choice until you get a chance to sneak away."

Luyu nodded. She took a breath and closed her eyes, squatting down.

"You okay?" I asked, squatting beside her.

"Scared," she said, frowning hard.

I touched her shoulder. "We'll be right beside you. If anyone tries to hurt you, they'll be very sorry. You know what I'm capable of."

"You can't take on a whole town," she said.

"I have before," I said.

"I don't speak Nuru very well," Luyu said.

"They assume you're ignorant anyway," I said. "You'll be okay."

We stood up together. Mwita gave Luyu a kiss on the cheek.

"Remember," he said to me. "I can only do it for an hour."

"Okay," I said. I could hold myself ignorable for closer to three hours.

"Luyu," he said. "After forty five minutes, find a place where we can hide."

"Okay," she said. "Ready?"

Mwita and I pulled our veils over our heads and settled ourselves. I watched as Mwita became hard to see. To look at someone who is ignorable is to feel your eyes grow painfully dry to the point of blurriness. You have to look away and you don't want to look back. Mwita and I wouldn't be able to look at each other.

We stepped onto the road and it felt like being sucked into a beast's belly. Durfa was such a fast town. I understand why it was the center of Nuru culture and society. The people of Durfa were hardworking and lively. Of course, much of this was to the credit of the Okeke who flooded in each morning from Okeke villages, Okeke who did all the work the Nuru did not want and felt they didn't have to do.

But things were changing. A revolution was happening. The Nuru were learning to survive on their own . . . after the Okeke had put them in a place comfortable enough to do so. All the ugliness was on the outskirts of the Seven Rivers Kingdom and Durfa people especially were indifferent to it. Though the genocide was happening mere miles away, these people were far removed. The most they saw was that there were significantly fewer Okeke.

It started before Luyu even made it to the first of the town's buildings. She was walking alongside the road when a fat bald Nuru man slapped her on the backside and said, "Go to my house." He pointed behind her. "That one just down the street there where that man is standing. Cook my wife and children breakfast!"

For a moment, Luyu just stared at him. I held my breath hoping she wouldn't slap the man in the face instead. "Yes . . . sir," she finally said submissively.

He impatiently waved the back of his fat hand at her. "Well, go then, woman!" He turned and strode off. He so assumed that Luyu would do his bidding that he didn't notice when Luyu kept right on going. She walked faster. "Best if I look as if I have somewhere to go," she said aloud.

"Help me with this," a woman said, roughly grabbing Luyu's arm, and this time Luyu was stuck helping a woman carry her textiles to a nearby market. She was a tall lanky Nuru woman with long black hair that crept down her back. She wore a rapa and matching top like Luyu except hers was the bright yellow of an outfit only worn once. Luyu carried the heavy bolts of cloth on her back. This at least got us safely and quietly into Durfa.

"Fine day, eh?" the woman asked, as they walked.

Luyu grunted vague assent. After that, it was as if Luyu weren't there. The woman greeted several people on the way, all of them well dressed and none of whom acknowledged Luyu's presence. When the woman wasn't talking to people in passing, she talked away on a black square-shaped device that she held to her mouth. It made a lot of staticky noise between when she or the other person spoke.

I learned that this woman's neighbor's daughter was the target of an "honor killing" to appease the family of a man the girl's older brother had stolen from. "What has the General made us into?" the woman asked, shaking her head. "The man goes too far." I also learned that the price of okada scooter fuel made from corn was going down and fuel made from sugar cane was going up. Imagine that? And that the woman had a bad knee, adored her granddaughter, and was a second wife. The woman could talk.

Mwita and I were forced to weave our way around, as we stayed close to Luyu. To stick too close would mean bumping into a lot of people, which would get Luyu into trouble. It was difficult, but what Luyu was doing was much harder.

The woman stopped at a vendor and bought Luyu a ring made of melted sand. "You're a pretty girl. It will look nice on you," the woman said, then she went back to blabbing on her device. Luyu took the ring, muttering a "thank you" in Nuru and slipped it on. Luyu held it up and turned it in the sunshine.

Twenty minutes later we finally arrived at the woman's large booth in a busy market. "Set them there," the woman said. When Luyu did so, the woman waved a hand at her, "Go on then." And just like that, Luyu was free. Within moments, she was asked to carry a bundle of palm fiber, then sweep out someone's booth, model a dress, shovel camel feces. Mwita and I took rests where we could, hiding under tables or between booths and letting ourselves reappear for a few minutes before going ignorable again.

When she was asked to pour okada fuel into containers, the fumes and her fatigue caused her to faint. Mwita had to slap her awake. The good thing about this job was that she got to do it alone in a tent and Mwita and I were able to help *and* take a break.

By this time, the sun was in the middle of the sky. We'd been in Durfa for three hours. Luyu got her chance when she finished pouring the okada fuel. As fast as she could, she ran into an alley between two large buildings. Clothes hung across it and I could hear a baby crying from one of the windows. These were residential buildings.

"Praise Ani," Luyu whispered.

Mwita and I let ourselves reappear. "Whoo, I'm exhausted," Mwita said, putting his hands on his knees.

I rubbed my temples and then the side of my head. My headache was flaring up. We were all sweating. "Luyu, much respect," I said, giving her a hug.

"I *hate* this place," she said into my shoulder, starting to cry.

"Yeah," I said. I hated it too. Just seeing the Okeke shuffling around. Seeing Luyu have to do the same. Something was wrong. . . .with *everyone* here. The Okeke didn't look too bothered as they worked. And the Nuru weren't openly cruel to them. I didn't see anyone beaten up. That woman had said Luyu was pretty and bought her a ring. It was confusing and strange.

"Onyesonwu, fly up and see if you can find the Conversation Space," Mwita said.

"How will I find you?" I said.

"You can bring people from the dead," Luyu said. "Think of something."

"Go," Mwita said. "Hurry."

"We might not be here when you get back," Luyu said.

I shrugged out of my clothes. Luyu rolled them up and put them against the alley wall. Mwita pulled me into a tight hug and I kissed his nose. Then I changed into a vulture and took off.

The midday's warm air current beckoned me to fly higher, but I kept low, near the buildings and palm-tree tops. As a vulture, I could actually feel my father. He was indeed in Durfa. I soared for a moment, my eyes closed. I opened them and looked in the direction that I felt he was in. There was the open Conversation Space. My eyes were pulled to a building just north of it. I knew it would have a blue door.

I circled, memorizing the way. A bird knows its location at all times. I laughed, the sound coming out as a squawk. *How could I think I wouldn't be able to find Mwita and Luyu?* I thought. As I flew back to the alley a glint of gold caught my eye. I turned and flew east to a wide street where a parade seemed to be going on. I landed on top of a building and assumed my vulture hunch.

I looked down and saw not just one glint of gold, but hundreds of round golden plates sewn into yellow-brown military uniforms. Each carried a large similarly colored backpack. They were ready for anything. People cheered as the soldiers marched. They were congregating somewhere I couldn't see. *We're too late,* I thought, remembering Sola's warning. Those armies couldn't leave before I did what I had to do, whatever that was.

I flew over the soldiers, low enough for them to notice me. I needed to follow their lines. I glimpsed their faces, young determined-looking men with golden skin so different from my mother's dark brown. They were marching into a huge building made of metal and brick. I didn't catch the name on the building's sign. I'd seen enough. They weren't marching out yet. Soon. Maybe within hours but not yet.

I flew back to the alley. Mwita and Luyu were gone. I cursed. I changed back. As I dressed, I sweated profusely and my hands shook. Right after I pulled my shirt over my head, I met the eyes of a Nuru man standing at the alley entrance. His eyes were wide as he had just gotten a view of my breasts and now was seeing my face. I put on my veil, made myself ignorable and ran around him. When I looked back, he was still standing there looking into the alley. *Let him think he saw a ghost,* I thought. *Let it drive him mad.*

I searched for several minutes. No luck. I stood there, in the middle of a large crowd of Nurus and the occasional Okeke. How I despised this place. I cursed to myself and a Nuru man passing by me frowned and looked around. *How do I find them?* I thought, desperately. My panic was making it hard to concentrate. I closed my eyes and I did something I'd never really done. I prayed to Ani, the Creator, to Papa, Binta, whoever would listen. *Please. I can't do this alone. I can't be alone. Watch over Luyu. I need Mwita. Binta should be alive. Aro do you hear me? Mama, I wish I was five years old again.*

I wasn't making sense to myself, I was just praying, if this was praying. Whatever it was, it calmed me. My mind showed me Aro's first lesson in the Mystic Points. "Bricoleur," I said out loud, as I stood there. "One who uses all that he has in order to do what he has to do."

I went over three of the four points. *The Mmuo Point moves and shapes the wilderness. The Alusi Point speaks with spirits. The Uwa Point moves and shapes the physical world, the body.* I needed to find Mwita and Luyu's bodies. *I can find Mwita,* I realized. I had a part of him in me. His sperm. Connection. I stood very still and turned inward. Through my skin, fat, muscle, into my womb. There they were wriggling away. "Where is he?" I asked them. They told me.

"*Ewu!*" someone yelled. "Look at it!"

Several people gasped. Everyone in the market suddenly stared at and moved away from me. I'd been so focused on the inside of myself that I'd become visible. Someone grabbed my arm. I snatched it away, became ignorable and pushed my way through the pressing crowd. Again, I wondered about these people who seemed so content and peaceful but changed into monsters when their sterile Nuru environment was even slightly compromised. There was chaos as they searched frantically for me. The news would spread, especially in a place like this where so many had those communication devices.

We were running out of time.

I ran, looking not so much with my eyes as with something else inside me. I spotted Luyu outside the large Conversation Space. She was standing with another Okeke woman. They were watching over a group of Nuru children while their parents went to the prayer space to pray. Luyu looked miserable.

"I'm here," I said, stepping beside her.

She jumped and looked around. "Onye?" she asked.

The Okeke woman standing near Luyu looked at her.

"Shh," I said.

Luyu smiled.

"Mwita?" I called.

"I'm here," he said.

"I saw soldiers preparing to leave. We don't have much time," I whispered.

A Nuru child of about two yanked on Luyu's sleeve.

"Bread?" the girl asked. "Bread?"

Luyu reached into the satchel beside her and tore off a piece of bread and gave it to the child. The child smiled at her, "Thank you."

Luyu smiled back.

"We have to go. *Right now*," I said, trying to keep my voice down.

"Shh!" Luyu whispered. "That woman will raise an alarm if I just leave. I don't know what it is with these Okeke."

"They're slaves," I said.

"Try to talk to her anyway," I heard Mwita quietly say. "Hurry!"

Luyu turned to the woman, "Do you know of Onyesonwu the Sorceress?"

She looked blankly at Luyu. Then she surprised me by looking around and coming over to Luyu. "I do."

Luyu was also surprised. "Well, what . . . what do you think?"

"I can wish, but that doesn't make it true," the woman whispered.

"Then wish again," I said to her.

The woman yelped, staring at Luyu. She stepped away, her eyes wide, her hands clutching her chest. She didn't scream or raise an alarm as Luyu walked away. She didn't say anything at all. She just stood there, hands to chest.

I made myself visible, pulling my veil over my face. Luyu and Mwita had to be able to see me. Only I could get us to the building with the blue door. For fifteen minutes, we ran. Because of the light skin of my hands, at first glance people assumed I was Nuru and that Luyu was my slave. And because we were running, I was gone before anyone had time to stop and consider me. We avoided speeding okadas and grumpy camels and passed Nuru children in school uniforms, miserable working Okeke, and busy Nuru. And then there we were, at the blue door.

Chapter 58

THIS BUILDING REALLY REMINDED ME OF THE House of Osugbo. It was made of stone, its thick outer walls were carved with designs, and it exuded a mysterious authority. The blue door was actually a painting of the white-tipped blue waves of a body of water. The unnamed lake? There was a stone sign in front of the building with an orange flag waving from a pole at the top. The following was carved deep into the stone:

General's Headquarters
Daib Yagoub
The Council of the Seven Rivers Kingdom

"I'll go in first," Luyu said. "They'll just think I'm an ignorant slave."

Before either of us could answer, she ran up the steps and opened the blue door. The door slammed behind her. Mwita took my hand. His hand was cold, mine probably was, too. I wanted to look at him but we were still holding ourselves ignorable. Several minutes went by. Behind us, people passed on camel, foot, and scooter. No one came or left the building. I venture to say that no one even looked in the building's direction. Yes, it was very much like the House of Osugbo.

"If she doesn't come out in another minute, she's probably dead," Mwita said.

"She'll come," I muttered.

Another minute passed.

"You think it was Daib who hung those two people in the cave?" he said.

I hadn't given it a thought. And I didn't want to think about it now. But it was just like Daib to kill a person and then make sure that the body couldn't rot.

"So who were the spiders, then?" I asked.

He chuckled. "I don't know."

I chuckled, too. Squeezing his hand. The blue door swung open with a loud slap. Luyu emerged, breathless. "It's empty," she said. "If he's here, he's on the second floor."

Without a glance behind us, Mwita and I became visible. "He's expecting us," Mwita said. We went in.

It was cool inside, as if a capture station was on nearby. From somewhere, a machine hummed. There were desks with dark blue tops and dark blue chairs. Office spaces. Each desk had a dusty old computer. I'd never seen so much paper. In stacks on the floor, in trash bins and many books, too. It was a wasteful place. A staircase wound up the far side of the room.

"I didn't go up there," Luyu said.

"Smart," I said.

"Stay here," Mwita told her. "Shout if anyone comes."

She nodded, putting a hand on one of the desks to steady herself. Her eyes were wide, tears glistening in them. "Be careful," she croaked.

Mwita and I made ourselves ignorable and went up. We stopped at the entrance. The large room was very different from the one below. It was as I remembered it. The walls were blue. The floor was blue. The room smelled of incense and dusty books. And it was eerily quiet.

He sat at his desk glaring at us. There was a large window behind him allowing sunshine in. It both threw a shadow over his face and bounced reflections off of the tiny disks sitting in a basket on his desk. He was both light and dark . . . but mostly dark. His large hands angrily grasped his chair's armrests. He wore a brilliantly white caftan with an embroidered neck and a thin gold necklace. His granite-black beard hung to his chest and the wooly black hair on his head was covered with a white cap. When he just continued staring right at us, Mwita and I took the hint and made ourselves visible.

"Mwita, my ugly apprentice," he said. He looked at me and I instantly went cold with fear, remembering the pain he inflicted me with just before he slapped the slow and cruel poison symbol on my hand. My confidence began draining from me. I was pathetic. He chuckled to himself as if he knew I'd just lost all my nerve. "And *you* should have stayed missing or dead, or whatever you were," he said.

Mwita strode into the room.

"Mwita, wh . . . what are you doing?" I hissed.

He ignored me, walked right up to Daib and grabbed the basket of strange disks. "Your brain is diseased," he said, shaking the basket in Daib's face. "Everything was destroyed in your house! Yet *somehow*, you saved *these?* You think I didn't know about your sick collection! I was cleaning your desk when I found these. I put one into your portable before the riots; I got to watch you beat a man to death. You were laughing and . . . aroused as you did it!"

Daib sat back and chuckled again. "I'm getting old. Sometimes a man needs a little help. My memory often fails me, too. Losing these would have been like losing a part of my mind." He cocked his head. "So is this what you came all this way to say? Is this why you pester me with your childish antics?" He snatched the basket from Mwita and reached in. All the disks looked the same but he was able to find the one he sought in a matter of seconds. He held it up. "For *this?* Your woman's honor?" He threw it at Mwita. It missed him, landing and rolling near my feet. I picked it up. It was barely bigger than my nail. Mwita looked at me. He turned back to Daib.

"Get out of here," Daib spat. "I have a plan to complete. Rana's prophecy to fulfill—'a tall bearded Nuru sorcerer will come and force the Great Book's rewriting.' What a different book it will be once I exterminate the rest of the Okeke." He stood up, a tall bearded Nuru man. A sorcerer with healing abilities. Just as Rana's prophecy had predicted. I frowned, questioning all that I had traveled for. Could Rana the Seer have actually been telling the truth? Was the prophesied one male, *not* female? Maybe "peace" meant the death of all Okekes.

"Oh, Ani save us," I whispered.

"But you, girl, I must also exterminate," Daib continued. "I remember *your* mother." He frowned. "I should have killed her. I let my men have their way and leave most of those Okeke women alive. Turning them loose is like sending a virus to all those eastern communities. The disgraced women run there to give birth to their *Ewu* babies. I brought that part of the plan to the Seven Rivers council head myself. I am her greatest general and my plan was brilliant. Of course she listened. She's a weak puppet."

He smiled, enjoying his words. "It's easy juju to work on soldiers. They become like cows, producing and producing milk. Me? I prefer to bash an Okeke woman's head in after I've had her. Except your mother." His smile faltered. His eyes went far away. "I enjoyed her. I didn't want to kill her. She should have given me a great, great son. Why are you a girl?"

"I . . ." I sighed.

"Because it's been written," Mwita said.

Slowly Daib turned to Mwita, really seeing him for the first time. Daib's motions were instant. One second he was standing behind his desk and the next he was on Mwita, his strong hands around Mwita's throat. A thousand things tried to happen in my body all at once but none of them allowed me to *move*. Something was holding me. Then it was squeezing. I wheezed and would have fallen forward if it weren't for the thing holding me.

I blinked. I could see it. A blue tubule had wrapped itself around me like a snake. A wilderness tree. It was cool, rough, and terribly strong, though I could see right through it. The more I struggled, the tighter it constricted. It was squeezing the air out of me.

"Always, so disrespectful," Daib said, baring his teeth as he throttled Mwita. "It's your *dirty* blood. You were born *wrong*." He squeezed harder. "Why would Ani give a child like you such gifts? I should have slit your throat, had you burned back to ashes so Ani could get it right the second time." He threw Mwita to the ground and spit on him. Mwita coughed and sputtered, trying to get to his feet. He fell back.

Daib turned to me. My face was wet with tears and sweat as the spirit plant released me. The world around me faded and then brightened. I opened my mouth wide as I inhaled and shakily got to my feet.

"My only child and *this* is what Ani gives me," he said, looking me up and down.

The wilderness rose around us. More wilderness trees surrounded us like gaping onlookers. Behind him I could see Mwita, his yellow spirit blazing fiercely.

"I've been watching you," Daib growled. "Mwita will die today. You will die today. And I won't stop there. I'll hunt down your spirit. You try to hide. I'll find you. I'll destroy you again. After I bring the Nuru armies and fulfill the prophecy, I'll find your mother. She'll bear my son."

I lost parts of myself with each of his words. Once my belief in the prophecy began to crumble, my courage went right with it. I was struggling to breathe. I wanted to beg him. Plead. Cry. I would crawl at his feet to keep him from hurting my mother and Mwita. My journey had been a waste. I was nothing.

"Nothing to say?" he said.

I sank to my knees.

Triumphant, he kept talking, "I don't expect . . ."

Mwita screamed as he launched himself at Daib. Then Mwita screamed something that sounded like Vah. He slapped his hand on Daib's neck. Daib shrieked and whirled around. Already whatever Mwita had done to him was working. Mwita stumbled back.

"What have you done?" Daib shouted, trying to reach behind him, scraping at his neck. "You can't do . . . !" I felt all the air in the room shift and the pressure drop.

"Come on then," Mwita said. He looked around Daib, at me. "Onyesonwu, you know *exactly* what's true and what are lies."

"Mwita!" I screamed so loudly that I felt blood burst into my throat. I started running toward them, barely aware of the deep bruises and lacerations the wilderness tree had inflicted on my body. Before I could get to them, Daib leaped at Mwita like a cat. As they both crashed to the floor, Daib's clothes split, his body undulating, thickening and sprouting orange and black fur, large teeth, and sharp claws. As a tiger, he tore at Mwita's clothes, slashed Mwita's chest open, and sunk his teeth deep into Mwita's neck. Then Daib grew weak and fell over, wheezing and quivering.

"Get *OFF* him!" I screamed, grabbing Daib's fur. I shoved him off Mwita. So much blood. Mwita's neck was half torn off. His chest gurgled out blood. I lay my left hand on him. He shuddered, trying to speak. "Mwita, shh shh," I said. "I'll . . . I'll make you better."

"N-no, Onyesonwu," he said, weakly taking my hand. How was he even able to speak? "This is . . ."

"You knew! *THIS* is what you saw why you tried to pass initiation!" I screamed. I sobbed. "Oh, Ani! You *knew!*"

"Did I?" he asked. Blood spurted from his neck with each beat of his heart. It was pooling around me. "Or did . . . knowing . . . make . . . happen?"

I sobbed.

"Find it," he whispered. "Finish it." He took in a labored breath and the words he spoke were full of pain. "I . . . know who you are . . . you should, too."

When he went limp in my arms, my heart should have stopped, too. I grasped him tightly. I didn't care what he said. I would bring him back.

I searched and searched for his spirit. It was gone. "Mama!" I screamed, my body shuddering as I sobbed. My mouth felt so dry. "Mama, help me!"

Luyu came in. When she saw Mwita, she fell to her knees.

"Mama!" I screamed. "He can't leave me here!" I heard Luyu get up and run out and down the stairs. I didn't care. It was all over.

Daib lay there, a naked human being, slobbering and shuddering. Still stuck to his neck was the piece of cloth scribbled with symbols. Ting must have given Mwita this juju. She had to have used the Uwa Point, that of the physical world, the body. The most useful and dangerous point to the *Eshu* born. As I held Mwita's body, a thought occurred to me. I grabbed and immediately acted on it. I didn't consider the consequences, the possibilities, or the dangers.

Mwita and I had not slept last night. I recalled how he'd moved inside me and released. He was still inside me. He was still alive. I felt them in me, swimming, wriggling. I was not at my moon's peak but I made it so. I moved my egg to meet what I could find of Mwita's life. But it wasn't I who joined them. All I could do was make it possible. Something else chose the rest. Something wholly outside of and unconcerned with humanity. At the moment of conception, a giant shock wave blasted from me, a shock wave like the one so long ago during my father's burial ceremony. It blew out the walls around me and the ceiling above me.

I sat there with Mwita's body, in the dust and debris, hoping something would fall on me and end my life. But nothing did. Soon all began to settle. Only the staircase remained intact. I could hear screams and shouts in the streets and buildings. All higher pitched voices. Female voices. I shuddered.

"Wake up!" some woman screamed. *"Wake up!"*

"Ani kill me too, *o!*" another woman cried.

I thought of the female apprentice Sanchi, who'd obliterated an entire town when she conceived as a student. I thought of Aro's reservations about training girls and women. And in my arms, I held Mwita. Dead. I wanted to throw my head back and scream with laughter. Was it the thought of our child in my belly? Maybe. The sinking shock I felt for the consequences of what I'd just done? Possibly. The clarity of mind brought by too little food and rest and too much distress? Maybe. Whatever it was, the clouds in my mind cleared to bring me to my dream about Mwita. The island.

Someone was running up the stairs.

"Onye!" Luyu shouted, leaping over a chunk of sandstone and a case of books that had fallen on Daib. "Onye, what happened? Oh praise Ani, you're all right."

"I know what we have to do," I said flatly.

"What?" Luyu said.

"Find the Seer," I said. "The one who made the prophecy about me." I blinked as it came to me. "Rana, his name is Rana."

Sola had spoken of Rana just before we left Jwahir. "This Seer, Rana, he is the guardian of a precious document. This must be why he was given the prophecy," Sola had said.

From outside, women continued to scream and wail. "Then . . . then say good-bye and let's go," Luyu said, putting her hand on my shoulder. "He's gone."

I looked at her. Then I looked at Mwita.

"Stand up," Luyu said. "We have to go."

I kissed his lovely lips one last time. I looked at Daib's naked quivering body and sneered. I had no saliva left in my mouth or I'd have spit on him. I did not kill him. I left him there, too. Mwita would have been proud of me.

You think that sand brick can't burn hot? It can. I would never have left Mwita's body there to be found and desecrated. Never. All things can burn, for all things must return to dust. I made the General's building blaze bright. Was it my fault that Daib was still in there? I doubt Mwita would have been angry at me for burning down the building while Daib happened to lie helplessly inside.

General Daib's building wouldn't stop burning until it was ash. Still, as we stood before it, I saw a large bat laboriously fly out the blaze like a piece of charred debris. It flew a few yards, dropped several feet, caught itself and then flew on. My father was crippled but he still lived. I didn't care. If I succeeded in what I had to do, he would be dealt with in his own time.

We walked quickly down the street as women ran amok. No one looked twice at us. We made our way toward the lake with no name.

Chapter 59

"I FEEL STRANGE," Luyu said. Then she ran to the edge of the river and vomited for the second time this day.

I stood with my face exposed waiting for Luyu to finish. No one cared about me. People may have heard things about a crazy *Ewu* woman but what was happening in the town of Durfa had usurped that. For the moment.

Every single male human in the central town of Durfa capable of impregnating a woman was dead. My actions had killed them. The armies I had seen, every single one of those men had instantly died. As we'd walked to the river, we saw male bodies in the street, heard cries from houses, walked past shocked children and women. I shuddered again, helplessly thinking about Daib . . . *He is my father and I am his child,* I thought. *We both leave bodies in our wake. Fields of bodies.*

"Are you finished?" I asked. My face felt hot and I too felt like I was going to vomit.

She grunted, slowly standing up. "My belly feels . . . I don't know."

"You're pregnant," I said.

"What?"

"So am I."

She stared at me. "Did you . . ."

"I made myself conceive. Something happened because of it. Something . . . terrible," I looked at my hands. "Sola said my greatest problem would be a lack of control."

Luyu wiped her mouth with the back of her hands and touched her belly. "So . . . not just me, then. *All* the women."

"I don't know how far it went. I don't think it touched the other towns. But where there are dead men, there are pregnant women."

"W-what happened? Why are the men dead?" she asked.

I shook my head and looked at the river. It was better for her not to know. A woman screamed from nearby. I wanted to scream, too. "My Mwita," I whispered. My eyes burned. I didn't want to look up and see bereaved women running amok in the streets.

"He died well," Luyu said.

"A son kills his father," I said. *But Daib isn't dead*, I thought.

"Apprentice kills his Master," Luyu said tiredly. "Daib hated you, Mwita loved you. Mwita and Daib, one can't thrive without the other, maybe."

"You speak like a sorcerer," I grumbled.

"I've been around enough of them," Luyu said.

"My Mwita," I whispered again. Then I remembered and reached into the folds of my rapa. I hoped it wasn't there. It was. I held the tiny metal disk up. "Luyu, do you still have your portable?" Inside a building across the road, a woman screamed until her voice cracked. Luyu winced.

"Yeah," she said. She squinted. "Where'd you get the disk?"

I stepped closer as she carefully slipped the disk in. My heart was beating so fast that I clutched my chest. Luyu frowned and held me close to her. There was a soft whirring sound as a tiny screen rose up from the bottom. Luyu flipped it over.

My mother was looking right at us as she lay in the sand. My father stabbed the silver knife into the sand beside her head. I noticed that its hilt was decorated with symbols very much like the ones etched into my hands. Ting would have known what they meant. He pulled my mother's legs apart and then came the grunting, panting, and singing, and the snarled words between the singing. But this time I was watching a recording, not a vision from my mother. I was hearing his Nuru words outside of my mother's perspective. I could understand.

"I've found you. You're the one. Sorceress. *Sorceress!*" He sang a song. "You'll bear my son. He'll be magnificent." Another song. "I'll raise him up and he will be the greatest thing this land will ever see." He burst into song. "It is written! I've seen it!"

Something made of glass flew out the window of the house across the road. It crashed to the ground. The sound of a sobbing child followed. I was numb to it all; the images of my mother raped by a Nuru sorcerer scorched into my eyes and my thoughts grew dark. I thought of the pained women, children, old men around me, wailing hurting, and sobbing; *they* had *allowed* this to happen to my mother. They wouldn't have helped her.

What would have happened if my mother had been the sorceress her father had asked her to be when Daib attacked her that day? There would have been such a battle. Instead all she had to protect her was her Alusi side.

"Enough," Luyu finally said, snatching the portable from me.

People were filling the streets. They ran, dragged themselves, walked up and down, to the side of that road, going to places that I didn't care about. Ghosts of their former selves, their lives changed forever. I stood there, my eyes unfocusing. My father actually *prized* this disk enough to keep it for twenty years.

"We have to keep going," Luyu said, dragging me along. But as we walked, tears dropped from her eyes, too. "Wait," she said, still clutching my arm. She dropped the portable. "Step on it," she said. "With all you have. Mash it into the ground."

I stared down at it for a moment and then stamped down with all my might. The sound of its breaking made me feel better. I picked it up and took out the disk. I crushed the disk with my teeth and threw it into the river.

"Let's go," I said.

When we arrived at the lake, we took a moment. I'd seen it before, yes, but during my vision I hadn't had a chance to stop and really take it in. Somewhere in the lake was an island.

Behind us was chaos. The streets were full of women, children, and old men running and stumbling about and wailing "How can this happen!" Fights broke out. Women tore at their clothes. Many dropped to their knees and screamed for Ani to save them. I was sure that somewhere, the few Okeke women left were dragged out and torn apart. Durfa was diseased and I had caused its disease to rise up like a fevered cobra.

We turned our back to all this. So much water. In the bright sunshine it was a light blue, the surface calm. The very air felt damp, and I wondered if this was what fish and other water creatures smelled like. A metallic sweet scent that was music to my sore senses. Back in Jwahir, neither Luyu nor I could ever have imagined this.

Several water vehicles came to a stop at the edge of the water. They cut and interrupted the water's tranquility. Boats, eight of them. All made of polished yellow wood with square blue insignias painted on the front. We quickly walked down the hill.

"You! Wait!" a woman shouted behind us.

We moved faster.

"That's the *Ewu* girl!" the woman said.

"Get the demon!" another woman shouted.

We started running.

The boats were small, barely able to hold four people each. They had motors that let out smoke and a belching noise as they churned the water. Luyu ran for a boat operated by a young Nuru man. I could see why she chose him; he looked a little different from the other boat operators. He looked shocked, whereas all the others were staring at me with horror. When we got to him, the same expression remained on his face. He opened the gate to his boat. We got on.

"You . . . you're the . . ."

"Yes, I am," I said.

"Move this thing!" Luyu shouted at him.

"That woman killed all the men in Durfa!" a woman running down the hill screamed at the men. "Get her, *kill* her!"

The man got his boat moving just in time. Smoke dribbled out and it made a sharp noise. He grabbed a lever and the boat shot forward. The other boatmen scrambled to the edges of their boats. They were too far to jump on ours. "Shukwu!" one of them shouted. "What are you doing?"

"Eh, he has already been bewitched," another boatman said.

A crowd of women were running down the hill. A stone hit the boat and then another hit me in the backside as I turned away.

"Where to?" the boatman named Shukwu asked.

"Rana's island," I said. "Do you know where it is?"

"I do," he said, turning the boat south, into the water's belly.

Behind us, the women quickly talked to the men. They started their motors and quickly gave chase.

"Stop the boat!" a man shouted. They were about a quarter of a mile from us.

"Shukwu, we won't hurt you!" another shouted. "We only want the girl."

Shukwu turned to me.

I looked him in the eye. "Don't stop the boat," I said.

We kept on.

"So are the rumors true?" he asked. "Have all the men . . . what happened in Durfa?" He had come from across the lake, possibly from Suntown or Chassa. News traveled fast. He'd taken a great chance coming across the water. What could I tell him?

"Why are you helping us?" Luyu asked, suspiciously.

"I . . . don't believe in Daib," he said. "A lot of us don't. Those of us who pray five times a day, love the Great Book, and are pious people know this isn't Ani's wish." He looked at me, inspecting my face. He shuddered and looked away. "And I saw her," he said. "The Okeke woman that no one could touch. Who could hate her? *Her* daughter could never do anything evil."

He was speaking of my mother going *alu* and trying to help me by telling people about me. So she was also appearing to Nurus. She was telling everyone what a good person I was. I almost laughed at the thought. Almost.

Despite their heavy loads, we couldn't outrun the other boats. Behind them, I saw five more boats full of men. "They will kill you," Shukwu said. He pointed to the right. "We just came from Chassa and all was fine. Please. Tell me what has happened in Durfa?"

I only shook my head.

"Just get us there," Luyu said.

"Hope I'm doing the right thing," he muttered.

They shouted curses and threats as they approached.

"How far?" Luyu asked, frantic.

"Look up there," he said.

I could see it, an island with a thatch-roofed sandstone hut on it. But the boat's motor was laboring, spewing out even more greasy black smoke. It started to make a chugging sound that couldn't have been good. Shukwu cursed. "My fuel is almost done," he said. He grabbed a small gourd. "I can refill . . ."

"No time! Go," Luyu said, grabbing my shoulder. "Change and fly to it. Leave me. I'll fight them."

I shook my head. "I'm not leaving you. We'll make it."

"We won't make it," Luyu said.

"We will!" I shouted. I got on my knees and leaned over the side. "Help it!" And I started paddling with my arm. Luyu leaned to the other side and did the same.

"Use these," Shukwu said, handing us large paddles. He gunned the motor to full power, which wasn't much power at all. Slowly we approached the island. Nothing was going through my head except, *Get there, GET THERE!* My blue rapa and white shirt were soaked with sweat and the cold water of the unnamed lake. Above, the sun shined. Overhead a flock of small birds flew by. I paddled for dear life.

"Go!" I shouted, when we got close enough. Luyu and I jumped out, splashed through the water and ran onto the tiny island that barely had room for a hut and two squat trees. Only a few yards to the hut. I paused to see Shukwu frantically paddling his boat away.

"Thank you!" I shouted.

"If . . . Ani . . . wills it," I heard him breathlessly shout. The boats of Nuru were closing in. I turned and ran to the hut.

I stopped beside Luyu at the threshold. There was no door. Inside slumped Rana's lifeless body. In the corner was a large dusty book. I don't know what happened to Rana. He could have been one of my victims, but did the death I accidently inflicted reach out this far? I'll never know. Luyu turned and ran back the way we'd come. "Do it!" she shouted over her shoulder. "I'll hold them off."

Outside as I was in that hut, those men who'd followed us saw her come out. Luyu was beautiful and strong. She wasn't afraid as she watched them step from their boats, taking their time now that they knew we were trapped. I think I heard her laugh and say, "Come on, then!"

Those Nuru men saw a beautiful Okeke woman protected only by her sense of duty and her two bare hands which had grown rough with use in the last few months. And they pounced on her. They ripped off her green rapa, her now dirty yellow top, the beaded bracelets she'd taken from the gift baskets only yesterday, a lifetime ago. Then they tore her apart. I don't recall hearing her scream. I was busy.

I was drawn right to that book. I knelt beside it. The cover was thin but tough, made of a durable material I couldn't name. It reminded me of the black cover of the electronic book I found in that cave. There was no title or design on it. I reached out but then hesitated. *What is . . .* No, I'd come too far to ask that.

When I touched the book, it was warm. Feverish. I rested my hand on the hard cover. It was rough, like sandpaper. I wanted to consider this but I knew I had no time. I dragged it into my lap and opened it. Immediately, I felt as if someone had hit me hard about the head causing my vision to go wrong. I could barely look at the writing on the pages, it bothered my eyes and head so much. I was focused, by now. I was there for only one purpose, a purpose that had been prophesied in that very hut.

I flipped the book's pages and stopped on a page that felt hotter than the rest. I lay my left hand on it. It didn't make any sense to me but I was inclined to do it, so sick the book felt. I paused. *No,* I thought. I switched hands, remembering Ting's words about my hand, "We don't know what the consequence will be." This book was full of hate and that was what caused its sickness. My right hand was full of Daib's hate.

"I don't hate you," I whispered. "I'd rather die." Then I began to sing. I sang the song that I had made up when I was four years old and living with my mother in the desert. During the happiest time of my life. I had sung this song to the desert when it was content, at peace, settled. I sang it now to the mysterious book in my lap.

My hand grew hot and I saw the symbols on my right hand split. The duplicates dribbled down into the book where they settled between the

other symbols into a script I still couldn't read. I could feel the book sucking from me, as a child does from its mother's breast. Taking and taking. I
felt something click within my womb. I stopped singing. As I watched, the
book grew dimmer and dimmer. But not so dim that I could not see it. It
hid there in the corner as the men burst in and found me.

Chapter 60

Who Fears Death?

CHANGE TAKES TIME AND I'D RUN OUT OF IT.

The moment I finished with that book, something began to happen. As it happened, I got up to run and realized I was caught. What I can tell you is that the book and all that it touched and then all that touched what it touched and so on, everything in that small sandstone hut began to shift. Not to the wilderness, that wouldn't have scared me. Someplace else. I dare say a pocket in time, a slit in time and space. To a place where all was gray, white, and black. I would have loved to stand and watch. But by then they were dragging me by my hair past what remained of Luyu's body, onto one of the boats. They were too blind to see what had begun to happen.

I sit here. They will come and take me. I have no reason to resist. No purpose in living. Mwita, Luyu, and Binta are dead. My mother is too far away. No, she won't come to see me. She knows better. She knows fate must play out. The child in me, the child of Mwita and me is doomed. But to live even for three days is to live. She'll understand. I shouldn't have made her. I was selfish. But she will understand. Her time will come again as mine will when the time is right. But this place that you know, this kingdom, it will change after today. Read it in your Great Book. You won't notice that it has been rewritten. Not yet. But it has. Everything has. The curse of the Okeke is lifted. It never existed, *sha*.

Epilogue

I SAT WITH HER ALL THOSE HOURS, typing and listening, mostly listening. Onyesonwu. She looked at her symboled hands and then brought them to her face. Finally, she wept. "It's done," she sobbed. "Leave me now."

At first I refused but then I saw her face change. I saw it become like a tiger's face, stripes and fur and sharp teeth. I ran out of there clutching my laptop. I didn't sleep that night. She haunted me. She could've escaped, flown away, made herself invisible, moved herself into the astral world and run off, or "glided" off as she liked to say. But she wouldn't do any of that. Because of what she'd seen during her initiation. She was like a character locked in a story. It was truly awful.

The next time I saw her was as they dragged her to that hole in the ground and buried her to her neck. They'd chopped off her long bushy hair and what was left stood on end, as defiant as she was. I stood in the crowd of men and few women. Everyone was shouting for blood and revenge. "Kill the *Ewu!*" "Tear her apart, *o!*" "*Ewu* demon!" People laughed and jeered. "The Okeke Savior is uglier than the Okeke!" "Sorceress indeed, she is capable of nothing but hurting our eyes," "*Ewu* murderer!"

I noticed a tall bearded man with a partially burned face, what looked like a severely mangled leg, and only one arm. He was near the front leaning on a staff. Like everyone else, he was Nuru. Unlike everyone else he was calm, observant. I'd never seen Daib but Onyesonwu had described him clearly. I'm sure this was him.

What happened when those rocks hit her head? I'm still asking that. There was light that flowed from her, a mixture of blue and green. The sand surrounding her buried body began to melt. More happened, but I dare not mention it all. Those things are only for those of us who were there, the witnesses.

Then the ground shook and people started running. I think in that moment, everyone, all of us Nuru understood where we'd gone wrong. Maybe her rewriting had finally kicked in. We were all sure that Ani had come to grind us back to dust. So much had already happened. Onyesonwu told the truth. The entire town of Durfa, all the fertile men were wiped out and all the fertile women were vomiting and pregnant.

The young children didn't know what to do. There was chaos in the streets all over the Seven Kingdoms. Many of the remaining Okeke refused to work and that caused more chaos and violence. The Seer Rana, who had predicted something would happen, was dead. Daib's building had burned to the ground. We were all sure it was the end.

So, we left her there. In that hole. Dead.

But my sister and I didn't run far. We went back after fifteen minutes. My sister . . . yes, I am a twin. My sister, my twin, she uses my computer. And she has been reading Onyesonwu's story. She came with me to the execution. And when it was all over, we were the only ones who returned.

And because my sister knew Onyesonwu's story, and because she is my twin, she was unafraid. As twins, we've always felt a responsibility to do good in the world. My status as one of Chassa's twins was why they allowed me to see her in jail. It's what drove me to take down her story. And it is what will help me fight to publish it and keep my sister and myself safe through the backlash. My parents were two of the few Nuru who thought it was *all* wrong, the way we lived, behaved, the Great Book. They didn't believe in Ani. So my sister and I grew up nonbelievers, too.

As we were walking back to Onyesonwu's body, my sister yelped. When I looked at her, she was floating an inch off the ground. My sister can fly. We would later find out that she was not the only one. All the women, Okeke and Nuru, found that something had changed about them. Some could turn wine to fresh sweet drinking water, others glowed in the dark at night, some could hear the dead. Others remembered the past, before the Great Book. Others could peruse the spirit world and still live in the physical. Thousands of abilities. All bestowed upon women. There it was. Onye's gift. In the death of herself and her child, Onye gave birth to us all. This place will never be the same. Slavery here is over.

We removed her body from that hole. It was not easy because all around her was melted sand, glass. We had to shatter it to get her out. My sister cried the entire time, her feet barely touching the ground. I cried, too. But we took her. My sister removed her veil and covered Onye's broken head with it. We used a camel to help take her body out to the desert, east of here. We brought another camel with us to carry the wood. We burned Onyesonwu's corpse on the funeral pyre she deserved and we buried her ashes near two palm trees. As we filled in the hole, a vulture landed in the tree and watched. When we finished, it flew away. We said a few words for Onyesonwu and then went home.

It was the most we could do for the woman who saved the people of the Seven Rivers Kingdom, this place that used to be part of the Kingdom of Sudan.

Chapter 61

Peacock

Chapter 62

Sola Speaks

AH, BUT THE GREAT BOOK HAD BEEN REWRITTEN. In Nsibidi at that.

Over those first few days in Durfa, there *was* change. Some women began encountering the ghosts of those men wiped out by Onyewson-wu's . . . impetuous actions. Some ghosts became living men again. No one dared ask how this was possible. Smart. Other ghosts eventually vanished. Onyesonwu might have been remotely interested in all this. But then again, she had other concerns.

Recall that the daughter of my student-gone-wrong was Eshu, a fundamental shape shifter. Onyesonwu's very *essence* was change and defiance. Daib had to have known this even as he flew from his burning headquarters where the body of Onyesonwu's dead love, Mwita, became ash. Daib, who was now crippled and could no longer see color or work the Mystic Points without suffering unheard of pain. Certainly there are things worse than death.

Indeed, Onyesonwu did die, for something must be written before it can be *rewritten*. But now, see the sign of the peacock. Onyesonwu left it in the dirt of her holding cell. This symbol is scribbled by a sorcerer who believes he has been wronged. Once in a while, it is scribbled by a sorcer*ess*, too. It means, "one is going to take action." Is it not understandable that she'd want to *live* in the very world she helped remake? That indeed is a more logical destiny.

Chapter 1

Rewritten

"LET THEM COME, THEN," Onyesonwu said, looking down at the symbol she'd scratched in the sand. The proud peacock. The symbol was complaint. Argument. Insistence. She looked down at herself and nervously rubbed her thighs. They'd put her in a long coarse white dress. It felt like another prison. They'd chopped off her hair. They'd had the *nerve* to chop off her hair. She stared at her hands—the circles, swirls and lines were woven into complex designs snaking up her wrists.

She leaned her head back against the wall and closed her eyes in the sunshine. The world became red. They were coming. Any moment now. She knew. She'd seen it. Years ago, she'd seen it.

Someone grabbed her with such roughness that she grunted. Her eyes flew open, bitter rage flooding her body and spirit. Bright red in the hot sunshine. She'd cured everything, yet in doing so her friends had died, her Mwita . . . oh, her beloved Mwita, her life, her death. The fury filled her. She could hear her daughter raging, too. Her daughter had the roar of a lion.

Six thick-armed young men crowded her cell to take her. Three of them had machetes. Maybe the other three were so arrogant that they didn't think they'd need weapons to handle her. Maybe they all thought the evil sorceress named Onyesonwu was resigned to her fate. She could understand why they'd made this mistake. She understood well.

Nevertheless, what could any of them do as a strange force shoved them all back? Three of them fell out of the cell. They all sat, lay, and stood watching, slack-jawed and horrified as Onyesonwu threw off her awful dress and . . . changed. She shifted, sprouted, enveloped, stretched, and grew her body. Onyesonwu was expert. She was Eshu. She became a *Kponyungo*, a firespitter.

FOOOOOM! She blasted out a ball of flames so intense that the sand around her melted to glass. The three remaining men in her cell were painfully scorched raw as if they'd been lying in the desert sun for days waiting to die. Then she blew into the sky like a shooting star ready to return home.

No, she was *not* a sacrifice to be made for the good of men and women, Okeke and Nuru alike. She was Onyesonwu. She had rewritten the Great Book. All was done. And she could never ever let her baby, the one part of Mwita that still lived, die. *Ifunanya.* He'd spoken those ancient mystical words to her, words that were truer and purer than love. What they shared was enough to shift fate.

She thought of the Palm Wine Drunkard in the Great Book. All he lived for was to drink his sweet frothy palm wine. When one day his expert palm wine tapper fell from a tree and died, he was distraught. But then he realized if his tapper was dead and gone, then he must be somewhere else. And so the Drunkard's quest began.

Onyesonwu considered this as she thought about her Mwita. Suddenly, she knew where she would find him. He would be in a place that was so full of life that death would flee it . . . for a while. The green place her mother had shown her. Beyond the desert, where the land was blanketed with leafy trees, bushes, plants, and the creatures that lived in them. He would be waiting at the iroko tree. She almost screamed with joy as she flew faster. Can *Kponyungo* shed real tears? This one could.

But what of Binta and Luyu, she wondered with a flicker of hope. *Would they be there, too?* Ah, but fate was cold and brittle.

The three of us, Sola, Aro, and Najeeba smiled. We (mentor, teacher, and mother) saw it all in the way that sorcerers, experienced and in training, often see things deeply connected to them. We wonder if we will ever see her again. What will she become? When she and Mwita unite, and they will, what will become of their daughter who laughed so gleefully inside Onyesonwu's belly on the way to the green place?

If Onyesonwu had taken one last look below, to the south, with her keen *Kponyungo* eyes she'd have seen Nuru, Okeke, and two *Ewu* children in school uniforms playing in a schoolyard. To the east, stretching into the distance, she'd have seen black paved roads populated by men and women, Okeke and Nuru, riding scooters and carts pulled by camels. In downtown Durfa, she'd have spotted a flying woman discreetly meeting up with a flying man on the roof of the tallest building.

But the wave of change was yet to sweep by directly below. There, thousands of Nuru still waited for Onyesonwu, all of them screaming, yelling, shouting, laughing, glaring . . . waiting to wet their tongues with Onyesonwu's blood. Let them wait. They will be waiting for a long long time.

Acknowledgments:

To the ancestors, spirits and that place so often called "Africa." To my father, whose passing caused me to ask, "Who fears death?" To my mother. To my daughter Anyaugo, nephew Onyedika, and niece Obioma for cheering me up when I was writing the parts of this novel that got me down. To my siblings (Ife, Ngozi, and Emezie) for their constant support. To my extended family, always my foundation. To Pat Rothfuss for reading and critiquing *Who Fears Death* in its infancy back in 2004. To Jennifer Stevenson for having nightmares spawned from this novel. To my agent Don Maass for his vision and guidance. To my editor Betsy Wollheim for thinking, seeing and being outside the box. To David Anthony Durham, Amaka Mbanugo, Tara Krubsack, and professor Gene Wildman for their excellent feedback along the way. And to the 2004 AP news story by Emily Wax titled, "We want to make a light baby." This article about weaponized rape in the Sudan created the passageway through which Onyesonwu slipped into my world.